I0760556

M. H. WOODSCOURT

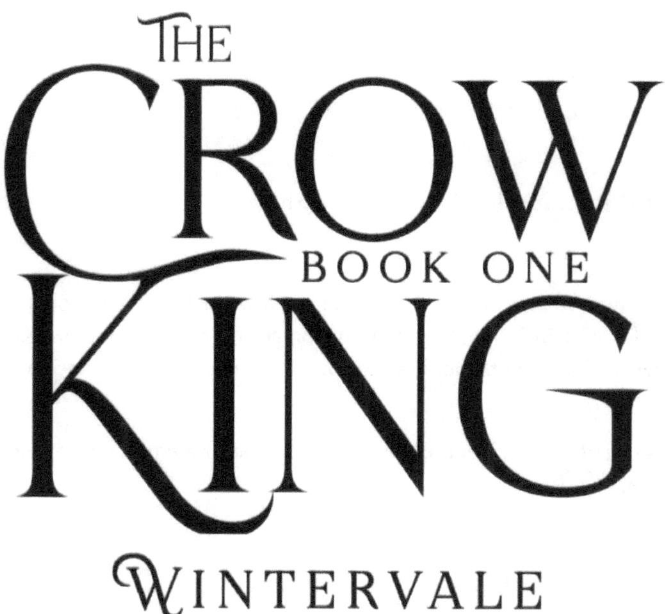

This is a work of fiction. Names, characters, and places are products of the author's imagination.

Cover art by GetCovers

Published by True North Press

www.mhwoodscourt.com

ISBN: (Hardback) 978-1-959619-07-9

ISBN: (Paperback) 978-1-959619-06-2

DEDICATION

To George Washington, whose life and character inspired Gwyn's story. May good folk always laud your name.

"Fairy tales are more than true — not because they tell us dragons exist, but because they tell us dragons can be beaten."

— G. K. CHESTERTON

Content Warning

The following pages contain fantasy violence, including war and death, as well as one case of a lovable but cannibalistic fae character.

There is also brief discussion about war crimes — including cannibalism — handled with delicacy. Topics of slavery, madness, and drunkenness are also touched on.

I write these things, not gratuitously, but with gravity, respecting the pain of history, with a strong determination not to repeat the missteps of the past.

Proceed at your own discretion.

—M. H. W.

Swan Castle
Ilid
Fraelin
Keep Canad
Keep Arch
Keep Montré
The Channel
Dorshen Heights
Mount Vinwen
Crane Castle
Hear ye, hear ye. No magic shall be used within the mighty realm of Simaerin, by order of the Crow King.
Charquae
Vinwen Province
Delesar River
Misoril Province
Keep Lirial
Trayton
Simaerin
Hesh-Kasal
Keep Talbethé
Yast Port
Kellion
Glashon Province
Londolin
Crowwell
Vaymeer Sea

PART I

THE QUEST TO SWAN CASTLE

Chapter One

Mist curled over the quiet hills of Vinwen. Somewhere a bird trilled, prophesying the coming dawn. The sun answered with a ring of gold spilling over the horizon as it peeked at the slumbering world. Lazy clouds drifted by, gray, dappled with faint pinks and yellows.

Sitting on the wooden fence, Gwynter ren Terare squinted against the hovering gloom in the valley below, eyes fixed on the road. He strained for any sound beyond the faint chirrup of crickets, the song of birds, the gush of the nearby stream. A crow cawed as it landed on the fence.

There. Just there. A faint neigh.

The rattle of a wheel against a stray stone.

A cracking whip.

Gwyn shoved against the rough wood post, leapt to his feet atop the fence, and wobbled once before he caught his balance. Perched, he soon made out the distant shape of the coming carriage, a single lantern bobbing to pierce the predawn shadows.

Gwyn grinned and jumped from the fence. The crow screamed and flew off. Gwyn loped along the streambank up toward the manor house. His light brown shoulder-length hair flounced in his eyes, but he ignored it as he cut through a protesting gaggle of geese and threw himself against the kitchen door to stumble inside.

"Mercy, child!" cried Mavell, spoon in hand. "You look a sight. What awful trouble could there be so early as this?"

Gwyn shook his head as he gasped for air, leaning forward, hands on his legs. He gulped a few times before he could utter a word. "Lawen's coming. Almost here. Down the road a bit."

He straightened and headed for a bucket of water on the table, took up a ladle, and helped himself to a long, cool drink.

The cook grabbed the ladle, poured water into a cup, and handed *that* to Gwyn. "Master Lawen, already? Surely not. He's not to come until tomorrow, so his letter said."

Gwyn drained the cup. He held it out to let Mavell ladle him another. "But he's always early. I had a feeling to watch for him, and here he comes."

"And how do you know it's Master Lawen?"

Gwyn smiled. "I always know."

She pursed her lips but didn't argue. There seemed no point, they both knew that.

"Well," the slender woman said, rubbing her hands against her apron. "If it *is* Master Lawen, oughtn't you go off and clean yourself up for his arrival? Your mother will have a fit if you greet him looking like a shepherd's boy." She swatted Gwyn's backside with the ladle. "Off with you, go on."

Gwyn chuckled, then trotted out of the kitchen and into a long gallery. His feet echoed against the flagstones. He cast a glance out the windows to find that full dawn had banished gray in favor of a thousand shades of green and brilliant gold. He could hear the geese and chickens griping and dogs barking as the carriage rolled along the private drive leading to the house. Gwyn thought he heard the crunch of gravel and his heart leapt.

Lawen! Home, at last. How long had it been? A year or longer. Mount Vinwen had felt hollow in his absence, though none of the others appeared to notice.

Gwyn reached his room, brushed off his trousers to dislodge any dirt or wood splinters, and changed his coarse shirt for fine woven linen. He slipped on stockings, yanked on a pair of polished boots, then caught his hair in a ponytail. A last inspection in his mirror. Gwyn awarded himself a curt, militaristic nod. He tugged one last time on his long tunic front, wrapped his belt atop it, clicked his heels, and headed downstairs.

In the main vestibule he found the rest of the ren Terares assembled, even Mother, though her lips pressed tight and her eyebrows arched above eyes sharp as needles. She turned toward Gwyn as he reached the bottom of the sweeping staircase and her gaze softened.

"Gwyn, dearheart. Thank you for *not* looking like a peasant this morning."

He kissed her cheeks. "Good morning, Mother. I thought this occasion warranted the change."

She sighed. "Yes, I suppose the master *is* home today."

Gwyn brushed off her tone, not willing to let it seep in. He could understand her resentment in a way. Last year Tynveer ren Terare — Gwyn and Lawen's blood father — had been killed in a skirmish against the savage Ilidreth. Now Lawen was the master of Mount Vinwen, and Mother, Tynveer's second wife after Lawen's mother had passed, now suspected her stepson would soon send her and her three children to live at another of his estates, but Gwyn knew better. There was no kinder soul in all Simaerin than his elder half-brother.

The sound of crunching gravel outside the front doors ceased. The carriage bounced to a stop. Gwyn's younger sisters laughed and tumbled forward as the servants pulled the manor doors aside to admit the Master of Vinwen.

"Sila, Neirin," said Mother. "Do *try* to behave like human beings." Though her tone was harsh, she wore a fond smile as she followed them out onto the wide porch.

Gwyn came last, clamping down on an urge to rush forth and barrel into Lawen as soon as he descended from the carriage. He couldn't wait to see Lawen in full dress: that rich red tabard bright over the full armor worn in the Crow King's service. The silhouette of a crow in profile painted against the gleaming breastplate. A broadsword strapped at the hip, heavy and sure in the possession of Lawen ren Terare.

The footman jumped from his perch behind the carriage and came forward to open the door. Lawen unfolded himself from within, and Gwyn felt his excitement crescendo—then die on a sour note.

Indeed, it was Lawen, though he wore no armor; instead, a shawl wrapped around his shoulders, plain travel garb beneath that. His complexion was pale, his green eyes sunken, black hair lank and damp with sweat. Even so, a smile adorned his ashen lips as he took in the sight before him.

"My beautiful family." He extended his arms to greet them.

Gwyn's heart wrung in his chest. He sprang forward to catch Lawen just as the man staggered. Gwyn steadied him, feeling the brittle thinness of his half-brother's arm in his grasp.

"My dear Lawen!" exclaimed Mother. "Are you wounded? We heard nothing of any battle."

Lawen shook his head. "Only a little ill, that's all. I've been granted an extended leave to care for myself until this passes. Don't fret over me." He turned to Gwyn. "My word, little brother. You've outgrown me, and only fourteen years of age. That should be against some ancient law of birthright." He coughed — a throaty, ragged sound. "I could do with a little water."

"Of course," Mother said, motioning inside. "Gwyn, take him into the parlor. I'll have Cook bring water and something to eat."

Gwyn guided Lawen inside and past the staircase into a parlor off the main gallery. He helped Lawen to sink into a plush wingback chair. Lawen panted and his hands trembled. As Gwyn stared at those thin fingers, his chest tightened around his heart.

Sila and Neirin hovered at the door, wide-eyed and speechless. Lawen smiled at them, then dropped his head against the chair-back. He closed his eyes. "Needn't worry so much. Just a bad cold."

Gwyn arched an eyebrow. "I've never seen such a cold as this."

Lawen's smile stretched. "You worry too much, Gwynny."

He drew back. "I'm not six anymore, Lawen. It's Gwyn now."

"Such a grownup." Lawen coughed until the fit doubled him over.

Gwyn watched with humming fear. His heartbeat raced in his ears.

At last the man sat straight and let his head fall back and roll to the side. He gasped. "You...really need to...enjoy your childhood a little...a little bit longer...you know..."

Gwyn tried a wry smile. "I'll not take that advice from a man who joined the Crow King's army to escape growing crops."

Lawen rasped out a chuckle. "Very well, very well. Your point is made, although one might argue that my advice is now the voice of experience. Enjoy your crops, Gwynny. Killing people isn't...quite the glory...our Sovereign King would like us to believe..."

Gwyn rested a hand on his brother's thin arm. "Enough of that for now. Just rest. You've come home to recover, not to pawn your estate off on me."

Lawen laughed again. "Justly rebuked. I shall repent by taking a nap."

Gwyn backed away from the chair, his smile warming. "Just so. But first, here's Mavell with your water."

❧

FOUR DAYS after Lawen's homecoming, Gwyn stood with the house steward and family physician on the landing of the manor's second floor. He listened to the rumble of the steward set against the treble of the physician, as they discussed the health of their master.

"I've bled him," the physician said. "But he only grows weaker."

Gwyn rubbed an itch on his neck, turning from the two men to study the world outside the nearest window. Little Sila chased the geese down in the courtyard, while Neirin looked on, laughing. Several milkmaids swept past them on their way to the barn.

Gwyn's eyes traveled to the forest beyond the estate's cultivated fields. A half dozen crows rested on the far fence. His neck itched again.

"Gwyn."

Mother's voice. He turned to find her cresting the staircase and offered a solemn smile. "Yes, Lady Mother?"

"A letter has arrived from Lawen's commanding officer." She held aloft the folded parchment. "I thought you and Doctor Hesegg should be aware of its contents." She swept forward, skirts rustling against the stone floor. "According to General Cadogan's personal physician, Lawen is dying."

Gwyn's heart convulsed. His light eyes danced between Mother and the physician, both shorter than him, and he felt as though they shrank in his sight, farther, farther. He was floating away.

Not Lawen. Please not Lawen too.

"Lawen knows," Mother went on. "He knows and he's said nothing."

Gwyn's feet found solid ground again. "He doesn't wish to worry us, Mother."

Her grip tightened on the letter, crinkling it. "Doctor Hesegg, is there anything you can do?"

The physician shook his head. "I've tried every treatment I know, my lady, and none have aided him in the least. All that's left in my power is to keep him somewhat comfortable until he either recovers or..." He offered a gentle shrug.

Gwyn slipped away from Mother, from the physician, and the steward, to approach Lawen's door. He entered the darkened room and choked on the close air. It smelled of sweat, blood, sickness. It reeked of death, just as when Father lay so still in his coverlets, ghost departed.

"Gwyn?" came a harsh whisper from the dark lump in the four-post bed.

He padded nearer. "Yes, Lawen. I'm here."

"You sound so grim. Is the doctor taking my cold too seriously?"

"General Cadogan sent a letter to Mother. We know how sick you are."

A deep sigh sounded in the gloom. "I'm sorry he did that, Gwyn. I didn't want to worry you."

Scalding heat speared Gwyn's heart and pounded through his head. He clenched his hands into fists and trembled against an outburst. When he spoke, his voice hung low and soft. "Did you think to deceive us until the very end, Lawen? Did you think the truth would be easier to bear when it became too late for farewells?"

The coverlet rustled and a thin hand rose from the darkness. "Come here, little brother."

Gwyn's fists loosened and his shoulders drooped. He knelt beside the bed and clasped Lawen's hand, seeking his brother's face in the gloom. There. Gaunt and tight, a sheen of sweat on his brow.

"Forgive me the coward's path," Lawen whispered. "I didn't think I could abide seeing my death reflected in your eyes. In truth I've been sick a long while. Father alone knew of it, but I begged him to say nothing. I've sought help from all sorts of healers, some less than reputable, but to no avail. And then Father was killed by the Ilidreth, and—" His voice broke. "Oh, Gwyn, I nearly died of guilt when we got word. Father went to the Ilidreth for my sake. He heard they could cure what others can't, but of course it was folly to try. The Ilidreth hate humans too much to hear a desperate man out."

Gwyn stared, a chill shooting down his spine as he imagined how Father must've begged to be spared — if only long enough to save his son. Rage rang in his ears, but he swallowed hard and urged it to be silent. Anger, Father had often told him, should never be given purchase in a man's mind. Not if he wanted to be respectable. Not if he wanted to be wise.

When the fury stilled enough, Gwyn squeezed his brother's hand. "I would forgive anything of which you're guilty, Lawen. But I don't see how you could be. I've never faced death for myself. How can I know how it feels?" He bowed his head to rest his brow against his brother's knuckles. He trembled. Lawen was so strong, so noble, an officer in the Crow King's army, yet...

He swallowed hard. “By Afallon, the Ilidreth are so cruel!”

“Not without reason,” Lawen said with a sigh. “We’ve stripped them of their pride and forced them deeper into the woods as we’ve cut down their forest. We’ve been cruel to them, far more so than they to us.”

“But the Ilidreth are a savage race. Had we not driven them back, they would’ve killed every last one of us.”

Lawen shook his head. “Would they, Gwyn? Or does the Crow King merely tell us so?”

Gwyn startled. He had never heard his brother speak of the king with anything other than the deepest respect. “Don’t say such things. If the king—”

“If the king weren’t so blind, perhaps we would live in harmony with the Ilidreth. Perhaps we wouldn’t be at war with Fraelin. Perhaps the sun would be just a bit warmer, a bit brighter, because those who live under it would do so without the eye of a tyrant bearing down on us.”

Gwyn shuddered. “You mustn’t—”

Lawen jerked his hand free and gripped Gwyn’s shoulder with brittle fingers. “Listen to me, Gwynter. It seems a bittersweet gift is born in a dying man to see what he couldn’t before. But perhaps my newborn sight will aid others where it avails me naught. The Crow King isn’t the great man we thought.”

“Lawen, you’re ill. You’re not thinking right.”

Lawen’s hand fell to the bed. He dragged in a rattling breath. “I served him... Served him with high honor... Drove Ilidreth to their deaths, and—and did so many other horrible things. Things...I would undo if I possibly could. The Crow King is mad, Gwyn. *Mad*.”

Gwyn’s throat constricted. He fought to swallow and took Lawen’s hand. “Hush, brother. You mustn’t speak like this. ’Tis treason.”

“What can the Crow King do to me now? I’m dying.”

Gwyn bit his lip. A crow beyond the curtained window gave a sharp caw. Wings beat hard against the air as it flew off, perhaps to the nearby wood. Gwyn let his mind's eye imagine the tall, ancient trees of that wood where the Ilidreth dwelt.

Father thought they had the cure.

He turned back to Lawen, but his brother had grown still, breaths deeper, though still so weak.

"You can't die, dear brother. I won't let you die."

Perhaps Lawen's reckless words against the Crow King were infectious. Gwyn felt nothing whatever about the king himself, but that defiant spirit filled his being like the low flicker of hot embers. Was it possible? Were the Ilidreth misunderstood — those strange, ethereal beings who dwelt in the wooded vales of the world?

Father must have thought so, and he'd perished for it.

But if there was a cure, dare Gwyn not risk it?

He rested Lawen's hand on the coverlet, stroked his fingers once, and rose. Gwyn was only fourteen years of age. But he was tall and strong, accustomed to hunting and riding, and he knew a fair stretch of the woods and how to navigate untamed lands.

Mother would never let him go, especially to save the life of Father's first wife's son. But Gwyn loved his brother more than anyone in the world. If there was a whisper of hope, he must answer.

Time stretched out of mind. Gwyn stared out at the distant trees and weighed the risks. Should he leave Lawen now, so frail and faint, when he chanced never seeing him alive again? Or should he remain here to watch Lawen fade, helpless, hopeless?

Gwyn curled his fingers into fists.

He would leave at once, under the pretense of the morning's chores. It would be hours before anyone missed him, and then Mother would search and discover a message explaining his departure. By then it would be too late to stop him. None of the servants, none of the serfs or slaves, would venture into the woods even for their master.

Gwyn left Lawen's room and made for his own to pack and to scrawl a hasty note.

Chapter Two

Woodland chatter filled the trees.

Gwyn guided Tia, his dappled mare, along the well-worn path. No Ilidreth would dwell so near cultivated lands; thus, humans used this stretch of the woods for lumber, trapping, hunting, foraging, or whatever else they could to secure a trade.

Gwyn often came here to hunt, or to study the lay of moss or the turning of a leaf, as Father had taught him. Gwyn had wanted to be a guide when he was younger, but when Lawen joined the Crow King's army, Gwyn had decided to follow in his brother's footsteps when he came of age. That would require many of the same skills he had spent his childhood honing.

It would be very handy now, when he left the path and entered less hospitable realms.

Gwyn had packed light, only carrying two extra sets of clothing to make more room for food and medicinal herbs, a hunting knife, bow and arrow, and a short sword. Tia bore her burden well, content to walk the familiar path as she had countless times, oblivious of their objective.

It was midday before Gwyn eased Tia off the path and into the thicker canopy of towering trees. Everything gleamed vibrant green after the night's spring rain, and rich loam taunted Gwyn's senses like a heady wine. Tia left prints in the soft soil for anyone to follow, but Gwyn knew they wouldn't.

Another twenty minutes passed with nothing but a distant wind sighing against the branches and the prattle of scampering squirrels. Tia nickered and shifted her hooves, ears flicking.

"Easy, girl," Gwyn said, running a hand along her neck. "Easy." He searched the surrounding trees but saw nothing strange. He urged her on. She tossed her head but obeyed.

Minutes later she faltered again and backed up with a snort.

"Whoa, Tia. What is it?" He leaned forward to pat her neck and stiffened. There, right of his course. A flash of color slinked behind a tree.

Gwyn straightened in the saddle and reached down to finger his hunting knife, wishing he'd had the sense to unstrap his bow from his pack before he'd entered the deeper wood. A stray breeze rustled the leaves overhead and tugged against Gwyn's ponytail. Something stirred behind the tree he studied, and he thought he smelled blood.

Movement came again. Red cloth. The fine material of an army tabard. There was no arm attached to that tabard, and it hung too high to belong to a man.

Hair rose against the back of Gwyn's neck.

He dismounted, wrapped Tia's reins around a branch of the nearest sapling, slid his hunting knife from the saddle scabbard, and crept toward the tabard.

He knew what to expect before he saw it. Rounding the tree, he lifted his gaze to find the empty red tabard pinned by arrows to the gnarled trunk.

Despite its color, Gwyn recognized the dark stains on its front for what they were: Blood. Lots of it, especially near the heart and neckline. Lowering his eyes, Gwyn discovered the telltale signs of a burial at his feet, where the ground had been raised and packed down under dancing feet.

The message was clear: Go no farther.

Gwyn returned to Tia, sheathed his blade, and swung into the saddle. He urged her onward again, grim but resolute. He knew the risks. The warning of the Ilidreth made no difference.

Despite the gruesome sign, there was no incident as the day wore on toward evening. Dusk settled over the wood early, stretching shadowed fingers across the green world. Gwyn knew better than to travel by night in this foreboding realm, and he set up camp at the first decent site he found. It was a wide dip in the earth, whose far side opened to reveal a trickling stream. Fallen moss-plagued logs and dead branches littered the ground. He gathered the branches, along with what dry kindling he could find, and used his flint and steel to make a flame. Soon a fire blazed, chasing off the growing chill.

Gwyn tied a canvas from the nearest limb of an old oak and stretched it down to the ground, pinned it, and unfastened his bedroll to spread out beneath the canvas shelter. He plucked a long, straight stick from the ground to draw a circle around his little camp, then fingered a leathern cord at his throat and murmured a prayer of protection to Afallon.

It wasn't much, perhaps superstition tied to faith, but Gwyn couldn't be too careful. Not in the territory of the Ilidreth.

He checked on Tia tied to a nearby tree, fed her a few oats and what wild grass he could find, and drew a circle around her to be safe.

A quick cup of hot tea, a few bites of bread and cheese, then Gwyn curled up for the night. Despite how weary he felt from the day's ride, his thoughts churned. For the first time he doubted himself. What had he been thinking, going off on his own in search of such an enemy? Yes, perhaps the Ilidreth did have a cure that would save Lawen's life. What good was that if Gwyn died here alone?

He turned onto his back and sighed, letting his thoughts drift out with his breath. The decision was already made, the journey begun. He couldn't turn back now; not when this was his last hope. If he succeeded, he would not only save Lawen's life, but in some sense he would be rescuing Father from this ancient wood.

No, Gwynter ren Terare would not return home empty-handed.

Chapter Three

At the first hint of dawn, Gwyn rose and broke camp, saddled Tia, and moved out.

Tia walked at her ease, untroubled by the memories of yesterday. Gwyn let her have the reins and she followed the stream until it disappeared underground around noon. Gwyn halted to let her enjoy the water at its end, while he ate an early dinner and filled his water flask before they started on again.

The sky darkened. Soon it began to rain, but the storm was fleeting, leaving the wood fresh and verdant as the grumbling clouds rolled away.

He drank in the scents, enjoying the solitude. He was accustomed to the lively sounds of the farm, the workers singing in the fields, the laughter of Sila and Neirin, the clucking of chickens, the rattle of wagon wheels as slaves and servants milled about performing their duties. So much hustle and bustle. Here, in this realm as old as life itself, the noise of wildlife, scampering or buzzing by, permeated the wood but it was ancient, hallowed. Somehow wise.

I could learn more about life in this place than I ever could in the busy streets of Crowwell or the thriving fields of Vinwen.

A startled sparrow fluttered from a flowering tree. Gwyn tensed, hands clutching the reins. He must remember why he'd come here. Not to learn from the trees, but to bargain with the Ilidreth.

Keep your head.

The woods, some said, could bespell you and make you lose your way.

He checked his bearings and sighed. He wasn't lost.

Tia halted, her body quaking. He patted her neck and glanced around.

The mare whinnied.

There. Gwyn sat up straight. This was no tabard pinned to a trunk, but a tall figure mostly hidden by the drooping leaves of a willow tree.

He swallowed to find his voice. "Hello?"

Leaves rustled.

Gwyn licked his parched lips. "I—I seek the Ilidreth."

The leaves whispered and the figure stepped into view, an arrow nocked and pointed at Gwyn's heart. The boy lifted his hands to show he held no weapons, his eyes wide as he stared for the first time upon a fae creature.

It was beautiful; tall and lithe, slender, with long hair of glossy black and slanted eyes of purest blue. High cheekbones and pointed ears framed the Ilidreth's face. He — for Gwyn thought it was a man — wore close-fitting clothes, deep greens and browns and purples and reds in motley patterns made from a material not unlike silk, though sturdier.

The creature glided forward, making the barest hint of noise. His arrow never strayed from its target and he halted several yards away, blue eyes burning into Gwyn.

"Were you but a year or two older you would already be dead, young one," the being said in a melodic tone that brought to mind twinkling stars and a burbling stream. "Why do you seek the Ilidreth?"

Gwyn steeled himself. "I need a cure for my dying brother."

The being's eyes narrowed a little. "You would ask for our aid?"

Gwyn nodded. "I would and I do."

The being canted his head. "So bold. What is your name?"

"Gwynter ren Terare."

"Ren Terare? I know the name. Another of your kin came here not many seasons past, seeking the same. He demanded we save his heir and when we refused, he tried to kill us."

Prickles clawed up Gwyn's arms. "Is that the truth of it? Yet you confess you would have killed me were I fully grown, before I had even a chance to speak. Did my father know better courtesy than this?"

The being's gaze softened, or perhaps the light overhead changed. "You ask a fair question. I did not expect such from ren Terare's ilk. Dismount and I shall show you courtesy, young Lord Gwynter ren Terare of Vinwen."

Gwyn hesitated. "What is your name, if you please?"

The being studied him for a moment. "Celin, perhaps, in your tongue. Come." He gestured for Gwyn to follow and glided back toward the tree where Gwyn had first seen him. The boy dismounted and followed, leading Tia. "Leave her," Celin said without glancing back. "Tamed beasts are not permitted in the glade beyond. She will be safe enough here."

Gwyn hesitated to leave Tia and his weapons behind but he followed the Ilidreth past the vine-like branches of the willow.

And gasped.

Before him stretched a vale, wide and bright with white light emanating from the sentinel trees whose crystal flowers shone in full bloom upon the twigs and branches. Celin stood before him, but where before his hair had shone black, now it gleamed white, and his raiment had become an intricate robe of woven silver. His eyes, however, were the same pure blue.

Celin wore a faint smile. "Welcome to the Vale of Life, where dwell the Ilidreth. Tell me, young lord, is this courtesy?"

Gwyn tried to drink in every detail. Water flowed like liquid silver, cascading down from a waterfall and into a glistening pool. Though moments before it had been daylight, here a black sky sparkled with myriad stars burning brighter than any Gwyn had ever seen. Strange constellations hung against the heavens, yet foreign names tumbled into his head as he stared at the shapes they sketched. Did something above whisper them to him?

"We cannot be in the same place."

Celin's smile grew. "We are not. The Vale is not of Simaerin, but of another Realm."

Gwyn took a step forward. "I don't understand. How can this be so?"

"It is magic, young lord. A thing humans have proclaimed as witchcraft performed by sorcerers. Yet the Ilidreth weave magic, no matter your commands, no matter the commands of your king." Celin's eyes narrowed, sharp as daggers; then his gaze softened. "Your father was not shown this sight, for he was forceful and impolite. Had he conversed with the Ilidreth as one man to another, as you have done to me, he might have lived."

Gwyn's heart constricted. "Did you—"

"Blow out your temper before it flames. I did not slay your father. 'Twas the deed of another, more prone to violence. Alas, there are many Ilidreth now aligned thus. That is the doing of man."

"We've been taught to fear and hate you. I believed you to be savage." He searched the Ilidreth's face.

Celin lowered his eyes. "And so we are becoming, one Vale at a time. Many of my kin are Fallen."

"But if humans knew of this beauty, surely they'd believe you mean us no harm."

Celin laughed lightly. "Most would not see this even should I lead them here. You, young lord, I have shown because your eyes are willing to see truth where others' are not. But I see that field of vision narrowing even now. A year or two more and you shall see as other men: a vision tainted by shades and shadows."

Gwyn bristled and heat bloomed against his cheeks.

"You see?" said Celin. "If an Ilidreth speaks truth, will you, so nearly a man, pay heed? Or shall you deny what you do not think to be right, proving thereby what I say?"

Gwyn bit his lip and shook his head. "I didn't come to argue, and I didn't come to learn your ways. I came to ask whatever price you require in exchange for a cure for my brother."

Celin canted his head. "And if my price were that you learned the ways of the Ilidreth? Or perhaps, the taking of one life in replacement of another? What if I should require the Crow King's head in order to save your brother?"

Gwyn's eyes widened. "That would be impossible!"

"It may be indeed. You are fortunate that I do not require such a weighty price."

"What then *is* your price?" asked Gwyn. "Will you help me after all?"

"I may, young ren Terare. But the cure is not so obtainable as you appear to assume. Have I a magic plant that would heal any disease? Even the Vales of Life are not so powerful. I do not know what ails your brother. How can I administer a cure?"

Gwyn's heart clenched. "Human healers have already tried everything. My father believed your people possessed something special. Something...*magical*." The word was heavy on his tongue. "Was he wrong?"

"We do not possess any such thing. But I begin to understand what it is your father sought." Celin turned east, his eyes boring into the trees, as though he saw something in the darkness. He lifted a hand, one finger stretched forth. "Travel by way of the *Serethenwé*, the ancient path of shades, until you come to a road of crystal. Follow that northward and you shall reach *Shaeswéath*, in your tongue called Swan Castle."

"I thought Swan Castle was just a myth."

Celin smiled. "To many, young Gwynter ren Terare, so are the Ilidreth." He lowered his hand. "Only in *Shaeswéath* may you find a cure so potent as you need, and then perhaps not. Beware: the road ahead is filled with snares."

Gwyn let his shoulders slump. Dread raked its cold fingers

through his limbs. "How far is Swan Castle? My brother won't last much longer."

The Ilidreth frowned. "Even should you ride without rest and encounter no dangers, it would take nearly two of your human months to return to Vinwen with the cure in hand."

Dismay tumbled over Gwyn, dragging his shoulders down more. "That's far too long!" He clenched his hands as they trembled.

"In truth, it will take much longer, for your mare will not survive the journey," said Celin. "Nothing so tame can long last in the True Wood."

"Then I must go on foot?" Gwyn breathed through his tightening ribcage. He lifted his head. "Due east will bring me to the path?"

"Never stray and, should you prove as resourceful as an Ilidreth, you might make it all the way. But afoot, never."

"Yet I can't bring Tia."

Celin nodded. "Just so."

"You give me little cause for hope."

"I mean not to. You should return home and make your brother's passing as comfortable as possible. This is wisdom."

Gwyn shook his head. "No. If I don't try, I will always see myself as a coward. I can't live with regret, knowing I turned back at the first difficulty." He held Celin's gaze. "What price do you ask for the information you've given me?"

The Ilidreth blinked at him, slow, deliberating. "You have but one task to perform. Upon reaching Swan Castle, you must kill someone."

Gwyn recoiled. "*Kill?*"

"There is a creature there, once of the Ilidreth but far Fallen. His name is Kive, though he probably does not remember it. Among all the Ilidreth, he is most foul. Your strike would be a merciful one. Kill him if you can. In exchange I shall provide a mount swifter than the fastest horse, and your journey there will take but a fortnight, provided you are not waylaid by the True Wood."

Celin lifted his hand. A rustle came from behind him. Before Gwyn could respond to the Ilidreth's offer, his mouth fell open as into view trotted the fairest horse Gwyn had ever beheld. No, not a horse. A white deer.

No, he realized with a jolt. "A unicorn!"

The fair, lithe creature glowed a white purer than the Vale itself. Its horn was of gold and silver twined into a deadly point; its hooves, golden and flecked with silver; its eyes, opalescent, filled with every color. It gazed at Gwyn with an expression not animal, nor human. Gwyn thought perhaps the unicorn held the world in its gaze and understood far more than any human ever could.

Celin rested his slender hand on the unicorn's head. "This is Aluem, my very good friend. He shall be your guide and your mount, for he chooses so to be. My advice remains that you should return home, but Aluem feels otherwise, and thus he undertakes to aid you. Treat him with respect, for he is no common beast."

Gwyn caught Celin's gaze. "I treat all beasts with respect, but I understand that this is no beast at all." He turned back to the unicorn and bowed his head. "I'm Gwynter ren Terare."

Rushing wind filled Gwyn's mind, followed by flute-like words both familiar and strange. *'I am Aluem in your tongue, young Gwynter. I journey with you now because the Weave has called you. Shall we go?'*

The wind ceased, the world stilled, and Gwyn caught his breath. His wits returned to him. "What of Tia?"

"I shall see her to the edge of Vinwen province," said Celin. "Look to yourself. Your danger grows, while your mare's has ended."

Gwyn nodded. "Then I just need to gather my supplies." He turned to head back to Tia, but hesitated, and turned again to peer one last time at the Vale of Life.

"Look well," said Celin. "You are unlikely to see a Vale again while you yet live. Though perhaps that is not so long a wait as you would wish."

GWYN REMOVED his packs from Tia's back and set them aside. He paused and fingered the saddle strapped to the mare. Would he require it, or would that offend Aluem? It felt wrong to confine the unicorn at all, even in order to ride him.

Wind rushed through Gwyn's mind again, and Aluem's clarion voice flowed into his thoughts. '*There will be no need of your saddle or reins. I am not a beast of burden, and you shall not direct my steps. Hold fast to my mane and all will be well. Never has anyone fallen from the back of Aluem, unless I desired it.*'

Gwyn nodded, strapped his hunting knife and short sword to his belt, and quiver of arrows to his back. He glanced at his packs as he adjusted his bow against his shoulder. "How will we carry these?"

'*Take from them what you need but leave food behind. I shall provide you with sustenance. Bring nothing you cannot carry in a single pack.*'

Rummaging through his meager possessions, Gwyn chose to keep only one extra set of clothes and the medicinal herbs. He hitched the pack to his shoulder, repacked the food, and tied it to Tia's back. On a slip of parchment, he scrawled a swift note for Mother to find:

> *I am well.*

Satisfied, he came around to rest his hand against the mare's head. "Be brave a little longer, my friend. Celin will take you safely home and, Afallon willing, I shall return to greet you once again."

The mare nickered and rubbed against his face. He laughed and stroked between her eyes, patted her neck, and turned to the unicorn named Aluem.

"I'm ready to depart."

'*Very good. Climb upon my back, young Gwynter, and we shall run swifter than the wind against the treetops.*'

Tentative, Gwyn reached out to touch Aluem's back. As his fingers brushed against the unicorn's coat, he started. It was nothing like a horse's coarse hair at all, but soft as velvet and cold as silk. Finding purchase, Gwyn pulled himself onto Aluem and gingerly gripped the mane.

He glanced at Tia one last time and found Celin standing beside the mare, his hair black again, his lean frame draped in motley hues, one hand on Tia's neck.

Celin dipped his head. "May the sun shine upon your purpose as the Weave directs your course. Do not forget our bargain."

Before Gwyn could reply, Aluem bounded forward, muscles taut, and the trees became a blur. Gwyn clutched the mane with all his strength and bent forward to keep astride. The world became a swirl of colors, faraway, filled with scents too fleeting to catch.

Cool relief surged through Gwyn's veins as he raced due east upon Aluem. He really might have a chance to save Lawen.

But...

Celin had asked him to kill someone. Could Gwyn do it? He'd never killed a man before, and while most would call Ilidreth animals rather than men, and though an Ilidreth himself had asked the price, Gwyn doubted it would be so easy as hunting food.

I never agreed to the price. I never gave my word.

But was he honor-bound just the same?

Chapter Four

Nothing slowed unicorn and rider through the long day's run. When night fell, Aluem let Gwyn take his own feet within a grove of willows whose swaying reeds cast undulating shadows across the packed earth beneath a full moon.

Gwyn circled the grove, gathering branches and twigs to build a fire, but Aluem's voice drifted through his mind, calling him back. He returned to the unicorn's side.

'*Do not make a fire here. We are too near the True Wood. We do not desire to call attention to you from that fell realm.*'

Gwyn laid the wood aside. He glanced toward the clear sky beyond the willows. "It will be a cold night."

'*I shall keep you warm.*' Aluem trotted forward and folded his legs beneath him, first the front and then the back. '*Lay beside me when you have eaten.*'

"What do I eat?"

Aluem turned his head and bowed it to point his horn at the ground. Just where moonlight trickled down from the treetops, cradled in a large magnolia leaf, lay a handful of berries and mushrooms. '*They will satisfy your appetite for the present.*'

Gwyn knelt before the leaf and sampled a berry. Strange to see berries this time of the year, but they appeared ripe. The sweet-tart taste lingered long after he swallowed, and his parched throat felt soothed. He finished the meager meal, crawled over to Aluem, and cautiously pressed his head against the unicorn's flank. Rather than the pungent aroma of a horse, Aluem smelled of rainfall and rich loam on a summer's night. Warmth radiated from his body, more pleasant than a flickering flame. Gwyn nestled closer and let his eyelids droop.

It had been a strange day. So much had happened, yet Gwyn felt at his ease, comfortable. Sleepy. Not hungry at all.

He dreamt of Lawen. Not the feeble man lying abed, but as he'd been before. Dressed in the bright armor of the Crow King's army, he wielded sword and shield. Enemy forces, both Ilidreth and human, fled before his might. But as his sword pointed ahead, blackness slithered near from behind. Dark clouds gathered overhead. Thunder rumbled, but it sounded of laughter, soft and cruel. The earth trembled.

'Awaken, Gwynter.'

He started forward. Aluem's head turned toward him, eyes bright with color, though night still clung to the world.

Gwyn shivered. "It's not yet morning."

'No, but something foul stirs around us. We must move, for when I run few things can catch me.'

Gwyn shivered again, though he didn't feel cold. His chest tightened as an urgent fear flooded his veins. He rose and snatched up his satchel while Aluem climbed to his hooves. Gwyn caught the unicorn's neck, swung up onto his back, and dug his fingers into Aluem's silken mane.

'Cling tightly. We are pursued.'

He leaned forward. The unicorn leapt ahead and broke free of the copse.

Cries erupted in the trees and the wild flutter of wings tore loose from the branches above. Gwyn glimpsed a crow winging toward him, but he whipped his head around as Aluem gained speed. The howl of wind flooded Gwyn's ears, drowning all other sounds.

Snatches of scent filled his nose: fresh rain, a flowering thicket, the minty green of herbs.

Beating wings broke through the wind noise, and Gwyn glanced right to catch sight of another crow, before Aluem dodged left and danced around a wide tree. The crow disappeared.

At such speed, Gwyn had no choice but to clutch the unicorn's mane and stay silent. Any question he asked would be torn from his lips and lost in flight.

By the time Aluem slowed to a trot, sunlight filtered overhead. Gwyn pried his fingers free of the mane and flexed them to bring back feeling. Still neither spoke until the sound of gurgling water welled up ahead. Aluem quickened his gait until the brook fell into view, and there he halted.

'*You may dismount and rest for a moment. Our pursuers are far behind.*'

Gwyn stumbled to the brook and sank into the mud, plunged his hands into the icy water, and drank from his palms. When he'd had his fill, he turned to the unicorn, who daintily drank nearby.

"What chased us?" asked Gwyn. "I saw crows, but nothing else."

Aluem flicked an ear and continued to drink, but his voice filled Gwyn's mind. '*The crows pursued us. They are not ordinary crows but bound to the service of the Crow King.*'

Gwyn arched an eyebrow. "Impossible. The Crow King can't control birds."

Aluem raised his head and turned to peer into Gwyn's eyes. '*How do you know this?*'

"Well, because he's human. Like me. Humans don't possess magic. The Crow King opposes magic. That's why he's so determined to destroy the Ilidreth. He calls them a perversion and an evil."

'*I am certain that he says such things. But many men say what they do not believe, in order to lead others astray. For greed and power and profit, what might a man not try? But, pray, young Gwynter: what am I? A perversion and an evil? And am I so because your king declares such to be truth? Was Celin'Laen an evil, though he aided you and spared your life? He must be, for the Crow King has made it so by royal decree.'*

Gwyn stiffened, his chest tingling. The Crow King was ordained by Afallon Above to lead the Simaeri. His rule was divine. Yet Gwyn had seen for himself the courtesy of an Ilidreth and the wonder of a unicorn, magic personified. Was Gwyn deceived? Was the Crow King ignorant?

An Ilidreth killed my father while another helped me.

Lawen's vehement words against the Crow King entered Gwyn's mind. Spoken in illness, could Gwyn believe them?

It was too soon to say. Gwyn shook his head. "I must withhold my judgment for now and let truth reveal itself to me in due course. You say crows chase us. Whether of the Crow King or not, why do they wing after us so relentlessly?"

'They are after you.'

"Me? Why?"

'You seek magic. No matter the reason, the crows are bound by command to stop you. Magic must not be awakened in Simaerin. The Crow King fears it.'

Gwyn frowned. "But if the Crow King wields magic, as you say, why would he fear it?"

'Because some men wield greater magic than their fellows. Oppressed, none can oppose the tyrant king. But should others rise with magic to rival or outmatch his, his reign might cease. This he knows.'

Gwyn turned his eyes to the brook. "But if the Crow King has magic, why does he not rule the world? Instead he contends with the Fraeli, and they're human like me. Couldn't he wipe his enemies from the land altogether with his magic?"

'The Fraeli have allied themselves with Ilidreth in the northeast — nor do they ban the use of magic in Fraelin — and so they are not without protections.'

Gwyn nodded as he stirred the water with a finger. It made sense, but that didn't make it true. He was loath to think ill of the Crow King. Wasn't he a benevolent ruler? Didn't everyone speak his praises? Father had been a loyal liegeman, proud of his many years of service under the Crow Banner. As Lawen had always been, until now in his fevered state.

Lawen.

Gwyn's heart flinched. Now wasn't the moment to worry about such lofty matters. "I'm ready to ride again." He stood up. "Are the crows still pursuing us?"

'*They will not stop until we reach* Shaeswéath.'

Aluem lifted his head and allowed Gwyn to climb onto his back. Gwyn shifted his satchel and twined his fingers into the mane, a frown on his lips. *Shaeswéath.* Swan Castle. He'd grown up on stories of the Ilidreth edifice, but it was only legend. A children's story. If such a place existed, would it be made of glass, crushed diamonds, and mirrors, like a castle of ice that never melted? So Mother had described it many times.

"Did the lady Shalesta truly dwell there?" asked Gwyn, though he hadn't meant to speak aloud.

'*Ah, yes,*' sighed Aluem. '*And fairer maid was never wed to any Ilidreth king of old. Nor was any Ilidreth ruler so just or kind as Lord Roth, with his lady at his side. Hold tight.*'

Gwyn leaned forward and Aluem sprang ahead.

Would Gwyn really see Swan Castle? Did it shelter the cure he sought?

He shut his eyes and thought of Lawen.

Please hold on, brother. I will return as quickly as I can.

❧

AS DUSK SETTLED across the forest, Aluem halted. Gwyn started to dismount.

'*Not here, young Gwynter. We must keep going. But look.*'

Gwyn raised his eyes and studied the trees ahead. These loomed older than the forest behind, stretching taller, and the world ahead looked somehow darker. He shuddered despite himself. This was no human domain. The air hung heavy and a weight pressed against Gwyn's mind.

This is an unholy place.

Foul things lurked in shadow. Lidless eyes looked on, invisible, malignant.

"The True Wood."

'*Indeed. Here we may be waylaid by more than the king's crows. Here even a unicorn must beware if a human rides upon him. The True Wood may perceive you as an enemy. Once, the Lady Shalesta tamed these trees, but upon her end the True Wood grew wild, and no human is permitted. And so I must ask: Does Gwynter ren Terare choose to enter?*'

Gwyn fingered the pommel of his short sword, drew a steadying breath, and nodded. "I have no choice."

'*There is always a choice.*'

"Nevertheless, I will go on."

Aluem nodded and started forward.

"Wait."

Aluem stopped.

"I don't ask you to come with me."

'*And that, Gwynter, is why I choose to come.*'

The unicorn trotted forward. No marker defined the border of the True Wood, but a tremor climbed Gwyn's spine as he and his ethereal mount crossed into the ancient realm. The world hushed. The trees grew closer together. The wind held its breath.

Within a few yards, the sound of Aluem's hoofbeats struck what sounded like stone. Glancing down, Gwyn found an ancient road beneath them, overgrown but still distinct.

'*We travel* Serethenwé, *the path of shades. In a few days we shall reach* Chesevwé: *in your tongue called the Crystal Way.*'

A few days. "We're making good time, then?"

'*Thus far. If we are not delayed, we shall reach our destination six days hence.*'

Six days was much better time than over a fortnight. "Celin estimated it would take longer."

'*Celin'Laen is a pessimist. That aside, six days will bring us to the gates of Shaeswéath only. It will be three days more before we reach the castle proper. It is a vast estate.*'

"Celin said an Ilidreth still dwells there. Why only one? Or are there more?"

Aluem sighed. *'There is only one. No other Ilidreth would dare to enter Shaeswéath now. It is Fallen. Twisted.'*

Gwyn frowned. "But it has a cure for Lawen?"

'If cure there is, no other place could it be found. But do not hope for too much, young Gwynter. Much may have changed since last I visited that once-fair realm.'

"What happened to twist it so?" asked Gwyn. "I was raised on stories of Shalesta and Roth, but the tales ended happily. If Swan Castle does exist, and it has fallen, as you say — why?"

'There is only one who knows, and he cannot now tell.'

Chapter Five

A crow's sharp cry jolted Gwyn from a heavy slumber. He shot upright and stared into the gloom, heart hammering in his ears. Two days' travel within the True Wood, the trees grew so close together and the canvas of leaves spun so thick overhead, he couldn't determine if it was dawn or dusk, noon or true night. Aluem could always tell, but the unicorn slept now, body rising and falling in a deep rhythm.

Gwyn climbed to his feet, careful not to rustle the undergrowth and foliage that nestled in around him. A crow had woken him, yet he thought he'd heard his name in its cry. Had it been a crow at all?

Gwyn.

He glanced at Aluem, but the unicorn remained asleep.

Gwyn. Help!

His heart stammered. Lawen's voice.

A twig snapped. Gwyn whirled toward it. "Lawen?"

Gwyn!

The desperate tone drove Gwyn forward. He plunged into the trees. "Lawen? Lawen!"

'*No, Gwyn. Do not follow the voice!*' Aluem's cry filled Gwyn's mind, but the beat of wings flooded his ears. His heart galloped against his ribs. Crows swooped from the trees and encircled him. Gwyn cried out and covered his face with his arms, stumbling forward, trying to escape.

Talons lashed out. Crows pecked at his flesh, drawing blood, shouting in a deafening frenzy.

Gwyn grabbed his short sword. Drew it forth. Slashed at the cloud of birds as he ran.

One screamed as his blade bit into its wing. He slashed at another.

The crows dispersed all at once, clearing his vision. A chasm, dark and wide, gaped ahead. Crying out, he stumbled over the ledge.

He scrabbled at the earthen wall as he plunged into darkness, blood roaring in his ears. His fingers snatched at the vines and roots jutting from the chasm's face until he snared a strong root and jerked to a halt, hands burning. His arms throbbed. He kicked the wall to dig the toes of his boots into the earth. Dirt filled his eyes as he squinted up.

Forty feet above, a dim crack of light revealed the chasm's mouth.

He risked looking down, but the darkness hung thick beneath him and he couldn't find the bottom. Gwyn shuddered. Acting like a fool, he'd come far too close to his death! Aluem would be right to scold him when he returned to their meager encampment — assuming Gwyn managed to climb out of this rift.

He set his jaw, dug his boots deeper into the wall, and reached one hand up to find a handhold. A root tickled his fingers. He snatched it and yanked hard to test its strength. It should hold. Gwyn sought a similar grip for his other hand, found one, and inched himself up. Burrowed his toes into a higher point in the earthen wall.

He repeated the process over and over, painstakingly inching upward. His limbs began to tremble. Sweat covered his brow.

Keep going. Just move.

Gwyn tried not to look up or down.

Just keep climbing. Ignore the fatigue. Ignore the distance.

He reached up for another handhold but found only dirt. He groped higher, but no root or vine hung within reach. Gwyn looked up. Five feet or more stretched between him and the surface. Sweat drenched his shirt. Stung his eyes. His throat burned. In the gloom he couldn't spot any plantlife except around the chasm's lip much too far to reach yet.

He licked his lips and tasted dirt.

What could he do? His arms ached and shook. He couldn't dangle like this much longer.

"You survived, Simaeri?"

Gwyn blinked and made out a silhouette hovering overhead. Not Aluem, for the voice wasn't in his mind.

"Will you help me?" asked Gwyn.

The silhouette laughed. "Why should I help you? Better that all Simaeri die. Why not like this?"

"You're Ilidreth." It seemed a reasonable guess.

"Just so. You are where it is forbidden to tread."

A dry smile touched Gwyn's lips. "I can see why. Chasms are difficult indeed to tread at all."

The Ilidreth chuckled. "At least you will die knowing you kept your wit until the end, if that is comforting to a Simaeri."

Gwyn's head pounded as the silhouette vanished from the opening. "Please wait!"

No answer.

Pressing his cheek to the wall, he shut his eyes and drew several breaths to calm his thumping heart. Musty odors filled his nostrils.

"Think, Gwyn. Is there another way?"

His eyes opened. He stretched his arm out to his right and found more vines. Gingerly, arduously, he inched toward them, and tried again to reach up for purchase. Protruding tree roots scratched his fingers; thick, strong. He started upward again, each movement an agony worse than the last, arms leaden. But he kept climbing.

His muscles screamed and his head hammered until spots appeared against his eyes.

Do not give up.

His foot slipped even as his fingers caught the edge of the chasm. He gasped, dizzy and euphoric. Clawing and scrabbling, he dragged himself, shaking, over the lip and collapsed in a heap. His body quivered and his head reeled. He was alive. He'd made it.

Cool wind breathed on his brow, lulling his mind into a doze. He lost track of time, lying still, letting his body recover as the forest groaned and whispered above him. His thoughts drifted into disjointed dreams of Mount Vinwen; of Lawen and his illness; of crows winging overhead, circling, circling.

Gwyn started up, still quavering, covered in sweat. His body throbbed and his head still spun. He staggered to his feet. He must return to Aluem, but which way should he go?

He cast his eyes to the forest floor, barely visible in the gloom. He bent and consulted the earth with his fingers until he found his frantic tracks heading from the forest southward. He set off, praying to Afallon that he wouldn't encounter crows or merciless Ilidreth.

Countless times, he stooped to find his haphazard tracks. Spots grew thicker against his vision. The world wobbled. His skin pricked with cold.

Wings fluttered. Gwyn whirled and stumbled.

A sharp point pressed into his back.

"I am impressed," cooed a soft, familiar voice. The Ilidreth from the chasm. "In a way it is better like this. It has been so long since I last met a Simaeri. I do long to torment you."

Chapter Six

Stupid. Stupid. Stupid.

Gwyn tested his bonds and winced as the ropes bit into his wrists. He lay facing a campfire, arms tied behind his back, legs bound, face burning with the fire's heat, eyes shut to avoid the drifting smoke. He could hear the Ilidreth close by, sharpening a knife judging from the grating noise of steel on whetstone.

Did the Ilidreth intend to torture him? Celin had shown him mercy for his youth; but then, Celin had implied not all Ilidreth were so courteous. This one dwelt in the True Wood. Did that make a difference?

Gwyn fought to keep his breaths even. Where was Aluem? The unicorn had kept him safe, even in these unhallowed woods. But though Aluem had called to Gwyn when he ran after that phantom voice, the unicorn hadn't followed. Did that mean Aluem didn't intend to rescue him? Perhaps the unicorn couldn't follow? Had the Wood harmed Aluem?

The scraping whir of the blade on stone ceased.

Cloth rustled.

The faint pad of approaching feet heightened Gwyn's dread and his heart raced. He opened his eyes and shifted to peer up. He caught a glimpse of the Ilidreth's face, though the fae man's features were contorted against the fire's glow.

"What is your name, Simaeri?"

"Gwyn," he whispered.

"Your full name."

He pulled his lips tight.

The Ilidreth knelt behind Gwyn and caught his arm. The sharp point of a knife dug into his back. "Your full name, or I will kill you."

Gwyn shut his eyes. His heart thundered in his ears. "Won't you kill me either way?"

Warm breath tickled Gwyn's ear as the Ilidreth whispered, "You are afraid."

Gwyn bit his lip to stifle a whimper. He didn't want to die.

Laughter, soft and mad, filled his ear. A hand stroked his hair. "You should be afraid. I shall not spare you pain, Simaeri. Until you tell me your name, your suffering will not end. And after that, long after that, I will kill you."

Gwyn inhaled a shuddering breath.

Please, Blessed Afallon above, lend me strength. Don't let me die here. I must save Lawen.

Lawen. Would he lie here and give up? No. He would fight for his brother until his last breath. Lawen didn't know how to give up. Gwyn closed his eyes and gathered what strength he had left. His arms ached with the recent memory of his climb. His head swam. But he couldn't die here; not now; not yet. Gwyn set his jaw and pulled against the cords binding his wrists. Strain coursed through his body, but adrenaline ran with it. A breeze brushed his skin. The cords snapped.

The Ilidreth cried out.

Gwyn twisted around and snatched the knife from the creature's hand. In one swift motion he cut the cords around his ankles, and trembling, climbed to his feet.

"I don't have time to be afraid, Ilidreth. I can't afford to be stopped. You must let me go on, or I must move you from my path. Which will it be?"

The Ilidreth, a ragged, emaciated creature with matted black hair, sank to his knees, hands lifted in entreaty. "Do not kill me. I will not stop you."

Gwyn kept the knife raised. "Have you seen my friend, a unicorn?"

A cruel smile crawled across the Ilidreth's face. "Your friend is dying. I stabbed him through. Even a unicorn can be killed if a fae strikes him down with the right weapon."

Gwyn's chest tightened. "Where is he?"

The Ilidreth pointed, chuckling. "Where you left him. Bleeding out."

Gwyn stared at the once-fair creature kneeling before him. Now twisted. Fallen. "What's your name?"

The Ilidreth sighed. "I remembered once. But that was long ago, when the castle stood bright, its lady fair, its lord alive. Long, long ago."

Gwyn turned away, clutching the knife. "Don't follow me." He darted through the close-knit trees, dodging branches and thorns as he could. Soon he picked his trail up and followed it until he reached the camp where he'd left Aluem.

The unicorn lay upon the forest floor, silver blood pooled around him. It glowed like moonlight on water, beautiful and terrible. Gwyn knelt beside his friend and rested a hand on his chest. It rose and fell so faintly.

"Aluem, please forgive a fool. I left you to chase after phantoms."

The knife had struck deep, but nothing vital, if Gwyn rightly guessed anything of the fair creature's anatomy. The problem was blood loss. Gwyn pulled off his gray vest, wadded it up, and pressed it over the wound.

He spotted his herb kit against a nearby tree. Stretched out his foot. Hooked the kit with his boot. Dragged it closer. Gwyn knew only a little herb lore, but enough to stop bleeding. He riffled through the kit for his jar of cayenne powder.

He hesitated. *Is unicorn blood different?*

It didn't matter. He must try.

He wiped his sweaty hands on his pants and continued to rummage through his kit. As he caught hold of the jar, his mind wrestled with a dismal thought: He had failed. Without Aluem, he could never hope to reach Swan Castle and return to Vinwen in time to heal his brother. Even if he saved Aluem's life here, the unicorn couldn't possibly travel on. They were stuck, lost somewhere in the True Wood, far from friend or shelter.

It's my fault. I fell for the crows' tricks and doomed my friend and my brother in the same moment.

If Aluem died now, Gwyn would be alone in this dread place.

His fingers moved deftly to bind the wound. He laid his head against Aluem's strong neck and listened to his deep breaths. "Please, Sweet Afallon, spare my friend. Let him live."

Afallon was the God of people, not of fae creatures. Would he listen to such a prayer?

❧

He couldn't say how, but Gwyn *felt* the dawn come. Somewhere beyond the True Wood the sun weaved golden threads of light across the greening world. He'd barely slept at all, too worried about Aluem to quiet his mind. Now Gwyn sat up and shifted to find Aluem's face. The unicorn eyed him back.

Gwyn started. "Aluem?"

'You move at last. Are you wounded, young Gwynter?'

Gwyn shook his head. "Not overmuch. Only a little sore. I might have been fevered but my mind is clear now." He brushed his fingers against the velvet coat of the unicorn. "How are you?"

'Healed, many thanks to you.'

Gwyn blinked. "Healed?"

'Aye. You stopped the bleeding and that allowed me to recover fully. The

only way to kill a unicorn is to rob him of his lifeblood. I owe you my life, Gwynter ren Terare.'

"No!" Gwyn's voice rose higher than he intended. He bowed his head. "Not true, Aluem. My reckless behavior caused your injury."

'I suspect not, for had we both been here, perhaps the Ilidreth would have killed you first, and then stabbed me. Who then would bind my injury? But tell me, what voice called you into the Wood? What occurred after you vanished?'

Gwyn recounted his misadventure and Aluem listened in silence. When Gwyn finished, the unicorn raised his head.

'You were blessed indeed, young Gwynter. It would seem your Afallon favors you.'

Gwyn smiled. "As He favors all people." The smile fell away. "I hope He'll continue to favor my quest. I fear for Lawen."

'May Afallon and the Weave keep him safe. Let us not tarry, for time is stretching on, and we must do our part in the work.' Aluem climbed to his hooves, shook his mane, and pawed the ground. *'Yes, all is well. We may ride on.'*

Hope soared through Gwyn's limbs, lending new strength. He pushed to his feet and rested a hand on Aluem's flank. "Are you certain?"

'Quite so, my young friend.'

Grinning, Gwyn caught up his meager supplies and mounted the unicorn. They began their journey again, slowed by the thickset trees.

Gwyn's mind felt fresh and strong despite his sleepless night. To harbor new hope after utter despair – it was the sweetest feeling in the world. For the first time in several days, curiosity prodded his thoughts. "Aluem? You've mentioned the Weave before. That it had chosen me. What is the Weave?"

'The Weave is life and the magic that runs through it. Some say your god Afallon and the Weave are one and the same. I do not know if that is true or if the two sources work in harmony, but harmonic is their tune nonetheless.'

"Then you believe in Afallon?"

'Not by the same name, but yes.'

Gwyn pondered the idea of Afallon being the source of magic. No doubt the Crow King would fight against any such notion — but then, he would also have Aluem burned alive. Gwyn ran his fingers through the unicorn's mane. "What did you mean about the Weave choosing me? For what?"

'*As to that, it is best I say nothing at present. For now, surviving the True Wood and obtaining your brother's cure are all that we should focus upon.*'

Gwyn nodded. "About that. Celin said nothing of what the cure might be. How will I find it?"

'*I do not know*,' answered Aluem.

They rode on in silence. Gwyn's thoughts lingered on Lawen until his heart grew heavy.

'*Tell me, Gwynter*,' Aluem said after a while. '*Why do the Simaeri fight against the Fraeli in this age? I have seen your battles from a great distance, but the reason for their battles escapes my understanding.*'

Gwyn raised his brow. "The Fraeli? Well. The Crane King broke a longstanding treaty with the Crow King and war has been waged these last thirteen years for that reason."

'*Ah. The breaking of oaths is an all too common sin in the mundane world if I rightly recall.*'

"The mundane world?" asked Gwyn.

Laughter rushed through Gwyn's mind. '*I meant no offense, but in hindsight perhaps the term is offensive. We of the Weave have always referred to those without magic as mundane or of the mundane world.*'

Gwyn shrugged. "It doesn't offend."

'*If I may ask, what treaty did the Fraeli break?*'

Gwyn frowned as he thought back on conversations between his father and Lawen over the years. "It has to do with the Ilidreth lands, I believe. Some of the Fraeli have tried to claim pieces of it for themselves, and rumors whisper of alliances between Fraeli immigrants and Ilidreth outposts. You mentioned such an alliance yourself. The Crow King claims that the forests belong to Simaerin and the Fraeli have no business taking any of it. Long ago, the Crane King acknowledged the Crow King's right to all this land, but since then his people have sailed the channel down from Fraelin to invade, nonetheless."

Aluem sighed. '*In truth, neither mundane king has a right to anything, for long before your peoples came to inhabit this land, the Ilidreth ruled all of this continent, then called Ilid, and all the isles around it. It is a pity that squabbles arise so, and many lives are lost, bathing the land in blood that taints its magics. The Weave is unsettled, and this war answers why that has been so.*' The unicorn sighed again. '*Though it would be unfair to say only the mundane have played a part in that. The Ilidreth, too, have shed blood unjustly.*'

Gwyn thought of Father, so desperate for a cure that he would demand one of what he believed was a savage race. And he had died for something he didn't gain.

Gwyn's heart throbbed and his throat tightened. There was no way to know now if Father's death was his fault or the fault of a Fallen Ilidreth.

Fallen. Celin wasn't Fallen.

"Aluem, you spoke before of one who knows why Swan Castle and the Ilidreth fell — but you said he can't speak. Why?"

'*I did not say he could not speak, but that he could not tell his tale.*'

"But why?"

Aluem softly sighed. '*You shall soon see.*'

Chapter Seven

Despite Gwyn's secret fears, nothing delayed the two companions further that day. At eventide Aluem halted and commanded Gwyn to raise his head. Weary but curious, Gwyn looked up and let out a gasp.

Before him stretched a pathway glowing like moonlight on water. It wended between the trees and out of sight.

'Behold Chesevwé — the Crystal Way.'

On closer inspection, Gwyn realized the path wasn't made of paved stones but was in fact a stream lighted by glowing stones deep beneath the flowing water. He tore his eyes from the view to look at Aluem.

The unicorn stepped forward. His hooves struck the surface of the water as though it *were* made of stone; he stepped fully onto the streamlet path. Ripples bloomed beneath the unicorn's hooves. Gwyn stared between the water beneath and the wending way ahead. Small wonder Celin had said Gwyn couldn't make it quickly on his own — if he made it at all.

Gwyn glanced at the trees surrounding the Crystal Way. "If Swan Castle has fallen, and everything there is twisted, why does this path remain beautiful?"

'The Lord and Lady fell, but some of their grace remains. If not so, perhaps all the world would be mad.'

"Not with Afallon's blessing."

'True. The Lord and Lady were not alone in blessing the world. But certainly without them the land is far less beautiful. So it is when tragedy and horror strike. But tell me, Gwynter, what is your perception of the world? Your king calls magic evil, and yet you sought the Ilidreth. Your people fight the Fraeli, but you are not a soldier. What way do you see the world?'

Gwyn frowned. "I hardly know the world if this journey has taught me anything. I came to the Ilidreth out of desperation, and so far, I've found allies and foes alike, and even one friend." He smiled at Aluem, but the smile faded. "Beyond that, I know very little. The Crow King and all who stand with him call magic evil. Should anyone learn what I'm doing here, I may be put to death. It simply can't matter to me. Lawen is the person I love most in the world. If I can save him, I'm under obligation to try."

'But if the Crow King is right, is not your soul forfeit?'

Gwyn's frown deepened. "The king's court would argue so. The church might agree. Yet I feel Afallon's blessing upon me. I'm unsure what to believe, Aluem. Could a provincial lord's son possibly know more than a king or priest about such matters? I just don't know."

His eyes sought the sky, visible like a wending crack between the woven branches overhead. "I had intended to join the Crow King's army, as my brother did. The fact remains, we're at war. People are dying. I'm under obligation to protect Simaerin, but from what threat I couldn't now say."

A crow's harsh caw rang from a nearby tree. Gwyn tensed and eyed the bird, black against almost-black green. A wall of trees towered on either side of the path. Did a thousand eyes watch from hidden places in the darkness?

'Fear not. The king's crows cannot come within the boundaries of Chesevwé.'

"You say the Crow King is trying to stop me, and certainly the birds are acting strangely." Gwyn sighed. "What must I believe? Am I a heretic? Is the Crow King evil?" He shook his head. "If the Crow King wields magic, why does he call it evil? And how does he, a human, wield magic at all? Isn't he, as you say, mundane?"

'*I never said humans could not wield magic, Gwynter,*' said Aluem. '*Many of the Crow King's generals do. They are mages — humans who wield magic are thus called. You, too, are a mage.*'

Gwyn started, sitting straighter. "I'm what?"

'*Did I not say upon our meeting that the Weave had chosen you? Have I not said it since? You are a mage.*'

Gwyn laughed. It was a ludicrous idea: He, a wielder of magic? "I'm only a fourteen-year-old boy — my father's second-born, and from his second wife. I know how to till the land and work the fields, and I've learned some forest lore, but I certainly can't work magic!"

'*You laugh, yet you are still alive.*'

"By Afallon's blessing and ample help from you, my friend," Gwyn replied, still smiling. "I can't credit myself for conjuring anything at all."

'*Except perhaps good instincts, strength enough to break Ilidreth bonds, and the ability to* see *within a Vale.*'

Gwyn paused. "I can't be a mage. I can't wield magic. Aluem, I'm barely noble. My father's lineage is weak. That we possess Vinwen at all is a boon granted by a past Crow King, several generations ago, for heroic service in his army. We can barely afford the servants we have; we can barely feed the slaves we house. We're nothing special by way of the world."

'*Who speaks of the world, but you, Gwynter? I said nothing of wealth or prestige. I spoke of magic, which may run in the veins of a pauper as much as a king. The Weave cares nothing for title or lands or jewels. You cannot buy its loyalty. Nor does it choose its wielders from only the most righteous or just men. Thus, those in the Crow King's service wield magic even for wicked deeds. But now and then the Weave* does *choose a champion. I believe that champion is you. I believe a great destiny rests upon your shoulders, should you choose to accept the Weave's calling.*'

Gwyn shifted and rubbed an itch on his neck. "A great destiny? I only want to heal my brother and return to my home. To join the king's army should he require my service. And after I've fought my war — if I survive it — I'll return to Vinwen and work the fields, raise a family to succeed me, and die of old age. *That* is the destiny my father set before me. That's all I can do."

'*And so your knowledge of the Ilidreth — of what they truly are — of what* I am, *means nothing? You will return to Simaerin and work the fields, forgetting what you have seen and learned in the True Wood?*'

Gwyn sighed, shaking his head. "If I thought I could help, if I thought my service would open the eyes of my Simaeri brethren to the truth — if it could stop the war between my people and the Fraeli — I would do it. But I haven't that kind of influence. I'm only a boy, not of age until six months hence, and my standing in the world is as humble as any nobleman could claim. It's simply impossible."

'*What is impossible is not simple, and what is simple is always possible, young Lord Gwynter. Do you stand by what you said? If you* could *make a difference, you would?*'

"I would have no choice should it be within my power. My conscience would require it."

'*Then let that be enough for now, Gwynter. Consider what you learn here; let your heart absorb it. And perhaps — should you prove to be more than you believe — just perhaps you will change the world.*'

❧

AT GWYN'S INSISTENCE, the two companions didn't rest that night. Fresh urgency flooded his soul as the weight of lost time pressed upon him. Lawen had been so fragile over a week ago. How must he be now? Could he already be dead? Gwyn tried not to think that way, but restless fears crept into his mind like spilled ink over parchment, staining every hope.

Then there were the crows.

The birds' numbers grew as unicorn and rider galloped along the stream; now the evil fowl resided on every tree in sight, eerily silent, as though they waited to snare Gwyn if he should step off the Crystal Way. Gwyn fought against a mad desire to flee, until morning finally dawned.

Aluem's pace slowed. '*Would you like to stretch your legs, young Gwynter?*'

Glancing at the trees, Gwyn shook his head. "I don't think that's wise."

'*The path is safe.*'

"I...I couldn't walk on it, surely. I'm human."

'*Even a human without magic could walk this path.*' The unicorn halted. '*Shall you not try?*'

Gwyn's limbs throbbed. He hesitated, then smiled. Swinging from Aluem's back, he struck the water and found it solid as ripples raced from his feet. Laughing, he studied the crystalline stones beneath the stream. Warmth pulsed from them as their light sparkled in the pale sunlight, dimming his fears.

'*They are called starstones in your tongue.* Léathial. *The Lord of* Shaeswéath *plucked them from the heavens to pave this pathway many ages past.*'

What a beautiful story. Gwyn stooped to rest his hand against the flowing water beneath, yearning to touch a starstone. He expected to meet resistance, but his hand passed through the water while his feet remained planted on its surface. Warm water bathed his fingers and his hand tingled. He brought his fingertips just shy of the nearest stone and hesitated. He glanced at Aluem, who watched him with twinkling eyes.

'*Do not fear. You can cause it no harm, and it certainly shan't harm you.*'

Gwyn let himself smile as he grasped the starstone. Warmth filled his body. His fears fled. Doubts melted. The forest grew brighter, and fairer, perhaps as it had been in an age long gone. Birdsong rang through his soul; almost words; almost human.

The wind laughed at him and tugged on his ponytail. *Come. Fly!* it warbled.

'*Come, Gwyn,*' Aluem said. '*We must not dally.*'

Startled, Gwyn dropped the starstone and the world dimmed. He pulled his arm free of the depths. The water rushed from his sleeve, his hand, his fingertips, leaving him dry.

He laughed. "Magic is wondrous."

'All of it, yes. Good and evil alike. That is why many are seduced by what is dark and forbidden. There is always wonder where there is power. But wonder is not the result, merely a symptom.' Aluem glanced up the path. *'The waters here shall long flow, but your time is short. We must move.'*

Gwyn mounted, still grinning. "If only I could bring back a starstone for Lawen. He would love to feel its warmth."

'Should we succeed, he will feel of something far better. Besides, these starstones cannot leave Chesevwé, *for the waters here bind them to this world. Otherwise, they would fade or fly again to the heavens as they chose, now that Lord Roth is not of this realm.'*

"Still, I would love to show him. But not at the cost of entering the True Wood a second time. I'll have to be satisfied with telling him of it. I confess I'm glad to have a story to match all his grand adventures." Despite Lawen's condition, Gwyn found his spirits much higher for touching the starstone. The feeling lasted all through the day, and still as the sun set, he felt warm and safe. Fears couldn't touch him.

That night, as he rested his head against Aluem's soft mane, he thought he heard the stars far above and close beneath faintly singing.

Chapter Eight

The Crystal Way flowed between enormous gates that formed great swan wings of crystalline stone. Early morning sunlight gleamed against the spanning feathers, casting rainbows before the gaping entrance. Gwyn stared when Aluem halted to give him a proper look.

These were the gates of *Shaeswéath*: the beginning of the land of Swan Castle; heart of that once-great realm of the Ilidreth in the days of Lord Roth and Lady Shalesta.

'*You may well be the first Simaeri to enter the domain of the fae in three hundred years,*' said Aluem in hushed tones, though his voice was in Gwyn's mind. '*Art thou prepared to enter?*'

Gwyn's fingers gripped Aluem's mane so hard he couldn't feel them any longer. His throat felt dry and closed. He forced himself to swallow.

For Lawen.

"I won't turn back."

Aluem bobbed his head and trotted forward. The gates lay open, and only now did Gwyn notice that one massive door hung by a single hinge. Swan Castle was indeed fallen. Beyond the gateway he looked ahead to find a rising slope. The Crystal Way flowed upward, leading them toward the castle proper still a three days' ride away.

"Surely other travelers have sought this place. Haven't any of them found it?" whispered Gwyn. Though the realm stood empty, he didn't want to disturb its peace. This place felt how he imagined a king's tomb: hallowed, ancient, sorrowful.

'*There are many who still seek this place, either to prove or disprove its existence. Most do not make it to the True Wood, and far fewer survive the True Wood to reach the Gates of* Shaesweáth. *If any pass through the gates, I little doubt they die before reaching the Castle.*'

Gwyn shuddered. "What foul thing resides here?"

'*A single Ilidreth. Kive by name.*'

"Kive." Gwyn swallowed. "The one I'm obligated to kill." His chest tightened. How could he accomplish this task if none before him had succeeded? He'd never killed anyone before. "Is he a dreadful specter?"

'*I do not know if your words do him proper justice. There is no Ilidreth so far Fallen in all the True Wood as is Kive. He alone dwells in* Shaesweáth, *and no sane Ilidreth will dare approach him.*'

"Please," said Gwyn through a shiver, "no more. I'm sorry I asked. I'll find out soon enough."

'*So you shall.*'

They traveled on in thickening silence. Gwyn's heart raced with the prospect of facing the coming terror. Would he have the strength to survive? Would he die here, in this realm so far removed from all he knew and loved? All alone, save for Aluem. Mother would despair when he didn't return. How could he not have considered her feelings until now? Hadn't she already lost a husband to the Ilidreth?

I can't change what I've done. Nor do I regret the effort to save Lawen.

The forest continued alongside the Crystal Way, somehow darker than outside this empty realm, though Gwyn hadn't thought that possible. But he noticed one welcome change.

"The crows are gone."

The unicorn nodded. *'None of them would dare to enter here in daytime. Tonight, we must remain alert.'*

Gwyn's one glimmer of hope expired.

Despite the looming trees, the sky hung more exposed, and Gwyn welcomed the meager sunlight, shadowed though it was. Its presence drove him forward, even as instinct screamed at him to retreat. His fingers stroked the hilt and pommel of his short sword. Onward, unicorn and rider trotted, slowly approaching the castle.

So slowly.

Darkness fell like a curtain. Gwyn glanced up and found black clouds gathered above. Thunder rumbled and the earth quaked.

Sweet Afallon, protect us.

The air tingled as the storm drummed against the sky. Was this magic?

Ahead, someone screamed.

Gwyn started up. Aluem's pace quickened and Gwyn drew his blade.

They crested another steep hill, and below — at the hill's base, just off the Crystal Way — hunched two figures. Gwyn shook Aluem's mane like reins, though the unicorn already charged toward the strangers. Another scream rolled across the air.

"I said no!"

Gwyn squinted until he made out the two figures. A pale-haired little girl pressed her back to a tree, while before her knelt a thin man with long, tangled hair of raven black. He reached toward her with slender fingers, as though to entice her. She looked petrified, eyes wide, face colorless.

Aluem came to a halt. The girl spotted him. Her blue-green eyes widened more at the sight of the unicorn and her mouth fell open. Slowly she looked up to meet Gwyn's gaze. He threw himself from Aluem's back and trotted from the Crystal Way, sword brandished.

"Fall back, stranger, before I run you through."

The thin man turned to Gwyn, who gasped. The stranger's irises were bloodred and glittering beneath his curtain of black hair. His clothes were in tatters, swaths of black, perhaps the remnants of robes. His flesh, though fair, held a faint sickly blue tint like a corpse. He smiled, and the motion sent a chill down Gwyn's spine.

Gwyn knew this man, this creature, for what he was. "Kive."

The Ilidreth blinked and canted his head, each motion slow and deliberate. "Does the rat know Kive?" he asked in a low, breathy voice.

Gwyn took a step forward, sword pointed at the Ilidreth's heart. "Back away, fiend."

"Be careful!" cried the girl. "He's very fast and very strong."

Kive turned back to the girl. "Hush, rat, and *let me eat you*." His voice drifted across the air, slow, lilting, somehow inviting.

The girl whimpered but lifted her chin. "I told you I'm not a rat. I'm a girl! You can't eat *girls*."

Gwyn inched forward to brush his sword-point against the Ilidreth's shoulder. "And I said to back away."

Kive considered the blade, then turned back to the girl. "Such a young juicy rat. Such big red eyes."

"My eyes aren't even red," cried the girl, half-shrieking. "They're blue. Green. Ish." She glanced at Gwyn and shrugged rather forlornly. He could see the wheels turning in her mind as she tried to plead for her life.

Kive looked again at Gwyn. "Rats always have red eyes."

Gwyn wasn't sure of that, but he shrugged, trying to show none of his fear. "I guess that means she's not a rat. Hers *are* a kind of blue-green. Look."

Kive turned to her. "So they are. A bird, then? Sooo crunchy. I like the wings best."

The girl let out a squeak. "I'm not a bird either. I don't even have wings!"

Gwyn pressed the sword a little closer. "Back away. You can't eat her."

With lightning agility Kive lashed out and knocked the sword aside. Gwyn staggered with it.

The Ilidreth's gleaming eyes considered him. "Should I eat this rat instead?"

"He's not a rat either," the girl insisted. "He's a *boy*."

Kive rose to his feet. "Rats often lie. But they taste good just the same. Hush, lying rats, and let Kive eat you."

"No!" said the girl, folding her arms as she swallowed. "We're not rats, and you can't eat us just because you want to. If a Kive eats what he thinks is a rat but isn't, h-he might get sick."

"I never get sick," said Kive, taking on a petulant tone. "Only hungry. Sooo hungry. But which are you? Birds or rats? Or are you flies? Oooh, I do love flies. Juicy flies, so tiny, so fresh." He closed his eyes, mouth working, as though savoring something delicious.

The girl looked ready to retch. "We're not flies either. I told you, I'm a *girl*. A girl named Nathaera." She glanced at Gwyn as she said that last. "And *he's* a boy named...?" She rolled her hand, urging him to speak.

"Uh, Gwyn. Gwynter ren Terare." He bowed his head, sword leveled again at Kive.

She managed a wan smile. "Ren Terare is of Vinwen Province, isn't it? I'm of House ren Lotelon of Crowwell."

Gwyn blinked. She was of high noble lineage indeed. But what in Simaerin was she doing all the way out here, and all alone — except for her deranged captor?

Nathaera turned back to Kive. "Besides," she said, voice quavering now, "you've eaten enough today. You must be full by now."

Kive paused, perhaps considering that. Then he shook his head. "Where there are rats, they must be eaten. Master said so."

"Well, there *aren't* any rats, so you needn't eat anything or anyone!"

'Besides, these two are not alone.'

Aluem's hooves whispered in the grass as the unicorn approached. Nathaera let out a gasp and her hands shot out as though she wished to touch the majestic creature. In the same moment Kive shrank back with a hiss.

"This is Aluem," said Gwyn. "My friend."

Nathaera nodded, her eyes riveted on the unicorn. "Yes. So he just told me. In my *head*." She slumped against the tree. "I'm not entirely sure I'm not *out* of my head."

Gwyn laughed softly, but as Kive shifted his smile vanished. Gwyn kept his blade trained on the fallen Ilidreth. "You mentioned a master, Kive. Is he here?"

Kive's eyes darted toward the sky. "Master is everywhere..." He flinched back as Aluem took another step.

"I've not seen anyone else," said Nathaera. "At least, not since... well, this morning."

Gwyn glanced at her and found her eyes red-rimmed. Her lips turned up in a tremulous smile.

"You were with companions until then?" He glanced at Kive, afraid to guess what had happened to them.

She nodded, eyes welling with tears. "I came with a party of knights in pursuit of Swan Castle. It was all Windsur's idea. He — he wanted to prove himself heroic, I suppose. Or maybe he was just a fool." She shook her head, a tear sliding down her cheek. "I only came to send him back home. I thought he'd turn about at the first sign of danger if I came along. But...he didn't."

Gwyn's brow lifted. "Windsur ren Cloven of Crowwell?"

"Yes," said Nathaera, lifting a handkerchief to swipe at her eye. "He's my betrothed — or, well, he was."

Gwyn's brow shot higher. "Betrothed?" She was such a wisp of a girl he'd assumed she was no older than twelve. But by the Crow King's law, a girl could only be promised to a man when she turned fifteen. Verbal arrangements might be made before that day, but one simply didn't speak of it until she came of age.

Nathaera eyed Gwyn with a knowing smile. "You thought I was younger than I am, didn't you? It's all right, I'm not offended. Everyone assumes I'm twelve or thirteen, but I promise you I've lived for sixteen entire springs. Windsur and I became betrothed last Autumn. It was our parents' wishes." Another tear slid down her cheek. "I can't say I loved him — those feelings can take time, you know. But I never would've wished our betrothal to end like this..."

Gwyn found his eyes resting on Kive. "How did he die?"

"S-swallowed," answered Nathaera with a shudder.

Gwyn's eyes widened. "He was *eaten*?" He shrank back from the Ilidreth, who had hunkered down against the unicorn's steady stare.

"No. Swallowed. By the trees."

Gwyn glanced at the girl. "The trees?"

Nathaera nodded. "The roots...just sprang up all of the sudden and dragged poor Windsur down into the earth. It was terrible. His screams lasted for several moments." She shivered and squeezed her eyes closed. "I'll never forget the sight of it. The sounds of his screams. Never."

Gwyn sheathed his blade, rounded Aluem, and knelt before the maiden. He rested a hand on her arm. "I'm very sorry for your loss. You've been through an awful ordeal. But I won't let anything happen to you now, while I have strength."

Her blue-green eyes opened, bright with tears. A faint smile touched her lips. "Thank you, Gwynter ren Terare. Despite everything that's happened, I do feel safer now that you're here." Her eyes slid to the unicorn and Ilidreth. "You and your, eh, companion."

Gwyn stood. "I'm a little pressed for time, so we must keep moving. If you don't mind riding a unicorn."

'*I can carry you both well enough,*' said Aluem.

Gwyn nodded and offered his hand to Nathaera. She took it and let him hoist her to her feet. She stood an entire foot shorter than him.

"Did all your party meet the same end?" Gwyn asked as he led the girl to Aluem's side. From the corner of his eye, he watched Kive slinking nearby, but not inching any closer to the unicorn.

"Some of them did," Nathaera said. "But others were eaten by the creature you call Kive."

Gwyn's step faltered. "He *ate* them?"

Nathaera gravely nodded. "That's why I was trying so hard to make him realize I'm a girl, not a rat. He seems to think people *are* rats, and he *eats* them. It's...the most dreadful thing I've ever seen... Not that I watched..."

Aluem caught Gwyn's eye. '*What befalls a twisted Ilidreth in the end. Thus, Celin wished for you to kill Kive upon your meeting.*'

"If I may ask," said Nathaera, "what are you doing all the way out here? And with such a magnificent acquaintance?"

Gwyn pried his eyes from Aluem's to meet the girl's gaze. "I'm seeking Swan Castle."

She grimaced. "Not to prove yourself heroic, I hope."

"No, nothing so grand as that. I seek a healing balm for my dying brother. It's the only hope he has to survive."

Nathaera considered Gwyn and a smile brushed her pale lips. "Grandness is nothing to nobility of heart, Gwynter of Vinwen. Small wonder your companion is a unicorn."

❧

"WHY HAVE I never seen you at parties?"

Nathaera's question brought Gwyn's thoughts up short. "Beg pardon?"

"Do the residents of Vinwen Manor never come to court? Surely your parents enjoy socializing, yet your family is never in attendance."

Gwyn frowned, eyes studying Aluem's twined horn as the company trotted along the watery pathway toward Swan Castle. He could hear the soft clop of Aluem's hooves and the faint rustle of Kive following close behind, just off the Crystal Way, hidden in the trees. He could feel Nathaera's warm hands on his arms from her place behind him. Otherwise all was still and faraway.

"My father died last year, and my mother has been in mourning. My elder brother is a lieutenant in the Crow King's army, and now he's taken ill. I'm afraid House Terare has been long absent at court."

"I'm very sorry," Nathaera said. "I didn't mean to provoke such pain. I merely wondered why I've not seen you before. I think I remember your parents from the Winter Festival two years ago. They were a handsome pair. But I would've thought I'd remember you too. Of course, I was too young to mingle yet, but my father hosted the event and I watched from the stairs above."

Gwyn smiled. "I wasn't in attendance."

"Were you ill?"

"No. I'm not yet of age."

Silence replied. After several heartbeats he heard Nathaera take a deep breath.

"How old *are* you?"

His smile widened. "Fourteen."

"Fourteen! Impossible. You must be seventeen at the least."

He laughed. "No, my lady, but my height confuses most people, just as yours does."

Nathaera's fingers tightened against Gwyn's arm and she leaned forward to crane her head. She stared at him for several long seconds. "Impossible. It's not just your height. You don't *look* fourteen. You don't *act* fourteen. You're not at all like a little boy."

"I don't consider myself to be a little boy. Though perhaps I am reckless."

"So is my betrothed and he's twenty-two. Was." She leaned back and loosened her grip. "Well. I suppose that explains everything."

Gwyn lifted his brow. "What does?"

"It's really very simple. You stole my height and kept it for yourself, you greedy little beast. Afallon above, some things are simply not fair!" Her tone danced with mirth and Gwyn couldn't help but laugh again.

"Forgive me, my lady. If I had it to do over again, I would return a few of your stolen inches."

"Just a few, mind," she said cheerily. "I wouldn't want you to look fully as young as you are. Fourteen."

"If it helps, I'm halfway to fifteen."

"Well, it's some relief. Just please don't grow anymore between now and then. You won't fit into any houses, and then you'll never be formally introduced at court."

"I would be fine with that, truth be told."

She craned her head to eye him again. "Why? Shy of strangers?"

"A little. Besides, I'm the firstborn of a second wife. My place isn't at court. It's in Vinwen's fields in times of peace and on the battlefield in times of war."

"But you must enter society sometime if you wish to raise a family."

"Likely my mother will make a suitable match for me, and I will be content."

Nathaera sighed. "It's remarkable just how unsuitable such matches turn out to be. But then, not every case is like my own. I'm not implying that Windsur is a bad match. Just a dunderhead sometimes." Her hands flinched. "Not that I would speak ill of the dead! Ah, Nathaera, you silly girl. I'm sorry, Lord Gwyn. Sometimes I say too much."

Gwyn shook his head. "I'm not offended, and I'll make no judgments."

"You really shouldn't give me such allowances. I'm far too free with my thoughts, and farther still with my words. Father says a little more of the former would do me better credit. He's right, of course."

"I don't mind." Gwyn felt more at ease now, in company with the young woman riding behind him. She gave him another reason to make it back home, even should he fail in his quest.

But I mustn't fail.

Chapter Nine

Night smothered the world in a breathless, deafening silence.

Nathaera slept nearby, half her face buried in Aluem's flank, her eyes swollen but dry now. When she'd first retired, Gwyn had listened to her quiet sobs, unsure how to comfort her. Eventually she'd drifted off to sleep.

A sliver of moonlight fell across Aluem and the girl. Gwyn studied each companion in turn, glad of the company. He was so near Swan Castle. So close to his goal. But would he find what he sought? Would it be enough to save Lawen?

He closed his eyes but sleep still wouldn't come.

A faint rustle sounded on his left, followed by breathing.

His eyes opened. "Kive, is that you?"

"Yes, Rat. I'm here," came the soft drawl of the Ilidreth.

Shivers prickled down Gwyn's arms and spine. "Do you intend to eat us?"

"Nice juicy rats. Such bright red eyes."

Gwyn shifted away. "My eyes are gray."

Kive paused. "So juicy."

"You, uh...like eating rats?"

"Delicious," said Kive in caressing tones.

Celin wants me to kill this creature. Gwyn drew a breath. "Why rats? Why does your master want them eaten?"

"Won't you let me eat you, juicy Rat? *Come away from the Shiny*."

Gwyn's limbs responded to the Ilidreth's command, as though his connection to his own will had been severed. He started to climb to his feet, but the pull faded, and he sat down again with a shudder. Did the Fallen Ilidreth have some power to control his movements? What a terrible talent. Is that why Celin had asked Gwyn to kill him?

I don't want to kill anybody.

"Kive, did you live here before? At Swan Castle? At *Shaeswéath*?"

The rustling ceased. Kive whispered the foreign word once, twice. The undergrowth stirred. Gwyn laid his hand upon his sword hilt.

"Shiny once." Kive's voice hung very near.

"Swan Castle?"

"So shiny and bright, like...like sunshine on water. Now all is dark. All is still as death. Except the rats. Master said I must eat them all. Allll the rats."

A suspicion dawned in Gwyn's mind. "Kive, are all the rats tall like me?"

"No, not all. Before, all the rats were tiny, but juicy. Tiny, but furry. Now all the rats are naked."

"Do you remember a time before you ate rats? When everything was — was shiny?"

"All is darkness now. Dark and soft like silken death. Cold and empty. The moon shrinks. The stars shrivel. All is silence, except when the wind screams. Screams and screams. She screams the last song before the fall of the world."

"She. The wind?"

"But she never screams on the lake. His lake. Her lake. Their lake. All there is still; all there is soft glow and moon's last stand."

"Are you talking about Swan Castle, Kive? Are you talking about Lord Roth and Lady Shalesta and their lake?"

A faint sigh drifted from the shadows. Silence followed. "Let me eat you, Rat. Let me swallow your juicy flesh."

Again, Gwyn's limbs answered. He moved toward the voice, its tones inviting, singsong, safe... He crawled into the undergrowth and knelt before Kive.

The Ilidreth smiled gently, his red eyes bright against the gloom. "Nice juicy rat. Let me eat you."

Gwyn raised his arm. Something screamed in his mind to stop, to flee, but his body was seized by a desire to obey. His thoughts ceased like slack water against the roar of a coming tide.

"No!" shrieked Nathaera. "No, Kive, please! Don't eat him!"

Her panic crashed into Gwyn with the force of a tidal wave. His mind and body broke free like taut ropes severing with a snap. He stumbled into a thicket. Thorns nipped at his skin. Nathaera knelt beside him and gripped his arm with trembling fingers, eyes wide.

"Are you all right, Gwyn? Did he bite you? Are you eaten?"

Kive scampered closer, eyes wounded, hands flexing. "Just one rat. Just one tonight. That's all. So juicy."

"*No*," Nathaera snarled. "No rats, you greedy Kive. You've had more than your share. You ate my friends. You *ate* them. I won't let you eat him too." With a sob she buried her face against Gwyn's shoulder.

"Rat is crying," said Kive, bewilderment in his singsong voice.

"I'm not a rat, I'm a girl," said Nathaera, muffled but firm.

Gwyn wrapped his arm around her quivering shoulders. "I'm all right. Kive hasn't eaten me."

"I saw him do that before. Sir Tarven just knelt down and let... let him..."

Gwyn tightened his grip. "Don't dwell on it. Banish the memory."

As the girl's sobs quieted, Gwyn found the Ilidreth's gaze. "I'm supposed to kill you, Kive. I probably should. You're a dreadful, wretched creature, with no conscience. But something holds me back. Maybe it's only fear. I don't know. Please leave. Don't follow us, or I *will* end your life." His hand trembled at the very idea.

"I must eat all the rats," answered Kive simply. "Master requires it." But he slinked into the brambles and vanished in the dark.

Chapter Ten

Kive stalked them over the next two days. Despite Gwyn's oath to kill Kive if the Ilidreth followed them, he couldn't bring himself to carry through with his threat.

Only if he comes too near, he told himself each time he heard Kive on their trail.

Along the Crystal Way, Aluem slowed.

As Gwyn and Nathaera stared at the ruinous edifice towering ahead, beyond the portcullis, Gwyn forgot about the fallen fae. Even in its decrepitude, it rose proud and graceful, all angles and sweeping arches, white stone sparkling like crystal, wrapped in ivy creeping to the highest turret. A lake spread before the castle and a winding road circled it, bringing unicorn and riders to its wide front gates. The gates hung limp and scarred, blackened in places from some ancient fire long extinguished.

"*No*!"

The inhuman shout brought Gwyn's head around, hand falling to his sword.

Kive stood upon the Crystal Way, red eyes burning under the sun, his hand stretched out, trembling. "Do not go into *Shaeswéath*, little rats. Do not. Please leave it be."

A breeze scattered Kive's tangled hair, revealing his expression. Against the madness, Gwyn caught a flicker of something deeper. Something shattered but achingly sweet.

"I must go in, Kive."

Kive moaned and pressed his hands to his face. "Not there. Not there."

"Poor creature," murmured Nathaera. "He's almost childlike."

Gwyn turned forward, a lump in his throat. "Keep going, Aluem."

The unicorn strode through the entrance and into the stone courtyard. Kive didn't follow. Though Aluem and Celin had called this place fallen and twisted, the word that entered Gwyn's mind now was *heartbroken*. The air tasted like tears and he thought he heard otherworldly sobs on the whistling wind.

"What a heartrending place," said Nathaera behind Gwyn. "I feel as though I might start crying."

The inner walls were carved with swan silhouettes and feathers, runes and symbols. Towering trees filled the courtyard. Grass and wildflowers sprang up from the cracked stones underfoot. A silent fountain brimming with stagnant water stood at the center of the courtyard, reflecting the sky. The statue of a tall figure, an Ilidreth, stood at the fountain's peak, arms extended in welcome.

Aluem carried his riders across the vast courtyard and into the palace proper through a portal whose door had been smashed into splinters. Cobwebs swathed the vestibule like shrouds for the dead. Broken and crumbling columns and statuary rose, pale and ghostlike.

Sorrow seeped deep into Gwyn's bones. Tears pricked his eyes. Outside, the tragedy was an ancient incident, but within the palace, the memories hung close, as though the very walls had absorbed them. As though the horror, whatever it was, had struck only hours ago, not centuries.

"Where do we go?" asked Gwyn above the echoes of Aluem's hooves on white flagstones.

'*Up. There is one chamber we must first try,*' answered Aluem.

"Which chamber?" asked Nathaera, evidently able to hear Aluem's thoughts at the same time Gwyn could if the unicorn so wished.

'The Lady's.'

No one spoke further as Aluem led them to a grand staircase arcing up to a second floor. Another flight of sweeping steps took the company to a third story; and here, Aluem trotted down the corridor. The wailing sobs grew louder as they approached a door at the corridor's end.

Aluem halted before the ornately carved door. *'Open it, Gwynter. This is your task.'*

Gwyn nodded and dismounted. Heart hammering, he reached the door. Caught the knob. Pushed it open.

A torrent of sunlight blinded him. Gwyn flinched and blinked until he could see, then peered inside. Drawing his shoulders straight, he entered the room.

Though the rest of Swan Castle stood covered in dust and cobwebs, this chamber stretched pristine, filled with sunshine, glittering with jeweled vases harboring roses fresh and blooming. The scent of greening spring clung to a wafting breeze. A wide bed stood upon a raised dais, and there — as though she only slept — lay a woman with raven hair, features fair and lovely, gowned in white silk. An intricate silver crown rested on her brow, set with a large gem like a sky of purest blue.

Gwyn's breath faltered. His knees weakened, and he sank to the floor, bowing his head. Awe clutched his chest.

Aluem's voice filled his mind with a rush of wind. *'Behold the Lady who slumbers evermore in these dread halls, slain by one whom she loved, thence fallen for his act of horror. This chamber shall never crumble to dust, and thus the palace will stand in part forever.'*

Gwyn's heart ached for Lady Shalesta, for her endless slumber, for the betrayal of her trust. The sorrow of this chamber enveloped his soul like a shroud.

"Kive killed her, didn't he?" whispered Nathaera from the doorway. "That's why he's so horrible now."

'None alive now know. Only the ghosts of this place remember, and they will not tell all that happened.'

Gwyn rose to his feet. "I don't know what I seek. How can I find the cure?" He kept his voice low, afraid to disturb the Lady's rest.

'Does nothing draw your eye? Does nothing call out to you?'

Gwyn glanced around. His gaze settled on the lady's crown. "Nothing I would take."

'Then you do see something?'

"The Lady's gem caught my notice, but I'll not take treasure from the slumbering dead. I don't believe the cure is in this room."

Heart panging, Gwyn turned from the bed, but a humming note filled his mind and he whirled back around. The crown blazed a brilliant blue. The ghost of wings unfolded from the circlet and spread forth to take flight. Nathaera's gasp assured Gwyn that she, too, saw the image.

The wings disappeared and the light faded. In the same moment, the gem slipped from the crown to tumble against the bed beside the Lady. Gwyn stared.

'It seems to me, young Gwynter, that your choice has allowed the gem to choose you instead. Thus, it is yours.'

Gwyn shook his head. "I can't take it."

"But you must if you wish to save your brother. This is the cure you seek.'

Gwyn stood still, heart racing, fingers clenched. On the one hand, Lawen lay dying. On the other, Gwyn would be robbing the dead if he took this precious stone. Was it even the cure? Aluem thought so, but he had said before that he didn't know what the cure might be. Did *Gwyn* know it was the very thing he sought?

Yes.

Something inside *knew* it was. But should he take it?

He had come here for Lawen's sake — a far-fetched but desperate measure. This would ensure his success if Lawen could hold on long enough for Gwyn to return to Mount Vinwen.

The Lady had no use of her treasures and Aluem claimed the gem had chosen Gwyn.

Should he take it?

He must.

Gwyn stepped forward. *Afallon above, forgive me if I'm wrong to do this.*

He reached the dais, padded up to the bed, and studied the Lady's face. But for her pallor, she looked so alive. Her fair skin and red lips against a frame of black hair stood in stunning contrast. Gwyn's heart throbbed. He stepped to the bed's head. Bent. Grasped the sky-blue gem in one hand.

"I'm sorry. Thank you," he whispered, and retreated.

He feared the chamber might crumble as he and his companions withdrew, but nothing changed. Only the whispering wind at their feet stirred. Gwyn closed the door and started down the corridor the way he'd come. The gem in his hand felt warm, and he thought he heard it humming.

Chapter Eleven

"May I see it?" asked Nathaera as soon as the three companions stepped from the palace into the less-dismal courtyard.

Lost in thoughts of Lawen, it took Gwyn a moment to understand what she meant. "Oh, yes. Of course." He held the gem up. In the sunlight it sparkled a hundred shades of blue, reflecting sky and water. Nathaera leaned close to study the gem, but she didn't touch it.

"Breathtaking. How does one use it?"

He shook his head. "I'm not sure." He glanced at Aluem, but the unicorn stared at the shadows of the courtyard's west side. Gwyn followed his gaze and tensed. A body sprawled across the ground near the remains of what might have been a pyre.

The unicorn flicked his tail. '*The remains are not eaten, so it is likely not the work of Kive.*'

Gwyn cringed. "Nathaera, please wait out—" The body twitched. A crow on the courtyard wall took flight with a scream. Gwyn watched its ascent with a growing chill. His heart thudded against his ribs. His eyes dropped to the body. "Aluem."

'*Does it yet live?*' The unicorn sounded surprised.

The figure moaned, lifting its head an inch or so.

"Windsur!" Nathaera bounded forward, long hair streaming in her wake. Gwyn dashed after her even as Aluem shouted a warning.

A shiver shot up Gwyn's spine. He caught Nathaera and dove aside as the whistle of an arrow brushed by his ear. Gwyn stumbled to his knees, clutching the girl and the gem. He searched the wall above until he spotted an Ilidreth silhouetted against the sky, a second arrow nocked and aimed at him. A mad laugh sang across the air.

Gwyn stiffened. This was the Ilidreth from the True Wood — the one who had intended to torture him.

"Hello, Simaeri," said the Ilidreth. "I am greatly impressed you have come this far, but you trespass upon sacred ground." The tone darkened. "Grave robber. Give me what you have stolen!"

Nathaera trembled in Gwyn's arms. "When I let you go," he murmured, "you must run as fast as you can to Aluem. He'll protect you."

She gave a small nod.

Gwyn loosened his grip and sprang to his feet. Nathaera bolted toward the unicorn. The Ilidreth hissed and changed his aim, but Gwyn darted forward to reclaim his attention. He kept the gem clasped in his hand.

"What do you think I've stolen?" asked Gwyn.

The Ilidreth sneered. "The Lady's burial treasure. Her life-gem. Give it to me, Simaeri!"

"I've stolen nothing. What I took was gifted by the Lady herself."

"Liar! The Lady would gift nothing to a Simaeri brute!" He released the bowstring. Gwyn had no time to dodge.

Lawen, I'm sorry.

A torrent of wind rose with an immense howl, lifting decayed leaves and dust from the ground. The arrow jerked off-course and landed with a clatter several feet to Gwyn's left.

The Ilidreth rapidly nocked another arrow. He let it loose.

Again, the wind rose, and the arrow clattered near its brother. Gwyn stared at the arrows.

What in the name of Blessed Afallon is happening?

"Do the spirits favor Simaerin now?" the Ilidreth shouted to the sky.

Gwyn caught movement from the corner of his eye. He glanced toward it, expecting to see the nobleman, Windsur. Instead, he found Kive crouched near Windsur, eyes riveted upon the Ilidreth atop the wall. Kive slinked to the ivy-covered barrier and started to climb, utterly silent, while his lips moved to form a familiar word: Rat.

Looking between the two Ilidreth, Gwyn sucked in a breath. Should he shout out a warning or let Kive have at his fellow madman?

Windsur groaned, drawing the mad Ilidreth's focus.

"Ah, my wounded prisoner. Hush now, don't worry, Windsur ren Cloven of Simaerin! I shall do as I promised — your life ends this day!" He nocked another arrow.

Gwyn reached out, as though he could stop the projectile weapon, and sprinted toward Windsur— but the distance was too far to outrun an arrow's path. He'd never make it.

The Ilidreth pulled back his bowstring. In the same moment, Kive leapt at him. The Ilidreth lurched backward. The arrow dropped from slackened fingers.

Gwyn skidded to his knees beside Windsur. The two Ilidreth plunged from the wall, disappearing on the other side.

One yelped, even as the second shouted with delight, "Nice rat!"

All fell still.

Panting, Gwyn turned his attention to Windsur. "Are you well, Lord ren Cloven?" He laid a hand on the man's arm, a stab of sympathy surging through him. He knew too well what terror Windsur must have experienced as a prisoner of the mad Ilidreth.

Windsur's eyes shot open and he knocked Gwyn's hand aside. "Don't touch me, sorcerer! I'm not deceived."

Gwyn frowned. "You're wounded and disoriented, no doubt, so I'll not take offense at your accusation. But I am no sorcerer, sir."

Windsur scoffed. "Do you think me blind? I saw your trick with the wind against those arrows."

"That wasn't me," answered Gwyn. "But I can see how it might be perceived that way." The slap of feet brought Gwyn's head around as Nathaera arrived, gasping for breath.

"Windsur, I'm so glad you're alive! Though I can't see how it's possible."

The soft clop of Aluem's hooves approached. '*Gwynter, Ilidreth do not perish by falling from such a small height. We must not tarry.*'

He nodded. "Can you move, Lord ren Cloven? We need to leave this place."

Windsur raised his chin. "Of course I can move. I'm no woman."

Gwyn lifted an eyebrow but said nothing as he caught Windsur's arm and hefted him upright. "Climb onto Aluem if you can manage it."

Windsur glanced at the unicorn and nodded. "Of course I can." He allowed Gwyn and Nathaera to help him stand. Gwyn noted several shallow cuts and bruises on the man's face, and he suspected worse wounds lay hidden beneath his shirt and vest.

Gwyn supported Windsur as the latter man limped toward the unicorn. But Aluem shied away, tossing his head.

"What is it?" asked Gwyn.

Aluem shook his mane again. '*He cannot ride me.*'

Gwyn glanced at Windsur, puzzled. The man stood shorter than Gwyn, though he was better built, having reached full manhood. Gwyn guessed they weighed much the same. "Why not?"

Windsur moaned. "What's the delay? I can't stand here all day."

'*It is a rare man who can ride me as you do, Gwyn. This one cannot. He is not pure.*'

Gwyn flushed as the implications settled in. But Windsur was betrothed to Nathaera. He was unwed. Surely that meant... Gwyn shook his head. It didn't matter what it meant. "Is it impossible or merely uncomfortable?"

"What the devil are you babbling about?" Windsur demanded. "Help me mount your confounded horse or release me to do so on my own."

Gwyn gaped at him. "My horse?"

"Yes, your horse! Are you simple, man?"

Nathaera spoke up. "Windsur, I know you're not well, but that's no reason to lose your temper when Gwyn is just trying to help."

"Help? Is that what you call this? Standing here, waiting to mount his blasted horse, losing blood the whole time? And after all I've been through, with the savages and the woods! I tell you, Nathaera, I've reached my limit."

The petite young woman reached up and rested a finger against Windsur's lips. "Hush. Shouting won't help anybody. Where are your manners, sir? Let Gwyn do what he can. He's rescued us both." She lowered her hand.

"This simpleton?"

Nathaera pressed her finger to his lips again. "That isn't nice, Windsur. There's never cause to be rude. And besides, Gwyn isn't a simpleton."

Gwyn turned from them to meet Aluem's eyes. The unicorn flicked his tail.

'*I can try to carry him, but our going will be much impeded. My speed, my very essence, will be diminished in his presence.*'

"Be that as it may, we have no other choice. He can't be left here."

Windsur gestured with the arm Gwyn wasn't holding. "See? He's speaking to himself. He's either a witch or a lunatic."

Heat flashed through Gwyn's frame. "I cannot be a witch, sir, for only women are witches. Men of that skill would be called sorcerers or warlocks. Nor am I a lunatic. I'm merely speaking with Aluem."

Nathaera nodded. "It's true, Windsur. Here, Aluem, speak to him."

'He cannot hear me.'

Nathaera frowned, apparently receiving the same answer as Gwyn. "But why not?"

'He sees me as a horse, not a unicorn. He wields no belief in magic or faith, despite his accusations. Thus, he cannot hear me.'

Windsur sighed. "This is madness. Just get me onto the horse and let's be underway. I can't abide this horrible place any longer."

Gwyn moved forward, and though Aluem tossed his mane, he held still and allowed Windsur to clamber onto his back. The company left the courtyard at a plodding pace. As they started down the *Chesevwé*, away from Swan Castle, Gwyn thought he heard a rustle in the brambles nearby.

The wind picked up, sounding like a thousand ancient voices sobbing, bidding a sorrowful farewell.

THEY PUSHED on until dusk crept into night. Gwyn ordered a halt, and despite his private misgivings so near the borders of the True Wood, he lit a fire to keep the wounded nobleman from catching a chill.

"Let me see your wounds," he said, kneeling beside Windsur, who rested against the hollow of an old tree.

Windsur turned a sneer on him. "I'd rather Nathaera attend me. I'm of noble lineage, and common filth should be more prudent with my person."

"Windsur!" cried Nathaera.

Gwyn lifted a hand. "It's fine, Lady Nathaera. I'm not offended." He turned back to Windsur. "If it eases your mind, I know something of herb lore, and—"

"And he's also nobleborn," Nathaera cut in.

Windsur's eyes widened. "Nobleborn?" He turned to stare at Gwyn. "You look so rustic! What of your homespun rags?"

Gwyn smiled. "Rags, they may now be, but they weren't spun at home. A few weeks ago, they were unspoiled if plain. Your own garb has suffered in this merciless place as well. But I confess I've been remiss. Forgive my slight. My full name is Gwynter ren Terare of Vinwen."

He understood the dawning expression on Windsur's face; the slight curling of his lips; the arching brow. "Ah," said Windsur. "Vinwen. Such a quaint little estate. Farmers, aren't you?"

Gwyn drew a long breath to stifle his churning temper. This wasn't the first time other lords had slighted his House.

Don't let him goad you.

He forced himself to smile. "We don't work farms, but plantations. Our food supplies the Crow King's armies."

Windsur's scornful smile grew. "How patriotic. It's good that you recognize your worth. After all, not everyone can be a knight's son. Someone must grow crops."

Nathaera made a strangled sort of sound. "Oh, Windsur. *Please*."

Gwyn riffled through his meager belongings and pulled out the herb kit. "We've digressed. May I be allowed to treat your wounds, sir?"

Windsur's smile faded a little. "You never said why *you* are traveling through these Afallon-forsaken lands. And how you ran into my betrothed, or when."

"I sought Swan Castle," Gwyn answered. He lifted a poultice. "This helps with bruising and infection. May I administer it?"

"Why were you seeking the castle?" Windsur asked, folding his arms.

Gwyn sighed and laid the poultice aside. "For personal reasons I'd rather not discuss. I met Lady Nathaera three days ago. Before that, I traveled only with Aluem as my companion. Have I answered your questions sufficiently, sir?"

Windsur shifted against the tree trunk. "Why have I never seen you at court?"

Nathaera chuckled. "I asked the same question."

Gwyn rummaged through his kit again. "Because I'm not yet of age." He glanced up in time to watch Windsur's mouth fall open.

"Just how old are you?"

"Fourteen and six months." He pulled an herb from the kit, chewed the leaves, then slapped them against a deep scratch on Windsur's hand. "This will numb some of the pain. Allow me to treat you, and then let us retire. We've got a lot of ground to cover tomorrow."

The lordling's lips stretched into a profound grimace as he stared at the chewed-up leaves, but he offered no protest. Gwyn quietly treated each wound, while Nathaera turned her back to give her betrothed his privacy.

Finished, Gwyn set to work on a meal. Aluem discreetly provided berries and Gwyn boiled an herb broth from his stores.

When the company had eaten, Gwyn slipped outside the encampment and settled on a half-rotted log nestled between two gnarled trees. Night noises filled the air around him, soothing despite the gloom of the woods. Nearby the Crystal Way glowed, illuminating the path ahead.

The starstones sang to their brothers above as Gwyn pulled the sky gem from his pocket and ran his fingers along each edge and smooth place. The gem still felt warm, as though it had captured some fragment of a summer morning sunbeam.

"May I sit?"

Gwyn started and craned his head to find Nathaera standing nearby, hands behind her back, a smile playing at her lips.

"Certainly." He motioned to the spot on the log beside him.

She circled the log and demurely took the proffered seat. "Your mind must be so full of hopes and fears. Are you tired at all?"

He nodded. "A little. But I'm too anxious to rest."

"Tell me about him. Your brother." She shifted on the log and folded her hands on her lap.

He stared at the gem, vision blurring as his mind conjured a clear image of Lawen in his armor, strong and lithe. "Lawen is the gentlest, kindest soul I've ever known. He's my lord father's only child from his first marriage. The birth was difficult for my father's wife, and she died within a few hours of delivering Lawen. The incident devastated my father, but he found solace in his son.

"It was ten years before he married my mother, who gave birth to me. Lawen never opposed the marriage, nor did he resent me — though he easily could have. The arrangement was harder on my mother, who wanted her own child to be the heir of Vinwen. Ironically, Lawen wants nothing to do with growing crops or managing a serfdom. He'd much rather travel the world, so he joined the Crow King's army."

"But you said he's very gentle. Wasn't that difficult for him?"

"Very, but he also believes in protecting the weak. Lawen has always felt that a knight or soldier *should* be gentle, not hard and cruel. It's the gentle souls who remember to stop fighting when peace has been achieved." He fingered the gem again as fear's claws raked against his memories, chilling his bones.

Let Lawen be alive.

"How is Windsur doing?" he asked.

"He fell asleep. I can't even imagine how exhausted he is, after all he's been through. Please forgive his ingratitude today. He's not usually so uncivil." Nathaera grimaced. "It's been a trying few days for all of us."

Gwyn offered a smile. "It certainly has. Don't worry, I meant it when I said I wasn't offended. Besides that, nothing he said was untrue."

Nathaera held his gaze. "Are you certain you're fourteen, Gwynter? You don't behave like any fourteen-year-old boy I've met."

He chuckled. "That's only true when I'm surrounded by imminent peril in a dark wood. It tends to sober even the most reckless and lighthearted souls."

"I suppose there's some truth in that." She glanced at the gem. "You know, when we were in that chamber back in Swan Castle, I really felt like you were meant to have this. Like it did choose you. It's strange, I know, and I'm not certain if I should say so, what with the Crow King's edict about magic. But it felt *good*, and...well, like it *wanted* to help you. If that's the case, Gwyn; if magic does want you to have it, to use it, isn't that a sign that your brother is still alive?"

Gwyn blinked. His smile grew deeper. "I hope you're right."

"I believe I am." She took his wrist and squeezed it. "I'll pray to Afallon for protection, both for us and for Lawen." She released him and stood, smoothed her stained skirt, and motioned toward the encampment. "I'd best go back in case Windsur stirs. I doubt he'd appreciate waking to an empty camp after everything."

Gwyn nodded. "I'll return shortly."

She retreated, her footfalls soft in the leaf mold.

Chapter Twelve

Despite a full night's rest, Windsur's mood didn't improve. On top of that, Aluem's pace slowed even more.

Gwyn glanced with dismay at the canopy of trees overhead, wondering how they could possibly reach Vinwen before Lawen ran out of time. Nathaera seemed to sense his growing anxiety, sending him encouraging smiles. He answered in kind, but his anxiety only grew until his head ached.

Windsur insisted on stopping to rest more than once, and though Gwyn hated to comply, he worried about Aluem's condition and relented.

When the company stopped to sup around midday, he leaned against a tree trunk and let out a deep sigh, shutting his eyes. The rustle of a nearby brush jolted him forward. He shot to his feet and drew his short sword.

"Kive, is that you?"

The rustling grew louder. A pair of red eyes appeared between the branches of a thorny bush. A drawling voice drifted upward. "Is the rat talking to Kive?"

Gwyn's heart fell. "I'm not a rat. I'm a boy. Remember?"

The rustling grew as Kive crawled from the bush, his tattered robes snaring on the thorns. He sat up, legs folded beneath him, mangled hair in his face. "Big juicy rat. Much better than the last one."

Gwyn swallowed and tried not to imagine Kive's implication. "You survived the fall."

"Oooh yes. I survive so many falls. So many falls."

Gwyn glanced behind him and found Nathaera sitting across the tiny clearing, eyes pinned on Kive. Windsur thankfully had fallen asleep. Gwyn turned back to Kive. "What happened to the other Ilidreth? The — the rat who fell from the wall with you?"

"I ate him. So juicy, so tender. I love rats. His eyes—"

"Please!" Gwyn lifted a hand. "Don't go on. I don't want to hear."

Kive licked his lips. "Nice juicy rat."

Nathaera rose and trotted to stand beside Gwyn. "Why are you following us, Kive?"

"Rat took the shiny rock. The shiny rock is here, so I followed. It called and I must follow wherever it goes. I must."

Gwyn and Nathaera exchanged a look.

"Does that mean we're stuck with him?" asked Nathaera.

"So it would seem." Gwyn crouched down and met Kive's gaze. He tried not to think about his deal with Colin.

I didn't give my word.

Besides, Kive might have answers Gwyn needed.

"Do you know what the rock is?" he asked. "Does it really call to you? Do you know how to use it?" He fingered the gem in his pocket but decided against pulling it out. Kive might snatch it. He might have come to steal it in the first place. But if so, couldn't he have stolen it from the Lady's chamber? Kive hadn't wanted to enter Swan Castle. Was that because he couldn't or wouldn't?

"The sky fell," said Kive, staring back at Gwyn, his eyes wide with wonder. Just as before, it struck Gwyn that Kive was rather childlike in spite of being a full-grown man. Despite his horrific desire to eat rat- and human-flesh, he was almost, dare Gwyn say, innocent?

The fallen fae spoke on. "The sky fell into shadows, swallowing the sun, swallowing the moon and all her stars. All but the shiny rock. All but that. All that's left. Only the shiny rock, cradled, cradled. A single piece of the heavens. Full of ocean and starlight."

"Do you know how to use the shiny rock, Kive?"

Kive went on, unheeding. "But the stars are silent. The songs are over. All finished, save one. One last lullaby, the lullaby of death. Dark, fallen. Allll gone."

"If he does know, I don't know if you can eke it out of him," said Nathaera. "He's so shattered. It's really very sad."

Gwyn sighed and straightened to his full height. Kive didn't seem inclined to attack them anymore. Maybe he was too full...or too interested in the gem.

Does that mean I can avoid killing him?

"We should keep going." Gwyn glanced down at Nathaera, so much shorter than him. "I think Aluem's rested enough now. Would you please wake Windsur?"

Nathaera walked over to her betrothed as Gwyn turned back to Kive. "I suppose you'll come along, whether we welcome it or not. But let me be clear: if you hurt any of my companions, I will be forced to harm you."

"Is Rat angry?" asked Kive, his eyes widening again.

"No, but I recommend you not make me so." Gwyn cautiously moved away from Kive to crouch before Aluem, who sat under a tree nearby, legs folded beneath him. "How do you feel?"

The unicorn raised his head. His opalescent eyes blinked once, twice. *'I will manage, but I am not at my best. I am afraid our progress is slower than I had estimated. I fear for your brother's well-being.'*

"I'm nearly as fearful for yours. Can I do anything to assist?"

Aluem began to toss his head, but hesitated. *'Perhaps if the gem were in my possession, if Lady Nathaera carried it, and sat upon my back with Lord Windsur? Its properties are such that it may rejuvenate me even as I am taxed.'*

Gwyn dug the gem from his pocket. "Let's try it." He rose and turned to find Nathaera. She knelt beside Windsur, speaking to him in low tones. The man looked irritated, disheveled, pale. When Gwyn had treated his wounds, he'd found nothing fatal, but lacerations could become easily infected in conditions like these. Speed was of the greatest importance for everyone in the company.

'*Gwynter.*' Aluem's urgent tone brought him around. The unicorn stood now, one ear flicking backward. '*We are not alone in these woods. A large force comes crashing through – not made solely of Ilidreth, for it is much too loud.*'

A chill rushed through Gwyn's frame like a biting wind. "How near?"

'*Less than a league away.*'

"Can we avoid them if we continue along our course?"

'*Only if we hurry.*'

Gwyn turned back to his human companions. "We must move now. There's something heading our way and we should avoid them if we can."

"What sort of something?" asked Windsur. "Ilidreth savages?"

"No, possibly Fraeli."

"Fraeli here?" Windsur scoffed. "No madness would drive them to come here."

"Oh, yes?" asked Nathaera, hands resting on hips. "Do you call yourself mad, Windsur? *You* came, after all."

The man scowled but said nothing. Gwyn approached and held out his hand. "We'll make better time if Nathaera rides with you. Come."

Windsur grudgingly accepted his hand. Gwyn hauled him to his feet and assisted him toward Aluem.

"The going will still be slow," Windsur said stiffly. "Your horse can't carry all three of us. He's done a poor job just carrying one."

Gwyn considered that as he cupped his hands and lifted Windsur by his boot to mount Aluem. When the man was seated, Gwyn walked around to face the unicorn. "Sir Windsur speaks some truth. I'll slow the company down. There may be one solution. If you will, my friend, please take the lord and lady to Vinwen. Fly as fast as you can, and once they're safely there, come back for me. It's the only way to ensure their safety, and you'll be able to find out if my brother still lives."

Aluem studied him, perhaps weighing Gwyn's resolve. He nodded. '*It will be as you wish, young Gwynter. But what of Kive?*'

Gwyn chewed the inside of his lip. "If he can sense the gem, Kive may follow you. You must outrun him."

'*And if he stays behind with you?*'

"He will be the least of my dangers."

'*You will likely not survive, my little friend.*'

Gwyn nodded. "I know. But this is the best plan I can think of. Better I perish alone than all of us together."

'*I wonder if that was not your brother's philosophy as well.*'

Gwyn turned from Aluem and found Nathaera standing close, her eyes bright and brimming with worry.

"You're staying behind?"

"I must. Aluem will return for me after you're safely brought to Vinwen. Once there, will you find Lawen and discover if he still lives?"

"What about the gem?"

"It must go with you." Gwyn gently took her wrist and pressed the gem into her hand. "Give it to Lawen. See what can be done to heal him if it's not too late."

She curled her fingers around the gem, tears sparkling in her eyes. "I promise I'll do what I can."

"Thank you, Lady Nathaera."

"Come on, Nathaera," said Windsur. "Let the boy play the hero. We must outrun the Fraeli."

She gathered her skirts and turned to Aluem. Gwyn helped her to mount behind Windsur.

"Be safe, all of you."

Nathaera turned to meet his eyes. "Stay alive, Gwyn. Promise?"

"I promise to try."

Aluem galloped into the trees, fast and fleet and nearly silent.

Gwyn stared the way they'd gone long after they vanished from sight. He shivered and bowed his head, allowing loneliness to settle over him like a heavy cloak. Then he bent down and caught up his pack, slung it over his shoulder, and started after them.

Kive followed closely in his tracks.

Chapter Thirteen

Despite Aluem's speed, it took well over a week to reach the edge of the forest and spot the lush, rolling hills of Vinwen.

Nathaera looked upon the open countryside and thought she might start to cry. Her body ached from the hard ride, from sleeping on the ground, from eating little besides berries and roots. She yearned for a bath. Windsur needed a doctor. She must find Lawen. Such thoughts had been her constant companions for so many days now, and here at last, she could accomplish all.

But her heart throbbed. Gwyn had stayed behind. Brave, quiet, determined Gwyn. Was he still alive, alone and afoot in that forsaken realm?

Aluem slowed his pace as a large stone manor house came into view, along with a windmill and several well-maintained outbuildings surrounded by stone- and wooden fences. Fields surrounded the estate, tender crops growing well, cultivated by slaves hard at work even so early in the morning.

As Aluem and his riders passed, the slaves lifted their heads, stared for a moment, then returned to their work. Aluem cut through a pasture and found a dusty road leading toward the manor house.

"I told you it was a quaint little place," said Windsur. "They don't even have a proper keep."

"I'm sure they have much more land and many more buildings than we see right here," Nathaera replied, fighting to keep her voice level. "Besides, wealth isn't everything. Consider sweet Afallon, raised in poverty before he ascended to Godhood."

A grunt was Windsur's answer.

Dogs barked as they neared the manor house. A man dressed in livery darted from the doorway, but as he comprehended the newcomers, hope left his eyes.

He thought we might be Gwyn, Nathaera realized, biting her lip.

She lifted her hand in greeting. "Are you the steward?"

"I am," answered the man, less courteous than he ought to be when addressing nobility. But then, she and Windsur didn't look noble right this minute. They could hardly look better than paupers.

"If you seek food and water, go around back and Cook will see to you. If you seek lodgings, be on your way. We can't put you up at present — unless you've a mind to work. The lass can help in the kitchen, and you, lad, can be of service in the fields."

Nathaera felt Windsur's muscles grow taut where her fingers clung to his shoulders. "How dare you?" he snapped. "I'll have you know I'm no beggar. I'm Windsur ren Cloven of Crowwell and this is Lady Nathaera ren Lotelon. We require your assistance."

The steward looked between them, brow pinched. "Forgive me, but you hardly look—"

"We met your master in the woods," Nathaera blurted out. "Gwynter ren Terare. He sent us on ahead, but we must hurry. Let us stay and I'll send Aluem back into the woods to retrieve him."

The steward's mouth fell open. "You met the master?"

"He saved our lives. Please, lodge us for now, and give water to Aluem before he returns to find Gwyn."

The steward glanced behind him as a woman appeared in the

open doorway, tall and willowy, with light brown hair that tumbled down to the tips of her lithe fingers. Her gray eyes were the same shade as her son's.

"What is all this, Rovare?"

"My lady, these travelers claim to have seen Master Gwynter in the woods."

"It's true!" cried Nathaera. "Gwyn saved us. He gave us Aluem to ride here ahead of him, but he's afoot and we must send Aluem back straight away. Fraeli might be on his very heels if they've not caught him already."

The noblewoman tensed. "Fraeli? In the woods?" She glanced at the steward and, after several heartbeats, nodded her head. "Water the horse, then let it go. I would speak with our guests."

"Yes, my lady." The steward laid a hand on Aluem's neck. Windsur dismounted, flinching, then aided Nathaera down after him.

"Are you all right?" Nathaera whispered.

"Nothing a goblet of wine won't fix," he replied, with a weak smile.

"Come inside," said the woman, hand beckoning. "First things first, you each require a hot bath to scrub away all that filth. I'll have the servants draw one immediately, and afterward you'll eat a hot meal. We'll discuss Gwynter at that time."

Nathaera followed Lady ren Terare inside but glanced one last time from the doorway to watch Aluem being led toward the stables.

❧

Lady Mair — for so she introduced herself — stared at Nathaera from across the long table. Windsur had also ceased to devour his food, one eyebrow arched.

Nathaera waited, praying to Afallon she hadn't made a mistake by explaining Gwyn's quest. But she must reach Lawen, and she doubted there was another way if she hoped to visit the dying man.

So far, Lady Mair had given no indication of whether Lawen was alive or dead.

"Nathaera," said Windsur, breaking the silence. "Have you even heard yourself? It's obvious that in his grief Gwynter went mad. Magic? It's...preposterous!" He glanced at Lady Mair. "I'm sorry if that hurts to hear, but Swan Castle is just a ruin. And magic is a myth. Were it not, even so, his quest would be folly. The Crow King considers the use of sorcery punishable by death."

Nathaera turned narrowed eyes on him. "Listen to yourself. Even the Crow King believes magic is real. Now, do try to be sensible." She turned back to Lady Mair. "Let me ask you frankly, Your Ladyship: Is Lawen still alive?"

The woman sat very still. "He is, but only just. Can he truly be saved?"

It struck Nathaera that this woman had no reason to want Lawen healed. Hadn't Gwyn said she desired her own son to be the heir of Vinwen? Wouldn't Lawen's death allow that to happen? Would Lady Mair prevent Nathaera from using the gem, assuming she could even find a way to make it work?

Well, there was nothing else for it.

I must risk it, nonetheless.

Nathaera nodded. "I believe he can."

Lady Mair rose from the table. "Come with me. I will take you to his chambers."

Nathaera sprang up and rounded the table to follow the noblewoman from the dining hall and its roaring fire, into a flagstone corridor lit by windows on the west side and the occasional torch against the east wall. Windsur followed, limping a little, a chicken leg in one hand.

The journey was short. They ascended a single flight of stairs and Mair stopped before the first door on the right. "This is his room. He's very weak and doesn't respond to anyone. Once in a great while he calls for Gwyn, but no one else." She turned the doorknob and pushed it open.

Darkness shrouded the chamber, caged by long curtains at a tall window. It smelled of death and blood and stale air. A four-post bed sat in the room's center, raised slightly on a stone dais. Nathaera squinted and thought she could make out the frail form lying in the bed.

She inhaled the fetid air, nose wrinkling, then stooped and pulled the gem from her stocking. She straightened and entered the chamber. She crossed the room and stood upon the dais to peer down at Lawen — what was left of him. He lay so thin, so pale, barely a wisp of a human. Once he might have been handsome, but his illness had ravaged his features, drawing the skin so tight against his skull that he might be mere bones covered in the thinnest parchment. Rattling breaths escaped his thin, bloodless lips. Each laboring moment, he grasped at life only to wait for his brother.

"Lawen," she whispered, heart panging. "I've come on Gwynter's behalf. He sent me to help you. He's returning even now. Oh, you should have seen how brave he was, all he went through, to bring you this."

She uncurled her fingers. At once the gem ignited, filling the room with blue light, ripples like water flung against the walls, illuminating Lawen's ravaged frame. His eyes fluttered open, a deep green shade, still sparking with life. Still clinging to it.

On impulse, Nathaera fell to her knees, caught his wasted hand, turned it palm up, and pressed the glowing gem against his parchment-skin. She leaned forward, lips nearly touching the gem. "You chose Gwyn, didn't you? You know what he sought. Please, save his brother's life."

The light from the gem flickered and died. Then it flashed, blindingly bright. Nathaera threw her hands before her eyes. Warmth washed over her. The room hummed a high note, long and hopeful.

All fell silent and dark.

Deep breathes came from the bed.

Nathaera lowered her hands and found the room darker than before. She climbed to her feet and rounded the bed to approach the window. A cloud of dust swirled into the air as she yanked the heavy drapery aside and drowned the room in sunlight.

Turning, she found Lawen sitting upright, a hand pressed against his eyes. "Too bright."

She caught the curtain again and pulled it mostly closed, leaving a gap wide enough to illuminate the foot of Lawen's bed. She caught up her dress skirt and hurried back to the bed. Glancing toward the door, she found Lady Mair and Windsur both standing at the threshold, gaping and silent.

Nathaera turned back to Lawen. "How do you feel?"

He lowered his hand gingerly, eyes mere slits against the gloom. "I feel like a whole new man. What happened? Who are you?"

"I'm Nathaera ren Lotelon." She curtsied. "I've come on Gwynter's behalf. He found a way to heal you. You're going to live."

His eyes grew wide. "Heal me? What—? Where is Gwynny?" He searched the room.

She bit her lip and shook her head. "I'm afraid he's in the woods. Far from here. He sent us on ahead to bring the instrument of your healing. You're holding it now."

Lawen uncurled his hand to reveal the blue stone. It shone dully in the dismal light.

"Isn't it lovely? He brought it from Swan Castle."

Lawen's eyes widened further. Then his gaze slid past Nathaera. "Lady Mother?"

Mair slipped into the room. "You've been sick for a long time, Lawen. Gwyn disappeared several weeks ago, leaving a note to say he'd gone for help. I knew nothing more until this young woman arrived. But it seems Gwynter did find a way to heal you. You look yourself again, yet only yestereve Doctor Hesegg said you might last only a day or two more."

Nathaera let out a breath. "Then Gwyn was right to send us ahead. He feared it might be too late already."

Mair met her eyes. "Had Lawen been anyone else, it would be so. But his bond with Gwynter is such that I think he held on long enough to say goodbye."

Lawen's gaze darted between the two women. "Gwyn is alone in the Ilidreth woods? Someone must go find him." He started to push his coverlet aside. "I should—"

"You should stay where you are," said Mair in a sharp tone. "Gwynter didn't risk his life so that you could run impulsively into the woods after him, catch a cold, and die on the very heels of gaining your health. Besides, this isn't a simple matter we might easily lay to rest. How do we explain your sudden recovery to Doctor Hesegg, or to anyone at all? If word of Gwynter using of magic gets out, we all risk burning at the stake. No, Lawen, you will remain abed for several days more, and we shall do all we can to make it appear that you're slowly gaining strength by Afallon's blessing."

"But Gwyn is out there." Lawen swung one leg off the bed. Nathaera flushed. It was bare. Realizing the same, Lawen threw his coverlets back over his leg. His hands clutched his sweat-soaked tunic. "I need clothes."

"You shan't have them," answered Mair. "You'll stay here and wait with the rest of us. Even should we send an army into those woods, we'd have little chance of finding Gwyn. He, at least, knows where to find *us*. Lie still, rest, and pray to Afallon that Gwynter's resourcefulness is enough to bring him home. That foolish, head-strong boy!"

Her outburst startled Nathaera, for Lady Mair had remained composed until now. But then, Gwyn was her child, her treasure, now utterly alone in a wood full of fallen Ilidreth and, possibly, Fraeli enemies.

Chapter Fourteen

One hand pressed hard against Kive's mouth, Gwyn balanced on the thick branch of an oak tree and waited for the Fraeli scout to pass. Perspiration trickled down his neck.

Too close. This one had come much too close.

Not surprising, for they knew he was out here, just as he knew about them.

After all, he'd spent the past three days slowing them down.

Kive had come in handy. His drawling tones could lure wildlife with a few silken phrases, and Gwyn had encouraged him to call for a fleet of rats to descend upon the Fraeli encampment as dusk settled in. A delighted Kive began to devour every rat he could snatch, while Gwyn stole through the chaos and cut the cords to at least two dozen horses. That's when they'd seen Gwyn — but catching him had been another matter.

It was clear from the Fraelis' chosen direction and accoutrements that their destination was Crowell, capital city of Simaerin. And certainly not to attend a festival. Whatever this new provocation, whatever the Crow King's part in it, Gwyn couldn't let

Fraeli forces stamp their way through Simaerin and kill innocents. At the least, he must see that their efforts were severely hampered.

Wings fluttered close by.

Gwyn glanced toward the sound as a crow landed on a branch of the oak tree. Gwyn eyed the crow. It returned his stare, tilting its head to one side. Gwyn's heart started to pound and sweat pricked his brow. It was just a normal crow. Please let it be a normal crow.

The crow opened its beak and let out a harsh caw.

The scout on horseback halted a few yards from the oak and lifted his helmed head. His absent smile faded. His eyes met Gwyn's. Gwyn released Kive even as the scout drew his bowstring and unleashed his arrow. Gwyn couldn't dodge in time — but the arrow shot past the tree and thunked against another trunk.

The scout blinked, then nocked a second arrow with fleet fingers. Gwyn dropped from the tree and sprinted into the dense foliage. The second arrow shrieked past his head and landed in a thicket. The scout let out a curse.

Kive ran beside Gwyn. "Should I eat the other rat? He looks so juicy. Those big red eyes!"

"He's not a rat, Kive," Gwyn said, dodging right. Kive kept an easy gait beside him. "He's human. I'm human. We're too big to be rats. We're human and you're Ilidreth."

"No, just Kive."

Gwyn weaved left and dropped into a shallow gorge he'd found earlier for just such a situation. He rolled beneath a slight overhang to hide in the long reeds and thistles, ignoring the pinprick pain of a million tiny barbs in his arms and legs. He drew shallow breaths, and strained to hear any sound over the thudding of his heart.

Kive nestled beside him, content to remain still. Listening. His red eyes locked onto Gwyn's gray gaze and he rested a finger to his lips. "*Shhh, little rat*. The other rat is cooomming."

As though an invisible hand clamped to his mouth, Gwyn was seized, unable to speak. Kive's command laced magic bonds around his soul. Gwyn reached out and rested his hand against Kive's lips, placing his free fingers to his own. Kive continued to stare at him, so still, unblinking, perhaps not breathing.

Soon Gwyn heard the crunch of feet against twigs and leaf mold above, but the sound faded before it ever came near.

The two waited for twenty minutes or longer. Gwyn's muscles ached and his flesh raced with chills by the time he allowed himself to roll from the niche and unfold his limbs. Kive followed with no evidence of discomfort. Gwyn massaged his jaw, relieved that the invisible hand had departed.

"Kive, we've done what we can to slow the army down on our own. But you've a gift we might make better use of than calling rats. Shall we test the limits of your strange magic?"

Kive licked his lips. "Calling rats is my favorite."

"I've no doubt of that." Gwyn pointed toward the sliver of sky peering down between the close-knit trees. "Have you ever called down rain?"

Kive glanced up. "Rain? No. Kive doesn't eat rain." He grimaced.

Gwyn gently took Kive's shoulders. "Try, Kive. The army of rats is coming to destroy my home. We must slow it down and get far ahead in order to warn my people."

"Rats like the rain," said Kive matter-of-factly.

"Not an army of them. Enough water will drown rats."

Kive's lips pulled in a fresh grimace. "Drowned rats aren't tasty. Only alive, juicy, with big fat eyes. And the tails. Mmmmm."

Gwyn swallowed bile. "Please, Kive. Please don't."

Kive canted his head, reached out, and very delicately patted Gwyn's hair. "Nice rat. Not so vicious as other rats. Nice rat. I won't eat you for now. Nice, quiet rat."

Gwyn managed a limp smile. "Thank you, Kive. It's fair that we both try not to hurt each other for now." He began to climb up the gorge.

He didn't want to kill anybody.

"Not yet," said Kive. "Not until the shiny rock says so."

Gwyn paused and glanced down at Kive. "Will the shiny rock say so?"

Kive shrugged. "Kive doesn't know. Kive is Kive. Shiny rock is shiny rock."

"Yes. And Gwyn is Gwyn. *Not a rat.*" He started to climb again, slipping twice against the slick surface and clumps of grass that tore loose as he gripped them. At the top he sat and waited for Kive to lightly follow, unencumbered by such minor inconveniences as muddy slopes.

Kive mimicked Gwyn in brushing himself off and smoothing his ragged clothes. He whipped aside a tangle of matted hair and glanced in the direction of the Fraeli army. "Does Kive call the rain now?"

"Not yet. Wait until we can almost see them. I might need to commandeer a horse, and I'll want to locate one before the torrent is too strong." That was assuming, of course, that Kive could summon rain, and a lot of it. "We should test it." He looked overhead. "See that cloud, Kive?" He pointed.

Kive glanced up with disinterest. "Yes, Rat. I see the cloud."

"It kind of looks like a rat," said Gwyn, cocking his head. "Doesn't it?" He saw no such shape, but it was worth a try.

Kive's attention fixed on the cloud. "Ooo, a rat-cloud!"

"Tell it to come nearer, just a little, so we can be sure."

Please, Blessed Afallon, let this work.

Kive raised his hands. "Come, rat-cloud. Coooome!"

Gwyn willed the cloud closer until his head began to ache. The cloud moved perceptively nearer in the sky, no longer lethargic. Gwyn blinked. It might truly work.

"Ask the rat-cloud to find its brothers, the ones who drink water, and tell it to bring them here."

Kive nodded and relayed the command in his singsong drawl. The cloud retreated. Gwyn felt a little uneasy altering Afallon's weather patterns, but he must do all he could to save Simaerin.

THE TORRENT KIVE summoned proved a double-edged sword, but Gwyn had anticipated that. He was a party of two on horseback, fleeing the raging storm, while the army could only hunker down and wait for the sun to return.

Gwyn had easily freed a single horse as blinding rain hammered the forest and tore buds and leaves from the trees. It took some coaxing to make Kive mount the gelding, but at last the threat of losing Gwyn and his shiny rock had been more than Kive could bear. He slipped onto the horse's back and clung desperately to Gwyn.

Only after they'd ridden in dreadful conditions for several hours did the sun chase away Kive's so-called rat-storm. Gwyn slowed the horse's pace and mopped his sopping brow.

"This is a strange rat," Kive murmured, patting the brown gelding's flank.

"It's not a rat, Kive. It's called a horse."

"I've never heard of a horse."

"Haven't you?"

Kive fell silent for a time. "Once there were horses. Looong ago. Clip-clop. Clip-clop."

Gwyn smiled. "Can't you hear the horse's hooves now? Clip-clop."

Kive leaned to one side, one pointed ear tilted to the ground. "Oh, it does! It does clip-clop! Ooo, a horse. I thought all the horses were gone. Clip-clop, Rat. Listen!"

"I'm not a rat, Kive. This is a horse, and I'm Gwyn."

"Clip-clop!" cried Kive.

Gwyn shook his head and guided the horse through a thick copse of trees. "I wonder if Nathaera reached Vinwen all right. Aluem must be near my home by now if they've not already arrived." He mopped his brow again and shivered. His chest ached and he cleared his throat. "Perhaps Lawen is better now. Perhaps when I arrive, he'll be standing in the doorway of the house, arms open to receive me." His throat itched. Gwyn coughed into his hand. "It seems I've caught a cold."

"You can't catch the cold," said Kive. "Only rats. Or birds. Or flies. Juicy little flies, buzzing, buzzing."

Gwyn smiled despite himself. "Humans catch cold. Especially when they don't sleep or eat well, and then ride through rain for hours." He wiped his face with his dripping sleeve. "Foolish, really. I don't have time to be ill. I need to get back to Vinwen. I need to see Lawen...to know..."

Kive patted the horse's flank. "Clip-clop. Clop-clip."

Gwyn's vision swam. His limbs grew heavy, then he was toppling from the horse, stomach fluttering. He expected to hit the ground hard, but something snatched his arm.

"Rat is falling," Kive said from far away.

Gwyn's eyes shut. The world was dropping, tumbling away. His mind spun into a dark place deeper than the True Wood. Deeper than the pit where he'd fallen so long ago.

Deeper than the black of a crow's wings.

Chapter Fifteen

The embers of a dying fire danced before his vision. The world hovered dark and silent, but for the pop and hiss of glowing logs. A blanket covered Gwyn, a bit damp, but warm. He tried to raise his head but found himself too weak. He lay still and wondered instead why he rested beside a fire he hadn't built, covered by a blanket that wasn't his.

"Your eyes ask many questions," said a male voice with a weighty accent. A Fraeli accent.

Gwyn stiffened and tried again to move, but his body refused.

"Relax. I will not harm a sick man."

Gwyn drew a breath to ask a question, but his lungs caught fire, and he broke into a ragged cough.

"You have been many days ill," said the Fraeli voice. "Lucky I came upon you, or you would long be dead. Your fever was fierce."

Gwyn closed his eyes and fought against another cough. His body throbbed and his mind pressed against his skull. "Who...?"

"I am the scout you managed so well to evade. But I had to find you. None before have dodged my arrows as you did. None in many years. That is thanks to my Ilidreth blood."

Gwyn's eyebrows knitted together. "But your accent."

"I am half Fraeli and half Ilidreth. A cruel fate for most, but I have managed to hide my roots. You are the first to know in long years. I tell you because it is important that you know. I saw you in that tree, Gwynter ren Terare. I saw you now, and long from now."

"I don't understand—" He coughed again — a long fit that seared his lungs. He gasped for air before the fit passed, throat raw and burning.

Shuffling sounds came from overhead. Fingers wrapped around the back of his neck and drew him up. A flask pressed against his scorched lips. He drank the water and welcomed the cool wetness against his swollen throat.

"I had to find you. To tell you." The man's breath tickled Gwyn's ear. "I saw you mounted upon a magnificent unicorn of purest white. You stood before an army of many banners. No arrow could pierce you, just as mine could not. You were mighty; mightiest of all. Kingdoms rose in your name. Kingdoms as none have known. Afallon and the Weave were your sword and shield. You are chosen for a great purpose, Gwynter ren Terare — warrior of the bright soul."

Try as he might to fight it, even as the Fraeli scout's alarming words thundered through his mind, Gwyn felt sleep's hand press against his eyes. Weariness washed over him. Heavy, deep.

When he woke again sunlight snaked through the treetops. The forest around him looked different from the place where he'd fallen from his horse.

Here the trees stood wide apart, and less undergrowth surrounded the meager camp. On the far side of a smoking fire's remains, tied to a tree, stood the gelding he'd stolen. It looked well fed and brushed. Beside it lay his pack, unmolested. He still wore the blanket that wasn't his. Then, his rescuer couldn't be a dream, yet it felt surreal now. Otherworldly.

"Is Rat awake?"

Gwyn started and turned his head to find Kive hunched beside a tall, straight tree, clutching a mess of blood and fur. The animal might still be writhing. Gwyn looked away, stomach churning. "Kive, please. Don't eat in front of me. If you must eat, do so alone." Why hadn't Kive eaten him while he was ill?

A cough ripped through Gwyn's lungs, doubling him over. The fit lasted several seconds, then he slumped back down and rolled over, shivering in the thin blanket.

The memory of the Fraeli scout's words returned as he stared into the charred fire pit. "Chosen to what purpose? Conquering the world?" He smiled dryly. He had no ambition to lead men into war and raise up kingdoms for himself. He was content with his lot. Mostly.

❧

THOUGH HE HATED THE NOTION, Gwyn remained in his camp for one more night to be certain he had enough strength to ride through the morrow. Kive appeared content to stay nearby and snare whatever poor creatures he found fit to devour alive. Gwyn did his best to ignore the horrible sounds.

As dawn spun fiery threads of light through the treetops, Gwyn abandoned the warmth of his blanket, rolled it up, and strapped his pack and roll to the gelding. He found a few unripe berries, mushrooms, and roots to choke down, all the while wishing Aluem were near to provide food as before.

But then, if Aluem were near, Gwyn would be much closer to home and less desperate for nourishment.

As Gwyn climbed onto the gelding's back, Kive emerged from the trees, mouth stained with blood. Gwyn cringed, but drew out a handkerchief from his pocket, still damp from the deluge. "Come here, Kive. Please."

The fallen fae obeyed and stood before the horse. "How is the shiny rock today, Rat?"

Gwyn reached down and wiped Kive's lips with the handkerchief. "The shiny rock wants us to keep moving."

Kive bobbed his head. "I thought so. Shiny Rock was eager to leave the shiny towers. Eager to be useful."

"I'm glad to hear it. Will you ride with me again, Kive?"

Kive glanced at the horse. "Oh. Clip-clop. Clop-clip. Horse. Yes, Kive will ride. And for dinner, Kive will eat Rat."

"I'm not a rat, Kive."

Kive flopped behind Gwyn. "Sooo many rats say that."

KIVE MUST NOT HAVE MEANT Gwyn when he referred to his dinner, or he forgot which rat he'd marked by the time Gwyn tethered the gelding for the night. Dusk had ushered in a cold wind, but Gwyn didn't dare start a fire. He huddled in his blanket and peered at the gaping sky above the canopy of leaves. A few stars winked back at him in an ocean of swirling clouds.

"Do you ever eat crows, Kive?" he asked, dropping his eyes to the Ilidreth seated across from him.

Kive's mouth glistened with blood from his recent meal. "Crows? Oh nooo. Never crows. No." He shook his head for a long time and murmured no to himself over and over.

"Is that because they also eat animals?"

"Crows, crows." Kive tucked his legs up to his chest and began to rock back and forth. "So many crows, feathers, feathers, flying, swirling, pecking." His chant faded and he held Gwyn's eyes, seized them, like an unspoken command. "He looks for you, little rat. Looks and looks. He sees you, but maybe he doesn't understand. Maybe you're just another rat to him. But you're not a rat at all. You're not a rat. You're not a rat."

His rocking grew faster. His eyes closed. He mouthed the same phrase again, again, again.

"What am I, Kive?" asked Gwyn, riveted by the Ilidreth's agitation, heart thudding.

Kive's eyes cracked open. "What are you? Not a rat. Not a bird or a fly. Not a crow. What are you? Are you a shiny rock? Nooo. Not a shiny rock." He gasped. Sprang to his feet. Clapped his hands together as a smile lit up his face. "You're a *shiny*, aren't you? Not a rat at all. You never were! You're a *shiny*!" He flopped to his knees before Gwyn and stared into his face, eyes wide and bright. "Shiny. Shiny. Shiny!"

He reached out and stroked Gwyn's hair with blood-stained fingers. Gwyn cringed, but didn't draw away. This was a new side to his peculiar companion — and who could say if Kive would stay docile should Gwyn react badly?

For a long time, the fae stroked Gwyn's hair, humming a tuneless song under his breath. At last, Gwyn gently took his wrist and lowered his hand.

"So, I'm not a rat now?"

"No," said Kive in hushed tones. "Not a rat, silly Shiny. You're a shiny."

Gwyn nodded, cool relief rolling through him. "Help me to understand, Kive. What makes a shiny a shiny?"

"Only a shiny can be shiny," answered Kive, smiling. The abrupt gentleness of his expression, the faint awe in his tone, was a welcome if perplexing change. Gwyn prayed it would remain.

He reached up and pushed aside the mangled hair in Kive's face. "You were once bright and beautiful as all the Ilidreth were, is that not true? I wish I could heal you somehow."

"Once," whispered Kive, "I was shiny. But now Kive is Kive. Kive is Kive is Kive is Kive is Kive."

"Kive, will you let me comb your hair? I don't know if I can keep its length with all your tangles, but I'll try. I think you might feel less miserable if you were clean and groomed." Gwyn reached into his pack and pulled out a comb carved from ivory.

"Shiny," cooed Kive.

Gwyn knelt behind Kive, gingerly took a handful of snarled hair, and began the painstaking process of working through the knots. Kive sat still, making no sound while Gwyn took strand after strand

and worked through each until, an hour later, the Ilidreth's hair fell smooth and straight down his back.

Gwyn massaged his wrist. "There. How is that, Kive?"

The Ilidreth reached back and felt his hair. "Ah, like spider threads! Not chewy spiders – just the threads." He spun around on his hands and knees. "Shiny, it's so soft!"

Gwyn laughed. "It certainly is. It will be even softer following a hot bath and a selection of fragrant oils. When we reach Mount Vinwen—" He broke off as a coughing fit took him. It subsided after a moment, and he sipped from his water flask to sooth his throat.

"Is Shiny all right?" asked Kive, pawing Gwyn's arm.

Gwyn bobbed a nod. "Yes, Kive. I'm all right. It's just a cough."

"Oh, cough. Cough is horrible. I don't like how it sounds."

Gwyn chuckled. "I don't like the sound of you eating rats, so I suppose we're even."

"Shinies don't eat rats," Kive whispered.

"No, we definitely don't."

"Only Kives eat rats."

"I wish they wouldn't." Gwyn slipped the comb into his pack. "Well, Kive. I must sleep until dawn. Then we ride on." He pulled the blanket close, checked that his short sword was near, rested his head against his pack, and shut his eyes.

"Goodnight, Shiny," whispered Kive in his singsong drawl.

"Sleep well, Kive."

"Kive doesn't need to sleep."

Gwyn smiled faintly. "Have a pleasant night then, Kive."

"If I see rats, I'll eat them. That will be pleasant."

Gwyn turned away from the Ilidreth. "Not in camp, Kive. Outside of camp only. I don't want to hear."

"Outside of camp, Shiny. I'll eat the rats there. Shhh, Horse. Shiny is sleeping. No clip-clop, clop-clip. *Shhh*."

The horse made no noise at all that night.

Chapter Sixteen

They stood silent as statuary in the dawn light, arrows nocked and pointed at his heart.

Gwyn sat slowly upright and lifted his hands in surrender. The number of Ilidreth surrounding his makeshift bed was hard to guess against the foliage. A lot.

One of the Ilidreth stepped forward. Gwyn's eyes widened. He recognized the white and blue tabard over the silver armor. Fraelin's Crane Knights.

His hands fell to his sides. "Fraeli allies?"

"Correct, Simaeri. You've caused our allies much grief the past few days. Do you deny it?"

He shook his head. "I've done what I can to save my lands from invasion. I deny nothing."

The Ilidreth smiled without humor. "He is rather honest for one of the Crow King's mages. Shall we perhaps skewer him right-side-up rather than by his toes to thank him for his integrity?"

No one laughed, no one smiled. The arrows remained pointed at Gwyn's heart, unwavering.

"It seems I am alone in appreciating your condescension." The

Ilidreth drew his bowstring back, arrow pointed at Gwyn's head. "Poor Simaeri. You must die this day."

Gwyn stared at the arrow tip, wondering if by some miracle it might miss its mark again even at such short range. He doubted it, unless it truly was Afallon's will that he live.

The bowstring hummed its tightest note. He shut his eyes.

"Stop!" cried a familiar voice. "You will not hurt Shiny!"

The arrows all lowered, compelled by Kive's ruling tone. The fallen fae dropped to his feet from a nearby tree and strode up to the commanding Ilidreth.

"You will not hurt Shiny."

The enemy Ilidreth glared at Kive. "An Ilidreth betrays his own to serve the Crow King?"

Kive flinched back, shoulders hunching. "I serve my master. But I will protect Shiny! You cannot hurt Shiny!"

"This is a dark mage in service of the Crow King, you pitiable fool." The Ilidreth stabbed a finger at Gwyn. "He is not some radiant creature to revere!"

Gwyn glanced between them. Kive was formidable, but against so many of his own kind what chance did he have? Gwyn rose gingerly from the ground, lifting his hands in a show of peace. "Perhaps shedding blood can be avoided. Let us go on our way and we'll hinder your forces no more."

"Oh, yes? Is that why you hastily charge toward the forest border to inform the nearest Simaeri outpost of our approach?"

Gwyn shrugged. "Would you do otherwise if our positions were reversed?"

The Ilidreth's expression softened. "Perhaps not. You behave oddly for one of the Crow's mages."

"I'm not a mage. I'm the son of a nobleborn farmer."

The Ilidreth raised his brow. "Not a mage? Yet you summoned a storm."

"No, Kive summoned that."

The Ilidreth shook his head. "The fae cannot summon or alter weather. It is not in our power. Even fallen and unfettered, he could not do so."

Gwyn faltered. "But I can't summon rain either. It wasn't me."

The Ilidreth stepped past Kive to search Gwyn's eyes. "You say you're not a mage. You say you did not summon rain. Yet you *are* a mage and you smell of summoning magic. Are you a liar or are you a simpleton?"

Gwyn's eyes narrowed. "Neither. I've been told by Aluem that I'm a mage, but I know nothing of magic. Nothing of summoning rain. Indeed, I've never heard of the Crow King using mages at all. He opposes the use of magic altogether."

The Ilidreth stared hard at him, then threw his head back and laughed outright. "This is beyond belief! A Simaeri farmer's son, unaware of magic, yet he summons a rainstorm, befriends a fallen Ilidreth, and converses with a unicorn. What has the world come to?"

He clapped a slender hand to Gwyn's shoulder. "I will allow you to live, Simaeri, but I will not allow you to leave these woods to warn your people. You are now my prisoner, and if your fallen friend wishes to come along, he certainly may. I am High Lord Bowrin in your tongue, commander of the Ilidreth Allies under the Crane King's illustrious banner. What is your name, Simaeri prisoner?"

"You may call me Gwyn, for that is all the name I intend to bestow."

Bowrin smiled. "Wise for someone so ignorant. Well, Gwyn. Come along. We've far to march before dusk."

"Don't hurt Shiny," Kive piped up.

Bowrin glanced at the fallen fae. "You keep strange company indeed, Gwyn. But where is Aluem?"

"In Simaerin," Gwyn answered, "though I suspect he'll come looking for me soon."

"A bluff?" Bowrin studied his eyes. "No, not a bluff. You are an honest mage, no mistake. The first I've met of the like. Now come, we must not delay." He lifted a hand, and all as one, the Ilidreth soldiers gracefully slung their bows against their shoulders and started to move through the trees. One Ilidreth untethered Gwyn's stolen gelding and rested a hand against Gwyn's shoulder.

"Do not hurt Shiny!" Kive insisted.

Bowrin laughed as he headed for the front of the moving force. "I think, young Gwyn, you will be the safest prisoner we have ever held. Have no fear on that account."

He chuckled as he walked on, Gwyn behind him, guided by the Ilidreth warrior who had laid claim to his shoulder.

Safe he might be, but he was still the prisoner of an invading army.

Chapter Seventeen

Seated on her packs, Nathaera waited, shivering in a woolen shawl borrowed from Lady Mair. The girl watched the nearest window two stories up in the manor house.

Any moment now he would emerge.

Any moment.

Come on.

A dark-clad figure appeared at the window. He swung out to cling to the creeping ivy that climbed the wall beside it and began his descent. Nathaera smoothed her dress, tightened her grip on her shawl, and waited until the figure dropped to the ground a few yards before her.

She cleared her throat. Lawen spun, his green eyes wide, reflecting moonlight.

"Good evening, Sir Lawen." She smiled.

"Lady...Nathaera, isn't it?" He glanced around. "Why are you here?"

"I've been waiting for you. The horses are saddled and tethered just there." She pointed to a patch of shadow beneath a large shade tree. "I doubted highly that you would remain in bed while your brother is missing. I also doubted I could sit idly either. It's a fool's errand we embark upon, no mistake there. But Gwyn saved my life, and he's out there somewhere, all alone." She bit her lip. Unless Kive was with him, which was hardly better.

She shuddered and pushed down the memory of Kive with his lips covered in gleaming blood.

Lawen regarded her with narrowed eyes. "You're coming along?"

"Of course. I'm not sitting here merely to ornament your lawn. Though perhaps some ladies would. No, Lawen, I'm not a brainless dunderhead, but rather a reckless one. I shall accompany you by choice or" —she held aloft a dagger— "you shall come as my prisoner. Whichever better sets your mind at ease." She smiled amiably.

He rested a hand on his hip, shook his head, and finally shrugged. "You can't possibly expect this trip to go well. We'll likely never find him."

She nodded in what she hoped was a sage manner. "I've considered the risks. Gwyn is worth them all. Now, shall we leave at once, or wait for dawn so the entire estate can see us off?"

He chuckled. "Perhaps at once, my lady. If you'll stand, I'll help carry the packs."

"I can carry one."

"I expected as much. If you're coming you can't become a liability, or I'll turn back at once, hogtie you, and leave you in a field for the crows."

Nathaera quietly laughed and hefted her pack. Lawen grabbed the second. Together they trudged to the horses.

"I like you immensely, Lawen ren Terare. You're much livelier than Gwyn painted you out to be."

The man grinned under the moonlight. "In his defense, I *wasn't* lively when last we spoke."

"You've a point there."

They reached the horses, tied on the packs, and mounted.

Lawen steered his mount around to face the woods. "We ride northeast for five days, then turn around. If we encounter Fraeli scouts before that time, we turn back sooner. War is brewing, and I won't drag you into the thick of it, dagger or no."

Nathaera nodded. "I'm in full accord, sir. I doubt Gwyn would approach the enemy anyway."

Lawen cast a sideways glance at her. "Oh? You don't know my brother very well, after all. He's resourceful, even clever. But he's also reckless. Or didn't you gather that from his mad excursion to Swan Castle? If any Fraeli force rides the woods, I'd wager a mound of gold he's doing all he can to thwart its advancement."

THEY RODE HARD until the forest grew too dense to manage more than a walking gait. Only then did Nathaera notice how quiet the world around her had become. None of the usual chattering wildlife abounded. The only living creature she spotted was a single crow upon the bough of a holly tree. Its beetle-black eyes follow their course until she and Lawen passed it by.

"It's unnatural," she murmured.

"Aye," whispered Lawen. "Almost unholy. It likely means the Fraeli are near. Few things can chase away wildlife faster than an army."

Nathaera clutched her horse's reins. "Great Afallon above, protect us."

A voice spoke ahead of them in the gloom. "Hold, Simaeri."

Nathaera drew up her reins and Lawen halted his mount. The voice came from ahead, but no one stood beneath the trees. On impulse, Nathaera lifted her eyes to the branches above. Sure enough, there stood a shadowed sentinel, arrow raised against them.

"What business brings you so deep into these woods?" the shadow demanded.

"We seek our lost companion," answered Lawen.

Nathaera piped up. "And now that we've answered, perhaps you'll explain what *you're* doing so deep in these woods?"

The arrow's point inched in her direction. "The only reason I've not killed you yet is because one of you is a woman. Simaeri have become foolish indeed to bring the fairer sex here."

"I brought myself," Nathaera said with only a little malice. "Thank you."

"I will rephrase my question: What brought your lost companion into these woods, so that you felt compelled to wander in to find him?"

"He came on my account," Lawen said. "Beyond that, I'll say no more."

"What are your names, intruders?"

"I am Lawen and this is Lady Nathaera."

"From where do you hail?"

Lawen replied without hesitation. "Mount Vinwen, westward. Pray, what is your name?"

"I am called Celin in your tongue. It seems you and I are acquainted with the young man you call lost: Gwynter ren Terare of Vinwen."

Nathaera gasped.

Lawen perked up. "You've seen him?"

"Alas, not recently. I saw him early in his quest. But you say he came here on your account. I had understood that he came seeking a cure for his brother."

"He did. I am that brother."

Silence. "Are you mended on your own?"

"Nay. He sent the cure ahead with Lady Nathaera. I'm healed thanks to him, but he's not come home. In our worry we seek him, though it's a foolhardy venture."

Nathaera wondered at the wisdom of explaining so much to a stranger. She urged her mount to take a step forward. "How do *you* know Gwyn?"

"I aided him," Celin answered, still hooded in the shadow of the trees. "My friend accompanied him to *Shaeswéath*."

"Do you mean— Might you mean Aluem?"

"I do," Celin said. "But if Gwynter ren Terare is lost, what became of my friend?"

With relief Nathaera explained the last leg of her journey to Vinwen and Aluem's return to the woods in search of Gwyn. Celin listened in silence until she'd finished.

"Leave the search to Aluem," he said. "He is swift and clever. You risk yourselves without need. If Gwynter can be found at all, Aluem will succeed where you cannot. Return to Vinwen. Wait for word. Even should Aluem have no success, he will not give up the search without letting you know."

"But—" Lawen began.

"*Go home.*" The man's tone was sharp as broken glass. "Would you waste the great gift your brother has offered you? Few are given such a chance as yours. Return to Vinwen and place your faith in Aluem and in Gwynter. They succeeded once. Shall you doubt them now?"

Nathaera flinched as though he'd slapped her across the cheek. Bristling, she clutched her reins tighter. "Listen here. We've not come all this way to turn back because it's a little dangerous. Gwyn's all alone, and we intend to go on searching for him. You've no right to tell us not to!"

"No right? Yet these are my woods. Mine and my people's. You are trespassing."

A chill charged up her spine. "You're one of the Ilidreth?"

Lawen glanced at her. "You didn't know?"

She shook her head. "I hadn't thought..."

The figure leapt from the trees and landed lightly before the two on horseback. "That is just the trouble with Simaeri. You rarely *think*." Celin's blue eyes caught and held hers. "You refuse to turn back?"

"As we said," Lawen answered, "we know already that it's foolhardy. But we can't sit back and do nothing."

Celin sighed, reaching up to finger his brow. "Am I to be plagued with all the kin of ren Terare? Very well. I shall guide you as best I can. Where Gwynter of Vinwen is, I cannot guess, but Aluem's tracks may be traceable if one knows how to look. We shall try that and discover in time if it is fruitful."

"Thank you," Lawen said. "But why trouble yourself?"

Celin gazed at him a moment before he answered. "Your brother survived *Shaeswéath* and found what he sought. He lived to speak of it afterward. You are alive because of his deeds. These truths puzzle me, but they speak most of Gwynter's soul. He may be something different. Something great. I wish to see what that may mean, for good or for ill."

"You'll be well compensated for your aid," said Lawen with a grateful smile.

"I do not desire the wealth or favor of a Simaeri. Threaten to reward me again and I shall leave you in the first pit I find." Celin turned his back on the travelers. "Follow. We will head east."

"That's the way we were planning to go," Nathaera said, to be clear.

Celin glanced back at her with a stony face. "Keep up."

Nathaera blinked and glanced at Lawen. He shrugged. She replied in kind, and they nudged their horses onward toward the True Wood.

Chapter Eighteen

"Kive, I don't have the shiny rock."

The fallen Ilidreth stared at him, uncomprehending.

Gwyn sighed. "I gave the shiny rock to Nathaera. I need you to go find her. Tell her that I — that *Shiny* — is with the enemy. With the bad rats. Can you tell her that?"

He glanced around to be certain none of the sentries were near enough to listen. He and Kive sat before a campfire in the center of the Ilidreth-Fraeli camp. Gwyn's hands and feet were bound, his shoes had been removed along with his weapons, and a noose had been slipped around his neck to discourage trying anything drastic.

Kive shook his head. "I must stay with Shiny."

"But what about Shiny Rock?"

"I must stay with Shiny."

Gwyn groaned, shutting his eyes. "Very well. We'll just have to pray to Afallon that He provides an opportunity to escape." Did Ilidreth pray to Afallon? He didn't know. Another coughing fit seized him, and he doubled over. The noose dug into his neck, but he ignored it until he gained control of his lungs again and gasped for air.

"Shiny?"

"I'm...all right, Kive. Just...fine."

"Shall I eat the rats, Shiny?"

"Don't eat large rats, Kive. Please."

"But Master said so. I must obey."

"Do you like eating large rats better than small rats?"

"Juicy," answered Kive.

"What about a nice chicken or some berries?"

Kive grimaced. "Kive must eat rats, or birds, or flies."

"Because master said so?"

"Master said so."

"I see." Gwyn's eyes strayed to the strange tents erected by the Ilidreth. Woven from leaves and branches, the tents blended so well with the woods, a stranger might wander into the midst of camp without recognizing that it was just that, until it was too late to run. The sentries were also difficult to spot, though Gwyn knew one hid near enough to spear him if he tried to escape.

He sighed and turned back to Kive, who fingered a stray twig. Gwyn studied his features, struck by the angular shape of the Ilidreth's face; the otherworldly beauty usually hidden in Kive's madness. He bore a strong resemblance to the other two Ilidreth Gwyn had encountered.

"Kive, do you remember before you fell? Did you know Lady Shalesta?" Stories of the Ilidreth always implied they were long-lived. Maybe even centuries old. Could Kive have been there when Swan Castle stood as the thriving center of trade with humans from Fraelin and Simaerin alike? When King Roth took to wife the beautiful Fraeli princess Shalesta?

The Ilidreth lowered his head, glossy hair slipping over his eyes. He plucked a bud from the twig.

"Did you know someone named Celin, perhaps?"

"Kive is Kive," whispered the Ilidreth in sorrowful tones. "Not shiny anymore. Not shiny. Just Kive. Just Kive..."

"Do you want to be shiny again?" asked Gwyn gently.

"Never again. Just Kive." He snapped the twig in two. Gwyn stared at the broken fragments until Kive lifted his red eyes.

"Shiny? Oh. Hello, Shiny. Nice Shiny." Kive crawled around the campfire and knelt before Gwyn. He began to stroke his hair. "Nice Shiiinyy." His cooing tones hung faint and singsong. As he chanted on, Gwyn's eyelids grew heavy.

He caught Kive's wrist. "Please, Kive. I'm trying to think, not to sleep."

"Does Shiny miss Shiny?"

Gwyn's brow furrowed. "What do you mean?"

"Does Shiny miss Shiny? You know. Shiny. The other one. Clip-clop, like a horse. But Shiny isn't a horse."

"Oh, you mean Aluem? You mean the unicorn."

"Uniiicorn? Ah, yes. Unicorn. Shiny Unicorn. Does Shiny miss Shiny Unicorn?"

"Yes, Kive."

"Shall Kive find Shiny Unicorn?"

The tension bled from Gwyn's muscles until his head felt light. "*Yes*. Yes, Kive. Can you find Shiny Unicorn? Can you bring him here?"

"Yes, Shiny. Of course, Kive can find Shiny Unicorn."

"Find him, Kive. Bring him to wherever I am when you do. Don't bring him *here* but bring him to *me*. To Shiny."

Kive nodded dreamily. "Kive will bring Shiny Unicorn to Shiny. Uniiicorn. I forgot that word. Uniiicorn. Shiiinyy." He smiled. "Nice Shiiinyy."

"Go, Kive. Hurry. Please."

Kive rose and slipped away. If the sentries noticed him, they did nothing to prevent his departure. Gwyn couldn't blame them. Kive was Kive, after all.

❧

Two days passed without any sign of fallen fae or unicorn. Fortunately, Lord Bowrin remained content to keep Gwyn whole, even in Kive's absence; perhaps because he suspected Kive wasn't far away.

The army maintained a rapid pace. Despite Gwyn's weakened condition, he refused to mention his fatigue. He stared at his feet, hands kept bound as he walked between two Ilidreth guards, his thoughts muddled but his willpower as stubborn as any ren Terare who had come before him.

Toward evening of the second day since Kive's departure, he stumbled, eyes too weary to keep open. A hand reached out and caught him. His personal guard. The Ilidreth helped him to regain his feet.

"Steady, Simaeri. Not much farther and we shall stop again."

Gwyn nodded and kept walking, footsteps pounding in his head. The last few hours of the march stretched on for an age as his mind struggled to think of anything to keep him upright and conscious.

Lawen. It always came back to Lawen. Had Nathaera made it in time? Had the sky gem worked?

His heart ached for home. For knowledge. For warmth and food and safety. For family.

Lawen.

A call came down the line. Shouts cut across the air. Gwyn's stomach fluttered and air caught in his chest. Had Kive succeeded? Had he brought Aluem? Stretching to his full height, Gwyn peered over the heads before him.

A flash of orange light lit the air. Fire exploded near the front of the line.

"A mage!"

"It's a mage! Run!"

"Hold your positions! To arms!"

Pandemonium rippled into defense as hundreds of arrows unleashed upon the flames. The arrows slowed. Halted. Spun and shot back at the soldiers, as though the wind controlled them. Ilidreth dodged and slammed into each other.

Someone shoved Gwyn against a tree and cut the bonds on his wrists.

A voice whispered in his ear, "Climb, Simaeri. Stay there. If I see you run, I will shoot."

Gwyn seized the first branch he could reach and pulled himself up into the tree. He climbed until he reached a limb far above the swarming soldiers and turned his attention to the burning forest. In the center of the Ilidreth forces, blazing with flames that seemed not to consume him, stood a figure cloaked in black, hand stretched forth. Fire licked his gloved fingers but didn't devour the cloth.

As Gwyn looked on, the figure turned its cloaked head in his direction. Hungry, smoldering eyes pinned him in place. Frost clutched his heart. His soul lay exposed.

Another torrent of arrows filled the air, but the mage waved his hand, repeating the same reversal attack. The forces broke apart, retreating, reforming. Another volley filled the air. Another effortless deflection.

The figure shook his head. He flicked his hand upward. The flames leapt into a raging fire, swallowing the cloaked figure. In the next instant, the fire died. The trees stood untouched. The figure was gone.

The back of Gwyn's neck prickled.

"I found you," whispered a wintry voice in his ear.

Gwyn shoved off the branch where he sat and tried to drop to the forest floor — but a hand snatched his wrist.

"Not so quickly, little mage. You've been summoned."

Gwyn dangled from the branch, wrist throbbing. He lifted his eyes and met the gaze above him: black eyes glittered beneath the hood. A grin stretched across the man's shadowed face. He murmured a phrase Gwyn didn't understand, and the air around him tingled.

A rush of wind filled Gwyn's mind.

'Gwynter, resist!'

"Aluem!" He released the branch with his free hand and slammed his fist into the cloaked man's restraining arm.

The man hissed and his grip slackened.

Gwyn wrenched free, letting go of the tree to tumble toward the ground. Aluem leapt up and caught him on its back. Together, unicorn and boy landed on the ground. Aluem pawed the earth and turned. Gwyn looked up just as the mage vanished from the tree.

'*Are you well, Gwynter?*' asked Aluem, turning his neck until his eye could meet Gwyn's.

"I am now. But we can't stay here."

'*Of course not.*' Aluem galloped away from the army as voices cried out. Gwyn didn't look back, but he heard the whistling arrows unleash. One shot past his shoulder, tearing his sleeve but drawing no blood.

He buried his face in Aluem's silken mane. "I'm so glad to see you. Did you reach Vinwen? Are Nathaera and Windsur well? And Lawen, what news of him?"

Aluem laughed in his head. '*All are well, young Gwynter. All of them are very well. Lawen lives.*'

Tears scorched his eyes and he laughed aloud. "Afallon be praised. I'm so glad."

Chapter Nineteen

A crow's shriek jarred Nathaera from a bad dream.

As she rolled over and stared into coals of the campfire, the memories of her dream slithered away, but the heaviness in her chest lingered. Dawn had come, slipping slender fingers of light between the branches of the trees overhead. The air hung crisp and sharp.

The crow called again. Nathaera sat up and spotted it hopping along the branch of a nearby birch tree. It eyed her and cocked its head one way, then the other.

The thud of approaching hooves tore her gaze from the bird. She staggered to her feet as Aluem appeared at the edge of camp.

Draped along his back, sound asleep against his neck, lay Gwyn.

Nathaera gasped and danced around the fire to kneel beside Lawen. "Wake up, wake up." She shook his shoulder hard. "He's here. Aluem found him. He's here!"

Lawen moaned and blinked a few times. "What's wrong?"

"Get *up*. Gwyn's here. Aluem brought him. Look!"

Lawen lethargically rolled over and lifted his head to follow her finger. His eyes widened and he surged to his feet. "A unicorn!"

Nathaera climbed to her feet beside him. "You see him? I mean, you really see a unicorn? Not just a plain old horse?"

Lawen shook his head. "I've never seen a horse like that before. It's beautiful!" He blinked. "Gwynny!" He sprang forward.

Gwyn barely moved as Lawen reached him. The elder brother grasped Gwyn by his arm and shoulder and, straining, lifted him from Aluem's back. Gwyn groaned and opened his eyes as Lawen half-dragged him to the fire.

"Gwynter, are you wounded? Tell me how you fare." Lawen guided his brother to his bedroll and helped him to sit down. He wrapped a blanket around Gwyn's shoulders.

"Lawen?" Gwyn's voice was a sleepy murmur. He raised his head and gazed into Lawen's face, blinking. "Lawen!" His arms shot up and he caught his brother in a bear hug. "You're well! You're truly well! Aluem said so, but I had to see — to know!"

Lawen laughed. The brothers embraced for a long, quiet moment, though Nathaera thought she heard Gwyn sobbing into Lawen's shoulder. Finally, they pulled apart. Lawen ruffled Gwyn's hair.

"You've been through a fair bit, trying to save me. What a bold and reckless fellow you are, Gwynter."

Gwyn grinned. "It was worth every step."

Celin's voice came from a tree. "Now that you have found him, through no effort of your own, you should hurry back to Vinwen. The woods are more unsafe than normal."

"Celin?" Gwyn's brow furrowed.

"Your acquaintance agreed to help us find you," Lawen explained. "But it seems your unicorn was enough, just as Master Celin said."

Aluem's tail flicked. Nathaera turned to the unicorn as he approached her, and she lifted her hand to rub his head. "Thank you, Aluem."

'The woods are crawling with Fraeli and their Ilidreth allies, along with other rather foul creatures. We must leave just as Celin'Laen says. Gwynter is most at risk.'

Nathaera turned back to the brothers. "Aluem says we need to leave immediately."

Lawen nodded. "I should say so. Gwyn, let's get you home." He took his brother's arm and hauled him to his feet. "Between all our mounts, we should make good time."

Aluem sighed. '*I suppose he believes that is so. I shall try not to gallop too swiftly for the sake of your beasts.*'

Nathaera laughed.

Chapter Twenty

Celin accompanied the Simaeri travelers until they reached the woods' southwestern border two days later. There he bade them to stop and turned his gaze to Gwyn. "You didn't kill Kive as I asked."

Gwyn shook his head. "I couldn't. I'm sorry. I will pay another price to preserve my honor if you will but name it."

"It does not surprise me that your hand was stayed in a fit of mercy, but he cannot remain in these woods. His power will taint the land further. He must go with you. Let this be your price."

Gwyn glanced toward the trees. "I'm afraid I lost him while I was a captive of the Ilidreth."

"But he has not lost *you.*" Celin pointed to a shadow among the tree trunks. "I suspect he desires to remain with you as well."

Nathaera groaned. "Yes, to eat us! He thinks we're rats."

"He doesn't think I am anymore," Gwyn said. "He calls me Shiny now."

Celin nodded. "Then it is fate. Call for him. If I find him in my homeland again, I will slay him and then I shall come after you. This is a promise, Gwynter ren Terare. Keep Kive away from these borders."

"Vinwen isn't very far away, you know," Nathaera said. "Won't that be a problem?"

"It is not my concern how or where Gwynter chooses to keep Kive, so long as he does not return here." Celin turned his blue gaze back to Gwyn. "One last thing: Hide your mark."

Gwyn started. "My mark?"

Celin took Gwyn's hand, turned it palm-up, and pushed his sleeve back to reveal a rune signifying death emblazoned on Gwyn's wrist. The symbol came from the Old Tongue in the age of the Kings of Wintervale. As Gwyn stared at it, a chill soared up his frame and settled against his mind, dizzying and cold.

"You have encountered one of the Crow King's mages," said Celin. "Should he or another of his order find you again, you are marked for execution."

"But why?" demanded Nathaera. "He's done nothing!"

Celin shot her a piercing look. "Has he not? Do you call the use of magic *nothing* in Simaerin, despite your king's edict?"

The girl bit her lip and lowered her eyes. "He only wanted to save his brother."

Lawen steered his horse nearer to Gwyn. "What is done can't be undone. We'll just have to hide this mark and keep our secret well. We must go." He inclined his head. "Thank you, Master Celin, for all you've done." He turned the horse toward Vinwen. "Come, Gwynter, Lady Nathaera. No doubt the residents of Vinwen are very anxious by now."

Gwyn glanced toward the trees. "Come, Kive! Follow me."

The Ilidreth emerged from the shadows of the foliage and gracefully loped across the open ground until he reached Gwyn's side. The fae man gingerly reached out and brushed his fingertips against Aluem's coat. "Shiny. Shiny Unicorn. Shiny." He smiled up at Gwyn with such guileless adoration, Gwyn couldn't help but smile back.

"Come along, Kive. We're going to my home." He looked up and found Lawen eyeing him.

"An Ilidreth will be difficult to hide."

Gwyn shrugged. "We'll have to find a way."

Lawen nodded and shook his reins. "We ride for Vinwen! Ha!"

The company started off. Gwyn glanced back once toward the woods. Celin had vanished.

❧

"GWYN!"

Mother raced down the front steps of the manor house and reached up for Gwyn before Aluem had a chance to halt. Gwyn leapt from the unicorn's back and wrapped his arms around the slight woman.

"Hello, Lady Mother."

"You fool. You reckless, brave—" She pulled back. "You're thin as a reed. And pale! Have you been ill?"

"Yes. But I'm over the worst of it. Only a cough now."

Her eyes narrowed. "What an exchange that would be, replacing one son for another. Had neither of you any thought for *my* feelings?" She sighed and caressed his cheek. "Come inside. I'll have Cook make you a feast. Some mulled cider will warm you up in the meantime." She turned to Lawen. "And *you*, back to bed."

Lawen started toward the door.

"Not that way. You'll go in by the same method you got out. See that the doctor doesn't spot you. I've had a terrible time keeping him out these past days. Shoo!"

Lawen chuckled and changed course for the side of the house.

Last of all, Mother turned on Nathaera. "You're not much of a lady, running off like that, but I'll ask you to at least *look* presentable." Her words cracked like a whip, but Gwyn caught the corners of her mouth twitching upward. "Your betrothed has been frantic. He borrowed a horse and has gone looking for you for several hours each day, but he's returned for the night. Go put his mind at peace."

Nathaera bobbed a curtsy and hurried inside ahead of mother and son.

Gwyn wrapped his arm around Mother's waist and ushered her up the steps and into the vestibule. "I'm sorry I worried you, Mother. But as you see, Lawen is healed. I could do no less than try."

She sighed. "I know, Gwyn. You're far too much like your father. I feared where you'd gone seeking help, and lo, I was right. What confounds me is how you survived it."

Gwyn's mind flitted to the arrows barely missing him again and again. "I must credit Afallon."

"Then it's a very good thing recklessness doesn't rob devoutness."

They walked along the gallery and into the dining hall. Heat from a roaring fire rolled through Gwyn, warming his cheeks and stilling the gooseflesh on his arms. He hadn't realized how cold he'd been.

"Sit down. I'll see what Cook has." Mother pushed him gently toward a chair, and Gwyn took it. Nathaera and Lawen were nowhere in sight. Gwyn smiled as he thought of his brother. *Healed.* It had worked! Every harrowing moment had been worthwhile. The weariness, the illness, the fear, the rats...

Kive!

Gwyn shot from his chair, scooting it noisily backward. He hurried from the dining hall, raced down the gallery, and darted through the front door. "Kive?"

The fallen Ilidreth danced from around Aluem's other side. "Shiny! Look at all the crunchy birds!" He pointed to the chickens.

Aluem turned his head toward Gwyn. '*I have been attempting to dissuade him from eating any.*'

Gwyn laughed despite himself. "I'm certain there are plenty of rats in the barn, Kive. Why not investigate there? But *only* little rats, all right? Don't eat any rats that walk about on two feet."

Kive cocked his head. "Two feet?"

Gwyn patted his legs. "One, two. The big rats don't crawl. Don't eat the big rats. Do you understand?"

Kive bobbed a vigorous nod. "Only little rats, Shiny."

Gwyn pointed toward the barn. "Try in there."

Kive started off at once, skipping lithely toward the large stone barn, humming a tuneless sound.

"I'm sorry I left you both alone." Gwyn inclined his head to Aluem. "Forgive me. It was thoughtless."

'*But understandable. You have been reunited with your family, following a traumatic journey. Now is the time for you to rest.*'

Gwyn stroked Aluem's muzzle. "And what of you? Is this where we part? You've done more for me than I could ever repay."

Aluem's opalescent eyes held his gaze and seemed to see all there was of Gwyn. '*Have you forgotten that you saved me also, Gwynter?*'

"Are we even, then? Where will you go now?"

'*Perhaps to the barn, to see that Kive does not eat any big rats.*'

Gwyn blinked. "Are you staying?"

'*I am for now. Your journey for your brother has ended, Gwyn, but not your peril from it. I will stay for a while and see if the storm clouds pass away unbroken.*'

Warmth flooded Gwyn's heart. He wrapped his arms around Aluem's neck and buried his face in the unicorn's sweet-smelling coat. "Thank you, friend among friends. But please don't put yourself at risk."

'*Nonsense,*' replied Aluem with a smile in his voice. '*Most men do not perceive me as a unicorn, and those few who may on their own, cannot, should I desire to disguise myself. As once I told you, Gwynter: You are a rare man to see me and ride me as you do. Thus, so long as you banish any thoughts of violence or greed, lust or cowardice, from your heart and mind, I shall stay until your need of me has ended.*'

Gwyn pulled back to study the unicorn's fair countenance. "If that day should never come? If I shall always need you?"

Though the unicorn's face remained serene, Gwyn sensed that Aluem smiled. A pleasant warmth rippled through Gwyn's frame, banishing the last of his chill. *'Then I shall remain at your side until the end of your days, for thus I would choose to be, friend of my heart.'*

"Unless I become greedy and corrupt," Gwyn said. "I don't want to be those things, Aluem. But I can be reckless and thoughtless, and I have a temper I'm learning only slowly to control."

'I do not ask you not to be human, Gwynter. I only ask that you not become a beast.'

PART II

THE TRIAL AT CROW CASTLE

Chapter Twenty-One

A harsh knock hammered the front door of the manor. Horses whinnied in the courtyard outside.

Gwyn sprang from his bed, raced to the window, and peeked between his dark curtains. In the pale morning light, he spotted two men in red tabards standing at attention. One held the banner of the Crow King.

His heart tumbled into his stomach. He quickly dressed, tied his hair back, slipped on his boots, and left the quiet of his room to creep down the corridor. Voices rose from the vestibule below. Gwyn paused at the head of the stairs to listen.

"I will ask you only once more. Is he or isn't he at home?"

Mother's voice dripped with venom. "Having been woken so abruptly from my slumber, how am I to know if he's gone already for the fields? Gwynter is a very difficult boy to keep track of."

"Please send a servant to summon him, then, and let us find the answer. We have an important message to deliver."

"Very well." Mother called for a chambermaid to locate Gwyn. "In the meantime, gentlemen, would you care for tea? I doubt Cook has anything more substantial so early in the morning."

"Thank you, no."

Silence followed as the chambermaid slipped up the stairs. She spotted Gwyn, but kept walking, as though he didn't exist. Mother had trained her servants well.

"Might I inquire after Lord Lawen's health?" asked the man below.

"His health has been lately very poor, but there's some hope for him."

"Really? I'm relieved to hear it. He's a good swordsman. A good soldier."

"Yes," Mother replied.

Gwyn drew a steadying breath, tucked his surcoat straight, and descended the stairs. Two soldiers stood in the vestibule. The nearest to Mother was tall and fair-haired, his tabard decorated with the Crow King's device: the silhouette of a black crow in profile. He cradled his helm in his left arm and held a scroll in his right hand.

"Are you Gwynter ren Terare?" asked the man.

"I am," said Gwyn. "And whom do I have the pleasure of addressing, sir?"

"Sir Pensivil ren Dorsen, adjutant to General Cadogan ren Silverard."

Gwyn clicked his heels together and bowed. "An honor, sir. May I inquire as to the nature of your visit?"

Lord Pensivil held out the scroll. "An order from his Royal Majesty the Crow King. You're under arrest for the deliberate use of magic, punishable by death under the law. You will accompany me now and remain in custody until the date of your trial to commence a fortnight and three days hence."

Gwyn took the scroll, broke the wax seal, and unrolled it. The wording echoed the lordling's pronouncement.

Mother took a single step forward, eyes blazing. "This is an outrage, sir. My own son, accused of such a heinous—"

Pensivil raised his hand and she cut off.

"No one here has the power to alter this, my lady. Your son must stand trial for the crimes of which he's accused. If you've something to say, say it there and then." The lord turned back to Gwyn. "Gather what you may need. Choose a horse and come with me now."

Gwyn nodded. "I understand. I'll be just a moment." He turned and started up the stairs, heart hammering, mind reeling. How did they know? The mage's mark? Could the crows in the woods really report to the Crow King, their master?

How could Gwyn avoid execution? He *was* guilty of finding and using magic. What would become of Kive? Would Lawen also face a trial for being healed? He'd not chosen it. What of Nathaera? She'd been the one to trigger the magic to heal Lawen. Would the Crow King demand justice of her also?

Blessed Afallon, let them be safe.

At the top of the stairs, beyond view of the vestibule, stood Lawen, Nathaera, and Windsur. The first two stared wide-eyed, robed, disheveled from sleep, while Windsur regarded Gwyn with a smug smile, his eyes dark and glittering.

And Gwyn understood.

Chapter Twenty-Two

Crowwell, the seaside capital of Simaerin, rose like obsidian before the bright southern Vaymeer Sea. Three hundred years ago, when the first Crow King ascended the throne, he had moved his court from the old capital of Londolin further west, erected an enormous castle of black stone, and called the surrounding land Crowwell. A city rose around the castle and thrived under his magnanimous hand.

Gwyn had never visited the capital before now. Whenever Father came to this enormous city on business, he'd either brought Lawen or his steward along, or he'd sent one of them in his stead. Since Father's death, the steward had continued to oversee such matters. Gwyn had seen no need to take a hand in that until he came of age.

He hadn't anticipated seeing Crowwell for another year, at the beginning of spring. Certainly, he'd never intended to come as a prisoner.

Now he rode Aluem over the crest of a hill and slowed to view the city spread wide before him behind enormous walls of thick stone. On an opposing hill rose the turrets of Crow Castle, banners flapping on the sea breeze. The castle nestled within a second square of walls, a fortress within a fortress.

Lord Pensivil allowed him a moment to comprehend the city, then he motioned his small contingent onward, guiding Gwyn and Aluem down the tree-lined highway to Crowwell, flanked by armored soldiers who raised the Crow King's banner as they neared the city gates. The gates drew aside to admit the contingent and slowly shut after the company rode into the cobbled thoroughfare.

The hustle and bustle of a city shaped by commerce closed in around him. A thousand scents and sounds assaulted him, and bright shade awnings fought to snare his attention as voices beckoned and shouted out wares of every kind.

To avoid harassment by the merchants, Gwyn lifted his eyes to Crow Castle looming dead ahead beyond the city. As he studied the dark stones of the mighty edifice, dread flooded his body, heavy and oppressive. The sounds of the port city rolled away as he contemplated what lay before him: a trial and death by fire.

Why? Because he couldn't let his brother die.

It didn't seem right to execute someone for using magic when that magic had done no harm. What of Aluem? Was the unicorn an evil just because the king said so?

But the Crow King was divinely appointed by Afallon, wasn't he? Besides, the Church of Afallon echoed the sentiment of their king. Doctrinally, only Afallon could perform miracles, while magic was declared the counterfeit of those miracles. To use magic was tantamount to heresy.

Why then did Gwyn feel Afallon had guided him, even protected him? Was that not a miracle too?

Gwyn now knew firsthand the horror of fallen magic. He'd seen Kive, watched him eat live rats, heard tell of him eating human flesh. Gwyn had also seen the state of the True Wood and of Swan Castle. He'd also seen Lady Shalesta caught in eternal slumber, lovely and pure and certainly not evil.

Wasn't it possible that Afallon could — as Celin and Aluem suggested — bless his children with magic to be used for good, as much as magic could be used for ill? Weren't people allowed choice in order to grow and shape their souls for Heaven?

Gwyn shook his head. He could ponder doctrine all day, but what use was it at this point? His fate was likely sealed. No one at his trial would heed his questions and give him an answer that satisfied all.

If I die here, I won't die in vain. Lawen lives. He's well. That's enough for me.

Crowwell stretched on longer than Gwyn could have imagined. It took thirty minutes or longer to cross the many squares of commerce and trot through the affluent streets that led gradually up a slope to a second gate. The sentries there granted the contingent access to a long tree-lined lane that curved up to the impressive facade of Crow Castle.

The third gate swung aside at a call from Lord Pensivil, and Gwyn rode into the bailey, where hooded men in black cloaks encircled him. Lord Pensivil drew out a scroll identical to the one he'd given Gwyn one week before at Mount Vinwen. He handed this one to a cloaked man who stepped to the fore of the group.

"Gwynter ren Terare, as requested," Lord Pensivil said.

"Thank you for your service," replied the cloaked man in a mellow tone. "You may report to General Cadogan. We will take the prisoner hence."

Lord Pensivil inclined his head. He nudged his horse toward a lane that led away from the castle proper, and his soldiers followed, leaving Gwyn alone with Aluem and the cloaked men.

The leader pulled his hood back to reveal a round face and light eyes framed by unruly auburn curls. "Welcome to Crow Castle, Gwynter ren Terare. The Order of Corvus will host you until your trial in one week's time. Come this way." His eyes lowered to study Aluem. He bowed his head. "We will see that your companion is well treated." He started to turn away. Paused. Glanced back. "Hurry along."

Gwyn frowned and said nothing. He and Aluem followed the stream of hooded figures along the main thoroughfare and past several buildings that looked like barracks. Soon they turned right and followed a moat until they reached a bridge.

Aluem crossed it, and Gwyn glanced down. The water of the moat stood still and clear. He looked up as they reached the other side and turned right again to follow a cobbled path running beside the castle's wall. Eventually the trail curved left and brought them to a wooden door standing ajar.

"Please, enter," the leader of the cloaked men said, gesturing. "You may ride."

Aluem paced through the doorway and entered a wide room lit by torches. Gwyn glanced around. The floor was made of dirt and the walls appeared scarred by deeply etched runes.

"Dismount," the man ordered.

Gwyn obeyed and rested a hand on Aluem's neck. His heart began to race and sweat trickled down the back of his neck. Here he would be separated from Aluem. He would be truly alone among strangers.

A hooded man came forward and gestured toward a side door. "Leave your mount here and come with me."

Gwyn turned to Aluem. "Goodbye, my friend."

Aluem eyed him somberly. *'This is not the end, Gwynter. Your purpose does not expire here.'*

Gwyn offered a trembling smile. "I'll see you soon, then." He turned from Aluem and followed the leader of the cloaked men from the room and into an earthy-scented passageway trailing downward.

"Your cell will be down here," the guard said. "You will be provided with a bed, food, and water. You should know, magic is suppressed in this place. You'll not be able to summon aid to escape."

"I don't intend to escape," Gwyn whispered.

At last they reached a corridor stretching left to right. The guard turned left and brought Gwyn to a door forged from steel. He pushed it aside and admitted Gwyn into a small room without windows. Gwyn gagged on the close, musty air. A pallet made with straw haunted one corner. Mice scurried in the dismal light of a single candle.

"Use your light sparingly," the man said. "There will be no replacement."

Gwyn nodded and moved to the center of the cell. He turned to face his warden. "Thank you."

The man barked a laugh. "So civil." He turned away. Paused. "You're allowed a priest to commune with you through the coming week. Do you want one?"

"Yes, please."

"Very well. I'll send for one in the morning. Pleasant dreams, ren Terare." The man shut the door softly, but the sound echoed through Gwyn's mind like a knell of doom.

He sank to his knees and prayed.

"AFALLON DEFEND US, but this *is* a dismal tomb."

The stranger's voice brought Gwyn upright. A single night in the cell had left him shaken, chilled, and desolate, as though he'd been locked away for a year.

"Please step inside," said a second voice from the open doorway.

Gwyn squinted against the shaft of light and found two figures. One was tall, the other short. The second figure entered, and the door swung shut behind him, near enough to brush his heels. The room turned black.

"Surely they gave you a candle."

Gwyn fumbled in the dark for the candle beside his bed. "Aye, but nothing to light it by, as I discovered too late."

The man grunted. "Sounds like the Order. Just a moment." Feet scuffed against the stone floor, then a fist pounded against the door. The rattle of keys sounded on the other side, and the door cracked open.

"Finished already, priest?"

"Nay, I can't even begin. We want some light, my good man."

The jailer heaved a long sigh. The door slammed shut and footsteps retreated down the corridor. A few seconds later the feet came scraping back, the door opened, and light flooded the cell. Gwyn shielded his eyes with an arm.

"Here. Bring the torch back out with you."

"Thank you, my son."

The door shut again. Gwyn lowered his arm, blinking to adjust to the light. He squinted at the priest until he could make out more than a dark shape. The man was short, plain of face, with merry eyes glittering black in the torchlight. The black and red vestments of the church draped his narrow shoulders.

The priest studied him back. His lively eyes dimmed and his brow furrowed. "Why, you're barely grown."

"I'm fourteen, sir."

The furrowed brow shot up. "Younger than you look! You're not even of age. How can they imprison you? What is your crime?"

Gwyn held his gaze steadily. "The use of magic."

The priest's lips parted. "I see. I see. But why did you dabble in what's forbidden?"

"Because my brother was dying, and I found the only means of saving him."

The priest stared. His lips moved, but he said nothing for a long moment. "You saved him? You actually saved him using magic?"

Gwyn nodded. "I don't regret that I succeeded. I knew it was against the law. I was willing just the same. For anything less than my brother's life, I'd never have tried. But for him, I would do anything."

The priest's face darkened. "Be careful of saying that, my boy. In this place, most of all, give no price for your service." He moved forward, his shadow shrinking behind him in the guttering flame. "You're a brave lad. No disputing that. But you might be less free with your confessions, even to a priest. Not everything is so black and white here as it might seem back home."

"I realize that," said Gwyn. "But I won't lie to a priest of Afallon. I feel what I did is not deserving of death, but if that's the price for saving Lawen, I'm glad to pay it."

"Lawen?" The priest's brow wrinkled. "What's your name, lad?"

He rose from the straw bed. "I'm Gwynter ren Terare of Mount Vinwen."

"Ren Terare? Really? Then you're Sir Lawen's half-brother, born of his father's second wife?"

"I am."

The priest looked him up and down. "You're taller than your brother."

"Yes, sir."

The priest shook himself, as though waking from a trance. "Forgive me, my lad. Here you are, frightened, even if you're prepared to face trial, and I'm standing here insensitive to your suffering." He strode closer and offered his free hand. "I'm Rindermarr Lorric, priest of the second order in service to Divine Afallon, Bless His Eternal Name." He traced a square in the air in reference to Afallon's Four Tenets. "I've been brought here at your behest in these last days before your trial, to impart wisdom and comfort if I can, and perhaps even to help you make a defense before the Crow King."

Gwyn shifted. "Would defending myself be of any help? I did break the law."

Rindermarr shrugged. "There are two ways of thinking on that. Some would call it folly. Most, in fact. But there have been a few — mind you *very* few — cases where the defendant was pardoned. Not found *innocent*, mind. But pardoned nonetheless."

Gwyn blinked. "How?"

"Before I answer, I must ask a question. What kind of magic did you use?"

Gwyn hesitated. Should he answer? Was this some sort of trap? Did it matter? "I don't know what kinds of magic there are."

"Did you conjure a healing or use an artifact of some kind?"

"Oh." Gwyn shrugged. "I used an artifact, I suppose. I know nothing of conjuring."

The priest frowned. "Then you aren't a mage yourself?"

Again, Gwyn hesitated to answer. "I don't believe so, but others have insisted that I am."

"What others?"

"Aluem. He's a...unicorn."

The priest blinked. "A unicorn? You're acquainted with a unicorn?"

Gwyn nodded. "He's my friend. He came here with me."

"Here?" The priest looked around as though Aluem might appear in the cell. "To the capital?" His voice lowered. "Are you mad? To bring him here..."

Gwyn lifted an eyebrow. "He wouldn't take no for an answer. Is it dangerous for him?"

Rindermarr sighed. "You know little of Crowwell."

"That's true. This is my first visit. Perhaps my last as well."

"Chin up, my lad. Afallon willing, you'll live to come of age. You may even be able to use that. Never before has someone of your years stood trial, and there may be some leniency."

Gwyn studied Rindermarr's eyes, trying to judge his sincerity. "Why would you aid me, sir?"

"Why?" The priest smiled. "Because justice should never extend so far that mercy is forsaken. You're just a boy. A very resourceful one, by the sound of it. Magical artifacts aren't often just lying around. Would you tell me your story, Master ren Terare?"

Gwyn searched Rindermarr's eyes. Gentle. Open. He nodded. "You may call me Gwyn." Glancing around the cell, he shrugged. "There isn't much by way of seating, but my pallet of straw can handle us both, I think."

Rindermarr glanced at the straw protruding from the canvas. "We can always pray." He shoved his torch into a rusted sconce and sat cross-legged beside Gwyn on the makeshift bed. "Very well, Gwyn. Tell me what you will."

Gwyn stared into the flickering firelight, assembling all the details of his journey. "I went seeking the Ilidreth..."

Chapter Twenty-Three

By all reports, Nathaera arrived in Crowwell two days after Gwyn had been imprisoned in Crow Castle. Traveling with her were Windsur and Lady Mair ren Terare, and in a second carriage, a carefully disguised Lawen and Kive. Lady Mair had brought a dozen men-at-arms from Vinwen's garrison to protect them during their week-long journey.

The entourage reached Keep Lotelon without incident, where Nathaera was greeted in the manor's foyer by her very relieved mother, Lady Yiara ren Lotelon.

"I've been ill with worry!" scolded Mother, squeezing Nathaera so tight, she thought her ribs might crack.

"I'm fine. I sent a letter ahead, didn't I? You've known for days that I'm well."

"In these dark times, anything can happen, even on a main highway. Besides, you can't expect me to trust you, after you ran off to find some mythical castle!" Mother turned toward the others, eyes scorching, no doubt about to scold Windsur next — but her expression altered upon seeing Lady Mair.

Mother caught up her dress skirt and curtsied. "Welcome, Lady ren Terare. Please make yourself comfortable during your stay at

Keep Lotelon. My daughter wrote briefly of your plight, and while I don't know the particulars, I understand that your son saved my daughter's life. If there's anything at all that I can do in return, you have but to ask."

"Thank you, Lady ren Lotelon," Mair said with a graceful curtsy of her own. "You're very hospitable. Please call me by my given name, as I am to be your guest."

Mother turned to a manservant standing at attention nearby. "Direct Lady Mair to her suite. See that she has whatever she needs."

The servant bowed and motioned to Lady Mair, who followed him down a long gallery, steps clipped and lithe.

When she'd disappeared around a corner, Mother let out a sigh. "She's always been a fearsome woman. Exquisite, but fearsome. If not for her meager wealth, I suspect that woman could lead the court from any corner of the world just by a look!" She shook her head. "Never mind that. Hurry and bathe, Nathaera. You've much to tell me of your horrible journey, and I'll expect *every* detail. Every last one. March, young lady."

"What about my other guests, Mother?" Nathaera said as quietly as she could.

"Oh, yes, yes. I'll see they reach the guesthouse unmolested." Mother pointed at another servant, who bowed and headed for the front doors, no doubt already aware to be discreet.

Nathaera hurried toward the bathhouse, eager to be clean after her week on the road. But her thoughts strayed to Gwyn as she walked. Was he well?

Of course not. What a foolish question.

She bathed as quickly as she could, dressed herself in a soft gown of pale pink, and allowed servants to plait her hair with fresh spring flowers. Nathaera then made her way to the west parlor of the manor, where Mother sat awaiting her story.

Nathaera seated herself across from Mother on a silken settee, and she relayed as much of her journey as she could recall. She left out no detail, aware that her best defense of Gwyn was in painting his character entirely.

Mother listened. She asked no question and made no comment. When Nathaera finished, Mother sat still for a long time. Finally, she pulled a handkerchief from her sweeping sleeve and dabbed at her forehead. "You brought a man-eating Ilidreth to my guesthouse, child?"

Nathaera nodded grimly. "Better to know where he is then to let him wander to Crowwell on his own. He wouldn't stay behind. He insisted on following Gwyn. He calls him Shiny."

Mother nodded faintly, eyes pinned on the fur rug beneath her feet. "I'm afraid Gwynter will likely be burned at the stake, Nathaera. I can't think of any way around it. A pity, though. He sounds like a unique young man. Stupid, tremendously stupid, but brave just the same. Still, I'll speak with your father. Perhaps his age will bear some weight in his favor. We'll see."

Nathaera tried to smile. "Thank you. I'd hoped you might agree to speak with Father about his case. I know Gwynter disregarded the law. But truthfully, Mother, I doubt I would do differently if I thought I could save you or Father that way."

"I dare say it would tempt me as well." Mother sighed. "Poor boy." Her eyes found the westward window where the sun sank toward the distant mountains outside. "To think he found Swan Castle. Extraordinary."

"He is, Mother. Gwyn isn't ordinary at all."

Chapter Twenty-Four

Keys rattled in the lock outside.

As the door to his cell swung open, Gwyn looked up, his muscles taut. His nerves hummed against his ears. Rindermarr stood in the portal, grim but smiling. Two guards in full armor flanked the priest, each with a spear in hand.

"It's time, Gwyn." Rindermarr motioned behind him. "Follow me. The Crow King awaits you."

Gwyn climbed to his feet, straightened his grimy clothes as he gulped a few steadying breaths, then strode to the door. Rindermarr turned and padded ahead of him, while the guards took up position in the rear.

The priest led the way from the earthen passageway and out into the fresh air. Gwyn drank it in, desperate for open sky and the wind in his face — but freedom was short-lived. Rindermarr soon stopped outside a second wooden door set in the stone face of the castle. He opened it and slipped inside. Gwyn followed.

Narrow, uneven steps eventually carried him up into a tower room, where the guards instructed him to wait with Rindermarr until the appointed hour of the trial. An altar stood in the room's center, a moth-eaten cloth draped over it.

"Pray with me, Gwyn," said Rindermarr, kneeling at the altar.

Gwyn knelt and bowed his head. His heart struck his ribs and his mouth tasted like sand.

This is it.

Very likely he wouldn't live to see this day end. He would never see Vinwen again or play in the fields with his little sisters. Never again gather his mother into his arms and hold her tight when she was sad. Never wrestle with Lawen, or wander the woods on Tia's back. Never see Aluem again to thank him for all his help, or bow to the fair Nathaera with her quirking smile. Never fulfill his promise to keep Kive out of the realm of the Ilidreth.

Please, Afallon Above. I don't want to die. Let me live. Let me live to repay my debt to Thee.

The tower air hung stifling and thick, even with an open window facing southward. Gwyn mopped his brow and tried to pray on, but his prayer changed little, repeating over and over in his mind.

He wanted to live. He wanted to live!

Please let me live.

The door beyond opened. "Gwynter ren Terare. It is time."

He staggered to his feet.

Rindermarr followed him into the adjoining chamber, where a circle of high-rising chairs loomed above him behind a short wall erected to keep him isolated. Two dozen men in black stared down from those lofty chairs. At their center, raised above the rest, sat the Crow King himself.

The man looked much like his portraits. Long dark hair framed an angular face and pale eyes of white-gray shone in the torchlight. He was robed in a white cloak lined with crows' feathers, and a delicate crown of black stretched above his brow, spired and sharp. He sat with one leg propped over the other, an arm draped casually over the side of his throne. Yet despite his nonchalant stance, his eyes were pinned on Gwyn and his gaze burned like sunlight on a frozen pond, fiercely attentive.

A hand seized Gwyn's shoulder and pushed him firmly forward

until he stood in the chamber's center. High above him, the domed ceiling came to a point, where a brass chandelier flickered with a hundred burning candles. Fanning out from the chandelier spread a mural of black wings along the ceiling.

Gwyn shuddered, nerves raw. His heart thundered in his chest and his stomach writhed like a million tiny ants hard at work. He struggled to keep his face still, eyes alert but not wide. He mustn't show fear or he might collapse in a heap and sob for mercy.

He mustn't begin to doubt his choice. He'd saved Lawen, and that was all he'd meant to do.

If that is a sin, I am guilty.

"Gwynter ren Terare of Mount Vinwen in the ancient land of Simaerin," boomed a voice among the dark figures above. Gwyn started and looked around but couldn't tell which man spoke. "You stand before Blessed Afallon and his servant, our Illustrious Crow King, to be judged according to your deeds. You are accused of seeking out and performing magic, which is a direct and malicious violation of His Majesty's edict against such use. How do you plead?"

Gwyn's tongue swelled. He swallowed, raised his eyes to meet the king's, and stated: "Guilty."

Murmurs stirred the looming men.

The booming voice spoke. "Have you a defense for this action?"

Gwyn nodded and curled his hands into fists. "I sought a cure for my dying brother. None could be found among men, and so I sought it from the Ilidreth, though I knew well it might cost me my life. When I crossed paths with one of their kind, he directed me to Swan Castle, where I acquired a small blue gem. This was taken to my brother, and it healed him of his illness mere days before he would have otherwise died. Beyond these facts, I present no defense. I'm ready for your verdict."

He bowed his head and waited. Waited.

"Tell me, Gwynter," said a soft, lulling voice overhead. The Crow King. "Should anyone who risks losing a loved one break the law, and pursue whatever course, in order to avert such a loss?"

Gwyn lifted his head and met those cold, burning, penetrating eyes. "I don't know if there is a blanket answer to that question, sire. Should they? Perhaps not. But will they? Almost certainly."

"Then your defense is the human condition?" asked the king, leaning forward in his throne. "'Impulse directed my feet, and my heart led me onward. I couldn't help myself.' This is your philosophy? This is acceptable?"

"I *could* help myself, Your Majesty," Gwyn said. "I chose not to. I weighed the risks, and found I was willing to pay the price. If the price is death, I must accept that."

"So noble," the Crow King murmured.

"Your Majesty," Rindermarr said, stepping forward to stand beside Gwyn. "May I speak?"

The king waved his hand before him. "Priest Lorric, certainly. Say on."

"It has been brought to my attention that this boy is not yet of age. A trial of this level may not have been appropriate. While it is obvious from his own confession that Gwynter did break the law, can he be punished to its full degree at the tender age of fourteen?"

The king blinked slowly, and his gaze slid back to Gwyn. "You are but a child?"

"I'll be fifteen in six months' time."

"You're very tall for your age," said the king. "And rather mature."

"Yes, sire."

"Well." The king leaned back and steepled his hands to tap his fingertips against his chin. "Well." He lowered his arms to curl his fingers against the armrests of his throne. "Where is the blue gem you used to heal your brother, Gwynter of Vinwen?"

"With me." Gwyn reached into his pocket and withdrew the gem Lawen had given him as they returned together from the Ilidreth realm. He held it out now for all to see.

The king's eyes widened. "How exquisite. And this is from the fabled Swan Castle?"

"The castle exists," Gwyn said.

The Crow King turned his gaze to Rindermarr. "Take the gem and bring it to me."

Rindermarr inclined his head and reached to take it, but the gem flashed with blue light, hummed a single note, and vanished. Gwyn stared at his empty palm. As did the entire room.

"Well," said the king, breaking the silence. "Such is the nature of magic. Fickle and fleeting. You're better off without it. So are we all." He turned his attention back to Rindermarr. "Thank you, priest. Is there anything else before you leave?"

"No, Majesty."

"Then you may go."

The priest bowed and turned to leave the chamber the same way he'd come. Gwyn watched him exit with dismay, but he steeled himself and turned back to the Crow King.

"You strike me as quite a remarkable child. Resourceful, willful, stubborn, yet noble and long-suffering. I find that I do not hate you."

Gwyn's brow creased. Hate him? Was so strong an emotion warranted?

"That said," the king went on, "you've broken my law more than once. And while your actions for your brother's sake might be commendable to some, what defense have you for your second infraction?"

Gwyn shook his head, perplexed. "What second infraction, sire?"

"You summoned a storm in the True Wood, did you not?"

Gwyn's mouth fell open. Why did everyone assume he'd done so? It wasn't possible. Kive had summoned that storm. "I don't understand, sire. There was a rainstorm in the woods while I was there, but I summoned nothing — although it was fortuitous, as it slowed the march of a Fraeli force considerably."

"An army marches this way?" asked the Crow King, smiling faintly. "And your storm slowed them?"

"Not my storm, sire," Gwyn said. "*A* storm."

"You refuse to confess? But this misdeed might be considered more noble, and certainly more patriotic, than your other. Would you refuse the credit?"

Gwyn didn't flinch. "I would confess, had I the responsibility."

"Hm." The king folded his arms. "You're either a stubborn fool or an ignorant one. I wonder which." He turned toward the men seated on his right. "Lord ren Lotelon, show me."

The familiar name startled Gwyn. A tall man rose from his seat, bowed, and moved behind the row of chairs toward stairs Gwyn hadn't noticed before. The man descended the few steps and approached Gwyn.

"Raise your arms." His voice rang familiar in Gwyn's memory.

Gwyn complied, raising them, palms forward. He flinched as the man caught his right wrist and held it higher. "Your Majesty, behold the mark."

"Ah *ha*," said the king, smiling softly. "Then this *is* the little mage, whatever he might say."

Gwyn's mind reeled. "B-but that means this is a mage as well, Your Majesty."

"Ah," the Crow King said, "then you no longer deny being a mage, Gwynter ren Terare?"

Gwyn flushed. "I only meant that he must be a mage, if he marked me, sire. Yet you don't accuse him of breaking the law."

The king quietly laughed. "True enough, young mage. Allow me to introduce you to Lord ren Lotelon formally. He is my master mage, head of the Order of Corvus, and my right hand. And you, should you prove as smart as you appear, shall be his apprentice." He smiled gently, but Gwyn found himself shivering as though the gesture had summoned an ice storm.

"If not," the king went on, "you may, of course, choose to burn at the stake instead. I'll not force you to stay alive."

A frown touched Gwyn's lips. "I don't understand this, Your Majesty. Your edict states that the use of magic is an evil and a blight. None may use it. But what of the Order of Corvus? What of your master mage? And I, his apprentice?"

"It is very simple," said the Crow King. "The law is to prevent the common masses from using what they don't understand. The consequences could rupture the very fabric of magic itself. Magic thrives by carefully heeding its natural laws. When broken, chaos reigns. Lord ren Lotelon will teach you how to abide by those laws, so that when next you summon a storm or use a gem to heal a family member, you won't compromise the very ground beneath your feet."

The king rose from his throne. "Besides, Gwynter ren Terare. I am the Crow King, crowned by heaven itself, divinely appointed by Afallon to lead Simaerin. What I deem truth is truth. What I call an evil is evil insofar as I declare. Thus it is." His eyes glittered in the guttering flames surrounding the chamber. "Now, make your choice. Make it carefully. There is no backward path from whichever you decide."

Chapter Twenty-Five

He wasn't a mage.

After a week of grueling lessons, Gwyn longed to concede defeat. Even Lord ren Lotelon, at first confident he could awaken something within Gwyn, began to doubt.

"You summoned a storm, didn't you?"

Gwyn lay sprawled on the floor of a private dueling hall within Crow Castle, sweat beading down his face, scorch marks covering his bare arms from the conjured fire of his mage opponent. Fire he'd managed to dodge, though it had singed him still.

"I told you," Gwyn said between panting breaths, "I summoned no storm, my lord."

"That storm wasn't natural. It was certainly the work of a mage, or I'd never have been drawn to its core. It must have been you."

Gwyn peeled his eyes open to stare up at the mage lord with pale hair and dark eyes. "It must have been an Ilidreth."

"Why would Fraeli allies conjure a storm that would slow their progress?"

"Not them," Gwyn said. "Perhaps one of the Ilidreth who detest Fraeli as much as Simaeri do. Could that not be possible?"

Lord ren Lotelon considered that. "But you reek of magic. You have it within you. It isn't merely from possessing an infused gem, or it would have worn off by now. You also rode a unicorn. You must be a mage." His tone strained with every word.

Gwyn struggled to sit up, muscles objecting. He'd been dodging fire for the past three hours, and he'd only been allowed to rest half the night before. "So even Aluem believes, but I've seen no trace of magic inside me."

"Are you certain of that?"

Gwyn started to nod but paused as he recalled the arrows that veered off course every time someone tried to shoot him. Should he say something? The alternative to training under Lord ren Lotelon was death. If the Crow King deemed him unable to use magic, Gwyn knew too much about the Order of Corvus now. He'd not be allowed to leave alive. But could he endure becoming one of its members?

The past week had been dreadful. Every waking moment, the master mage worked to stir his dormant magic until Gwyn collapsed. He still slept in the windowless cell, not yet to be trusted.

But why did the Crow King bother to train him at all? What did anyone have to gain by forcing Gwyn into service? Why not execute him and be rid of a potential threat to the laws of magic?

"You've thought of something?" asked ren Lotelon.

Gwyn shook his head. "I merely wondered why the Crow King desires you to teach me magic. Aren't I more of a liability than not?"

"The Crow King always has his reasons. Rise. We'll go again. This time try to strike me. Stop defending. Fight back. Conjure fire, or storm, or anything at all."

Wincing, Gwyn pushed to his feet. His leg twinged, an earlier burn flaring up. "How is Lady Nathaera?"

Lord ren Lotelon tossed fire at his face.

Gwyn dodged left — back — slid to one knee to miss a third bolt of fire. He hadn't been able to determine whether Lord ren Lotelon was Nathaera's father, uncle, or a more distant relative. He knew the line of Lotelon was an old one, and well protected by many heirs. He could be a cousin. Whatever his relationship to the young woman, he refused to divulge it.

Fire loomed ahead. Gwyn flinched and narrowly escaped losing a limb. His skin stung. Smoke filled his nose.

"Too close. You're growing sloppy. Attack me!"

Gwyn sighed and raised his hands. "I can't go on this way. I must have rest."

"Magic often stirs when you're on the very brink of death, ren Terare. You will either awaken to your power or you will burn. Here or at the stake. More likely here. Now attack!" The mage lord summoned wreaths of fire above his hands and threw them hard at Gwyn.

Gwyn remained still, too weary to dodge. The fire would consume him or it would miss its mark — just like those arrows.

But the fire did neither. It stopped just short of Gwyn's face; and in a puff of dark smoke, it vanished.

Lord ren Lotelon pointed at Gwyn. "There! You see? What do you call that?"

Gwyn frowned, shaking his head. "But I feel no different. I gave no command. Are you certain *I* did that?"

"None but a mage could destroy my work, and I certainly didn't." He strode close and seized Gwyn's shoulders with each hand. "You're a mage. I was right about that. Now to discover how it works."

"I still can't summon storms or fire," Gwyn said.

"Yes, yes. So you say. Perhaps it's true, but that doesn't matter now. We must learn what form your magic takes. Not all mages are conjurers, though it's the most common manifestation." He released Gwyn and began to pace. "Is yours purely a defensive form? Does it respond to your distress? Perhaps you summoned a storm in defense."

Gwyn stifled the urge to refute bringing the storm. It might be best if they believed he'd done it. He certainly didn't want the king or his order to find out about Kive. He hadn't even told the priest that part of his tale.

Is Kive all right?

Before he left Vinwen, he'd begged Nathaera to try keeping the fallen fae hidden unless it risked herself. She'd smiled with perfect confidence.

"I'll see to it," she'd vowed.

Gwyn felt ill at the very thought of what Kive might be doing now. Had he reverted to eating people, or had someone taken Kive's life instead? Might that be better? Should Gwyn have killed him after all? The thought sent a shiver down Gwyn's back.

"You, boy."

Gwyn blinked at the finger hovering in his face. "Yes?"

"Has anything like what you did to my fire ever occurred before?"

Should he mention the arrows? He already knew the answer. If this man could teach him, if Gwyn did possess magic, shouldn't he learn it? Full disclosure would bring him closer to knowledge.

Gwyn nodded. "Several times arrows missed me, yet those who shot them were skilled. It was like a great wind rose up and flung them aside."

The master mage tapped his chin. "That still suggests defensive magic. Useful in some situations, though not the most impressive manifestation. Even so, if your magic could be used in defense of others..." He turned away and paced again.

Gwyn watched him, thoughts straying back to Swan Castle. To the Ilidreth shooting arrows at him. To the wind that rose to protect him. Had he assumed at the time that it was the spirits of that place, just as the Ilidreth had? *Would* they protect a Simaeri against one of their own? Had *he* knocked the arrows off course? Had *he* perhaps conjured that storm, and only assumed it was Kive?

Was he a mage? *He*, second born of a lesser lord, and from a second wife?

Then again, if Afallon above sought followers from the

humblest huts, and if magic *was* Afallon's domain as Aluem had eluded to, why couldn't Gwyn wield magic as greater lords did?

"I've spared you too much," Lord ren Lotelon said.

Gwyn winced, anticipating the mage's next words.

"Your magic thrives under threat. I can't hold back if I'm to waken it fully." The mage grasped the hilt of his broadsword and drew it with the scrape of metal against his sheath. "Prepare. I shan't hold back any longer. Either you will awaken or you will die this day, ren Terare."

Gwyn moved back, staggering in his haste to escape the blade swinging at his face. The lord was *fast*. He swung the opposite direction and Gwyn dropped to one knee to avoid being cloven in two. He rolled back, rose, and charged toward the far end of the dueling hall. Lord ren Lotelon raced right on his heels.

"Running is rarely the best defense, boy."

Gwyn had no alternative, unarmed and unused to magic. Unless his power stirred on its own, he would soon be a dead man.

The blade swung again, humming across the open air. A wisp of Gwyn's hair floated to the floor as he scrambled from death. But the mage lord was faster still.

The blade whistled toward Gwyn. He winced.

No escape.

His heart stopped.

The world stopped.

Sound stopped.

He spun, arm raised. The lord swung his blade, but his motion was slow, as though ropes restrained him as he fought to break free. Gwyn's hand moved on its own.

He caught the blade between two fingers. Snatched the hilt with his other hand. Yanked it free.

The world moved again. Lord ren Lotelon tottered forward, disarmed, eyes wide and clouded.

Gwyn dropped the heavy broadsword to the floor with a clatter. He gasped for air, as though he'd run ten miles rather than the length of the room. Sweat ran down his face. He wiped his brow with his tunic sleeve. With a groan, he sank to the floor, too weary to stand.

"Congratulations," said ren Lotelon. "You've come into your power, little mage."

Gwyn shivered, limbs trembling. He bowed his head and concentrated on breathing.

"It will be a few days before you recover. Despite that, you'll need to train during this time. If you don't, your magic may grow dormant again, and you'll have to start over."

The master mage's words gave Gwyn pause. Hadn't he taken sick just after the storm struck in the True Wood? Did that mean he *had* conjured it?

"Get up."

Gwyn lifted his head slowly. "I don't think I can."

Lord ren Lotelon bent down and took up his sword. He turned it over and examined the blade. "I think I can persuade you." He swung straight down.

Gwyn couldn't move—

—but he did.

In an instant he stood across the room, wind rushing around him. The sound of metal striking stone rang through the hall. Gwyn turned as the lord straightened, sword in hand.

"Excellent. Again."

Gwyn tripped backward and leaned hard against the wall. He shook his head, panting. "I...can't."

"You must." Ren Lotelon pointed his blade and charged.

Gwyn pushed himself from the wall and tried to run. Staggered. Fell. He caught himself, hands smarting against the marble floor. His neck tingled. He glanced up, rolled to his side, and lifted his hand in the only defense he had.

The sword shattered. Shards of metal flew in every direction — except toward Gwyn.

Lord ren Lotelon wiped a trickle of blood from his cheek and examined a cut in the fabric of his sleeve. "Well done, ren Terare. Again." He drew a dagger from his belt.

❧

WHEN GWYN STUMBLED to his straw pallet, he collapsed and closed his eyes, listening to the scraping sound of the door locking. The rattle of keys. The retreating footsteps.

He didn't bother to light a candle with the flint and steel given to him after his trial. He laid in the dark long after the warden's footsteps faded, leaving the faint sound of his own breathing and the soft scuttle of mice wandering the cell.

Lord ren Lotelon had pushed Gwyn for hours. Pushed him until he finally passed out. The mage lord then woke him with a bucket of water, ordered him to rest, and assured him training would recommence before dawn the next morning.

It was almost morning now. He imagined he could feel the sun beginning to rise. He would barely have enough time to dream before his tyrant mentor returned to claim him.

Gwyn yearned to bask in silence, in not moving. He almost didn't want to sleep, just to soak in one moment of solitude.

His body trembled. He'd reached his limit long ago, and like an overwrought horse, he feared his heart might burst at any second. Gwyn willed his thoughts to wander, anywhere, any place but this wretched circumstance.

Think of Vinwen, of Mother and Lawen, of Nathaera. Even of Kive. Anything but here.

The clatter of keys intruded on his thoughts. Dread doused him, colder than the mage's bucket of water. Had dawn come already? Surely, he'd only lain here for a few minutes, not a few precious hours.

He tried to lift his head, but he couldn't move. His body shook more for his effort, that was all.

The door swung open on shrieking hinges. Faint light flooded the room behind him. Gwyn tried, but he couldn't turn his head toward the door to see the master mage's face.

Silence filled the open space of the little cell. A heartbeat. Two. Three.

"Shall you not rise for your king?" asked a soothing, silken voice.

Gwyn twitched. The Crow King had come here? In the dead of night? To what purpose? Gwyn tried to raise his head, tried to push himself up by his hands, but he only twitched again.

"Lord ren Lotelon tells me you've awakened to your power at last. I am glad. It means you're more useful alive than dead." The soft tap of boots against stone approached Gwyn. He heard the rustle of cloth, and faint breathing close by. "Are you ill, ren Terare?" The king was very near, leaning close.

"Yes, sire." His voice rasped, faint and hoarse.

A cold hand touched his brow. "So you are. But your training has only begun. Can you endure it?" The hand withdrew. "I thought to inspect the strength of your magery for myself. Shall I?" Cloth rustled again. "Turn over."

Fingers caught his arm and pulled Gwyn onto his back. He stared into the shadowed face of the Crow King. Pale eyes studied him back with a strange hunger smoldering in their depths.

"You intrigue me, Gwynter of Vinwen. You bewilder me. To love your brother so much that you would risk all. You, second born, second always. You could have been heir of Vinwen. Or was that too small a realm for your ambition?" The king leaned closer and his voice turned into a whisper. "I have heard a rumor that you desired to join my army."

Gwyn held his gaze, though his frame shook with tremors. "I did."

"And now you have. Rejoice."

Gwyn said nothing.

The Crow King drew back with a soft laugh. Jewels sewn into his cloak glittered in the torchlight beyond the open door. "You are mine now, Gwynter. There is no greater station for a Simaeri than to be at my side. You will become one of my elite within my order of mages. You will defend my lands against Fraeli and Ilidreth. You will protect your people. This is an honor." He climbed to his feet. "I expect great things of you, *Gwyn*. Very great things."

Chapter Twenty-Six

Nathaera marched into the dim stable with hands on her hips. "No, Kive! How many times must I tell you, *you can't eat the stable boy*!"

Kive's mouth snapped shut and his hands fell away from the boy's shoulders. As the Ilidreth sank back to rest against his heels, the stablehand scrambled to his feet and scurried away, pale and shaking.

Nathaera sighed. "You're not supposed to be in the stables at all. We've talked about this."

"But all the rats are *here*. Allll. And now the big juicy one got away."

"Remember what Shiny said?" She strode forward and knelt beside Kive, ignoring the dirt and hay that clung to her dress. "You can only eat the little rats. Got it?"

"Shiny said that?" asked Kive, perking up.

"Yes, he did. Remember?"

"Shiny?" Kive scooped up a handful of hay and squeezed it between his hands. "Where is Shiiinyy? I need to seeee him." His drawling tone pitched into a whine. "Shiny is gone. So is Shiny Unii-icooorn."

"I know, Kive." Nathaera rested a hand on his shoulder. "I miss them too. But there's no word of Gwyn being burned at the stake. Father says he's fighting hard to get Gwyn released, and Father has some sway with the king. But these things take time, Kive, and we must be as patient as you or I have any hope of being. Which isn't much, I will grant."

She sighed and flopped into the haystack behind her. Kive crawled close, heaved his own sigh, and flopped beside her in almost perfect mimicry. Both stared at the loft above. The sun streamed through tiny flaws in the wooden beams revealing a swarm of dust motes.

Warmth curled over the air. The sweet fragrance of grass and unfurling blossoms wafted into the dusty stable. Were it not for Gwyn's circumstances, it might be one of those perfect spring mornings; the kind that seeped into one's memory and remained forever, sweeter to taste than wine.

"This is a surprise."

Nathaera opened her eyes, wondering when she'd closed them. She smiled up at Lawen, who stood above her, grinning.

She shook her head. "You and Kive are both impossible. You're supposed to stay in the guesthouse. Don't think our servants won't gossip, whatever we might command."

"It's all right. General Cadogan knows I'm here. I wrote to him, and he said he'd heard about my healing and doesn't believe there will be any charges laid against me. After all, I couldn't even move to protest. I asked if I might return to his service. Maybe there I can do something for Gwyn."

Nathaera sat up. "But you're still recovering."

"I'm fully recovered, dear lady. I have been since the moment I was first healed. There's nothing but a few roads between me and Gwyn, and he's locked up somewhere, undergoing who knows what sort of cruelty, all for my sake. I can't sit here any longer, waiting and wondering. I didn't come to Keep Lotelon to hide. I came to help my brother."

She studied the earnestness of his face, the determination

shining in his green eyes, and a smile crept onto her lips. "I'd be a fool to stop the ren Terares from doing whatever they feel strongly about." Nathaera lifted her hand to him. "Help me up, my good man."

Lawen caught her hand and lifted her easily to her feet. She laughed. While he wasn't as tall as Gwyn, nothing of his former frailty remained. He stood around six feet, well-toned, with the same quiet manner about him as his younger brother.

"How old are you, Lawen?" she asked.

He raised an eyebrow. "Nearly twenty-six years. Why, my lady?"

Hardly older than Windsur, yet the contrast was striking. "Oh, just wondering at the world and all its varieties. It makes one fully appreciate the vastness of it all." She shrugged and started toward the stable door. "Come, Kive. You at least should stay in the guesthouse."

"Lady Nathaera?"

She turned and found Lawen standing still, green eyes vivid in the dim light, his expression grim. "Someone reported what Gwyn did. Someone must have."

She blinked. "But no one knew."

"A few knew."

Her brow wrinkled. "But none of us would say anything—" She cut off and her eyes widened. "Windsur! He— Might he? But why would he? Gwyn saved our lives. He had no reason to—"

"None? Is your intended not a jealous man?"

She started to shake her head. Stopped. Shook it again. "But he had no reason to be jealous."

"Does he know that? You did run off to rescue Gwyn after you reached Vinwen the first time. Any proud man might perceive that as a threat. I know it might make me uncomfortable, especially if I were uncertain of my lady's feelings on our union."

Her mouth fell open. "But that's ridiculous. Gwynter is my friend. He saved my life. Of course I would want to find him, to help him. Of course I would. *Anyone* would!"

"Anyone, my lady?"

She threw her hands up. "But to condemn a man to trial and execution? It's horrible." Yet though her mind reeled, her heart pounded. It *was* Windsur. She had no proof, but she knew it to be true.

"Oh, that dunderhead," she whispered, dropping her head into her hands. "Poor, foolish, stupid, jealous Windsur. Was it worth a life?" She lifted her head. "I have to help him. I must make amends. If Gwyn is executed, it's as much my fault as Windsur's. Please, Lawen, what can I do?"

He shook his head. "Nothing for the present. I'm heading out now to report to General Cadogan. When I've found out anything more, I vow you'll learn all I discover. In the meantime, Nathaera, look after Kive. It's what Gwyn asked of you."

"Of course. I'll do my best."

Chapter Twenty-Seven

"How is your new apprentice?"

The voice rolled like thunder across the plains.

Gwyn's eyes snapped open. He tried to turn over onto his back, but his body protested and a wave of nausea rushed over him. Bile burned in his throat.

"He's ordinarily a more impressive specimen, but I've attacked him for six hours without a rest. He passed out."

"Does he have much potential? What sort of magic does he wield?

Through a haze of exhaustion, Gwyn began to recognize the voices hanging overhead. One must be Lord ren Lotelon. The second took longer to pinpoint. Where had he heard that deep voice before? Oh. General Cadogan ren Silverard, his brother's commanding officer and head of the Crow King's armed forces. The two had met only once at the funeral for Gwyn's father.

Gritting his teeth, Gwyn rolled over. He blinked until his vision returned and found the two men peering down at him. Lord ren Lotelon clutched his replacement broadsword. General Cadogan ren Silverard stood with hands behind his back. He was garbed in the red tabard and black armor of the Crow Army's leaders. Brunett hair fell past his broad shoulders and eyes of deep brown studied Gwyn's face.

"His magic is defensive," ren Lotelon said.

"That's disappointing. We need more warriors, not more shields."

"His defenses appear to become offensive if provoked. I'm testing that presently to be sure."

General Cadogan lifted an eyebrow. "Rumor at court claims the boy performed magic to save his brother."

"That is so."

"I frankly can't blame him. Lawen is a good man, one of my best. I hated the thought of losing him, but none of my physicians were of any use. I even asked a mage healer for assistance, but he said it was beyond his skill. What sort of magic did the boy invoke?"

"An Ilidreth gem, or so he claims."

Cadogan looked down at Gwyn, dark eyes catching his. "Is that so, boy?"

Gwyn nodded gingerly. A headache settled in, throbbing like a hammer-strike against his skull.

"What does the Crow King intend with him?" Cadogan asked, turning his eyes toward the mage lord.

"I'm uncertain. But he insists that I bring out his full potential. He wants him fully trained by his coming of age."

"Ah, yes. I recall Lawen saying his little brother was tall for his years. Even lying down, it's rather apparent." Cadogan rubbed a scar on his chin. "Well, I'll leave you to your work. When you've got his power harnessed properly, call for me. I'd enjoy a spar. Defense mages are always interesting opponents."

"This one may be more so than you expect." Lord ren Lotelon bowed his head. "Good day, General."

"Good day, my lord." Cadogan inclined his head, turned, and strode away, footsteps an even click against the marble floor.

"Up with you," the mage said, adjusting the blade in his hands.

"You've had long enough to rest. We've much to do before nightfall."

Gwyn set his jaw and staggered to his feet. His head swam and nausea rushed through him again. "I might take ill."

"Your stomach?"

Gwyn nodded.

"Resist your body's weakness. Defend yourself. Use your magery."

Gwyn nodded even as his stomach churned and his throat tightened. He wasn't certain he used his magery at all. Instead, his magery used him.

Lord ren Lotelon charged him, sword raised, eyes hard as a blacksmith's anvil.

Gwyn threw out his hand, concentrating on his enemy's blade. It shattered, but ren Lotelon flung the hilt aside as metal scattered across the floor, already pulling free a dagger. At the same moment, the mage summoned fire.

Wind circled Gwyn and the fire died. The dagger missed his face. Gwyn knocked ren Lotelon's arm aside, and the man staggered back.

"Good. Better. Again."

Chapter Twenty-Eight

Following Lawen's departure, a fortnight passed before word of the ren Terare brothers reached Keep Lotelon.

As the courier rode away, his horse kicking up gravel, Nathaera broke the seal of the letter he'd brought with trembling fingers, chanting a prayer to Afallon under her breath.

I have confirmed that Gwyn still lives. Beyond that, very little. Only that he is housed by the Order of Corvus, which can mean nothing good. No word on the king's verdict at his trial. All is eerily silent. Will write again with any news at all. Pray for Gwyn.

—L.

The hasty scrawl sent a tremor through Nathaera's body. She knew little about the Order of Corvus. Only that they were the king's personal guard. Rumors whispered more: That they were assassins and torturers.

If they held Gwyn, was he being tortured? Was using magic so horrible that he deserved such treatment?

She stomped her foot. *Preposterous.*

Slipping through the open door of the manor house, she raced down the steps and crossed the extensive lawn, heading for the stables. She always found Kive there. He was terrifying, even disgusting. But though she'd witnessed him do unspeakable things, she found a strange sort of comfort in the fae man's company. Kive behaved like a small child or a feral kitten: he didn't understand when he did bad things, and the rest of the time, he was almost cute.

Or perhaps I'm becoming calloused.

She couldn't say.

Pushing the stable doors aside, she spotted the fallen Ilidreth standing before one of the stalls, stroking the muzzle of a chestnut mare, cooing in his lilting drawl. "Niiiice soft horse. Niiice horse."

The horse stood still and allowed it. Nathaera wondered if it felt safe or, more likely, Kive had commanded it not to move.

"Hello, Kive," she said, approaching.

He turned his bright red eyes to her. "Hello, Rat."

"No, Kive. I'm a girl."

"Rat." Kive turned back to the stall. "Horse."

She sighed. "If I can't be a girl in your head, Kive, can't I be a different animal? Do I look like a rat to you?" She lifted her arms and twirled. "See? No tail. No sharp teeth. I'm not a rat. Remember, you thought Shiny was a rat, but he's a Shiny, right?"

Kive eyed her. "Are you...a bird?"

"You still eat birds, don't you? No, Kive. I'm not a bird."

"Are you a fly?"

She laughed. "Some might think I'm enough of a pest for that. But Kive, you're not thinking big enough. That's a horse, isn't it? You'd forgotten about them. There are hundreds, even *thousands* of other animals besides just rats, birds, and horses. There are all kinds! Cats and dogs and beavers and — and wolves. Deer. All kinds."

Kive canted his head. "All kinds? So many?"

"Yes. Maybe I'm a deer, or, or an elephant!"

His eyes widened. "El...eh...faunt?"

She laughed. "Yes. Maybe. Do I have a long, long nose that can uproot trees?"

His mouth hung open. "*No*. You can't be an eleph..." He trailed off.

"Elephant. No? Maybe a tiger. Do I have stripes down my back?" She turned and pulled her hair aside for his inspection. Gentle fingers brushed against her back, then withdrew.

"No. No stripes."

She turned and tossed her hair back. "Hmm. Maybe I'm a beetle."

"A beetle? Noooo." Kive shook his head. "Not crunchy."

"There, see? You know what beetles are." She folded her arms. "Tell me honestly, Kive. Do I look like a rat to you?"

He regarded her like he'd never seen her before and shook his head. "No. No, you're not a rat at all. Not juicy like a rat. Not sneaky."

"Well," she laughed, "not *always* sneaky. So, what am I?"

"I don't know," said Kive. "So many aneeemals I don't know. So many aneeemals. Do *you* know what you are?"

"Well." Nathaera tried to think of any she'd ever related to. "Maybe a cat or a deer. I do like birds, but you eat those." She unfolded her arms and clasped her hands behind her back, tilted back onto her heels, and thought. "Do you know, Kive, there are thousands of kinds of birds? Black birds and blue birds and sparrows. Cranes and crows and swans."

"Swans," crooned Kive. "Lovely white swans, swimming, swimming. Cutting through the water. Swimming."

"Yes, swans are lovely." She smiled. "You like swans, Kive? Not to eat, I hope."

"No, Kive doesn't eat swans. No." His eyes filled with a haunted light. "Swans are all sleeping now. No more swimming. No more cutting through water."

"I like swans," she said quickly. "I like sparrows and wrens, too." She chuckled. "Did you know there's a kind of bird called a fairy wren? Isn't that pretty? I want to see one someday."

Kive tilted his head one way, then the other. "Fairy wren?"

She nodded. "I've heard they can be pink or blue, but that may be a myth. They sound beautiful."

"Beautiful." Kive reached out and ran his finger down her cheek, his touch light as a feather quill. "Fairy wren. Fairy wren." He met her eyes and held them. "Hello, Fairy Wren."

She laughed. "Well, all right. Hello, Kive. That doesn't mean you'll eat me, does it? Fairy wrens aren't to be eaten."

He shook his head. "No, Fairy Wren. Kive doesn't eat fairy wrens. Not fairy wrens. Hello, Fairy Wren." He stroked her hair.

She grinned. "Hello."

Chapter Twenty-Nine

The Crow King granted Lawen the right to visit Gwyn if General Cadogan accompanied him. Fortunately, the general agreed.

"I saw your brother recently, and I'm intrigued to learn of his progress. He appears to have great potential," Cadogan said when he joined Lawen at the north entrance to Crow Castle. Together they traveled along the corridors leading to the south wing where the Order of Corvus made its quarters.

The general's words set off alarms in Lawen's head, but he said nothing. He would learn their meaning soon.

They reached the entrance to the south wing after a long walk down wending passageways lit by sparse torches. Lawen knocked on the wooden barrier and waited, resisting the urge to tap his fingers in his impatience.

Gwyn was somewhere on the other side of the door.

Finally, it opened, and a short, black-cloaked man peeked out at them. "Yes?"

"General Cadogan and Lieutenant Lawen to see the head of your order," Lawen said.

The man squinted at each of them, then pushed the door aside. "We've been expecting you. Come in, General, Lieutenant."

The two men entered and followed the shorter man across the antechamber and into a larger room where a fire crackled in a great hearth. A polished mantelpiece above brandished the Crow King's crest.

Glancing left, Lawen spotted a familiar man seated at a desk, one hand pressing a bloodstained handkerchief to his cheek. The man's eyes fixed on Lawen.

"Hello, Lord Lieutenant."

Lawen found his voice. "Lord Traycen?" He couldn't believe he stared at his host, the father of Nathaera ren Lotelon. *He* was part of the order holding Gwyn captive?

The lord rose from his chair. "You look bewildered. I'm sorry, but my deception couldn't be helped. The Crow King himself requested the strictest confidence until Gwyn's initiation was complete."

"Initiation?" asked Lawen, voice weakening. He swallowed and rubbed a palm against his pantleg.

Traycen ren Lotelon glanced at General Cadogan. "Can we trust your man to keep his silence?"

"I trust Lawen," Cadogan replied. "And the Crow King has agreed to let him know all. It's clear that Lawen and his brother share a deep bond. Do *you* want to upset Gwynter at this stage?"

"No, indeed not." Traycen nodded. "Very well. Be seated, gentlemen." He gestured to the chairs before his desk, then folded back into his own, dabbing his oozing cheek. "Lord ren Terare, your brother is a mage."

Air caught in Lawen's throat. "Impossible."

"So even he believed, but I assure you that he is. Not only that, but he's one of the most powerful mages I've ever encountered. His abilities are...unique. Defensive magic I understand well, but this is something else. Almost without exception, a man's magic is defined by his character, and I have reason to believe that's the case this time. That's *why* he's so powerful. Your brother's nature is complex. Thus, so is his magic."

Lawen shook his head. He must feign ignorance. "I don't understand. Why are you exploring Gwyn's magic? Isn't that against the law?"

Traycen nodded. "Except under very strict circumstances, yes. But this is that circumstance. Your brother is about to be sworn into the Order of Corvus — the king's army of mages."

Lawen closed his eyes. Dread flooded his limbs. Not that. Anything but that. "But why, my lord? The king's edict... The trial..." He opened his eyes and stared at Lord ren Lotelon. "Does Gwyn want to join the order?"

"He chose that over death by fire. A wise choice. Wild mages aren't tolerated in Simaerin, Lieutenant. Only mages of the Order of Corvus are exempt from the edict, and we heed only the Crow King's commands."

Who could have guessed his little brother to be so powerful? But then, perhaps it wasn't strange. Hadn't Gwyn tamed a fallen Ilidreth and won the favor of Celin and the loyalty of a unicorn? Hadn't he survived the perils of the True Wood to save Lawen's life?

Lawen inhaled. "May I see Gwynter now?"

"Certainly. But I must emphasize that all we've told you is a secret sealed by magic. To reveal anything here may cause your untimely death — something I suspect you don't want to risk so soon after your brother's efforts."

Lawen stood up, schooling his face. As the other two men followed suit, Lawen caught Traycen ren Lotelon's eye. "Your daughter is very worried about Gwynter. You might give her *some* peace of mind."

The man's eyes hardened. "I'll give her peace of mind only when I feel it's appropriate. In the meantime, patience is a lesson it's about time she learned. This way, please." He moved toward a door on the far end of the room.

The man's present attitude stood in sharp contrast to how he treated his family at Keep Lotelon. Lawen had suspected from

Traycen's smiles — and the gifts he brought home every chance he got — that he spoiled his daughter. Was that a show? Or was this the performance?

Now wonder there'd been no repercussions for Nathaera, despite her involvement in Gwyn's quest.

The door opened to a small stone chamber furnished by a single chair. There Gwyn sat, head bowed, wrists bound.

Lawen resisted the urge to run to his side, to gather him in his arms. He planted himself beside Cadogan instead, studying the bruises and welts along Gwyn's exposed arms. He wore a sleeveless gray tunic, tied at the waist by a cord, opened at the chest to reveal more abrasions and welts.

Lawen's blood turned to ice. He glared at Traycen ren Lotelon. "Is torture part of his training, sir?"

"Not usually, but in Gwynter's case it has been crucial."

Lawen curled his hands into fists and worked air through his lungs. He must keep his temper or risk his brother's life. He turned back to Gwyn and found the boy's head raised, gray eyes pinned on Lawen.

A broad smile spread over Gwyn's lips. Relief washed through Lawen like a breath of spring wind, melting the ice in his blood. Gwyn's body was bruised and battered, but his mind hadn't shattered.

Lord Traycen motioned Lawen forward. "He's been waiting for you."

Lawen reached Gwyn in a few bounding steps. He knelt before his brother, caught his arms where the bruising looked slight, and they searched each other's eyes.

"Hello, Lawen," Gwyn whispered. "I've missed you."

Tears pricked Lawen's eyes. He ran a hand over Gwyn's loose hair, trying to swallow back his emotions. "I've been so scared for you, Gwynny. You're so thin. Are you eating?"

Gwyn bobbed a nod, but beneath Lawen's fingers his body trembled.

Lawen pulled his brother into a tight embrace. "I'm so sorry. This is my fault."

He felt Gwyn's head shake against his shoulder. "It's not. How could it be? You would have done the same for me."

Lawen clung tighter. It was true; they both knew it. To save the other, each would travel to the very ends of the world. He pulled back, turned his head toward the two men at the door, and speared Lord Traycen with a look. "What becomes of him now, my lord?"

"He will swear fealty to the Crow King as the newest member of the Order of Corvus. Just in time, I might add. Fraelin invades our lands this moment."

The brothers exchanged a look. Lawen read the fear in Gwyn's eyes, but also his determination; that strange fire that always burned there. It always had, even in the first moment Lawen saw him as a quiet newborn in Lady Mair's arms. There was something remarkable about Gwynter. Something inborn. He could lose his temper as other people; could make bad judgment calls; could follow a foolish impulse. But he was special. Lawen would swear to that on his very soul.

His little brother belonged to a kind of otherworldly caste. He saw things others couldn't.

Would Gwyn step into his destiny now? Or had the Crow King done all this to bind him, to shackle his potential?

A few months ago, Lawen had come to realize the depths of the corruption in Crowwell, and that the king himself oversaw it. But what could anyone do to stop him? Did he fear Gwyn's latent talents?

Why not kill him then? Does he intend to use Gwyn for his foul purposes?

Gwyn rose from his chair, and Lawen followed him to his feet. The brothers stood facing General Cadogan and Lord Traycen.

"You'll swear fealty to king and country at dawn tomorrow," Traycen said. "Three days hence, the Order of Corvus marches with General Cadogan's regiment for the North Marches on the edge of Siaan Wood. There we will meet the Fraeli forces in combat. As you're already aware, they have Ilidreth allies in their company. Be ready."

Lawen clapped his hand to his chest in salute. "Will Gwyn be permitted to leave the castle in the meantime?"

"No," answered Traycen. "He must finish his training, and until his loyalties are proved, he'll be under constant watch. You'll see your brother again in a few days, Lieutenant. You're free to say goodbye."

Lawen clenched his jaw and turned to Gwyn, urging his anger to roll away. Looking into the eyes of his younger brother, Lawen could dismiss the present company and his frustration. He rested his hand on Gwyn's arm.

"You don't need me to tell you this but be strong. I'll see you soon."

Gwyn smiled, eyes ablaze with the firestorm that never extinguished. "Take care of yourself."

❦

As Lawen walked down the castle corridor beside General Cadogan, his heart hung heavy in his tight chest.

"You ought to thank me," Cadogan said. "Were it not for my petition on your behalf, you would not be coming with me into battle beside your brother. The Crow King worries about your influence over the boy. His allegiance to his king must come first, even above his family. Such is the way of Corvus."

Lawen's brow creased and he stared at the flagstones before him. "Thank you, *sir*."

"Don't take that tone, Lieutenant. You're lucky not to have been burned at the stake yourself. Your actions before your return to Vinwen might be considered treasonous, and the only reason I dismissed them then was because you were dying. Make another mistake, and you'll not be so lucky now that your health is nearly perfect."

Lawen halted, knuckles white, jaw locked. The general stopped ahead of him and turned.

"Do you have something to say, Lawen?"

"Sir, I tried to spare the life of a *child*."

"A child who broke the law."

Lawen said nothing.

Cadogan sighed. "I understand how you feel."

"Do you, sir."

The general's eyes gathered darkness. "Tread carefully, Lieutenant. You're in the King's Keep."

Lawen gave a curt nod. "I will curb my tongue, sir. But I will *not* stand by if my brother is in danger, Order or no Order."

"Do not cross the Order of Corvus, Lieutenant."

Lawen held his chin high. "Then they had better not cross *me*."

Chapter Thirty

Gwyn stood before the tower window, watching the sun climb over Crowwell nestled in the greening valley far below. Golden strands of fire glistened on the dewy hills around the city, and birds trilled in a copse of trees below the tower where Gwyn had spent his night.

Soon the door would open, and he would be summoned to the trial chamber again, this time to swear an oath of fealty to the Crow King. He had no choice if he wanted to live, yet his skin prickled at the idea.

The Crow King ruled Simaerin. Protected the beautiful country from outside threats. Contained wild magic to keep the innocent from being harmed. Weren't those noble acts? Wasn't the Crow King doing what must be done, not unlike Gwyn's quest to save Lawen?

Yet Gwyn couldn't bring himself to believe his thoughts. Executing mages merely because they found magic within themselves — because they weren't useful enough to integrate into the Order of Corvus? That wasn't reasonable. It was cruel.

On his deathbed, Lawen had called the Crow King a tyrant.

What had caused his brother, once so loyal to crown and country, to alter his philosophy?

Is the Crow King a tyrant?

Did it matter?

Gwyn would die if he refused to swear an oath, and what good would that accomplish? He loved Simaerin and his newfound magic could now be used to protect the kingdom from foreign enemies. Wasn't that reason enough to join the Order of Corvus and stand as a mage soldier under the Crow King's banner?

He could protect his family, his friends, his lands from the Fraelin-Ilidreth invasion, allowing Simaerin to thrive. Whatever his feelings toward the Crow King, it didn't mean Gwyn would stand by and watch his beloved country burn.

He would swear the oath, and he would mean it. For crown and country, he would fight until death; for freedom and life, he would join the Order.

The door opened and Gwyn turned. A man in dark robes beckoned him into the room beyond. "Come. The Crow King is ready to see you."

Gwyn stepped into the trial chamber and found the same sight as before: Rows of cloaked men loomed overhead. The Crow King sat upon his throne, leaning forward this time, elbow propped on his leg, chin in his hand.

"You enter this hall to become a free man in service to the crown," said the Crow King, smiling gently. "What say you, Gwynter ren Terare? Shall you serve me?"

Gwyn strode to the center of the room, placed a hand to his heart, and held his chin high. "I swear to serve king and country for its greatest good, Your Majesty."

The king's smile widened to show his teeth. "Very good, young lord. And I accept you. Welcome to the Order of Corvus."

Chapter Thirty-One

Nathaera stared at Lawen's grim face. She sat with him in her family's orchard, beneath the blossoming branches of an apple tree. Her eyes drifted to Kive crouched nearby, eyeing a beetle crawling along his hand and murmuring how delicious the poor insect would taste.

"I'm sorry," she said, dragging her gaze back to Lawen, "but I don't think I heard you. You see, a bumblebee flew by my ear and whispered a ludicrous tale about tyranny and magic and wicked mage cults all under our own banner and in our very own country. Which simply cannot be the case. Silly bug. Please, do go on."

Lawen lifted an eyebrow, then he threw his head back and laughed. "Oh, Nathaera." He shook his head, chuckling, but his smile faded.

The two sat in silence until a real buzzing insect flew by Nathaera's ear. "I wish you weren't in earnest, Lawen. I can hardly believe Gwyn has entered the service of the Crow King as part of a magical order sanctioned by the throne. It's...it's so awful. So twisted."

"It's delicious."

Nathaera blinked and turned to stare at Kive, who munched on something. The beetle had vanished.

Nathaera gagged and turned away, lifting a hand to her lips. After she felt certain she wouldn't retch, she lowered her hand. "What will Kive do? He's barely willing to stay with me. I've promised him he'll see Shiny soon, but if Gwyn goes to war, I'm afraid of what the poor creature might do. I try not to envision him terrorizing the streets of Crowwell, eating babies, and cooing after his *nice juicy rats*. It's a horrible portrait."

Lawen's lips pulled down. "You raise a good point. But he's too obviously an Ilidreth, and we can't hide that fact. I can't bring him along, or he'll be killed. Not to mention what methods he may employ to obtain his supper."

She grimaced. "Then what's to be done?" She looked down to study her fingernail, screwing her face up in concentration. The idea dawned like a glorious sunrise. She snapped her fingers. "But of course! I'll come along."

Lawen started. "You'll do no such thing."

"No, listen. It's the only way. If Kive and I travel very sneakily behind the army, that will satisfy Kive somewhat, and I can keep an eye on him."

"And when he eats one of the sentries, or even *you*, Nathaera?"

"He won't."

"I won't eat Fairy Wren," Kive chimed in. "Kive doesn't eat fairy wrens. Only rats, and birds, and flies." He smiled. "And beetles. So delicious."

Lawen moaned. "Does Kive *know* what fairy wrens are?"

She nodded. "But they're not crunchy like other birds. Kive said so."

"Uh huh. I see." He sighed. "You can't, you absolutely can't follow us. It's too dangerous. You're a woman."

Nathaera bristled. "And I suppose that makes me incapable? I seem to recall that you let me come along with you to the True Wood to search for Gwynter. What's different about this?"

"A hundred thousand things. First of all, you're not trained in combat. Second and more importantly, you have Kive with you. Until he eats you."

"I don't eat fairy wrens," Kive stated, lifting his chin. "Only rats, and birds, and—"

"And beetles, yes, yes, I know."

"And *flies*," Kive added.

"Right. Flies, yes. I feel so much better about your situation now." He scrubbed at his face.

"You should!" said Nathaera. "So long as Kive doesn't plan to eat me, he's about the safest place to be. And if it's true that the Crow King isn't what we thought he was, I don't feel so secure in Crowwell as once I did."

Lawen hesitated. "There is something else, Nathaera. It's difficult..." He trailed off.

"Yes?" she asked, cocking her head.

"It's about the head of the order. He's..."

"Yes?" She leaned nearer.

Lawen sighed. "Nathaera, the head of the Order of Corvus is your father. Lord ren Lotelon. He's a mage. He's...the one who's... training Gwyn."

Her faint smile slipped away. "I'm sorry. I don't think I heard you. A little ant came along, you see, and whispered a silly thing about my father lying to me all this time, and hurting Gwyn, and..." She bowed her head. "Are you certain?"

"I'm afraid so. I'm very sorry."

She shook her head. "No, no. Don't be sorry. I just...need to comprehend what all this means." She looked up. "But isn't all this dangerous for you to tell me? Won't they know?"

Lawen shook his head. "No. At least, I think not. You see, I'm a mage too."

Chapter Thirty-Two

The Crow King's army amassed on the north hills of Crowwell. Banners streamed in the high wind. Armor glinted in the bright sun. The tumultuous sounds of the cavalry forming ranks, the clink of metal as blacksmiths repaired shields and helms in last minute preparation, and the mingled odors of charcoal and sweat, flooded Gwyn's senses.

His nerves strung taut. Perspiration beaded on his brow. He strode beside Lord ren Lotelon, searching the din for any sign of Lawen or General Cadogan.

Men and horses parted for the mage lord and his apprentice. Whispers followed them, while the rest of the Order of Corvus trailed in their wake. This was an important campaign indeed if the Order had joined with Cadogan's regiment to wage war.

Gwyn fidgeted with the red tabard draped over his armor, wondering how many of the soldiers understood about magic. Were they sworn to silence or were they ignorant? How did the Order work magery in war without word of their deeds inundating the streets of every city, port, and village in Simaerin?

Soldiers swore an oath. Did that oath entail a bond of silence? Could they say nothing? Or did the Order march only under strict conditions? Fraelin hadn't invaded Simaerin so boldly in an age. Perhaps there had been no need of magery before this day in many long years.

Even so, rumors last for years and turn into legends. Magic must be involved in stifling the knowledge of the Order's purpose. It was the only way the Crow King could be certain his people didn't discover the truth.

Lord ren Lotelon spoke. "You will sleep in my tent and stay by my side in daylight. Is that understood, Gwynter?"

Gwyn looked at the man beside him. "Yes, Master Traycen."

"General Cadogan will join us in the evenings for meals, and that is where you will have a chance to see Lieutenant Lawen. Only then, until we engage the enemy. Understood?"

"Yes, Master Traycen."

"Good." The lord led Gwyn through the throng of marshaling soldiers, to a corral holding several dozen black horses. Traycen motioned to a young boy, who raced forward and bowed low.

"Yes, Master?"

"Bring Gwynter his horse."

"Very good, Master." The boy sprinted toward the corral's gate, climbed over it, and disappeared among the stallions.

"A special provision has been made for you, Gwynter," said Traycen. "The Crow King is very generous."

As the boy reappeared with Aluem following meekly on his heels, Gwynter's heart leapt.

"Aluem!" Gwyn raced to the wooden barrier and reached his hand between the posts, stretching to touch his friend.

Aluem's voice rushed like wind in his mind. *'Gwynter, are you well?'*

The boy led Aluem through the gate and walked beside him until they reached Gwyn. The boy then bowed to Traycen and padded away. Gwyn caught Aluem's muzzle in his hands and pressed his forehead to the unicorn's. He closed his eyes, nerves relaxing, mind and heart calming.

'I told you, did I not, Gwynter? You are indeed a mage.'

Gwyn chuckled. "So you did, and so I am. You were right."

'You will find, my friend, that a unicorn very often is.'

The din behind Gwyn fell away and murmurs hushed. He released Aluem and turned. His eyes fell on a black horse climbing the hill, its regal rider tall and proud, black cape flapping behind him, black crown glistening under the sun like obsidian. The Crow King had arrived. He'd brought no escort.

The soldiers bowed their heads, making no noise beyond the faint rattle of their armor. Gwyn bowed his head with them, as did Traycen. Even the horses kept still.

The king rode through the ranks and reined up before Gwyn and his master. "Your maiden battle awaits you, young Gwynter. I do hope you excel upon the battlefield and bring glory to my kingdom."

Gwyn lifted his head to meet the king's eyes. Knots writhed in his stomach. "I will do all I can to protect my beloved Simaerin, Your Majesty."

The Crow King smiled. "I think I understand you, Gwyn. Your heart is very pure. The unicorn is proof." He inclined his head toward Aluem. "To the Ilidreth in ancient days, unicorns were said to bring good fortune to riders in battle. Let us pray to Afallon that is so, hm? A good journey to you both." He shook his reins and moved on down the line, approaching the banner of General Cadogan.

Gwyn's gaze trailed to the general who came forward to greet his king. Lawen stood at Cadogan's side in full armor.

"You needn't come with me, Aluem," whispered Gwyn. "I don't ask you to."

'I know, Gwynter. Still I shall come.'

The Crow King addressed the army, his voice ringing across the green hills. Gwyn heard none of what he said. His eyes found the highway crawling along the northern hills. His heart raced. He'd long dreamed of going to war. Of fighting under the Crow King's banner, near his brother's side. Now here he stood.

Am I frightened or proud to serve my kingdom?

Both, perhaps. He might die for a king he feared, but then, he might die for the land he most loved.

Better to stay alive.

Whatever happened, he must find a way to kill.

A shadow fluttered at his feet. He glanced up to find a flag streaming in the morning breeze. The Crow Banner. Once a symbol of awe and reverence, now a dread hand hovering above Gwyn, directing his course.

The king's speech wound down. Now he spoke the words Gwyn had heard Lawen repeat a dozen times. Gwyn turned to watch the king, to listen and take what inspiration he could from rote sentiment.

"Serve well and faithfully, people of Simaerin, and by Afallon's grace, we shall be victorious!"

The men cheered, spears and banners bobbing. The army surged with fervor, ready to begin the long, arduous march northward. To face an invading force. To face the Ilidreth. To perform magic.

Chapter Thirty-Three

The days of marching droned on.

Gwyn was fortunate enough to ride rather than walk; but even so, at the end of each day he dismounted, sore, weary, and irritable. The only glimmer of hope along the march came when evening halt sounded, and Gwyn knew he would soon see Lawen.

The brothers were allowed no privacy at dinnertime. Master Traycen and General Cadogan remained present, dominating the conversation as they debated tactics for the coming engagement. Lawen and Gwyn sat on opposite sides of the officers' table, glancing between the map sprawled across the wooden surface, and one another, offering supportive smiles.

Worse than the grueling march under a brutal sun was the countdown to Gwyn's maiden battle. Would his mage training be enough?

Master Traycen drilled Gwyn as they rode, but the man never dueled against him now. Perhaps he'd decided Gwyn needed *some* level of rest before he faced the enemy.

On the ninth day into its march, the army remained camped at General Cadogan's behest. The horses rested while the soldiers mended tack and weaponry and washed up. At dinner, the officers would converge to go over strategies for the anticipated battle two days hence.

In the late afternoon, General Cadogan allowed Lawen and Gwyn to bathe, and even pointed out a wide stretch of water farther upstream, apart from the bulk of the army. He remained beneath a shade tree, letting them stroll upstream alone after he nodded toward a sentry stationed on a moss-covered boulder nearby. He said nothing, but Gwyn understood his warning. It was unnecessary. He had no intention of running, though he doubted the sentry's arrow would hit its mark if he tried.

After stripping down, Lawen waded into the stream ahead of Gwyn, sighing as he sank into the flowing water. He tipped his head back and doused his shoulder-length hair.

Gwyn hung his clothes over a low pine branch and slipped into the water, cringing as the icy current climbed his shivering body.

"Enjoy it," Lawen said, lifting his head. "In late summer, you'll think of this cold and crave it. By then the streams are too shallow and muddy for a proper bath. It's sponge bathing or nothing. I won't mention the mosquitos."

Gwyn grinned. "No wonder you've become such a priss about baths."

"You've nooo idea." Lawen waded to the far side, propped his elbows against the bank, and scrutinized Gwyn. "How are you, really, Gwynter?"

Gwyn smiled and lowered his eyes. Warmth flowed through him. "You worry too much."

"It's my right to worry. What they've done to you, how they've shackled you — it's infuriating. You're not yet of age. You shouldn't have to go to war this time, Gwyn. And all this talk about how powerful you are, and how *involved* the Crow King is... His interest in you..." Lawen shook his head. "I don't like it. It's not normal."

"It worries me too," Gwyn murmured. "I'm frightened, Lawen. I don't want to kill people. But part of me feels excited too."

"Of course. You're a young man going into battle for the first time. Excitement is *necessary*. It helps you to survive. That, and your good sense, will keep you from making grave blunders, which may save you out there. It's an ugly place, Gwynter. It never leaves you once you see it, once you take part in it. The battlefield stains your soul. I don't want that for you."

"I know. Me neither." Gwyn looked up. "But as you once said, that's why *I* need to go to war. I won't want it to go on. I'll want to fight and win quickly, so that peace can come again. That's why Afallon lets people like you and me go to war. To *end* it rather than prolong it." He sighed and gazed at the treetops. "Lawen."

"Yes?"

"The world is beautiful. Even the dark places, even the True Wood and the ruins of *Shaeswéath*, are beautiful. You remember Celin, the Ilidreth who helped you search for me?"

"I remember."

"He could have killed me, yet he didn't. I met another Ilidreth who tried. I had to threaten him in order to get away, and later Kive...ate him." Gwyn shifted. "I heard ghosts weeping in Swan Castle. I saw a fair woman lying as though she were sleeping, but she had long been dead.

"After that, the Ilidreth force allied with Fraelin captured me. I spoke with their commander. I've met the Crow King, and I've stared into his eyes in the dark of my cell. I've heard the silken tones of his voice and seen the madness lurking in his gaze.

"But the world *is* beautiful, Lawen. Even its shadows." Gwyn dropped his gaze to find his brother. "I want to save this world. I want to help it to understand peace. I wish I had that power."

Lawen smiled faintly. "No one alive has that power all by himself, Gwynny. But sometimes one person can draw all those who might make a difference together. Maybe...maybe someone will be able to do that for Simaerin."

"I pray to Afallon that someone appears soon," Gwyn murmured. "The world seems to be on the brink of something. Like it's holding its breath."

"I know what you mean, little brother. This battle is different from others I've faced. I don't know just why, but *something* has shifted. Like the earth is stirring or a storm is brewing. Yet despite the fear it brings...I don't know if this will make sense, but...it feels somehow *right*. Necessary. Something akin to that."

Tension bled from Gwyn's shoulders. Lawen had put into words the very feelings he'd held. Hearing them aloud, knowing he wasn't alone, brought a kind of comfort despite the looming battle ahead.

"By the way," Lawen said, tone grim.

"What is it?"

"I've meant to tell you for days, but we're always watched. It's important Traycen ren Lotelon doesn't overhear me. Nathaera is on our trail." Lawen's voice was barely loud enough for Gwyn to hear over the rushing stream. "She brought Kive. It was the only way to keep him docile. He's very determined to find you."

"*She's following us?*"

"I begged her not to, but that woman has a mind of her own. The most stubborn creature I've ever encountered. What's worse, she can say the most foolish things imaginable and make them sound rational."

Gwyn groaned. "I begin to doubt that she attended Windsur on his quest only to convince him to return home."

"It does seem more likely that she goaded him on. She's got a craving for adventure, I suspect."

Gwyn shook his head, swallowing back nausea. "She's being foolish. Does she not understand what she's walking into?"

"I tried to explain that very thing to her, but she looked at me as though *I* were the fool." Lawen chuckled. "She's a very rare young woman, no mistake. Where did you say you found her? Perhaps her blood is part fae."

"Well," Gwyn said, studying his palms. "Her father is a mage. Perhaps there *is* something in the blood."

"Mages aren't fae. Only humans can become mages. Fae magic is altogether different."

What an odd thing to say. Gwyn fixed a pointed look at Lawen. "How do you know that?"

Lawen started, as though his thoughts had been far away. "What?"

"What you said. How do you know so much about magery and fae magic?"

Lawen blinked and a frown shadowed his eyes. "I've encountered enough of it to know, Gwyn. It isn't as though I learned of magic *after* your trial. The king outlawed it for a reason, though the fact he uses it in secret does raise some rather poignant questions. Few know he's established an order of mages."

"Lawen." Gwyn hesitated. "What did you mean when you called the king a tyrant? Just before I left for the woods, you called him such, and claimed he's mad. Why?"

His brother let out a heavy sigh. Gwyn noted the weariness in Lawen's face, the slump of his shoulders, the guilt burning in his eyes. "Gwynter, I also told you I did horrible things. Things I can't...things I won't explain in any great detail. But yes, the king is a tyrant, and yes, he's mad. Only a madman would murder children to keep them from growing into mages. Only a madman would order the weakest Ilidreth prisoners to be drawn and quartered to..." Lawen squeezed his eyes shut and looked away "...to feed the rest of the Ilidreth prisoners with the flesh of their own kin, as well as the remains of Simaeri mages. Children mages, Gwyn. They were *eaten*."

Bile scorched Gwyn's throat. He gagged and turned away from the haunted expression on his brother's face. "Why, Lawen? Why do you still serve him?"

"Because," Lawen whispered, "I'm still alive."

Gwyn recoiled, struck by words he never thought he'd hear his brother say. He bit his lip and ran a wet hand over his face. "You wanted to die."

"Oh, Gwyn. No. No, that's not what I meant."

The splash of water brought Gwyn's head up, and he found Lawen wading toward him. His brother reached him and rested a hand on his shoulder.

"Gwynter, don't mistake me. I'm grateful that you healed me. I didn't want to die. But I swore an oath to serve the Crow King until I do. A binding oath, Gwyn. Much as yours is binding. We're soldiers now. We serve king and country and magic binds us to that service. We must serve the rightful king of Simaerin."

Gwyn nodded, lowering his gaze to the water rippling before him. "But does a king forfeit his right to rule after an act of tyranny, brother? Does the Crow King deserve to lead us?"

"No. He doesn't even march at the head of his army into battle. The man is a coward, as well as mad. Except when addressing those about to march to war, no one even sees him leave Crow Castle. Sometimes I wonder if he's not a prisoner of his own making. Sometimes it feels like Simaerin is *in* a prison."

Lawen's words pierced something inside Gwyn and a swell of wonder raced through him. "Simaerin is a prison?" he whispered.

"It is for us, sworn to the mad king."

"It's deeper than that, Lawen." Gwyn looked into his brother's green eyes. "You've struck upon something. I only wish I knew what."

A bell rang downstream. Gwyn and Lawen jumped, and the latter sighed.

"Best finish washing up. The officers' meeting is about to start."

Gwyn nodded and waded toward shore, but he couldn't shake the image of chains.

But where there are chains, there's a key.

Chapter Thirty-Four

The quiet chirp of crickets did nothing to sooth Nathaera's nerves.

She thought she'd grown accustomed to sleeping out of doors, but the open plains were altogether different from the close confines of a forest. Here, she stood exposed for miles all around. It made following the army challenging. She remained a day behind them, for any closer would send her galloping into the very clutches of Simaeri scouts.

Kive, at least, proved eager to help.

While he didn't seem inclined to eat rabbits, he could catch them easily. At first Nathaera convinced herself she could use the little animals to supplement her store of food, but upon meeting the gaze of Kive's first four-legged capture, Nathaera's heart melted.

She kept the rabbit; not to eat, but for company. It was a rather cuddly companion, so long as one held it snugly until it stopped striving to wriggle free. The few times it managed to escape, Kive promptly brought it back. After a few days, the rabbit had come to accept its new fate as a comfort object for a very silly girl.

For Nathaera *knew* she was a silly girl to come all this way on horseback, with a fallen Ilidreth as her bodyguard, and only a single pack of essentials. But she also felt she had little choice. Even so close to Gwyn, Kive champed at the bit, resolved to run ahead to locate his Shiny.

Nathaera kept insisting that Shiny was too busy to be disturbed right now, but she suspected Kive didn't comprehend what that meant.

Lying under the stars now, Nathaera watched her breath appear in puffs as she shivered under her blankets. She'd brought some padding to sleep on, but it did little against the cold and lumps in the ground.

A full moon glared down at her, almost accusing, and Nathaera imagined Mother's face within the glowing sphere. Mother would be livid when she found the letter Nathaera had left behind, detailing an elaborate fib about running off to sea, and that she might be back someday, weather permitting. Nathaera knew better than to explain the truth this time. Otherwise Mother would send Keep Lotelon's sentries after her. They would find her and drag her home kicking and thrashing.

"Is Fairy Wren sleeping?" Kive's voice drifted toward her from his perch on a craggy pile of rocks which might be a cairn.

Or maybe I'm overreacting.

Hundreds of rocks stood in mounds along this stretch of the king's highway. It numbered among the most desolate landscapes in Simaerin, far too rocky to cultivate.

"No, Kive. I'm not."

"Is Fairy Wren looking at the heavens?"

"Mm-hm. It's very pretty, isn't it, Kive?"

"Very pretty," he repeated, tone forlorn. "On they sing. On and on and on and on. Always singing."

"Do you mean the stars?" asked Nathaera, sitting up. She looked at Kive in the darkness, and found his red eyes, so bright under the moon.

"Stars," Kive whispered. "Yes. Stars are always singing."

"What do they sing about? Do you know?"

"Many things. Too many things. Things that do not matter

anymore. All must be darkness and sorrow, and the silly stars don't understand. On and on they sing of worlds and dreams and pretty things."

"But Kive," said Nathaera, kneeling on her pad. "There truly are dreams and pretty things left. So many. Don't be so sad. I know you've had a dreadful life — I can't imagine that you came to be as you are unless it was worse than anything I could conceive of. But can't you see that not all is ended? You have friends now, in Gwyn and me. We can help you not to be alone; to learn to smile and laugh, and maybe even eat normal, decent food."

"Master says I must eat rats. And flies. And—"

"Who is your master, Kive?"

"Master is master."

Nathaera frowned. "What does he look like? Can you describe him? What color are his eyes? What color is his hair? Is he tall?"

"Master is master."

"Does he have a name?"

"Master."

"I suppose I should have expected that answer." She patted the ground before her. "Come here, Kive."

He slipped from the rock pile and padded forward on bare feet. Knelt, and rested his hands in his lap. "Hello, Fairy Wren."

"Hello, Kive. Listen. What does your master look like? Is he an animal?

"No, Master isn't an aneeemal."

"Ooh, what approach can I take...?" She pressed her thumbs together. "Okay, let's try this. Are Master's eyes red, Kive? Like yours?"

"Rats have red eyes," Kive whispered and licked his lips. "Soooo juicy."

"Yes, we've established all that. Are Master's eyes red?"

"No."

"Are they blue?"

"Blue?" asked Kive, canting his head.

"Green, maybe?"

"Green?"

Nathaera grimaced. "You don't understand colors any more than you understand gender or humans, do you? Hmm. See the moon up there, Kive?"

"Yes."

"*That* is silver. Ish. Yellow. Oh dear." She sighed, but the memory of Swan Castle's gem tumbled into her mind. "You remember the shiny rock, Kive?"

"Yes. Shiny Rock."

"It was *blue*. That was its color. It looked blue, like rats' eyes look red. Do you understand?"

Kive stared at her for a moment. "Blue. Like the sky? Not this sky, but the other sky?"

"Yes, yes, exactly. Well done, Kive! That's blue."

"Blue. Blue." The ghost of a smile haunted his lips. "That's a funny word."

"Isn't it?" Nathaera glanced around, but hues were so dim in the dark, she wondered how to help him learn other colors by sight. "Um. Oh. Shiny Unicorn."

Kive straightened from his slouch. "Where?"

"He's not here, Kive. But his color is *white*."

"White."

"Yes. White. And you know what the sun is, right? The big burning ball in the blue sky?"

Kive nodded.

"The sun is yellow. That's its color."

"Yellooow."

"Exactly." She pointed to a distant copse they'd passed earlier that day. "Trees. The trunks are brown. Usually. The leaves are green. Brown trunks. Green leaves."

"Brown. Greeeen."

"Very good, Kive." A thrill raced through her as she glimpsed a light in Kive's eyes. He stared at the shadowy copse, soundlessly repeating the colors he'd learned.

"You already know what red is."

"Rat eyes." Kive looked at her. "Blood. Dying. Screams."

She swallowed. "Yes. But also roses and cherries and other beautiful things."

"Beautiful." Kive's tone rang flat.

Nathaera pointed at the sky. "Black. The night sky is black."

"Black." Kive looked up, but the wonder had fled from his eyes. "Like crows. Death. Silence."

Nathaera's heart throbbed. What terrible, shattering things had he seen to become this way? "Perhaps. But also like a beautiful sky filled with stars, Kive, and velvet cloth. Like a fast-riding stallion. Like the hole where moles live."

Kive frowned and dropped his gaze to her. "Moles?"

"Little animals who live underground in burrows."

"Burrooows."

She laughed and nodded. "Another silly word." She caught his hands in hers. "Look at me, Kive. You're still full of the wonder of life, whatever's happened to you. You're not too far gone, or you'd already have eaten me. Let me help you, Kive. Let me show you worlds, and dreams, and pretty things."

He started to shake his head. "Master wouldn't—"

"Master isn't here," Nathaera said.

"He would know. He watches, always. I must eat rats. I must cower before his greatness. I must—" He cut off as Nathaera released his hands and clamped her palms to his cheeks.

"Phooey on your master, Kive. You're not a slave. You're not a servant. You're a Kive, right? Don't let anyone walk over you as though you were a rug underfoot."

He blinked. "But Master..." He took her hands and gently pulled them to his lap. "But Master would be angry if he heard. *Shhhh, Fairy Wren*. Or Kive will have to eat you."

Nathaera's eyes widened as she realized she couldn't speak. He had bound her tongue.

"Shhh, Fairy Wren. Kive doesn't want to eat you. Kive doesn't want to, at all."

Chapter Thirty-Five

One day's march from the borders of Siaan Wood, a rain of arrows fell upon the forces of Simaerin. No one heard it coming, no one saw the Ilidreth upon the westward hills. Over a hundred cavalry men fell to the ground, dead or wounded, before an alarm sounded.

Most of the fallen were mages.

Gwyn and Aluem galloped through the volley, none hitting their mark. Cries filled the air until the arrows ceased their song. Gwyn had a mere moment to glance around for Lawen before a second volley whistled through the air — but this time he was ready.

Gwyn lifted his hand, summoning his strength. The arrows disintegrated in the air, turning into dust swept north on a faint breeze.

A third volley darkened the sky. Gwyn kept his palm raised and the arrows dissolved again at his will. The Simaerin army regrouped, horses and men closing in around Gwyn, cheering.

A captain lifted his voice. "Ready! Aim!"

Simaerin bowmen turned their arrows to the west hills.

"Fire!"

The volley unleashed, screaming through the air. Cries sounded on the hillcrest as the projectiles fell upon the hidden enemy.

"Corvus, reform your line!"

Gwyn wheeled Aluem toward Traycen's voice. The unicorn raced across the plain and halted beside the master mage on his black stallion.

Traycen's dark eyes caught Gwyn's gaze. "Good work, Gwynter. Keep up our defenses. Don't let any more arrows hit their marks. Remain near the rear to avoid risk to yourself. Remember your magic has limits."

"Yes, sir."

Gwyn let Aluem guide him as he lifted his hand against another Ilidreth volley. Turning the arrows to dust weakened him. He couldn't maintain that level of destruction. Instead, he swept his hand across the air.

The arrows spun and shot the other direction, down into the enemy lines beyond the hill.

Hidden cries followed.

Gwyn allowed himself a grim smile to stifle the pang in his heart.

I'm killing people.

He was also protecting people.

A tingle ran down his spine. Gwyn nudged Aluem around and his eyes widened. Creeping upon the Simaerin forces from the east, the Crane King's banner waving under the high sun, another contingent of soldiers trooped near, clad in glistening silver armor.

"Master Traycen!" Gwyn wheeled Aluem back around.

The unicorn charged through the ranks of Corvus, heading for Traycen, who bellowed out attacks. The air around the mages shimmered as conjurations joined together to create a twisting pillar of fire.

"Master Traycen!" Gwyn cried. "Enemies at our rear, sir!"

As he spoke, the approaching Fraelin army unleashed a volley of arrows. Gwyn gritted his teeth and threw his hands into the air.

The air pulsed, throwing the arrows off course. Sweat beaded on Gwyn's brow. Dueling one on one was nothing to this.

"Concentrate on holding the Fraeli off," Traycen barked. "The rest of the order will defend against the Ilidreth and their magic."

Gwyn nodded and the unicorn sprang toward the coming force.

'*You cannot withstand them alone. I shall aid you, Gwynter.*'

With Aluem's words swelled a rush of strength. Gwyn's mind quickened. His heartbeat evened out and his breathing leveled.

'*Nock your arrow.*'

Gwyn shook his bow from his shoulder, snatched an arrow from its quiver, and strung it.

'*Aim high. Summon wind.*'

Gwyn released the arrow. It soared high, arcing toward the enemy, one weapon against five thousand strong. Wind rose behind Gwyn, following the arrow's course. The gust picked up speed, rushing over the army, throwing many from their feet. The arrow landed in their midst. Wind formed a funnel at its center. Screams filled the air as the gale flung men to and fro.

Gwyn swallowed. *Don't hesitate. This is war.*

If he didn't strike fast and first, he would die rather than them. He mustn't lose his momentum.

He nocked another arrow and released it overhead, even as the vortex lost its strength. The Fraeli began to regroup, rising from among those who would never stand again. A second gale rose to carry the arrow. Again, the vortex formed and tossed men and horses across the plains.

The vortex collapsed.

The wind ceased altogether.

Gwyn frowned, shot another arrow, and waited. The wind didn't follow. Any hint of a breeze had died.

Someone had blocked it.

Gwyn searched the plain. There, riding toward him across the field. A man with long pale hair, sword drawn, charged forth. As he neared, Gwyn caught the fire in the man's pale eyes. Gwyn drew his blade, adjusted his grip, and urged Aluem forward.

Swords met, singing.

Gwyn's gaze caught and held his opponent's.

A young man, scarcely older than himself.

"I am Gwynter ren Terare of Vinwen."

"And I," said the young man in a thick accent, "am Adesta Gilhan of Seabrelle in Fraelin. It is an honor to kill you, mage."

"There is little honor in killing anyone," Gwyn replied. "The honor comes only in protecting life."

"An honorable Simaeri mage?" Adesta Gilhan scoffed. "Is such a thing possible?"

Gwyn directed Aluem to step back, pulling his sword with him. "Just as there are fallen Ilidreth and those who still dwell in vales. Just as there are Fraeli thieves as well as Fraeli priests. So, too, Simaeri come in all varieties and shades."

Adesta Gilhan grinned, baring his teeth. "Well said. I shall rephrase: It will be an honor to meet you in combat, Mage Gwynter."

"Likewise, Mage Adesta. Well met."

They raised their blades and urged their steeds forward. Swords clashed. Withdrew. Aluem danced around the Fraeli's larger mount. Gwyn pressed his advantage, forcing mage and horse to fall back. His magic funneled through his body, tingling as it guided his actions. He could feel the force of the Fraeli mage's shield of magic.

Defense mage against defense mage.

Adesta blocked Gwyn's blows as he maneuvered his mount. Aluem forced the pair right, backward, right again. Hard left. Adesta gritted his teeth and swung.

Gwyn answered, striking the man's sword hard enough to send a jolt up Adesta's arm. He poured magic into the assault at Adesta's weak point. The soldier gasped and dropped his sword.

Gwyn touched his sword tip to Adesta's chest. "Do you yield, sir?"

Adesta scowled. "I do yield, Simaeri, though I do not understand why you do not pierce me through."

Gwyn lowered his sword and pointed toward the northern hills, motioning Adesta to ride with him. "As I said, the honor is not in killing someone, but in protecting life. If you would please, Master Gilhan, I need the wind freed."

Adesta brought his horse alongside Aluem. "I have yielded, sir, but I cannot let you take back such an advantage, lest you rend my compatriots as though they were wheat under a sickle."

Gwyn nodded. "I understand well how you feel, but my purpose is to act as a shield for Simaerin. As my prisoner, you must relinquish all your weapons. Even the magical ones. Or must I render you unconscious?"

"Perhaps you must." Adesta reined in his horse and turned in his saddle to meet Gwyn's gaze. "I cannot give you power over the wind of my own choosing."

Gwyn sighed and raised his blade to Adesta's chest. "Very well. Dismount."

Adesta obeyed and stood before him, arms raised in surrender. Aluem pranced behind the young man and, wincing, Gwyn slammed the pommel of his broadsword against Adesta's skull. The man crumpled. Gwyn's hair shifted in a stirring breeze and he raised his hand. The gale rose and chased after the advancing Fraeli, knocking them from their feet.

"Now what?" asked Gwyn, turning back to Adesta lying on the ground. "Have we a place for prisoners to reside?"

'Fall back to the supply caravan. Surely someone there will know what to do with prisoners of war.'

Gwyn climbed from Aluem's back and hefted Adesta onto the back of the Fraeli stallion. Gathering the horse's reins, Gwyn remounted Aluem and galloped toward the caravans hovering far back from the fray.

Chapter Thirty-Six

Evening fell.

The armies withdrew from the battlefield until dawn. In the failing light, Aluem trotted toward the command tent. Gwyn struggled to keep his eyes open and stay on the unicorn's back. He'd used his magic far more today than in an entire week under Master Traycen's tutelage.

For the first time, Gwyn felt a sliver of gratitude toward the man for pushing him so ruthlessly.

Lawen waited outside the command tent. "Gwyn, you were magnificent! I hear tell you won your first battle duel and took a live prisoner. I suspect even Lord ren Lotelon is pleased."

Gwyn tried a smile. "In his pleasure, I hope he intends to reward me with one night of uninterrupted sleep."

"Perhaps that much I can provide," said Traycen as he bent through the opening to stand beside Lawen. "Your efforts today saved the lives of many soldiers. More impressive is how you defeated a Fraeli mage. But why did you spare his life?"

"He yielded." Gwyn swung down from Aluem's back and gently stroked his mane. "I will not kill an unarmed man." He bowed at the waist. "I've returned, Master Traycen."

"Be welcome, apprentice. Enter and sup with us." Traycen stooped through the doorway, and Gwyn followed. He straightened within as Lawen slipped inside to stand beside him. A long table stood in the tent's center, over a wide rich-colored rug. General Cadogan and several captains from the other regiments dined on smoked pheasants, sharp cheeses, and mulled wine.

"Well, well," called a captain, saluting Traycen with his pheasant leg. "This must be the whelp who came in so handy today. The Crow King's chosen one, they say." He laughed and stripped meat from the leg with his teeth.

"Aye," Traycen answered. "This is the whelp, and he's far stronger than most of Corvus, so beware lest you offend the boy."

The captain's eyes caught a twinkle. "Stronger than you, Master Mage?"

Traycen smiled, but his eyes glittered with frost. "Not quite. And he's still very inexperienced. Even so, the Crow King expects great things from him someday."

"I see you've found yourself an heir," the captain said, shrugging. "Good to know even mages worry about successors. It seems you're not immortal after all." He chortled.

Traycen's coldness spread across his face. His body went rigid. "Tread lightly, Captain Harrevin. I'm in a rather violent mood, following the day's events. I will only warn you once."

The mockery fled from Captain Harrevin's face, and he turned back to his dinner, muttering under his breath.

Traycen strode to the head of the table and sat beside Cadogan. Gwyn and Lawen took places opposite each other beside their commanders.

"The wine went to his head," Cadogan murmured. "Try not to threaten my men over every little slight."

Traycen grunted and speared a pheasant wing with his fork. "Promote more intelligent men, then, and I'll have no cause to threaten — or follow through with it."

Clinks and clatters filled in the cracks of silence for a while before another of the captains broached the subject of the day's battle. With eager bravado, other officers piped up, offering exaggerated tales of their personal glories, each more farfetched than the last.

Gwyn listened with growing amusement as Lawen mouthed corrections to him. Captain Lishtil hadn't singlehandedly cut the heads off five men at once, but he *had* cut off one poor soldier's head, which Gwyn suspected wasn't as easy or glorious as the captain declared.

The levity heightened as the wine made several more rounds. Gwyn's eyes grew heavy in the candle smoke. He began to nod and shook himself to stay awake, but the voices drifted far away, and his vision stretched.

A loud laugh jerked him upright. He'd fallen asleep.

"Wine doesn't agree with you, boy?" asked one of the nearer captains. Gwyn didn't know his name.

He stared at his untouched goblet, his empty plate, and realized he'd eaten and drunk nothing. His stomach clawed and growled for sustenance, but weariness held a stronger claim to his body.

Gwyn glanced at Traycen. "May I go to sleep, master?"

The man nodded. "You've earned it. Your brother will see you there."

Gwyn rose and swayed, his vision reeling. His head and limbs felt as heavy as... He couldn't find a comparison. Lawen appeared beside him, took his arm, and led him from the tent. The chill night air needled Gwyn's muddled thoughts into some coherency.

"Are you all right, Gwynny? Just sleepy, or were you wounded?"

Gwyn shook his head. "I'm not hurt. It's just...my magic is so new...and I used so much of it..."

Lawen chuckled. "You look drunk."

"I didn't drink any wine."

"I know. I watched you. But you sort of act like you are." Lawen led him to the tent Gwyn shared with Traycen. Inside, he spread out Gwyn's bedroll and patted it. "I'm not a betting man, Gwynny, but I'd wager you'll not stay conscious to reach your pillow."

Gwyn knelt on the bedroll.

When he looked up, it was morning.

THE SIMAERI COMPANY intended to battle at dawn, but the enemy forces had withdrawn during the night.

"They must have run back to their stolen keep," General Cadogan growled.

His officers, along with Traycen and Gwyn, stood poring over a map of the surrounding plains.

The general stabbed the map with a finger, where a fortress was depicted in fat ink strokes. "It's magically fortified by both Fraeli mages and Ilidreth scum. Though I anticipated this happening, it's still unfortunate. I suppose they were overwhelmed by our success yesterday, despite taking us by surprise. Now they'll hunker down for a siege and pick us off a little at a time."

"It changes little," said Traycen. "Our original strategies involved laying siege to Keep Lirial."

"Still," Cadogan said with a sigh, "sieges are difficult at the best of times." He looked up and caught Gwyn's eye. "Your defensive magic will be an asset in protecting my men as they charge the gates."

"Yes, sir."

"He can be even more useful than that," Traycen said. "His affinity with defensive magic could turn the tables if he can unmake the very defenses of the keep. Theoretically, it might work. Each manifestation of magic follows its own laws. Anything defensive, anything *defensible* may respond to his command, either to strengthen or — if my theory holds — *weaken* the shield: be it physical, spiritual, or emotional. Of course, the level of manipulation would depend entirely upon the mage's magical and emotional strength. A normal defensive mage couldn't touch a physical fortress in the manner I'm proposing. But I suspect Gwyn may stand a chance of it."

"But he's had no practice," Cadogan said.

Gwyn looked between them, wondering if it might be possible. Such a power could reshape the playing-field. He wandered from the table as the two men debated his chances, and whether they could risk trying it — and *how*. How was the real question.

Gwyn sat on the floor in the shadows of the command tent's south wall. To summon power, to wield it well, he needed to know exactly what he intended. In the past his magic had acted for him, based on desperate desires in harrowing moments. This wasn't like that.

Between dueling matches with Traycen, the master mage had lectured him on defensive magic. He claimed Gwyn had latent potential like few defensive mages in history.

But could he manage this? Could he unmake a structure like the keep's outer walls?

To unmake something meant to revert it back to a previous state. To rocks and mortar?

He frowned. No, unmaking something was impossible. Rocks still *existed*. He couldn't unmake them, for if they weren't rocks, they would be dust and minerals. They would still *be*. He couldn't unmake anything. He could only *remake* it. Reforge it. Transform it.

If he wanted to bring a wall tumbling down, he needed to turn it into something different, but equal to its original proportions. A paved highway, for instance, or a watercourse. He merely needed to teach the stones to move.

Gwyn smiled grimly and stood up. As he approached the table, every officer looked toward him, some casually, most with curiosity.

"I can do it." He paused. "At least, I believe so."

"Really?" asked Cadogan, tone skeptical, one eyebrow arched.

"I have an image in my head now, and I understand how to achieve it," Gwyn answered. "It's little different from calling forth a gale."

Cadogan glanced at Traycen. "Very well. Send your pupil forth like a gale and let us see the measure of his skill."

HIGH NOON REIGNED as the hour of full strength for a mage, so Traycen claimed. Gwyn must test that now, for he needed all the power he could muster if fending off arrows and dueling a single mage had taxed him so dearly yesterday.

He rode ahead of the army, alone but for Aluem.

A part of Gwyn resisted the idea of destroying Keep Lirial. It was a fortress of high reputation and a relic from an age before the first Crow King rose to power by Afallon's will. It had been the final defense of the last reigning Wintervale king. The royal line fell into ruin when their House displeased Afallon. Though the keep still stood at the end of that bloody campaign, none of House Wintervale had survived.

Of that victorious day, one historian had penned the declaration: *Winter fell at long last.*

Now Gwyn would reform the keep, destroying a shard of history. A lamentable thought.

The keep rose before him, seeming to grow as he raced toward it. He felt certain he could alter the structure of the outer walls, assuming none of the enemy mages thwarted his efforts as Adesta Gilhan had the day previous.

He could only try.

Gwyn leaned forward to speak above the wind into Aluem's ear. "Bring me to the very walls, my friend."

Aluem's gait quickened. Unicorn and rider flew over the plain, wind whistling in Gwyn's ears. The gates loomed ahead, set into high-rising walls of gray stone topped by a parapet.

Arrows shot past Gwyn's head. He leaned closer to Aluem's neck. An arrow sliced through his sleeve but drew no blood. Another arrow missed his ear by a millimeter. He'd chosen not to wear armor today to avoid hampering Aluem's speed. Even Lawen had agreed. It was the safest way to ensure Gwyn escaped, even at the risk of being shot.

He'd felt confident he wouldn't be wounded. Whether by magic or the will of Afallon — or both — he had remained unscathed so far. If that changed, he would be no worse off than any other soldier in combat.

'Prepare yourself.'

Gwyn nodded and stretched out his hand. Aluem ran straight at the wall beside the gate.

At the last possible moment, the unicorn veered sharply left. Gwyn whipped out his hand to run his fingertips along the rough rocks. Blood smeared the wall, trailing behind Gwyn's hand as he poured his will into the stones.

To defend, break the defense.

"Go!" he cried, pulling his arm in, fingers cracked and bleeding.

Aluem raced from the keep.

Arrows descended, hundreds of them.

Voices rang overhead, barking orders, screaming for his execution.

Gwyn slumped against Aluem's neck, drained and dizzy. A mighty crack boomed behind him and the earth shook. His vision darkened. His mind tumbled into a chasm beyond fatigue.

❧

"BY AFALLON, HE DID IT." Cadogan laughed. "He actually succeeded!"

Lawen stood beside the general, grinning from ear to ear, heart swelling. Gwyn and his unicorn galloped toward the encampment. Behind them, cracking and rumbling like a thunderstorm, the walls of Keep Lirial tumbled.

"That boy's magic is something else," Cadogan said, shaking his head. "He'll turn the tide of this war. The Fraeli won't be able to hide now and their morale will be trounced. The Ilidreth will slink back to the woods and leave us in peace."

"Don't celebrate victory prematurely," Traycen murmured. "When those walls have crumbled, we have our own conflict to meet, and Gwynter will be too tired to assist us. He's played his part in this battle. It will be days before he recovers enough strength to dodge a single arrow."

Lawen scurried forward as Aluem approached. The unicorn came to a sharp stop and Lawen pulled Gwyn from his back. "Gwynny?"

Unconscious and flushed, covered in a sheen of perspiration, Gwyn didn't stir.

"I'll take him to a healer." Lawen swung Gwyn's arm over his shoulders and pulled him upright.

"Be quick. We ride to battle soon," said Cadogan.

"Yes, sir." Lawen started for the nearest mage healer's tent. Aluem trotted beside him as he struggled to hold Gwyn up.

"You did well, brother," Lawen whispered. "I'm so proud. Rest easy in the knowledge that you've done your part."

As Lawen left Gwyn with a mage healer, cries broke out among the Simaeri soldiers.

He trotted to his general's side against a surge of darting men. "Sir?"

Cadogan caught his arm. "The scouts I sent to assess Gwynter's work have returned. The Fraeli brought a dragon."

Chapter Thirty-Seven

Nathaera sang snatches of lullabies and sea ditties she'd learned in her childhood — which wasn't so long ago, she supposed. The horse she rode seemed to enjoy the songs, if she read the flick of its ears right, and Kive hummed along tunelessly. The rabbit rode morosely in her arms, her only critic.

Around noon, Nathaera contemplated halting for a bite to eat, but the neigh of horses ahead brought her up short for a different reason. She slipped from the horse's back and crept up the steep hill. She peeped over the other side and groaned. The army's supply train nestled in the valley below, and from the look of things, a battle waged beyond that.

She should have guessed she'd caught up, after she'd stumbled onto the remains of a battlefield last night.

"Use your head now and then, Nathaera, won't you?" she muttered as she backed down the hill and remounted her horse. She'd best circle around and see what she might of the ensuing fight. Perhaps, just maybe, she would spot Gwyn or Lawen.

"Come along, Berry ren Cream." She nudged the mare onward. The horse nickered and trotted along the course Nathaera cut toward the line of trees bordering Siaan Wood.

Kive kept up, still humming.

The three companions sneaked through the trees until Nathaera judged she'd come far enough alongside the army to risk a glance. She tethered Berry ren Cream to a sapling and crept forward, Kive on her heels. The two peeked between the trees as the clash of arms rang in the air. She expected to find soldiers fighting brutally — but far worse than that unfolded before her.

The blood rushed from her face and a cry tore from her lips.

Huge and black, wings spread wide and snout streaming smoke, a dragon wheeled in the sky.

She forced herself to search the battlefield again, heart thumping in her ears. So many Simaeri soldiers were sprawled across the ground, some blackened husks. Smoke curled from their remains.

Nathaera swallowed down bile. "K-Kive, do you see Shiny? Please tell me you see Shiny!"

Kive lowered his eyes from the circling terror above. "Fairy Wren, there's a giant lizard in the sky!"

"Yes, Kive. Yes. That's a dragon, and if he has his way, we will be crisped like those poor soldiers out there."

Kive shook his head. "Lizards can't eat Kive."

She choked down more bile. "Kive, listen for a moment. Do you see Shiny anywhere?"

"Shiny?" Kive tilted his head to one side. "Is Shiny here?"

"Somewhere in that mess, yes."

"Oh, we must go find Shiny!"

Nathaera snatched Kive's sleeve. "Hold a moment, O eager one! Don't you remember what I said about crisping? I, for one, prefer to keep my skin." Her voice broke as tears welled in her eyes.

Kive's red gaze flitted between her and the battlefield. "But *Shiny*!"

"Don't be so dramatic, Kive. Please! We must handle this strategically. One cannot run pell-mell into the open when a—a dragon is winging overhead." She yanked him down beside her. "Think with me, Kive. We must be as smart about this as two brash young people can be." She paused, wondering how old Kive must be to remember when Swan Castle once thrived. Three hundred years at least. "Or two brash young-*looking* people."

She turned her mind back to the present dilemma with a shake of her head.

Concentrate on what you can control. Nothing else.

"Fairy Wren, does the lizard need to go away so we can find Shiny?"

She turned back to Kive, eyes narrowing. "If you told the—the lizard to go away, would it listen, Kive?"

He bobbed his head. "Oh, yes. Lizards are very good listeners of Kive."

She clicked her tongue. "That won't work. You would need to get very close to shout, and there's a rather strong chance you'd be crisped before you got to open your mouth. I won't risk it."

'*What if I carried him close enough?*'

Nathaera whirled with a shriek. "Aluem!" She rushed to the unicorn, who stood just within the trees, and wrapped her arms around his neck. "I'm so glad to see you! Where's Gwyn? Is he all right? And Lawen? The d-dragon — it didn't crisp them, did it?"

'*I have lost track of Lawen, but Gwynter is safe for the present. I sensed your nearness and intended to make use of it. Kive is exactly the best way to stop the dragon's rampage.*'

"But you'll both be in danger," Nathaera said, pulling back to look into the unicorn's eyes.

'*Not much. Dragons cannot easily harm a unicorn, nor are they eager to try. He will likely avoid me as best he can, but if I challenge him, he will accept and fly close enough for Kive to order him away. That should break whatever force has harnessed him to such a fell purpose.*'

"You make it sound very simple, but still I worry."

'*I will not fault you for feeling a human emotion. You can hardly do otherwise.*' Aluem turned to Kive. '*Will you ride upon my back, Ilidreth? We must tell the flying lizard to leave, or he may hurt your shiny friend.*'

Kive pawed Aluem's neck. "Oh, no! He mustn't do that. He

cannot hurt Shiny." He leapt onto the unicorn's back. "Come along, Shiny Unicorn. We must protect Shiny!"

As the unicorn bounded toward the battlefield, fire filled the sky. The dragon wheeled wide across the field. Screams erupted below, agonizing and horrible. Nathaera flinched and trained her gaze on the galloping unicorn.

"Please, Sweet Afallon. Keep them both safe."

At first the dragon circled away from Aluem, but the unicorn bayed a singsong cry, and the dragon circled back at once and flew lower. A tongue of flame streamed from the dragon's mouth, but Aluem's horn pulsed with an iridescent light that swallowed the fire at once.

Kive called out his command, tone like a cracking whip across the field. "Go away, Lizard! You will not hurt Shiny!"

The dragon lurched back. Its wings beat the air and it rose higher, higher. The soldiers on the ground froze and stared up until the dragon disappeared into the blue horizon above Siaan Wood.

One man's cheer rose from the battlefield. Another, another. Shouts and whoops filled the sky.

So many soldiers lay dead, most of the Simaeri forces had fallen. Tents smoldered. Untethered horses had bolted. But the dragon was gone, and with it the last threads of the Fraeli army's morale.

A horn called and the Fraeli troops pulled back. Not one Simaeri soldier gave chase.

The battle had ended — but amid the destruction Nathaera couldn't guess which force claimed victory.

Aluem trotted toward her in the trees, Kive still on his back.

"I told Lizard, Fairy Wren. He can't hurt Shiny anymore. I told him not to, and he left."

Nathaera beamed. "Well done, Kive! I saw the whole thing. You did very well."

The thunder of approaching hooves seized Nathaera's attention. She stepped around Aluem and her eyes widened. Coming fast, eyes blazing, Father galloped toward her. Nathaera stepped back into the trees, praying he hadn't seen her. Praying he chased after a deserting soldier, or — or anything else.

She gasped. He'd seen Kive. He *knew* about Kive. Mother had told him. And even if he didn't think Kive was the same Ilidreth, he certainly knew an Ilidreth riding a unicorn had commanded the dragon to leave.

"Not good, not good, not good." Nathaera caught Kive's arm and stared up into his pale face. He still sat on Aluem's back, eyes bright, humming.

"Kive, you need to hide. Go! Aluem—"

An arrow whistled past Nathaera's arm and stuck to a tree trunk mere feet away. She yelped and Aluem reared up. Kive clung to the unicorn's mane to keep astride.

"Don't move!" Father's voice rang out.

That settled it. He'd seen her. The black stallion halted just outside the trees. Lord Traycen ren Lotelon dismounted, cape billowing in a menacing fashion.

The looming man stalked through the undergrowth, eyes smoldering as they flicked between Nathaera, Kive, Aluem, back to Nathaera. He stopped before her, folded his arms, and in a voice like thunder, said one word: "Well?"

She did her best not to quiver, and but for her lips, she thought she did a fair job. "Hello, Father."

His eyes narrowed.

She gulped. "I'm fine, by the way. Not a scratch on me."

His eyes turned into slits of fire and ruin.

Nathaera winced. "I had no choice, you see. Kive here, well, he wanted Shiny. And I couldn't let him wander off looking for Shiny on his own. If I did, he'd eat everybody he saw along the way, and that would be on *my* conscience. I've been teaching him, Father. He's learning about colors, and what sorts of animals are edible, and which aren't. He sees people as animals, so I thought, if I could teach him different kinds of animals, he might not think we're all rats, and fewer people would be in danger of being eaten."

His anger was nearly palpable.

She took a step back. "I am sorry to worry you, but Kive wouldn't harm me. In fact, he's been my bodyguard. He took care of that dragon, didn't he?"

"Did Gwynter put you up to this?" asked Father in a quiet, rumbling tone.

"No! No, no. I put myself up to this. I've not seen Gwyn since Mount Vinwen."

"Lawen, then."

"No, he tried to stop me!"

"So, he knew."

Nathaera bit her lip. "I mentioned it only in passing, and he berated me for the idea. He didn't have any notion of my actually undertaking it."

"Your Lady Mother sent me an urgent missive that you'd run away to sea. You *lied* to her."

Nathaera ducked her head. "I knew she'd send someone to collect me if I told the truth."

"You should have stayed home!"

Kive slid from Aluem's back and jabbed a finger at Father. "Don't shout at Fairy Wren, Rat."

Nathaera caught the Ilidreth's arm. "It's fine, Kive. Please don't interfere."

Father's eyes rested for a long, dark moment on Kive. "This *thing* must be executed, Nathaera. A twisted fae is far worse than you can fathom. He's beyond saving."

"No, he's not! He's learning all kinds of things. Except for his eating habits, he's really very gentle."

"He's not a pet, Natty."

Nathaera flinched. These days Father only used her childhood pet-name when he was very, very angry.

She released Kive's arm and held out her hands. "I'm sorry for upsetting you and for running away from home. I'm sorry for worrying you. But I still feel I did the right thing. And I feel that the right thing *now* is not to hurt Kive after his victory against the dragon. He saved the Simaeri army, Father. That must count for something."

"He's a fallen Ilidreth," Father answered. "The Crow King's law on this is very clear." He caught the hilt of his sword.

Nathaera grabbed his wrist. "No, Father. Please!"

"Stand aside, child."

Nathaera stomped her foot and tightened her hold. "I'm not a child! I'm of age, a daughter of nobility in an enlightened kingdom. We're not barbarians! Kive has done an immense service for our country, and he'll *not* be executed without a trial! If you wish to harm him, know that you must first harm me."

"Move, Nathaera."

She tightened her hold. "I won't. Bring him before the Crow King. Let him stand trial to weigh his actions. He's only helped us!"

"He's an Ilidreth, Natty. He can't be granted a trial. It's the law."

A singsong bay filled the air. Aluem trotted forward, horn lowered to point at Father's chest. Wind circled Kive, and whatever the unicorn said to Father drained the blood from the man's face.

'Let your father go, Nathaera. He will not harm Kive. The Ilidreth will stand before the Crow King.'

Nathaera uncurled her fingers and stepped back. Father's shoulders slumped a little, but his eyes burned brighter.

"I never thought my own daughter would betray Simaerin."

Nathaera cringed and her chest clenched. "This isn't treason, Lord Father. It's protecting a friend."

He scoffed. "You will ride with the Ilidreth by the prison wagons as we return to Crowwell. He will stand trial before the Crow King. But Nathaera, the outcome will not change." He started toward his horse.

She bit her lip and nodded. "Are we...are we returning then? Is the war over?"

He froze and turned to eye her. "Look around the field, daughter. See what remains of our army and then tell me we have the strength to pursue the Fraeli northward. Idiot child." He mounted his horse, took up the reins, and glowered at Kive. “I’ll escort you to the wagons. Hurry.”

Nathaera scurried to Aluem’s side, fighting tears. She swallowed down a lump. Pressure built in her forehead. She *would not* cry. “C’mon, Kive.”

“Is Shiny there? Where we’re going?”

“He’s very close.” Nathaera mounted Aluem. The unicorn brought her first to where Berry ren Cream remained tethered, and she took the reins to lead the mare toward camp. Kive leapt up behind her, and the unicorn followed Father’s stallion from the stand of trees, out into the scorched plains.

Moans rose around Nathaera, and she choked back bile as she glanced down to find a man nearly cloven in two. A tear rolled down her cheek.

Somehow this scene hurt worse than watching Windsur’s men devoured by trees or Kive. Kive was almost an animal, not human. He didn’t understand. But this...

“This is war,” Father said, eyes staring straight ahead. “Take a long look, and reconsider your inclination to do as men do.”

Fire seared her stomach. She clenched her fists. “I didn’t come here to fight, Father.”

“You came here to find adventure. Mark this: Adventure is a myth. Reality is war, destruction, death. There’s nothing thrilling, nothing exciting, about it.”

She eyed Father’s back. “Is adventure a myth just like magic?”

He didn’t so much as twitch. “Magic isn’t a myth, Nathaera. It’s a tool. Most use it for ill, and so the Crow King keeps it in chains.”

“I wonder,” said Nathaera, “what that says of those who wield it in his behalf?”

Chapter Thirty-Eight

The ground rattled.

Gwyn pried his eyes open and stared into the gray sky.

I'm in a wagon, he realized as the oversize contraption jostled and rocked over a rut in the highway.

Several blankets shielded him from a chill wind, and a feather pillow guarded his head from the wooden slats of the wagon-bed beneath. He could hear the crunch of hooves and the nickering of horses around him. Faint murmuring voices. The clatter of wheels.

He dragged a hand across his face to swipe aside his tangled hair. His muscles throbbed like he'd run a thousand miles.

He swallowed hard against a parched throat, tasting grit and iron. His head pounded against his skull.

All signs of using too much magic.

Ah, yes. He remembered commanding the walls of Keep Lirial to reform into a stone foundation spreading across the plains, depicting a likeness of Swan Castle. It was all he could think of at the time and somehow it felt right.

"Good evening, Lord ren Terare. How do you feel?"

Gwyn turned his eyes toward a face peeking down at him from

the wagon's gaping rear. The man sat on horseback, cantering along, a smile on his lips.

"I'm better than I was," Gwyn answered, voice hoarse.

"You'll be wanting water, I wager. Also, your brother. He said you would. I'll be back." The man wheeled his horse around and trotted out of sight.

Gwyn stared at the sky and tried to stay awake, too weary to contemplate anything of consequence.

Hooves approached. "Ho there, little brother."

Gwyn turned a smile on Lawen as the man climbed from his horse and into the wagon-bed.

"Hello, Lawen."

"You look a little less pale. That's something. How do you feel?"

"Heavy."

"It's all that height." Lawen rested his hand on Gwyn's forehead. "Your fever seems to be gone."

"Lawen, how did the battle go? Did the keep fall? Were we victorious?"

"Your part went wonderfully well," Lawen said, "but we didn't expect to unleash a dragon. I'm afraid we're in retreat now, and while the Fraeli also retreated to the sea border, I don't think we can call this a victory for Simaerin."

Gwyn stared at him. "A dragon? A real dragon?"

Lawen nodded. "Just like a real unicorn or a real mage. Only a *lot* bigger."

"But how did the army escape? Don't dragons breathe fire?"

"Aye. And we were all about to succumb to his fiery wrath, but for a stroke of luck that's since gone bad. Kive showed up and told the dragon to leave, and it did."

Gwyn's head spun. "Kive?"

Lawen nodded. "He surely did. But as I said, luck went bad. Lord ren Lotelon discovered both the Ilidreth *and* his companion. I'm afraid Nathaera is in for a storm when we reach Crowwell. Ren Lotelon is none-too-pleased.

"He can't be blamed for that. It would shock any father to find his daughter so near danger."

"Yes, well, he seemed equally upset about the fallen Ilidreth's presence. Rumor has it Nathaera pleaded for Kive to stand trial, rather than face immediate execution. Lord ren Lotelon relented, but with great reluctance."

Gwyn set his jaw and raised himself up by his elbows. "Where are they?"

"Near here, with the prison wagons." Lawen helped Gwyn fold forward, and repositioned his pillow, to let him lean against the wagon wall.

"He locked his daughter up?" asked Gwyn, incredulous.

"No, but she's commanded to stay with the prison wagons to keep Kive in them. Your unicorn is with her."

"I must speak with Master Traycen."

"Not right now." Lawen's tone was firm. "There's little you can do at present. Besides, the mage lord is very busy with what's left of his order, trying to protect the remnant of our forces. I doubt he's in a mood to discuss an Ilidreth's fate just now."

That was likely true. Gwyn nodded. "How many men were lost?"

"Well over six thousand. We were slaughtered out there."

So many men, gone forever. And why? Because of a war whose purpose remained veiled. Yes, the Fraeli invaded, but to what end? They'd allied themselves with the Ilidreth, who felt that the Simaeri had stolen *their* land.

Who was right? What did anyone gain compared to their losses?

Gwyn fought to protect his home and lands. Could others say the same? How much of the fighting had become about gain and glory, rather than self-preservation?

"We'll reach Crowwell in about one week's time." Lawen patted his arm. "Rest until then. We'll find some way of helping your friends."

"The Crow King will kill Kive," Gwyn whispered.

"Possibly."

"Definitely." Gwyn looked into his brother's eyes. "Tell me I'm wrong."

Lawen lowered his gaze. "I'm sorry, Gwynter. But maybe it's best. Kive *eats* people. Don't tell me you've forgotten that."

"I know. But there's something... He's broken, but he's not hopeless. Maybe he can come back. Maybe there's a way to rescue the fallen. Doesn't Afallon love all people?"

"Some argue that Ilidreth aren't people," Lawen quietly said.

Gwyn frowned. "I've met several of them. I've walked into a Vale. I know better. They're people, just like you and me. They're being slaughtered like vermin, but why? Because the Crow King has commanded it. Why, Lawen? Why is he so determined to exterminate them?"

Lawen shook his head. "I couldn't say. They keep to themselves well enough. If we stayed out of their woods, they'd not harm us."

"Yet," Gwyn said, "the Crow King burns the trees, captures and tortures them, *feeds* them their own kin..." He broke off, thoughts falling on Kive. His master had insisted that Kive subsist on rats — or on what he *perceived* were rats. But was it possible? The Crow King was a relatively young man, perhaps in his fortieth year. Kive had fallen three hundred years ago, or so Gwyn had assumed.

Maybe Kive hadn't been warped so long as that. Perhaps...

But why would the Crow King seek out an Ilidreth only to twist him? There was no rhyme or reason to it. When would he have done so? How?

If not the Crow King, perhaps one of his mages?

Gwyn sighed and closed his eyes. *I'm too tired to come to any sound conclusions.*

"Go back to sleep." Lawen brushed his hand against Gwyn's head. "Whatever plagues your thoughts should wait until you've recovered your strength. There's nothing you can do in this moment."

"You're right," Gwyn murmured. "Thank you, Lawen."

His brother helped him to lie back down. Gwyn tried to dream, but his thoughts grew dark and shadowed, and doubts haunted his heart.

GWYN MOUNTED Aluem on the last day of the army's march. The grassy hills surrounding Crowwell rolled like waves upon the ocean, familiar and green under a brilliant sun, while a strong wind brought the scent of brine from the nearby ports.

He had no chance to speak with Master Traycen of Kive's fate, or even of Nathaera's. Perhaps the mage avoided him on purpose, or perhaps military affairs occupied every moment. In a way, Gwyn didn't mind. It was beyond the lord's power to do anything now, so near the royal capital. Messengers had already ridden ahead days before, bearing news of all that had transpired on the plains near Keep Lirial.

Gwyn hadn't been allowed to see Nathaera or Kive. He'd been stuck in a wagon until this morning, when General Cadogan asked him to stay near the head of the column, as one of the few remaining representatives of Corvus. He wielded the Crow King's banner.

At least Aluem could reassure Gwyn his friends were well, considering the circumstances. Nathaera acted little changed, and Kive stayed content with an occasional rat, except when he pined for Shiny.

Nearing the city, Gwyn's nerves grew taut. Another trial stood before him and he had little hope of saving Kive from execution.

A tiny voice inside kept asking why he wanted to. What about Kive made Gwyn desire to keep him alive? Could he be redeemed? Could an Ilidreth return from such darkness? He ate people, for Afallon's sake. Even Celin, one of Kive's people, had required Gwyn to slay him. Yet Gwyn couldn't, and strongly felt that he *mustn't*.

"Aluem?"

'Yes, Gwynter?'

"Could a fallen Ilidreth ever be healed? Does Kive stand a chance of being saved?"

'*Is that the real question?*'

"Isn't it? What should I ask?"

'*Whether or not a person such as Kive can be saved, should you not strive regardless? Bear in mind: Nothing can be undone of itself. It is through action and interaction that something can be changed. Kive is altered. He cannot undo what has altered him. But perhaps he can be altered* again, *and thereby overcome what has broken him. Wind shapes the mountain peaks. Become Kive's wind, Gwynter, and see what shape you might forge in his world, and perhaps the world at large.*'

"But how?" asked Gwyn, shoulders drooping. "Now he must face the Crow King. How can I save him from that?"

'*It is possible you have more influence over the king than you perceive.*'

As the column trudged on toward Crowwell, Gwyn contemplated the unicorn's words. Midafternoon brought them up the last crest before the swelling hills gave way to the low valley dotted with trees and the sparkling ocean beyond.

Crow Castle stood tall and ominous over the city. Gwyn shuddered as the burden of what lay ahead pressed against his body. He would have to meet the Crow King again, and he dreaded the prospect even beyond his need to plead Kive's case.

He rested a hand on the unicorn's head. "Aluem, I'm afraid."

'*Then all is well. Bravery cannot be proved in the absence of fear. Be stalwart and know your cause.*'

The army started down the hill along the tree-lined highway. Ahead, the gates of Crowwell opened while horns sounded the clarion welcome. When Gwyn passed through the giant gates, he found a somber crowd assembled on either side of the wide thoroughfare. News of the army's defeat had indeed arrived ahead of it.

Despite Gwyn's heavy heart, despite his dread of future meetings, he lifted his chin and gripped the Crow Banner tighter. While Simaerin had been wounded, he'd fought to defend it, proud to serve his beloved kingdom. And he still lived. No need to despair. One engagement had ended, but the war was not decided. Fraelin had also taken a hard blow. Both armies would rebuild and fight again.

The procession through Crowwell took much longer than Gwyn's first passage to Crow Castle. His insides writhed by the time the army entered the castle bailey and stood at attention before the barracks.

General Cadogan dismissed the archers, cavalry, and foot soldiers. Only the officers and the remnant of Corvus crossed the moat and rode to the castle's main gate. If Nathaera and Kive came with them, Gwyn didn't know. He didn't dare crane his neck to search for them among the contingent. A soldier must look ahead.

The castle's second portcullis rose on a windlass. Gwyn tensed as he spotted the figure highlighted under a shaft of sunlight in the opening. The Crow King sat on horseback, so still, so silent, Gwyn wondered if he only imagined him.

The press of soldiers halted. A hush fell over them, long and breathless.

Slowly, very slowly, the Crow King raised his horse's reins and snapped them. The sound echoed across the bailey behind Gwyn.

The horse started forward, hooves beating against the cobblestones, his rider erect and intent until he pulled the reins before Traycen ren Lotelon.

"Where is he?" asked the king.

His tones were deadly soft yet carried as a shout across the open air. Traycen flinched but didn't reply.

"Where is he, Traycen?"

"He — he escaped, sire."

"Escaped." The Crow King's voice whispered like silk against a dagger's edge.

"Last night." Traycen's shoulders quavered, as though he resisted a desire to fold in on himself.

"How?"

Traycen bowed his head low. "Forgive me, sire. It seems my own flesh has betrayed you."

"Your child. The girl."

"Yes, sire. She helped him and a Fraeli prisoner to escape, but I will find them all, and she will be severely punished."

Gwyn touched Aluem's neck. The unicorn understood and moved forward, forcing the other officers to part for him. The movement caught the Crow King's eye and his pale gaze pinned on Gwyn.

"Ah. The boy mage. Come." He lifted a slender hand and Gwyn thought it trembled.

He approached, stopping before the king, eyes never leaving his liege lord's face.

"Is it true you found the fallen Ilidreth in the True Wood, Gwynter?"

"Yes, sire."

"You brought him to Mount Vinwen?"

"Yes, sire."

"You persuaded Lady Nathaera to bring him to Crowwell?"

Gwyn hesitated for a single heartbeat. "Yes, sire."

"Now he's escaped."

"So it sounds, sire."

"Are you not the least bit alarmed about this? He eats people as though they were rats. What of your lady friend? She is in danger."

"Kive won't hurt her, sire," Gwyn said.

The Crow King flinched. "Kive, you say. That is his name?"

"Yes, sire."

"This is very troubling." The king ran a hand up his arm, shivering. "Very troubling. You know not what you've unleashed, Gwynter ren Terare. This Ilidreth is dangerous above all others."

Celin's similar warning resounded in Gwyn's ears. "I don't understand, sire, how that's true. Why is Kive so dangerous? What might he do?"

The king sighed. "This is not a discussion to be had under the full sun and in such numbers. Traycen, Cadogan, and the brothers: Lawen and Gwynter — you four shall accompany me to my private wing. The rest are dismissed. Reports of the Fraelin-Ilidreth engagement will wait. The matter of Kive is far more pressing." He steered his steed around. "Come."

Chapter Thirty-Nine

The Crow King's private chambers flickered in the candlelight. Drawn curtains rustled in a stray breeze while the remains of a fire smoldered in the hearth. The air smelled of dust and beeswax. Before the fireplace, a fur rug stretched across the flagstones, and a single wingback chair of dark velvet stood to guard the flames.

The party of four stood before their king, Gwyn with hands behind his back, trying not to shift his feet as he waited for his liege lord to speak. The Crow King stood before the hearth, his back to his audience. Gwyn's heart beat against his ears. He thought he heard Lawen's as well.

A hushed voice broke the stillness. "The Ilidreth would destroy us all if we were not stronger than they."

No one replied.

"We must eradicate them, or they will overwhelm us at some future point. To leave them alone would allow them to breed and grow in magic. That must not be permitted. And so, we hunt them to keep their numbers small." The Crow King turned, eyes flickering as though they had absorbed the firelight. "But Kive is a danger far greater. Do you know what he is, Gwynter?"

Gwyn shook his head. "A fallen Ilidreth, sire. That's all I know."

"No, Gwynter. He is far more than that. He is an Ilidreth prince. Fallen, but still powerful. Broken, but for how long? If his mind were to right itself, if he were to regain his senses, he might raise an army brimming with such magic, Simaerin would crumble at the first blow. He would be our undoing, Gwynter. Do you understand?"

Kive? A prince? Gwyn stared at the Crow King. But that meant — could it be — he was the child of Lord Roth and Lady Shalesta? Poor, pitiful, frightful Kive?

It was unbelievable...and yet Gwyn considered all that had transpired. All Celin had said of destroying the fallen fae — perhaps to spare his prince from insanity. The fact that Kive roamed Swan Castle, the one Ilidreth unafraid to dwell there. And a master — perhaps the one responsible for the castle's fall in the first place? — who kept Kive in constant dread and under strict command. Why? To keep him from rising up again and uniting the Ilidreth?

Standing before Gwyn, the Crow King watched. A man determined to keep the Ilidreth scattered, who somehow knew of Kive's ancient title.

How was it possible? Had the line of Crow Kings for the past three hundred years maintained the same hold over the Ilidreth heir? This Crow King knew of magic and ruled over it in secret. Did he possess it as well?

Gwyn took an unwitting step forward, staring into the peculiar eyes of his lord and king. "Sire, how do you know of Kive's lineage?"

The Crow King smiled faintly. "Does one ruler not recognize another?"

"You've seen Kive before?" asked Gwyn.

"Often."

"You're his master." It wasn't a question.

"Ah, Gwynter. You little fool." The Crow King sighed. "Could you not leave well enough alone? Must you discover all of my secrets?" His eyes flicked to a point behind Gwyn. "You and your brother are thorns in my side. So inquisitive. So impulsive. I spared

Lawen once, which I now see was a mistake. Ah well. You are both sworn to my service, and I shall never discharge you. You are my liegemen and shall die as such."

The king stepped forward and stretched out his fingers to brush them against Gwyn's face. Gwyn shuddered. "I should like very much to kill you now, Gwynter ren Terare. I am very tempted. But your power is useful, and I dearly delight in keeping you near. I sense your distrust. I sense your disdain. It is delicious to me."

Staring into the king's eyes, Gwyn witnessed the depths of the man's madness. No mere hunger for power turned to maddened fervor, but a genuine sickness, dark and swirling against the pale light of his ancient eyes.

So much like Kive's madness. So much like the fallen Ilidreth who had held Gwyn captive in the True Wood.

Could it be possible?

This man, this creature, didn't wish to preserve Simaerin, but to enslave it. To reign supreme. To conquer all who stood in his way.

"You're Ilidreth," Gwyn whispered.

The Crow King smiled. "Clever boy." His fingers trailed to Gwyn's throat and he snatched it. Gwyn gasped, wincing as the grip tightened. The king pressed his other hand to Gwyn's lips. "Silence be thine and mine. You are sworn to the king of Simaerin by blood and bond. None but the king shall unbind thee."

Gwyn reached up and caught the king's wrist, pulling his hand from his throat. He wheezed for air and narrowed his eyes. "But you aren't the king of Simaerin," he whispered. "You're an imposter. You're a fallen fae."

"No. I have conquered your kingdom. You shall obey me and pay homage. I am the Crow King in Crow Castle. *Jevye croe-kyné yith croewéath.*" The king's eyes flicked to the men behind Gwyn. "See that the ren Terare brothers are kept apart from others for a few days. They will be allowed time to consider whether they shall serve me willingly or in shackles. I am content either way."

Gwyn turned on Cadogan and Traycen. "You knew of the Crow King's origins? You willingly serve an imposter?"

Cadogan smiled faintly. "The Crow King's reign will never end by my hand. He is my sire. Simaerin thrives by virtue of his divine will."

Gwyn's hands curled into fists, nails digging into his palms. He sought Lord ren Lotelon's eyes.

Traycen's expression burned like frost. "Be honored to know the truth, child, and serve His Majesty by choice."

Gwyn turned last to his brother, whose expression reflected his own confusion and mounting horror.

Of course Lawen didn't know. He's no traitor.

"Go, General," said the king. "Lead them to the tower to ponder the strength of their loyalty." The Crow King tapped Gwyn's arm to seize his attention. "Nothing has changed except you, Gwynter ren Terare. I am exactly as I was, as are these men. All you need decide is how *you* will respond to truth."

❧

"HOW CAN I serve a man like that?"

Gwyn looked up from the strand of straw in his hands, to find Lawen standing at the sliver of a window in the tower, his back to the room.

"It isn't a *man* we should serve," Gwyn said, "but an ideal. Afallon's ideal."

"Quoting scripture hardly helps us in this matter. The church has declared the Crow King divinely appointed. How can we argue with that?" Lawen turned to Gwyn, eyes bright in the fiery glow of the setting sun. "Gwynny, I'm lost. I've always been proud of my king and my country, as my faith has dictated. But everything now feels like a lie. What can I believe?"

Gwyn lowered his gaze to the bit of straw and twirled it between his fingers. "What do you *want* to believe, Lawen?"

His brother barked a laugh. "Apparently what cannot be. A king worth serving, a god worth worshiping, a country worth saving."

"Then you have two of the three still in your favor." Gwyn

dropped the straw and looked up. "Afallon hasn't forsaken us, Lawen. And while the church sanctions the reign of the Crow King, how can we know that they aren't deceived? Even clergy are mortal. Even they can succumb to magic. And Simaerin is still full of Simaeri. Good men and women, humble, hard-working, and faithful. That has never been otherwise."

He scooped up a handful of straw from the pile he sat upon. The tower was a small, circular room, with a trapdoor in the center, by which Gwyn and Lawen had entered their prison a few hours before. But for the pile of damp straw and the tiny window, the room stood unadorned, stinking of mold and dust.

Gwyn studied the handful of straw. "We're forced to make a difficult choice. We're forced to serve the Crow King in one of two ways. They're hardly different. But one might give us a little more freedom than the other. I, for one, want to move about and become indispensable. Once that's so, the Crow King can't rid himself so easily of us. Already something holds him back. I want to understand *what*."

"You propose that we agree to serve an Ilidreth imposter?" Lawen shook his head. "Gwyn, I can't. After all he's done, all he's made me do, and now this...I just can't."

"Lawen." Gwyn squeezed the straw. "If we don't stay alive, what's the use of learning what we've discovered? Alive, we can make a difference. Perhaps we can stop the Crow King, once we understand what he's trying to accomplish. How he came to sit upon the throne. How long this deception has been going on. I will serve him in order to understand my enemy. In order to topple him."

"Gwynter, are you hearing yourself? You assume we can make that much of a difference. We're just two people."

"I'm also a mage," Gwyn murmured.

"A mage bound to serve the king of Simaerin."

Gwyn nodded. "I know. But that's just it, brother. The Crow King *isn't* the king of Simaerin. He can't be. He's Ilidreth. That means the line of kings since Crowwell rose isn't the true line.

Perhaps..." He hesitated. "Perhaps the line of Wintervale destroyed by the first Crow King didn't displease Afallon at all but was wiped out in order to steal the throne."

"If that's the case," Lawen said, "then there is no true line left. It ended at Keep Lirial and upon the shores of Londolin three hundred years ago."

"It may be so. Either way, I swore an oath to the true king of Simaerin, and if none such exists, I am bound to no man. I am free."

"No, you're locked in a tower within Crow Castle, Gwyn. We're prisoners, caught between two evils: serve willingly, or serve nevertheless. Some piece of me would rather die."

"What of Mount Vinwen?" asked Gwyn. "What of our lady mother and our little sisters? Our servants and slaves? Do you think that if we choose to gallantly burn at the stake, rather than serve a tyrant, they will be spared?"

Lawen's brow furrowed and he lowered his eyes to the floor with a heavy sigh. "You're right. I hadn't thought this through." A smile brushed his lips. "Dear little Gwynny, you're a far-thinking young man. Let us hope that your arm can be as far-reaching. Very well. For Vinwen and our family, I will serve the Crow King." He crossed the room and sat in the straw pile beside Gwyn. "There's one other matter I should—"

Gwyn raised his hand to silence his brother. "Not here. We're in the crow's domain. What we've said already is no surprise to him, but anything more, anything he doesn't know, should be discussed only far from Crowwell."

"Very well, I'll say nothing at present. Just know, Gwynter, you're not alone in this. I will stand by your side no matter what the Crow King tries."

"Thank you, Lawen. Please know that I feel the same."

PART III
THE SECRETS OF ILID

Chapter Forty

Eighteen months later

"Happy birthday, Sir Gwynter."

Gwyn turned and found a goblet lifted in the Crow King's slender fingers. Gwyn raised his own goblet to acknowledge the gesture and watched his king take a sip. Obligation took Gwyn's feet through the crowd gathered at the Crow King's side near the head of the great hall.

"Thank you, sire," Gwyn said, bowing his head.

The Crow King's eyes caught his as he straightened. "You've had an excellent campaign in the north, by all reports. Indeed, your men praise you highly. Lord ren Lotelon has even hinted that he would like you returned to his service to assist in our sea battles. What say you to that?"

Gwyn inclined his head. "I am flattered, but of course it's your will that matters, Your Majesty."

"Just so." The king smiled.

Music started up and a dance line formed in the hall's center. Gwyn's gaze drifted toward it, mesmerized by an ocean of colors as men and women began bobbing down the line, handkerchiefs stretched between them to keep from touching one another's hands.

"Do you dance, Sir Gwynter?" The king came to stand closer to Gwyn, having extricated himself from his many sycophants.

"Not lately, sire, though I do enjoy it."

"You're sixteen years old today, aren't you? One year out from your coming of age, yet you spend so little time socializing. Am I to blame for this oversight?"

"Perhaps partially, sire."

"Always so diplomatic." The Crow King stepped before Gwyn, blocking his view of the dance. "You've become one of my most successful officers. You've managed to squelch most of the unrest in the north, despite the ineptitude of your late superior."

Gwyn stifled a grimace. Ten months ago, he'd reported to General Kydess of Keep Arch on the northern border of Simaerin and Ilid. The general had been grossly self-indulgent, his soldiers sloppy and unkempt. Most were drunk more often than sober. General Kydess had blamed the state of things on the dangers of being stationed so near the Ilidreth and Fraeli and often cursed the inhabitants of Crowwell for their ignorance and security.

While Gwyn agreed that the royal capital knew little of what lay beyond their own walls, the laxness of the general and his officers had set Gwyn's teeth on edge. He'd gone there alone. Apparently the Crow King wanted to keep him far from Lawen's side, even after proving himself in two campaigns before that.

Things were different at Keep Arch now. At first, Gwyn had no choice but to work around the general. He'd found those men who still cared about Simaerin, who still had a shred of decency, and cultivated them. As positions of power opened up following bloody skirmishes against the Ilidreth, Gwyn had systematically brought their skillfulness to the general's attention and each was promoted in their turn. They answered to Gwyn.

At first, General Kydess had recognized none of Gwyn's machinations, but once he'd finally worked out what the boy officer had been orchestrating, he rampaged. In response, Gwyn soothed and coddled him. The general went back to nursing his bottles. The keep's defenses improved. By his fifth month Gwyn had won several engagements beyond the keep, forcing back the Fraeli-Ilidreth invaders so often, morale within Keep Arch improved drastically. Gwyn cracked down on excessive drink, gambling, and vulgar activities. He encouraged the keep's soldiers to attend church services and pray often to Afallon for safety.

"Fear Afallon and his servant Gwynter more than invaders, and we shall never be invaded," became the keep's mantra. His fellow officers called him invincible. No arrow ever hit its mark, though Gwynter rode more than once into a maelstrom with no more than a short sword and his unicorn.

Word of Keep Arch's recent string of victories had ostensibly reached Crowwell and the Crow King's ear. An invitation arrived at the keep last month. And here Gwyn stood, on his sixteenth birthday, honored by king and country for his efforts. General Kydess had come with Gwyn, expecting to receive the credit for all that had transpired, but when he bowed pompously before the Crow King, he'd been seized by two guards and sentenced to death for treason and the practice of magic. General Kydess was burned at the stake this morning.

Gwyn tried not to feel guilty, but in his mind, he couldn't help blaming himself for the general's death. Certainly, the man was a pathetic soldier, dimwitted and petty, but a traitor? Never that. Gwyn knew better than to believe Kydess had a shred of magic in his blood. The man had been superstitious and terrified of magery. Gwyn didn't doubt that the accusation of magic usery was the king's favored excuse for disposing of those he found unsightly or inconvenient.

The Crow King spoke, breaking into Gwyn's thoughts. "I want you to maintain Keep Arch, General Gwynter ren Terare."

Gwyn blinked. General? He was already a lieutenant, a prestigious rank for someone so young and inexperienced. "But sire—"

"I insist. The documents are already drawn up." The Crow King presented a scroll sealed with his signet ring, though where he'd stowed it until now, Gwyn couldn't say. "Take it."

He accepted the scroll. "Thank you, sire. I'm honored by the position, though I feel utterly inadequate."

The Crow King rested a hand on his arm. "Your humility does you credit, Gwynter. As do your merits at so tender an age. I am very pleased to call you mine."

Gwyn stared into the imposter's eyes, glimpsing the triumph hidden behind his praise. But there was more than that. The Crow King didn't trust Gwyn any more than Gwyn trusted him. Their game of camaraderie would continue, it seemed; the king always a portrait of civility, and Gwyn the model of a respectful subject. Neither fooled the other, but the world at large carried on in ignorance, convinced Gwynter ren Terare was the king's man.

"I have a gift for you," said the Crow King, smile widening.

"My new rank is gift enough, sire. You're too generous."

"Nonsense. This is your birthday. Besides, your coming of age last year was spent at the Battle of Forger's Bay. Allow your liege lord to spoil his faithful subject before all of Simaerin." He motioned at the hall. "Music, dance, drink, a new title and — tell me I am not the cleverest gift-giver — your dearest friend in the world." As his eyes flicked past Gwyn, the boy's heart somersaulted.

He spun. Standing before the servants' entrance, dressed in army red, stood Lawen. The master of Mount Vinwen raised his arms, eyes bright, a warm smile on his lips. He looked a little gaunt, perhaps. His dark hair hung longer and loose against his shoulders, and his skin glowed with the sun's frequent kisses. Gwyn ran to him, heedless of decorum or the esteemed crowd looking on.

Lawen caught him and pulled him into a bear hug so tight neither man could breathe.

Gwyn choked back tears as he and Lawen embraced for a wonderful, ageless moment.

Lawen pulled back. "Let me see you." He laughed. "You're huge! You've turned into a giant, Gwyn. Afallon is cruel to elder brothers to allow this injustice. Why must you be both tall *and* handsome? How many fair ladies' hearts have you broken this past year?"

Gwyn only laughed.

The Crow King approached, drawing the brothers' attention.

"Good evening, Captain Lawen." The king's smile sparkled like icicles under a cold sunrise. "I'm very pleased you could make it tonight. Tell me, have you had any success in your mission?"

Lawen's eyes dimmed. "Not yet, sire."

"A pity. I had hoped for yet another gift this night. Ah well. Redouble your efforts when you return."

Lawen bowed his head. "Yes, Your Majesty."

Gwyn looked between them. He and his brother corresponded often, but both knew better than to include anything approaching treason in their letters. They kept to general information about the war against Fraelin and exchanged news of Mount Vinwen if they chanced to hear anything. Beyond that, nothing.

Still, Gwyn could guess what Lawen might be undertaking. Of late, his brother's letters were far more vague than usual, and sometimes a bit peculiar. Gwyn suspected the Crow King had charged Lawen with the task of finding Nathaera and Kive, but after a year and a half, there was small chance of success. No one had seen or heard from them.

An ache filled Gwyn's heart as he thought of the two exiles, on the run, or perhaps dead by now. Where could a disgraced noblewoman and a fallen Ilidreth possibly hide for so long? Certainly nowhere in Simaerin. That left only two feasible possibilities, but no one would say it: They were either dead, or they had reached Fraelin. To most, either possibility amounted to a death sentence.

Lord Traycen ren Lotelon had publicly disowned his daughter. Windsur ren Cloven had become betrothed to another noblewoman of some distinction, insensible to the damage he'd inflicted on Gwynter's family and Nathaera.

At least, Gwyn prayed Windsur was unaware. Otherwise, he might not be able to keep his temper in the man's presence. Best to pretend Windsur was the dunderhead Nathaera had once called him.

"I should congratulate you." Lawen's voice broke into Gwyn's thoughts. He turned to smile at his brother.

"For what?"

"I was rather proud of my promotion, but you outrank me now. Tall, handsome, and powerful." Lawen's eyes twinkled.

Gwyn grinned. "I would much rather remain a lieutenant. Or better still, a nobleman farmer. I miss Vinwen."

"Then you shall enjoy the last of my gifts," said the Crow King. "You've spent the past ten months mucking out Keep Arch. I suspect you require a brief respite to maintain your health. I've granted you three months' leave. You and your brother."

Gwyn stared at the king, then turned to Lawen, who laughed.

"I received my papers of leave this morning from General Cadogan," Lawen said. "It's all arranged. We travel on the morrow."

Giddiness washed over Gwyn like he'd plunged into Temm River near Mount Vinwen. Home. He could go home! He'd last seen his mother on the steps of the manor house nineteen months ago. His sisters must be so big. The fields would be approaching harvest-time by now. Mavell might be baking pies all week, their aroma wafting from the kitchen windows to torment the stablehands working outside.

Shaking himself of his thoughts, Gwyn bowed at the waist to the Crow King. "I thank you, sire. Your gifts are most generous, and I humbly accept them."

"Now, now. Don't grow soft on me, Gwynter. I expect this time to buoy you up, not turn you into a sopping dish rag, do you understand? At the end of three months, return to Crowwell before you head for Keep Arch. Strange things are brewing in Fraelin, and closer still. Unrest grows. Return to me soon, so that we may head it off."

Chapter Forty-One

Gwyn sought out the royal stables where Aluem stood in his private, immaculate stall.

Through an open window, moonlight streamed in and distant strains of music haunted the wind. Gwyn's birthday party would go on all night without him. He doubted anyone would notice. Lawen had already retired to catch a little sleep before the dawn arrived.

Aluem turned his head from the night sky beyond his window. *'You are troubled, my friend. What has occurred?'*

"The Crow King is sending us home, Aluem. He's given me three months' leave."

'Quite generous.'

"Too generous," Gwyn muttered. He stalked across the stall and stood beside Aluem at the window. "It makes me very nervous. What does he intend by this gesture? I can't believe it's merely a kindness."

'Perhaps not, but you do require a respite. You have taxed yourself beyond enduring several times of late, particularly this past winter.'

Gwyn shrugged. "I agree that a reprieve shall do me good, and Lawen looked haggard tonight."

'Lawen?'

"Oh, yes. Lawen is here. He'll return with us to Vinwen. The Crow King orchestrated it."

'I am glad for you, but it is *alarming that the king would sanction sending you both home. He's kept you apart for so long.'*

Gwyn studied a winking star against the velvet sky. "I suppose there's nothing we can do but wait. If the king intends something, we'll soon find out what it is." He turned to Aluem. "You've remained with me for so long. Are you homesick? We'll be near the True Wood soon. Shall we say goodbye there?"

The unicorn tossed his head. *'Always this question: shall I leave? Are you so eager to be rid of me, my friend?'*

Gwyn shook his head. "Of course not. But I fear I've become reliant upon you, and already I despise the idea of losing your companionship. The longer you're with me, the more I dread your departure, but that's just it. If you must go, please go soon rather than late." He laced his fingers through Aluem's silken mane and pressed his forehead against the unicorn's. "Apart from Lawen, there's no one I love more than you."

The horse in the next stall nickered.

'Dear, tenderhearted human child, your words stroke my heartstrings like an Ilidreth harp. What is more, the music of your words holds no guile or greed. Blessed boy, meet my gaze.'

Gwyn stepped back to take in the opalescent eyes of his fae friend. Something hung on the air, like a tingle or a humming note, harmonic and ethereal.

'Gwynter ren Terare, the Weave is a force that entwines all life unto itself, but there are few outside the ties of the fae who recognize its bonds. The connection shared between all life is deep and beautiful. When such a connection is severed, it can cut sharper than a dagger's edge and cause more harm than death. Few of the fae reach beyond their own to forge such bonds. Dragons alone seek it out of need, and they do so often at heavy cost. Unicorns rarely, if ever, desire such a connection. Yet I would extend such an offer. I would bond with thee, human, and thou wouldst be my brother and my kin.

'Of course, this I will only do if you desire it. T'would mean that I will remain at your side through all your life. I cannot grant you immortality, but your life would be long, barring fatal injury. You would be able to wed a human if you chose, but I must warn you: any infidelity or promiscuity on your part would shatter our kinship, for a unicorn cannot be bound to something impure — and as I warned, it would be more painful than you can fathom to lose such a connection, once formed. That said, I suspect that a man of your character would resist any such temptation.'

Gwyn stared at his friend. "But, Aluem, does that mean you could never return home?"

'I could visit my Vale at any point, and you would be welcome to travel there with me. We would be kin, Gwynter. Brothers. I would not estrange myself from my own but would add you unto it.'

"But..." Gwyn lowered his gaze to the floor. "Why would you choose me? I—I'm...overcome." He wrapped his arms around Aluem's neck. "Thank you. Yes, please. I accept. Thank you."

'We shall perform the ceremony of kinship when we reach Mount Vinwen. It is best to do it on the soil of your birthplace.'

A pleasant warmth flooded Gwyn's body. For the past year and a half, he'd feared Aluem would soon announce an end of his adventures with Gwyn. That he would tire of human politics and war and return to his homeland, apart from all the turmoil. Each day the idea of losing his unicorn friend became harder to bear. Now he had nothing to fear. Aluem would be family.

A knock sounded behind Gwyn. Alarmed, he spun to face a cloaked figure at the stall's doorway.

The figure dipped his cowled head. "Forgive the intrusion, but I couldn't resist greeting an old acquaintance."

"Are we acquainted?" asked Gwyn. "Your voice isn't familiar to me."

"No, I suppose it wouldn't be after so long." The man raised a hand and drew back his cowl. "I am Rindermarr Lorric, a priest of Afallon. We met in one of your darkest moments, I think."

Gwyn's eyes widened. "Of course. I remember your face well.

You were a boon to me in my despair, and while I have no proof, I believe you swayed the king in his verdict."

Rindermarr smiled. "So it would seem. Yet now you're highly favored of him. I would never have wagered on that, even were I a betting man. You've climbed a high ladder in a very short time, Master ren Terare." He paused. "Forgive me, it's General Gwynter now, isn't it?"

"News travels with the swiftness of a unicorn. Yes, I suppose I'm a general now."

Rindermarr shook his head. "And only sixteen years old today. You'll make enemies for that, but I suspect you already know it."

"Quite well," Gwyn replied. "But should I fear such from the church, Rindermarr, or may I count you as a friend?"

"You're direct, aren't you? Have no fear. For my part, I would rather be a friend of mages than not. Particularly with your growing reputation, both as a proficient soldier and as the king's favored mage."

Gwyn glanced past the priest as a chill climbed his spine. "Be cautious, friend. Your language is bold outside the castle walls. Is talk of mages allowed in public places these days?"

"Allowed or not," Rindermarr said, "talk is being had. Despite the Crow King's ban on magic, it's stirring in Simaerin. More and more mages are surfacing, particularly in the northwest, near Mount Vinwen."

Gwyn perked up. "Vinwen? Is there any guess of why?"

The priest shook his head. "None. It has the Order of Corvus very concerned, especially since it's still limping a little after the Battle of Drakefield. That was your maiden battle, wasn't it?"

"It was," Gwyn said, nodding. "A lot of mages died, among many more soldiers."

"True. Quite true. While the army has been rebuilt, it isn't as though mages can be recruited in the same fashion. And now rogue mages are burgeoning with unchecked power, faster than the order can squelch it. People are talking. Where rumor dwelt before, now there's knowledge and suspicion — and many, many questions. The church is bearing the brunt of it, in many ways. The line between tradition and doctrine needs to be redrawn. Too long the church has preached of magic as an evil, but people are seeing men under the king's banner wielding it to stop mere babes from using magery. Will the king demand children burned openly at the stake, or will he recruit them into his order? Will the people stand for it? Who can say?"

Gwyn canted his head. "Why speak with me about this?"

"You once faced death at the king's hand. You chose to serve him in order to stay alive. You now have his favor. But tell me, Gwynter, does he have your heart? Do you serve the Crow King or Simaerin?"

Gwyn frowned. Was this a ploy? "Are they not one and the same, priest?"

"Is that how you see it?" asked Rindermarr, eyes dark and glittering in the gloom.

"I have sworn an oath to the true king of Simaerin, and this country will I serve until I die," Gwyn said softly.

"Carefully crafted words." Rindermarr nodded. "I believe I understand you. Thank you for your time." He turned away but paused and glanced back. "I think your trip to Mount Vinwen will be educational for you, but not necessarily restful. If you wish to understand how things are shaping in Simaerin, visit Charquae during your stay. There's a man there: Towwen Brym. He wrote a pamphlet which is turning heads. Find him. Read his words. They may interest you. Good night, General Gwynter. Safe journey."

Until the priest's footfalls faded, Gwyn stood beside Aluem in perfect stillness.

"What do you think?" he whispered, turning to the unicorn.

'I believe, young Gwynter, the Weave is breaking its bonds. I feel the kings of old stirring in their tombs. Something shifts to change the world.'

Chapter Forty-Two

Five days into their journey, Gwyn and Lawen stopped at a ramshackle inn for a night's rest indoors.

The Crow's Nest crawled with insects but felt like a palace after the stormy nights spent on the roadside. Only now, nestled under the inn's leaky roof in a private chamber, did Gwyn feel safe enough to relate his conversation with the priest to Lawen. The brothers sat on the room's single bed, the odor of mildew drifting from the damp coverlet.

Rain drummed the world outside. The rhythmic drip of water landing in a bucket in the nearby corner caught Gwyn's eye, and he watched it drip, again, again.

"I've heard of Towwen Brym."

Gwyn dragged his eyes from the bucket, back to Lawen. "You have?"

His brother nodded. "He's labeled an extremist. He's outspoken in his opinions, and when he draws his quill, its nib is sharper than a sword, so people say. General Cadogan calls him an eccentric fool. I understand Towwen used to live in Crowwell, but his opinions weren't well received by higher circles, and the Crow King disdained him. What's remarkable is that Towwen Brym garnered such a reputation among nobility. He's not nobleborn, but a tailor by profession."

"A tailor who can write?" asked Gwyn, surprised.

"So it seems. He now runs a small printing shop in partnership with an inventor named Brioc Ffyr."

"A printing shop? That's a peculiar profession outside of Crowwell. There aren't enough literate people to support a shop of that nature, are there?"

Lawen shook his head. "That might have been true a while back, but from what I've gathered, there's been a movement in Charquae and neighboring towns to teach children to read and write. Even slaves are being educated. It seems Towwen Brym and Brioc Ffyr offer free lessons to anyone wishing to learn."

Gwyn lifted his brow. "That's remarkable."

"And terrifying for some," Lawen said. "Cadogan went off one evening about how literacy among the common folk will make it harder to control them. They can be more easily swayed by opinions not in keeping with the king's philosophies."

"Such as Towwen Brym's." Gwyn rubbed his chin. "Does this extremist intend to promote open rebellion against the crown?"

"People aren't happy," Lawen murmured. "The Order of Corvus recently closed Bayton's gates to commerce, after they discovered several attempts to smuggle mage children from the port city. There's been a lot of unrest."

Gwyn sighed. "Even you know of this. It seems the Crow King has kept me in virtual isolation in the north, but why? It isn't as though I could stop the order or the people's outrage."

"I think the Crow King is afraid of you, Gwynter. Your magic is strong, especially for a defensive mage, and especially as young as you are."

"Then why not kill me?" Gwyn's fingers curled into fists. "Why this pretense, this charade? I know my magery is useful, but if he's so concerned, he should have burned me at the stake. If that's too public, he could order Traycen or another mage to end my life. It isn't as though I'm invincible. I bleed as any other man."

"I confess," said Lawen, "I've wondered the same thing. The Crow King sees you strangely, Gwynter. He doesn't treat you as he does anyone else. It's almost as though..." He hesitated. "I don't know quite how to put this... It's almost as though he's in *awe* of you. He fears and reveres you. It's just the feeling I get."

Gwyn met Lawen's eyes as a tremor ran down his limbs. "I think I understand that. I feel the same way about him."

Lawen opened his mouth to speak but stopped. He shook his head with a sigh. "Are we truly alone, or does the Crow King watch you even now?"

Gwyn shivered. "I don't feel alone, but I can't say it's more than paranoia. When I hear the cry of a bird, or the beat of a wing, I flinch. Roving eyes alarm me. Whispers frighten me. Silence is worst of all." He ran a hand through his wet hair. "I wish I knew *why* he sets me apart in his head. Why me? But perhaps it's very simple: The Crow King is mad. A fallen Ilidreth. Does he need a reason at all?"

NOON on the seventh day brought Gwyn and Lawen to the border of Vinwen's estate. Broad fields of wheat stretched before them, shimmering like gold under the influence of a laughing breeze. Beyond the fields, on a familiar hillside, stood the manor house of Mount Vinwen under a brilliant Autumn sky.

"I would race you," Gwyn said, turning a grin on Lawen, "but I already know the outcome."

Lawen laughed. "You could give a man a sporting chance."

"Aye, but Aluem could not. When he races, he slows for no man." Gwyn patted Aluem's neck. "Shall we?"

The unicorn broke into a full gallop along the road, stones flying behind him. Gwyn let out a whoop. Wind filled his ears like rushing tides. Lawen called out to him, but he never looked back, eyes fixed on the high turrets of his home.

Aluem carried him up the slope, past the gatehouse, straight to the front steps of the manor, where Gwyn swung to the ground. "Mother! Mother, I'm home!"

Two slight figures burst through the front doors in matching dresses. They tripped down the steps and flung their arms around Gwyn's waist.

"Gwynny!" cried Sila.

"You're back, you're back!" sobbed Neirin.

A third figure appeared at the door, bringing Gwyn's eyes up from his sisters. His grin widened. "Hello, Mother."

She descended the steps like flowing water, reached her hand up, and cupped it against Gwyn's cheek. "My beautiful son, welcome."

The pounding of hooves sounded behind the party and all turned to watch Lawen canter toward them.

Lawen waved. "Ho the house!"

"Welcome home, Lawen," Mother said, smiling as his horse came to a stop. "I see you've lost weight again. Cook will be delighted to fatten you up." She turned back to Gwyn, eyes bright. "I suspect you eat like a horse these days to maintain your height. Will you ever stop growing?"

Gwyn laughed, then turned to Aluem. "I must go inside and see the old place, my friend. I'll come out later to make certain you're comfortable, but please do as you wish meanwhile."

'*I understand perfectly. Take your time and enjoy your home.*' Aluem trotted toward the stables even as a servant ran to guide him.

Gwyn wrapped an arm around his mother's slight shoulders. Lawen seized her other side and together they drew her toward the front door. Neirin and Sila ran inside ahead of them, giggling.

The family settled at the servant's table in the large kitchen, rather than in the dining hall. A merry fire roared in the hearth. Mavell presented more food than the little gathering could eat in a day. Still, Gwyn and Lawen did their best to clear the platters, while they listened to the little girls chattering about the goings-on in Vinwen Province. Not much had changed in their view. If political unrest had arisen, Sila and Neirin remained ignorant.

"I *told* Stefa not to ride that wild colt, but she wouldn't hear of anything else," Neirin said, sighing. "The problem is, she's so nearly wild herself. Theolin said she's practically an Ilidreth. Not like Kive, mind, but—"

Gwyn started as Mother dropped her fork with a clatter.

Gwyn looked sharply at Neirin. "You remember Kive?" After so long, he didn't expect the child to remember the Ilidreth's name so well that she would reference it in natural conversation.

"Of course I do. He ate live rats! No one else I've ever met does that. Nathaera mentioned—"

"Bless you, child, but you do go on," Mother said with a threat in her tone.

Gwyn turned his gaze to the lady of the house. "There's a secret among you."

"Easy, Gwyn," Lawen said. "After the meal."

Gwyn turned on his brother. "You too?"

"Down, boy," Lawen replied, smiling grimly. "It's not a secret by choice. Clean your plate and we'll adjourn to the south parlor."

Chapter Forty-Three

Seated among the furs and cushions in the south parlor, Gwyn stared at his mother and brother, waiting with what patience he could muster. Sila and Neirin had been banished upstairs. A fire blazed in the hearth to chase away the chill as evening set in.

"You're a much-scrutinized mage, Gwynter," Mother said. "Nothing you do goes unnoticed these days. We couldn't risk telling you something of a delicate nature until you arrived here. Even now, the danger is great. There's no way to tell if you're watched in this very moment."

Gwyn's annoyance shrank a little and he relaxed his shoulders. What she said made sense. "If the danger grows in my knowledge, must I learn it?"

"You more than anyone," Lawen said. "It impacts you directly."

"You mean to tell me something of Nathaera," Gwyn guessed.

Mother and Lawen glanced at each other. Lawen shrugged. "He's no fool."

"No, that he's never been," Mother said, sighing. "Only occasionally foolhardy."

"Tell me," Gwyn said. "I've ached for news of her. Is she safe? Did she sail the channel to Fraelin?"

"All questions best answered by herself." Mother lifted her eyes to the door. "You may come in now."

As the door opened, Gwyn sprang to his feet. In stepped a familiar girl with bright eyes and a warm smile. Nathaera stood no taller than she'd been, but Gwyn found her fairer, with rosy cheeks and longer hair, soft and golden in the firelight. She wore a flattering gown in a fashion unfamiliar to Gwyn, perhaps a Fraeli design.

Their eyes met. Nathaera let out a cry and launched herself at Gwyn, wrapping her arms around his neck. She clung to him, head pressed against his chest. "It's so good to see you, you wonderful, giant boy!"

Gwyn stood stunned, hands frozen at his sides. He stared at the crown of her head. "You're here."

Laughing, Nathaera pulled back. "Your wits have slowed, alas. Of course I am. Could I hug you if I weren't?"

He shook his head. "But, Nathaera. You shouldn't be here. It's terribly dangerous." His mind moved at a snail's pace. His body tingled. She was supposed to be far away and safe. In Fraelin. With Kive. That was how he imagined them.

Gwyn blinked. "Where's Kive?"

Nathaera's smile died. "Well...that's why I'm here. At least, that's why I'm here *now*. He sort of sped things along..."

His feet felt far away. "What do you mean?"

Nathaera shook her head. "He simply couldn't take it anymore, poor soul. I learned not to mention you in front of him, or he went off on Shiny needing him, or finding Shiny, or riding Shiny Unicorn. Eventually he calmed down and stayed rather content. But I foolishly let your name slip when I was speaking with Adesta about a month ago. Kive overheard me, and...and he disappeared. I knew where he'd gone to. Where else but Simaerin? To find you."

Gwyn's mouth fell open. "Kive is *here*? In Simaerin? Alone?"

She bobbed a nod, biting her lip. "Isn't it dreadful? I mean, he's gotten much better about not eating people. Only a few are rats in his eyes. I've taught him a *lot* about different animals, and he's gotten very good at naming people lots of kinds of beasts. He's got an entire menagerie in his head! But still some people are rats. I think he's actually very good at distinguishing between people of good character and people of bad. But that doesn't mean he doesn't get confused sometimes."

"Oh, Nathaera," Gwyn said quietly. "Kive could be anywhere."

She nodded. "He doesn't know where to look for you. He must be so frightened."

Gwyn's chest tightened against his lungs. "The Crow King is still searching for him. And for you, too. Coming back here for Kive was extremely reckless."

She laughed. "This coming from the young man who braved the True Wood and Swan Castle to find a cure that might not exist? Afallon above, but you *are* a funny one, Gwynter ren Terare. I couldn't well let Kive alone, after all he and I have been through.

"It's not been easy, you know, living in a foreign land, even with Adesta's help. Most people there don't like Simaeri after everything. It took a while to gain any trust. Kive helped with that, actually. Being Ilidreth, people were inclined to sympathize, even though he's fallen. Fraeli believe the Ilidreth can be saved, and they want to help them reclaim what's been taken from them. It's awful, what the line of Crow Kings has done to the Ilidreth in the past three centuries."

Gwyn ran a hand over his face. "Slow down a moment. Adesta? The name is familiar somehow, but—"

"Oh, *you* know. Adesta Gilhan. The defense mage you trounced that day with the dragon. He's told me all about it, somewhat grudgingly. He respects you a lot, especially once I informed him that you beat him after only a few *weeks* of mage training. He also despises you, and that's also because you trounced him after only a few weeks of training." She laughed. "He's here, by the way. I brought him along. Or, rather, he brought me. We came across the channel with the Fraeli delegation."

Gwyn blinked. "What delegation?"

"Oh, well, it seems the Crane King of Fraelin — he's rather nice, by the way. Very generous — anyway, he's seeking a peace treaty with Simaerin. It all hinges on whether the Crow King will leave the Ilidreth in peace. If not, the war may go on indefinitely, although I've heard the royal coffers of both countries are being rapidly drained by all the fighting."

A sue for peace? Gwyn wondered if the Crow King would listen. He had mentioned a shift of some kind in the days and weeks to come. Was this what he'd meant?

An accented voice drifted in from the open door that led into the corridor. "Nathaera, may I come in now?"

"Oh," Nathaera spun toward the door. "Yes, yes of course. Come in, Adesta."

A slender figure stepped into view, pale-haired and handsome, just as Gwyn recalled. As he strode into the parlor, Adesta Gilhan met Gwyn's gaze. "Greetings from Fraelin, Lord Gwynter of Vinwen. We are well met, I trust."

Gwyn nodded. "Hello, Lord Adesta Gilhan. For my part, it is an honor to meet once more."

"Then it is a dual honor," Adesta said. "Lady Nathaera has said much of your exploits in the True Wood. I have also heard of your deeds at Keep Arch. It seems the Crow King favors you highly, and why not? Your reputation is well deserved by all reports. You're a keen warrior and a merciful enemy. Your name has even reached the Crane King. His Illustrious Majesty is hopeful of peace by your example, particularly because of your sympathies toward the Ilidreth."

Gwyn frowned. "My sympathies do not reflect the opinion of Simaerin's court, I'm afraid. And while the king does favor my skills, we do not share a common view of the world, nor does he seek mine to alter his."

"Adesta knows all this," Nathaera said. "So does the Crane King. But that's not exactly what he means."

Gwyn arched an eyebrow. "What does the Crane King hope to accomplish?"

Adesta piped up. "He wishes to ally himself with *you*. The delegation to Crowwell is a farce to distract your king from the true negotiations."

"I don't understand," said Gwyn, shaking his head. He glanced at Lawen, wondering if their desire to rally against the king was further along than anyone had let on. Lawen smiled at him, eyes twinkling. He knew something Gwyn didn't.

"Well, Gwyn," Nathaera said, drawing every eye to her. "You see...there's a reason it took me so long to return to Simaerin. I was pursuing something. Trying to solve a puzzle presented by the Fraeli. Adesta's been helping me. We finally found the answer. The key to open rebellion against the Crow King. Up to now, Simaeri have been frightened of defying the crown. The church sides with the Crow King, supposedly because he has the divine right to reign."

"But he doesn't," Gwyn said, nodding. "I know this already. The Crow King shouldn't rule because he usurped the throne, and he's not even Simaeri."

"Yes, that's true," Nathaera said, "but that's only half the reason. One might easily argue that after three hundred years of Crow Kings ruling, they have a certain right."

"He," Gwyn said. "There's only ever been one Crow King, I believe. He's merely feigned a succession by magically altering his appearance. He pretends to die of old age, his supposed child becoming heir. But there is no child. Only him, stepping in to fill his own shoes. It explains why there has always been a male heir."

The others exchanged looks, nodding.

"It fits with the legends," Adesta said.

"But you imply there's another reason why the Crow King shouldn't rule?" asked Gwyn.

Nathaera bobbed a nod. "Because, Gwyn, the line of the old

kings hasn't failed. The Crow King couldn't destroy them. He *magically* could not."

Gwyn stared at her. "What?"

Mother answered, her voice low and faint. "'Twas an oath sworn by King Roth of the Ilidreth five hundred years ago to the line of Cygmund Wintervale, first of the Crane Kings in Crane Castle. 'By blood and bond, thy line shall never fade, except by the will of thine heirs.' That's how the legend goes, at least."

"That is how it reads in Fraelin as well," Adesta said. "Thus, we know the true line of Wintervale is not ended."

Gwyn searched every face, hairs on his neck tingling. "But how can we trace such a line? No doubt its heirs had to hide from the Crow King — if they even know the legend by now."

"It was never hidden nor forgotten. Not by the heirs of Wintervale," Mother whispered. "The Crow King can't destroy it, you see. But he can suppress it. One hundred years have passed since the last male heir was born to the rightful line of kings — until now." Her eyes bore into Gwynter like burning coals.

Gwyn shook his head, refusing to understand even as dread swept through him, cold as the heights of Keep Arch in dead winter.

Mother stood and stepped forward, her hand extended. "You, Gwynter, are the rightful king of Simaerin by my blood."

His mind wobbled. His heart wavered. Silence screamed in his ears as every pair of eyes considered him with a reverent awe that shook his very core. He sat down in a wingback chair. "No." His voice rang cold and firm. "I'm not a king. I am not *the* king."

"But, Gwyn," Nathaera piped up. "You really are. Adesta and I traced the line as far as we could, and your mother's history fills in the rest."

"I've always known it," Mother said, "but I dared say nothing to anyone after I bore a son — the first male heir of Wintervale in a century. It meant something. Even the Crow King knew it. He visited here after you were born, claiming to be on his way to the woods. Perhaps he was. But he came here first, and he stared at you in such a peculiar way, I knew he understood what you were. But he didn't try to kill you, because he knew he couldn't. He could only suppress your magic."

Gwyn said nothing, hands clasped in his lap, heart thundering. This wasn't real. It was a lie. A dream. Something made up.

Lawen spoke. "I didn't know, Gwyn, until a few months ago. Honest to Afallon. But it stands to reason. The facts are verified. Everything makes sense."

Gwyn shook his head. "No." His mind detached from his body, as though he floated far above, voices muffled like they traveled through water to reach him.

Lawen went on. "Even your birth — the first male heir in a century — has an explanation. At least, I have a theory."

"An eruption," Adesta said.

Lawen nodded. "Exactly. The Crow King made certain the heirs of Wintervale were never male, because a male heir's magic acts in righteous defense of Simaerin. Thus, the heir would have the power to overthrow the usurper. But as a direct result, the defensive magic had nowhere to go, and it built and built upon itself until it finally exploded, driving its will into Lady Mair, as its last surviving heir. She bore a son, rather than a daughter, because the magic demanded it. The same must have happened one hundred years ago, but that male heir was born mad. Thus, he was harmless against the Crow King."

"I confess," said Mother, head erect, "I have always harbored hope that Gwyn would bring about the revival of our rightful claim. Wintervale was meant to rule Simaerin. Gwynter, you have the power and right to take back our throne."

Gwyn bowed his head, trembling. "No."

Lawen knelt before him and rested a hand on Gwyn's arm. "I imagine this is a great shock. You need time to think over—"

Gwyn shook off his hand, jerked away from his brother, and rose to tower over every staring face. "I'm not a king. I won't be a king." He marched to the door, shoved it aside, and darted for the stairs.

"Gwynter!" cried Mother.

Lawen's inquiry followed. "Gwynny?"

"He's frightened," came Nathaera's voice, chasing him up to the landing above. Gwyn didn't stop until he'd safely locked himself inside his bedchamber.

But he didn't feel safe.

He felt hunted.

Chapter Forty-Four

"I'm going up after him." Nathaera started for the parlor door, her stomach tied in knots.

Lawen caught her arm. "Give him a little time to sort all this. It's more than a mere shock. His entire world is upended."

Adesta stepped up beside Lawen. "Indeed. Imagine being told *you* are intended to rule, but first you must overthrow the very sovereign who has enslaved you and your countrymen."

She looked between the two men. "I can't even begin to fathom how that must feel. But he can't be left alone. I'm not going up to try to persuade him, or even to comfort him, for I can't imagine my words would provide any solace. I'm merely going up to be with him, so that he feels less alone. Please unhand me, Lawen."

He released her. "Go, my lady. Be with him."

She ran up the stairs, feeling eyes on her back until she crossed the landing and disappeared from their view. She hesitated outside Gwyn's door, aware of the impropriety of entering, and nervous of intruding on his privacy. Drawing breath, she knocked.

"Gwyn, may I come in?"

Silence followed. Then the door cracked open, and Gwyn

peeked out at her, pale and grim, his gray eyes stormy but contained.

He studied her and she studied him back. He looked older, taller and — dared she think it? — more handsome. But he also looked leaner, which he could scarcely afford. Dark circles marked his eyes, hinting at bad dreams and restless nights. He'd been plagued before today's revelations. Had Nathaera brought too heavy a burden for the young man? He was sixteen years of age, despite his copious maturity. She always forgot he was still so young.

"I'm sorry, Gwyn, for putting so much on your shoulders. It's not fair to you, is it? What we've said. What it means. I would be terrified to learn what you have. It's a very great responsibility."

"I don't want it," he murmured, a flash of panic brightening his eyes like lightning in a storm. "I'm a farmer, Nathaera. The son of my father, nobleborn, but not a king's heir. I've not got the skill, the aspiration, the...the ambition. Two years ago, I craved joining the Crow King's army to fight and gain glory. But war is ugly. I've had my fill of it. I just want to stay home and tend crops, oversee the slaves, and..." He grimaced. "Even that sounds so ugly. Slaves, Nathaera? People. People in bondage to me, as I'm in bondage to the king. When did that happen? Why is everything so ugly?"

"Because," Nathaera whispered, "we're led by a tyrant. But Gwyn, you could fix things."

He shook his head. "Who would follow me? Who would accept the distant heir to a long-forgotten line of kings? Those who do know of that line believe the Wintervales displeased Afallon, and he cursed them to death and ruin. I would sooner be burned than crowned if I stepped forward to claim an old birthright."

"Once, perhaps. But not now." Nathaera waved her hands before her. "Think of all that's changed since you came into your power. The people are waking up, Gwynter. They're seeing the king's true colors, as he executes infants, as he wages an endless war against a nation suing for peace. If Simaerin learns that the Crow

King is no Simaeri at all, but one of the very race he persecutes? Oh, Gwyn. Now is exactly the time to act."

He scowled. "I do not dispute the need to end his reign. Already Lawen and I have discussed it, and we know of others who feel the same. But I won't be the next king, Nathaera. Besides all my other reasons, I've a strong distaste of their kind presently."

"I can certainly appreciate why, but the Crane King is a good man. Not all kings are wicked." She grimaced. "I didn't come here to persuade you to take up a crown. I came because I didn't want you to be alone. The fact is, Gwynter, you *are* an heir of kings, and the Crow King knows it. The fact is, he must be overthrown. The fact is, Kive must be found before the Crow King finds him." Her heartbeat quickened. "The fact is...I love you, Gwynter ren Terare. *Those are facts*. Now, I'm going outside before my face is entirely red. You — you just stay here, and keep your peace. Good afternoon, Gwynter. I'll see you at supper." She whirled and bolted down the corridor, cheeks flaming like a blazing fire.

Chapter Forty-Five

"Did you know, Aluem?"

The unicorn regarded Gwyn from the far side of the barn, near a pile of hay left by a servant who couldn't tell Aluem apart from horses.

'There are many things I know, Gwynter,' replied the unicorn.

"Wintervale," Gwyn said.

'Ah. She told you.'

"You knew."

Aluem crossed the hay-strewn floor without a sound. *'You are upset.'*

"I'm frightened and confused." Gwyn shrugged, stepped to a second, closer pile of hay, and sat in it. "What am I to do?"

Aluem folded his legs beneath him, settling down beside Gwyn. *'What you feel to be right. Is that not how you have always tried to conduct your life?'*

"But, Aluem, I can't be a king. I'm...I'm a farmer and a soldier. I'm ill-suited to politics."

'Do you think anyone else would feel better suited in your position?'

Gwyn hesitated. "Lawen would be one hundred times better."

'Perhaps, but would he feel one hundred times better about the concept? It is easy to assess your own flaws, for you live in your own head. It is equally easy to project greatness or superiority onto another. But it is not fair to do so. Indeed, no one is immune to doubts and demons, Gwynter — but the thing to fear is the man who ignores his doubts and idolizes his demons. A man without flaw is no human, but rather a creature cloaked in human flesh and intent upon the fall of those around him. That is how he feasts and thrives: He builds his glory on the rubble of other men's dreams.

'You are not such a man, or you would not heed the fearful cry of your mortal confines. What you must do, Gwynter, is sooth your fears with the aid of your soul — for all souls begin in glory, filled with light. Pray, Gwynter, to Afallon, who gives you strength. There you will find your answers. After that, you must accept those answers, whatever they be, and strive to achieve them. Beyond this, I cannot say more. In the end the choice is only your own.'

Gwyn considered Aluem with a blend of dread and affection pressing against his chest. "You're wise, my friend, and I'd be a fool to disregard your words. I will pray, as I should have from the first. Thank you." He paused. "Aluem? Nathaera told me that she loves me. It was very sudden, and my thoughts were already so full, I couldn't be certain that she meant it — though I can't imagine she would say anything she doesn't mean. Yet, do we know each other well enough for such feelings? We've not spoken until this day for nearly two years. Back then we were barely more than children... I'm not certain what I should do. How I should behave. I hardly understand my own heart."

He rested a hand against his chest. "I do care about her, but is it in the same way? Should I even entertain such feelings in these turbulent times? My head won't stop spinning."

Laughter like rushing wind filled Gwyn's mind. '*Can I know your heart better than you? Do not run through such emotions. Rather, stride and view each as you would study every flower in your path, until you comprehend what they signify. Give yourself time, young Gwynter, for the answer is not required at the first of a journey but is discovered along the way. Did we find Lawen's cure at the start, or was there much toil before we reached your goal and gained your reward? Do not be so hasty.'*

Gwyn smiled. "Am I losing patience, Aluem? I hadn't meant to. My mind is just so full." He stroked the unicorn's mane. "Kive is missing. He came back to Simaerin by himself, which is what brought Nathaera so suddenly. I'm worried — for both of them. Especially for Kive. The Crow King is still adamant about catching him. I'm not certain where to look for Kive if he isn't at Vinwen. Where else might he go? I fear to the capital itself..."

'It is grim news indeed. But there is one place which may beckon him more strongly than his bond with you.'

Gwyn shivered. "Swan Castle? But Celin forbade him from entering those woods again. He said he would kill him."

'So he did, and I believe my friend intends to follow through on that oath if required. There is only one question for you to answer: Shall you seek out Shaeswéath *once more in search of Kive or let his fate alone. You have long been apart. Is there yet an obligation?'*

Gwyn pushed himself from the straw. "Yes. Celin charged me to keep him near, and I've failed that in every way. I owe Kive much, not the least being my life. And Nathaera is fond of him. She would blame herself should he die. There's also the Crow King. I won't allow him the satisfaction of such a victory."

'Your leave may not be sufficient time to return from Shaeswéath, *even should we find Kive without incident.'*

Gwyn nodded. "Yes, but I suspect we won't be alone in searching for Kive in the True Wood. We may encounter the Crow King en route. So my gut says, and in matters of the king I've learned to heed it. Should that be the case, my tardiness will hardly matter." He smiled grimly. "I can make my report more conveniently this way."

The barn door swung open. "Gwynny, are you in here?"

"Yes."

Lawen's head appeared in the crack of the doorway, haloed in sunlight from outside. "We have a guest. He's asking specifically to see you."

"Who is it?" Gwyn asked, striding toward the door.

"Towwen Brym. He's come on a matter connected with a certain genealogy."

Gwyn's heart withered and dropped into his stomach.

Chapter Forty-Six

"No call for secrecy on my account," declared Towwen Brym, shaking Gwyn's hand with the vehemence of a hurricane. "I've been in correspondence with the Gilhan family of Fraelin for several years, so I know everything. Adesta's father was ecstatic upon discovering the lost line of Wintervale, and he couldn't bear not to write to me and spill everything. But rest assured, he divulged the facts by way of a code we conjured up long, long ago."

"Actually," piped up a second man seated in the parlor, a cup of tea in one hand, "the code is mine, as is the correspondence. But Towwen enjoys riffling through the personal belongings of others and making their affairs his own." He rose and inclined his head. "My name is Brioc Ffyr. It's a true honor, sire." A smile quirked at his lips. "That wasn't intended to rhyme. At least not consciously."

Gwyn looked between the two men, bewildered by their sudden appearance in his home, forty miles north of Charquae. Towwen Brym was a small man, slender of limb, with unruly hair wisping about his head like a flimsy halo tinged with premature gray. His apparel was of coarse cloth, smudged with ink and patched haphazardly. Brioc Ffyr, meanwhile, looked well-groomed, a little on the plump side, with an amiable air and grounded eyes. He wore clean, simple clothes. He must be a decade older than his business partner, even as he appeared healthier.

"Why are you here?" asked Gwyn. He swallowed to wet his parched mouth and resisted an urge to twist the front of his tunic.

"I already said—"

Brioc cut his friend off. "We were sent for several days ago. By Lawen."

Gwyn turned toward his brother, nerves humming in his head. "When?"

"At the inn. I sent a messenger pigeon while you were asleep," Lawen said.

"Why?"

"Why?" laughed Towwen Brym. "Why else? To meet our king!"

Brioc offered a kind smile. "True enough, we wished to meet you. That, and we always come when we're called by the head of our order."

Gwyn stared, mind reeling. "Your order? I'm sorry, I don't understand."

Lawen smiled his fond smile. "I meant to tell you so many times, Gwynter, but the Crow King always watched you. Always kept us apart. And before that, you were still young."

"Tell me what?" Gwyn asked.

"I'm head of the Order of Cygnus. We stand against the Crow King and Corvus, though until recently our numbers have remained small. Our father led the Order of Cygnus before me."

The implications dawned on Gwyn like a bleak winter sunrise. "You're a mage."

"I am. Conjuration is my skillset. It's very potent and therefore often lethal. My magic was killing me until you found that cure."

A knock sounded at the door. Before anyone could answer it, the door swung open and in stepped Mother and Nathaera.

"I hope nothing significant was discussed without us," Nathaera said. Her gaze met Gwyn's, and though her cheeks reddened, she didn't look away. Her eyes shone bright and filled with what Gwyn thought might be defiance.

"Nothing much," replied Towwen. "Just catching His Majesty up to speed."

Gwyn flinched. "Please don't call me that."

"Oh," Nathaera said over him, "on which matters?"

"I told you once that I'm a mage," Lawen said.

The girl nodded. "Yes, I remember."

"I'm also the head of an order of mages in rebellion against the Crow King. I just explained as much to Gwynter."

Nathaera laughed. "What a day for revelations! It's wonderful." She turned to the two guests. "And what are you?"

"Mages of the same order," Brioc answered.

"Superb!" She drifted toward a couch and sank into the cushions. "So then, are we planning to openly oppose the king soon?"

"Well," said Lawen, glancing toward Gwyn. "We intended to use the heir of Wintervale to draw numbers to us. Legends do exist in Simaerin concerning an heir who would rise up to free the slave, enrich the common man, and overthrow the tyrant king. Now the stories are growing. People are praying to Afallon for deliverance. Towwen uses his printing press to circulate the stories more."

"People can't read," Gwyn murmured.

"Aye," Brioc said, "but *priests* can, and we've a few of them in our pockets."

"Rindermarr Lorric," Gwyn guessed.

Brioc nodded. "To name one."

"I can't go to war yet," Gwyn said. The room fell still. "I have to find Kive. He's key in all this. If the Crow King finds him first, we shall likely lose. I don't know quite why, or how I know it, but so my gut tells me, and that I must heed."

"But the Ilidreth is lost," Mother said. "Where would you even begin?"

"*Shaeswéath*," Gwyn replied. "Swan Castle. I believe he went home, and the Crow King knows it."

"You can't," Mother said. "It's a wonder you survived those woods the first time. I forbid you to go."

"But go I must and shall. Mother, I'm no longer a child, but a man and mage. The True Wood cannot claim me, no matter its will. But I won't go alone. Aluem will come with me." He gently smiled. "You needn't fear for me unless the Crow King follows. And even then, I'd be in no greater danger than I am already."

"What if you do face the Crow King?" she asked. "Have you the power to slay him?"

Gwyn shook his head. "No, but if what you've said of my heritage is true, he can't kill me either. I'm not chasing the king to end his reign, not yet. This is about my peculiar friend, one who deserves the chance to live and heal. I'm going."

"Then I shall go with you," said Nathaera, rising from the couch.

Mother gasped. "You can't. It's far too dangerous for a lady."

"But I'm not a lady! My father disowned me ages ago. I'm hardly more than a ragamuffin, and as such, I'm free to do as I please. Ragamuffins do, you know."

"I shall also come."

Everyone turned toward the accented voice in the doorway. Adesta Gilhan glared at Gwyn, issuing a silent challenge.

Gwyn sighed. "It is not for me to say who will enter the True Wood and risk his life. Let every man choose his own path."

"Every man," chimed in Nathaera, "and every ragamuffin."

"I'm not going," Towwen Brym said. "I'm not a warrior mage. Words are my skillset, and I'll be little use in such a place as that. I like Ilidreth at a safe distance and no closer."

"I would follow you, sire," said Brioc Ffyr, "if not for the fact I'm also of little good on such a quest. I will remain behind, rallying our forces and recruiting, as I pray to Afallon for your swift and safe return."

All eyes shifted to Lawen. His eyes gleamed dark and troubled. Gwyn knew his thoughts. Lawen was a leader and he understood his duty to his men, but he also cared about Gwynter. Could he step back and let his little brother and his small band journey through the True Wood to face death or worse? After a moment, Lawen's face cleared and light ignited in his gaze.

"I feel that the two choices before me are really just one," Lawen said. "We talk of defying the king. We talk of rebellion and warfare. Well, the battle has already begun. The next engagement will likely be at Swan Castle, and so it is to there I set my path. I'll come with you, Gwynter, and I'm glad I do so with a light conscience."

Gwyn's heart loosened, though he hadn't known it had been bound. "I gladly accept your company."

"Besides," Nathaera said, "you're the true king, Gwyn. We really *must* follow you. That's how it's supposed to work."

Towwen Brym barked a laugh, but Gwyn felt the blood rush from his face. Everyone here already accepted him as their ruler, a man set to lead the way into a brighter future, filled with wealth and prosperity, fulfilled dreams and blue skies.

He nearly opened his mouth to refute them again. He wasn't king. He would never agree to be king. But he hesitated and shook his head. Even if he spoke with thunder in his words and lightning in his eyes, he doubted they would heed him. Their heads were full of summer dreams, while he saw winter coming on.

Better that he steeled himself for the inevitable. The future of Simaerin depended on the Crow King's defeat. Gwyn must face him first of all.

Chapter Forty-Seven

The search party struck out from Vinwen at dawn.

Irritation clawed at Gwyn's insides as he led the way into the woods, retracing his route from what seemed ages past. He'd intended to head out the night before, alone but for Aluem. Together they could race all the way to Swan Castle as swiftly as a windstorm. Instead, well-meaning snail-paced friends slowed them down.

It wouldn't last. Gwyn had spoken with Lawen already, and they agreed that those on horseback could ride with Gwyn as far as Celin's Vale. After Kive's survival was assured, Gwyn and Aluem would ride on, the others following as quickly as they could, in case Gwyn never made it to *Shaeswéath*. He might be immune to death at the Crow King's hand, but he was *not* invincible.

The first night in the woods passed quietly. Toward dawn, Gwyn rose from his bedroll and stood at the edge of camp, straining his ears for any sound. All held still and silent, like the dread anticipation before a siege. No breeze stirred the boughs.

The Crow King is near.

A familiar voice spoke. "You've invited death into these woods."

Gwyn started and spun toward the newcomer. Not the king, but another Ilidreth, his tone silken and soft. Celin stood beneath an ancient elm, adorned in the rich motley colors of his kind, an arrow aimed at Gwyn's heart.

Gwyn inclined his head. "I came to find my charge. Have you seen Kive?"

"I warned you," Celin whispered. "Had I seen him, he would be dead. It would be better so. But you are not alone in seeking him."

"I know," Gwyn whispered. "I must find him first. You consider Kive's death a mercy, but I'm afraid it's otherwise."

"Your Crow King wants him alive," Celin said. "Is that not reason enough to end him?"

"But Kive is your prince."

Celin stiffened. "My prince is dead. All the royal house is dead. They fell on the night of blood, and none can bring them to their feet again."

"But Kive *was* your prince," Gwyn insisted. "You don't really want to kill him, do you? You wish to end his suffering. What if there's another way, Celin? What if he's healing? What if — as the Crow King fears — Kive can mend his mind and raise an army of Ilidreth to stop the king from conquering the woods?"

Celin laughed without humor. "Does the Crow King fear such a thing? Can he fear anything?"

"I think he fears a great deal. I believe he fears most of all an alliance between rightful kings he cannot slay, who would unravel his claim to land and woods."

"The line of Lord Roth and his lady fair is broken, and the line of Wintervale is bone and ash." Celin lowered his bow. "The Crow King has won."

"Kive *is* mending," Gwyn said. "He doesn't see me as a rat, but as a Shiny. He sees Nathaera differently too."

Celin shook his head. "Mending or not, he remains fallen. A fallen Ilidreth cannot be saved. His magic is dark, his soul twisted."

"But that isn't fair," said Gwyn, a fire igniting in his chest. "Kive didn't have a choice. He didn't want to fall."

"In the end, he gave up."

"The Crow King *tortured* him! How long could anyone endure such conditions? I've seen the king's cruelty. I've heard what he does to Ilidreth prisoners. How can you call that a choice?"

Celin blinked. "Then you know?"

"I guessed that the Crow King was Kive's master, and after that I realized he's Ilidreth."

"I see. Then you know only half the story." Celin sighed. "It hardly matters. Go. Find Kive and try to spare him. You will fail. But your efforts do you some credit. Farewell, Gwyn. Do not seek me again. We are not allies." He started into the trees.

"Wait!"

Celin paused.

"You know the story. You know how Swan Castle fell. Why the Crow King betrayed his people and tortured his prince. But Aluem said no one now remembers."

"One should not trust a unicorn's memories of such events. They are pure and peaceful creatures and do not long recall the pain and anguish of war. Nor do they wish to. I am surprised that Aluem has remained so long at your side, battle mage."

"I'm equally surprised, but he wants to stay even now. He wishes to make me his kin. We'd intended to perform the rites already, but Kive's situation has delayed us."

Celin's eyes widened. "He wishes to bind himself to you? A *battle* mage? A Simaeri? Perhaps the world is wholly mad at last."

"Celin," whispered Gwyn, "tell me of the Crow King. Why did he betray his people?"

"I do not know why!" Celin lowered his head and sighed. "Very well. Come, Gwynter ren Terare. If you are to fight him, it is best to know all that any can discover."

Gwyn followed the Ilidreth bowman. Soon he found himself in the silvery Vale he'd thought never to see again.

Celin guided him to the shimmering pool, bent down, and played his fingers across the water as though he plucked a harp. Humming music filled the air, and the ripples in the pool stretched and grew, forming the image of Swan Castle in its age of glory, bright and glowing.

"Behold *Shaeswéath*, during the reign of Lord King Roth ave'al Edelin. At his side stood Lady Shalesta of Fraelin, chosen queen of the Ilidreth kingdom, though she was of human blood." From the pool, water bubbled up, growing higher and higher until it coalesced into the shape of a man and woman standing hand in hand, erect and graceful. Prisms of color faintly painted their forms, and Gwyn recognized the raven-haired beauty long asleep in Swan Castle.

"Behold their two sons, Kovien ave'al Edelin, heir to *Shaeswéath*, and Kive ave'ar Edelin, second-born."

The watery shapes frothed and writhed, changing from the Lord and Lady into their sons, tall, fair-haired, comely. Gwyn's heart constricted as he stared into — not one — but two familiar faces. Kive, the younger, slightly shorter, did not surprise him. But staring into the fair and gentle face of Kovien, now the maddened, cruel Crow King, rocked Gwyn to his core.

Gwyn bowed his head before the fluid shapes. "But why? Did the Crow King not love his family? How could he destroy his own kin?"

"I do not know," Celin whispered. "None now living knows. Perhaps once his younger brother understood. The Crow King, as now he is called, held the young prince captive for many long decades within Swan Castle. Held him and did unspeakable wrongs against him. But as Kive's mind is, even he no longer knows his brother's motivations. Indeed, he does not know his brother at all. Kovien is dead, just as Lord Roth and Lady Shalesta are dead. Kive alone remains, for he has not forgotten his name. Once he does forget, the kingdom of Ilid shall fade forever, no longer rooted to the world."

"Has the Crow King forgotten his own name, then?" asked Gwyn.

"Far worse. He has forsaken it, as he forsook his people."

Gwyn shook his head. "But why? He was the heir to his throne.

Heir to magic. His parents were benevolent and kind. What could he gain in betraying the Ilidreth?"

"Nothing," Celin answered. "That is the question that has plagued me longest. No Ilidreth who remembers can find the answer. We only know that Prince Kovien invited an evil into the True Wood, brought it to the very heart of our lands, and cast its spell across the whole of our domain. It has claimed most of us. It will claim the whole of us in the end. The Vales are fading. Memory is fading. Beauty is fading. Soon all shall be lost."

"No," Gwyn whispered, clenching his fists. "*No*." He turned to the Ilidreth. "Fight with us, Celin. Simaerin will stand against the Crow King. Bring your kin, whoever will fight, and stand with us against his madness."

"What chance have you against the Crow? Simaerin loyalties remain with the crown, and none believe he is a usurper."

"Some know," Gwyn said. "And..." He inhaled. "The line of Wintervale isn't bone and ash."

Celin's eyes widened. "*You*, Gwynter. You are a king? Yes, I see it in your eyes. Even that first day we met, I saw it. Do you know when the Wintervale line gained its magic? It was granted to them by Lord Roth five hundred years ago. Shalesta's brother Cygmund, first of the Crane Kings, had two sons. The eldest became his heir. The second allied himself with Simaerin through marriage and became king upon the passing of his wife's father. The Wintervale line grew and prospered until the Crow King crushed it. But here you stand, the last remnant of ancient roots. The Weave has chosen you. Aluem has chosen you. Perhaps even your Afallon has chosen you."

"I don't desire to be a king," Gwyn said, "but I cannot deny what I am by blood. If it gives me the power to defy the Crow King, I must use what I have. Wrongs must be righted." He extended his hand. "Will you and your kin stand with me?"

Celin considered him. The silver blossoms of the Vale swayed on a fragrant gust. "You will try to save Kive and overthrow the Crow King? Do you not hear the folly of your own words?"

“The greatest folly would be in doing nothing to change the evil of now.”

Celin frowned. He sighed and shook his head. “I am sorry, heir of Wintervale, but I will not risk the remnant of the Ilidreth against such a force of arms. Better to fade in our home than leave it behind to be slaughtered en masse.”

Gwyn stifled his disappointment behind a soft smile. “I understand. Though if death were the only outcome I could see either way, I would choose to stand against the delivering hand — if only to claim I never gave into it. As it is, you’ve already handed the Crow King your sword. You are defeated.”

“Perhaps that is so.” Celin turned toward the pool and the shapes flowing above its depths. He swiped a hand through the air and the water broke apart to fall back into the glistening pool as pattering droplets. “Go, Gwynter ren Terare of Wintervale. Fight your battle. Attempt to win. But first, gaze a last time on the Vale, for soon it will fade.”

“I will fight.” Gwyn’s voice cut through the ancient realm of light and life. “And though you remain here to hide, I will struggle to keep this Vale and all those like it from fading. Such beauty should never be lost. It should never be forsaken.” Gwyn looked around the glowing Vale, drinking in the wonder of its magic. He turned and reentered the mundane world.

He headed back for camp, lost in his thoughts, until the sound of approaching feet brought his head up, hand falling to his sword. Lawen stepped into view among the trees, relief washing over his face.

“There you are. Are you well?”

Gwyn offered a grim smile. “I found Celin.”

“And? What did he say of Kive?”

“Still alive. I must go on ahead.”

Lawen nodded. “I understand. Let’s break the news to the others.”

Chapter Forty-Eight

Unicorn and rider pressed so fast that Gwyn lost track of hours and days. His mind burned with a kind of fever, his body throbbed, and only his magic sustained him.

The silence of the woods persisted, growing thicker as the two companions entered the True Wood. Gwyn's blood stirred. Perhaps his magic responded to the Crow King's presence. The sensation never ceased.

On they raced, and Gwyn's thoughts fluctuated between concern for those traveling behind him, and fear of where Kive might be. Had the Crow King caught him? Was Gwyn too late to save the wretched creature he'd grown strangely fond of? It had been so long since Gwyn had seen Kive, yet his memories of the fallen Ilidreth were sweeter at each reflection, and his desire to aid the tortured soul burned hotter.

Compassion spurred Gwyn on — and rage. Rage toward the Crow King. To torment and destroy one's own kin was unfathomable. Gwyn had risked his life to save his brother. He had no doubt Lawen would do the same in return. How could anyone do otherwise?

Perhaps the Crow King had been tortured himself. *Was* the king responsible for his actions, or had he been driven to them as Kive? None now knew. Did Gwyn have the right to condemn the Crow King, or should he pity him and try to save him as he intended to rescue Kive?

Gwyn didn't want to pity the Crow King. While Kive had appeared monstrous at first — while he'd eaten what he perceived to be rats — even back then there'd been a childlike innocence in him. He was more animal than man, and not deliberately cruel. Meanwhile, the Crow King destroyed and tortured his own people, knowing well who they were and who he'd once been. He made them *eat* their own. He delighted in war. Chained magic. Murdered mage children. Whether or not he'd chosen this course on his own, he couldn't be allowed to continue upon it.

Gwyn must stop him one way or another.

The Crystal Way glistened under a full moon. Autumn breezes kissed its surface. Aluem trotted along it for several paces, then halted, ear flicking toward the southwest. Gwyn strained to hear above the chill wind.

There. A rustle in the brush. Was that a footstep or his imagination?

A figure appeared in the moonlight, cloaked and cowled.

Gwyn snatched his bow and nocked an arrow.

"There is no need of your weapon, Gwynter ren Terare."

Starting, Gwyn lowered the bow. "Celin?"

The figure glided nearer. "You are a difficult pair to catch."

Aluem flicked his ears and pawed the water.

Celin inclined his head. "Greetings to you as well, my friend. Is it true that you intend to bond with this boy?"

If Aluem responded, Gwyn didn't hear his words.

"I once thought you the wisest of your kind. But it is not my affair." Celin lightly shrugged and pulled back his cowl. "I shall accompany you to *Shaeswéath*, though it may doom us all. Your words struck my soul deeply, Gwynter, and few can manage that in this age. Thus, I shall see for myself whether you are a man worthy of Ilidreth loyalty. Shall we?" He motioned to the Crystal Way.

Gwyn smiled. "I would be honored by your company. But we ride swiftly."

"Yet I have found you. Show some faith. I shall manage."

Chapter Forty-Nine

"I realize he's worried about Kive. I am as well. But to ride ahead all alone! That's exactly what we came along to avoid." Nathaera wrung the reins of her steed like they were Gwynter's neck. "He's always so reckless with his life."

"I'm worried for him, too," Lawen said. He rode beside her, one hand draped over the pommel of his sword. Adesta rode in the rear, a bow at the ready. The prolonged stillness of the trees clawed at Nathaera's nerves, and the little company moved as carefully as their trot allowed. Even at this speed, Nathaera knew Gwyn rode days ahead by now. Soon he would reach Swan Castle and face the Crow King utterly alone.

"Stupid, foolhardy..." She sighed, more scared than angry. Gwyn had to ride fast. Already it might be too late. But couldn't he have taken her with him? They could both ride on Aluem's back and still race as fast through the True Wood.

She'd scarcely spoken to Gwyn since she'd confessed her feelings a week ago. It seemed a lifetime now since Vinwen. Perhaps the trees had swallowed up time.

Gwyn had never responded to her confession. It was possible, even probable, he harbored none of the affection she so keenly held.

I'm just a spindly wisp of a girl, while he's a tall, noble, fool-headed, reckless, self-serving—

Nathaera knocked a fist against her forehead. Even her thoughts had turned prejudiced in her worry.

Her horse's step faltered.

Lawen snatched her reins. "Hold up." He drew his blade. "I think someone's watching us just ahead."

Adesta's bow hummed a note as he tightened its string.

Lawen urged his horse forward a pace. "Whoever you are, reveal yourself."

A cloaked figure staggered from the trees, slumped over, breathing hard. The figure raised its head, strands of long black hair tangled against a blue-tinged pale face and blood-colored eyes.

Nathaera gasped. "Kive!"

She threw herself from her horse and raced ahead of Lawen, even as he shouted a protest. Nathaera reached out and caught Kive's thin arms in her fingers.

"My poor Kive, where have you been? Let me look at you. Are you well?"

Kive stared, lips parted, eyes vacant. "Little rat, little rat. How juicy you are." He reached up and stroked her hair.

Nathaera flinched. "Oh, Kive. No, no. I'm not a rat, remember? Dear Kive, I'm Fairy Wren, remember? It hasn't been so long as all that. You can't have forgotten me already, after everything. We went to Fraelin together, remember?" She looked over her shoulder and found Lawen and Adesta standing close, weapons ready but not raised. "See there, Kive? Remember Rabbit? He brought you such nice rats in Fraelin. You remember him, surely." A sob caught in her throat.

Kive's eyes wandered to Adesta. "Nice juicy rat."

"No, Kive. Rabbit. And I'm Fairy Wren." Nathaera snared Kive's face with her hands. His eyes met hers. "Fairy Wren, your friend. And Shiny — Shiny's nearby too. You went looking for him, right? Well, he's here. You must remember Shiny, Kive. You simply must."

He considered her, his eyes searching, lost and tinged with feral instinct. "Fairy... Wren?"

"Yes, that's right. I'm Fairy Wren, Kive."

"Fairy Wren. Shiny's Fairy Wren?"

She flushed even as she laughed. "Yes, yes, Kive! Shiny's Fairy Wren. You *do* remember." Fresh tears welled up.

"You must come. I found you." He caught her wrist and pulled it from his face. "You must *come with Kive*." His airy, breathless tone seized her body and she followed him, her mind reeling.

"Where are we going, Kive?"

"Master said to bring Shiny's Fairy Wren. Bring her to him. I must bring Shiny's Fairy Wren."

"Stop, Kive," cried Lawen.

Adesta raced forward and snatched Nathaera's free arm. "Release her. She can't go with you."

Kive turned a cold stare on Adesta. "*Release Fairy Wren and let us go.*"

Adesta gasped as his arm dropped to his side. Kive pinned his gaze on Lawen.

"You will stay. *You will not follow*."

Lawen remained where he stood, sword in hand, eyes blazing. "Where will you take her? To Swan Castle? Is that where your master is?"

"Come," Kive said, tugging Nathaera forward. "Master awaits."

She stumbled on his heels. As Kive pulled her into the trees, she glanced back and caught Adesta's stricken stare and the frustration gathering against Lawen's brow.

"Gwyn will find me," she called. "Please don't worry!"

They disappeared beyond the trees and Nathaera straightened to gaze around her. The forest stretched high overhead, cold and ominous. She dropped her gaze to Kive's back.

"Please try, Kive. Try to remember me."

The fallen Ilidreth didn't respond, but dragged her ever deeper into the woods, where the trees grew close and confining, like bars in a dungeon window. Nathaera shivered and sent a prayer up to Afallon.

Evening crept into the wood, casting a deeper gloom. Droplets of water dripped from the canopy above and Nathaera wondered if a storm hung low in the sky. Kive led her into a clearing, where the trees grew in a near-perfect circle, though the sky remained invisible beyond a thick canvas of leaves tinged with autumn gold. A little brook burbled through the clearing, and Nathaera's parched throat tightened.

Kive dragged her to the bank. She sank to her knees, dipped her free hand in the cold water, and drank handful after handful. Kive said nothing until she finished, then he tugged her to her feet and plunged into the brook. The water reached his ankles. He pulled Nathaera in after him. She squeaked as freezing water drenched her slippers. The current yanked against the hem of her coarse gray dress — attire borrowed from Lady Mair's cook for the journey.

Kive reached a hand toward the leaves overhead. "*Amondel ré tiéthwé Shaeswéath.*"

Black tendrils of ink-like liquid shot from his hand and the flutter of wings echoed across the air. Light filled Nathaera's vision, blinding yet dark as pitch. She flung a hand over her eyes. The world contorted. Her head spun. Wind rushed through her ears.

A high-pitched note, nearly a scream, caught on the torrent.

All fell still. Nathaera lost her footing and landed against cold stones.

A silken voice floated down to her. "You must be the girl who has caused me such trouble. I am glad to meet you at long last, Nathaera ren Lotelon."

Nathaera lowered her arm. Icy fear pricked her skin like thousands of needles as her eyes sought the fair face of the Crow King. "Your Majesty."

He smiled gently where he stood upon a crystal dais. Behind him, faintly glowing like moonlight, rose two thrones carved from a peculiar, opalescent wood shaped to look like swans' wings.

She knew at once where she was. Swan Castle.

"Well done, Kive. Thank you for your obedience." The Crow King extended a graceful hand. Kive scurried forward to take and kiss it. He fell to his knees upon the dais steps and bowed his head, trembling as he released his master's hand.

The Crow King considered Kive with a kind of condescending affection. Nathaera studied the mad king where she sat upon the floor in the ruined throne room swathed in ancient clouds of spiders' webs and curtained in dust.

The king's expression darkened. Cruelty curled the corners of his mouth and he lifted his hand. Kive flinched. His shoulders hunched and he closed his eyes. The king struck his cheek. The slap resounded across the vast chamber. Kive slumped sideways, then coiled into himself, cowering.

"Master, please...Please, no."

"You've disappointed me, Kive. You've wounded me by your betrayal." The king's tone glided across the air, soft, gentle. "Have I not given you all the rats you need to live? Have I not protected you from the cruel men who would have destroyed you? Yet you choose Shiny and his ilk? Why, Kive?" He stooped and caressed Kive's matted hair. "Do you not love your master?"

Kive sobbed and turned his head to rest it against the Crow King's palms. "Master, please." He snatched the king's wrists and pulled them close to kiss the knuckles of his hands. "I serve my master only. Forgive Kive. Forgive me." He pressed his forehead against the king's hands and wept.

"I know you serve me, though not as faithfully as you should. But, Kive, you haven't answered my question." The king bent close to the fae's pointed ear. "Do you love master?"

Kive bobbed his head and choked out his answer: "Yes, yes, Master!"

"Ah, Kive. Why then did you betray me?"

Kive wailed and dropped his head to the steps. He looked so wretched, tucked into himself, swathed in tangles of his long hair, cloaked in tatters, barefoot.

Nathaera's heart throbbed until she thought it might burst. Not long ago, Kive had been well groomed, hair neatly braided, adorned in fashionable apparel from Fraelin. She'd even managed to convince him to wear boots in public. He knew to eat his rats alone at night, away from people. He'd learned so many animal names to give the people in his life: Rabbit, Deer, Purple Giraffe — a personal favorite. The dignitary so named had been likewise delighted. Kive was learning his colors. Learning about plants and seasons, even numbers, so long as he pretended to count out rat tails: 'One rat tail, two rat tail, three rat tail.'

But all of that, a year's worth of healing, had faded away in the mere weeks since. Had crumbled before the wrath and majesty of his tyrant master. Kive had fallen again into the pathetic, miserable creature skulking in shadows, dining on human flesh.

Tears wended down her cheeks, hot and bitter. Her throat burned. "Please leave him alone!" She meant to speak, perhaps only to whisper, but the words came out as a scream, hoarse, hysterical. "Haven't you hurt him enough? Haven't you—" She choked on a sob.

The king stroked Kive's head as he might stroke a bird's feathers. His pale eyes lit on Nathaera. "This is your doing, not mine. Kive was not conflicted before. He knew his place, understood my expectations. You and Gwynter are the ones who have hurt him most."

Nathaera's lips parted. She shook her head. "You don't really believe that, surely."

The Crow King rose and stepped from the dais, leaving Kive to weep alone. The king approached Nathaera, tall and graceful, cloaked in deep red velvet. Crow feathers trimmed the cloak's lining, glossy even in the faint glow that streamed through the broken ceiling above. A full moon poured light into the chamber. Night had fallen. Under the moon's influence, the king's head appeared crowned in light.

"Gwynter rides this way," the Crow King said. "But even upon the back of his noble friend, he will not arrive tonight. Indeed, the wait may be several days. You will need shelter and food in the meantime. Perhaps a tower room will suffice? Kive already occupies the dungeon, you see. He favors it for all the rats."

"Why are we waiting for Gwyn?" asked Nathaera. "What are you plotting?"

The gentle smile stretched a little wider. "I must put to rights what he has broken, and for that, we must have three things: A private place to conduct our negotiations, leverage worth negotiating over, and a lure. Kive has been the lure. This castle is the most secluded realm of any land across the world. And you, my dear lady, are the perfect leverage."

"What has he broken?" demanded Nathaera. "You're the tyrant who's done so much harm. How many have you killed in all, Crow King? How many infants, how many children?"

The king laughed. "I've lost count. But each death was necessary. Quite, quite so."

"Necessary for whom? Why? What is your aim?"

His smile dropped away. "There is no reason at all why I should answer any of your questions. You are nothing. Now, Gwynter. *He* is worth my time, worth my attention, and even my patience. Him, I shall await."

Chapter Fifty

Swan Castle sparkled under the noon sun.

Gwyn's skin prickled as he drank in its grand construction for a second time, so delicate yet so solid. And, most of all, sad. Even in the full light of day, sorrow clung to the air, just as it had on his last sojourn to this hallowed place — yet this time, the wails rose higher. The taste of tears pressed against Gwyn's tongue.

"Come, Aluem. The Crow King is already here. We're late."

The unicorn carried Gwyn ever nearer to the ancient edifice, Celin pacing at his side, unwearied. As Gwyn studied the spires and tors shining like ice against the sun, he tried to unknot his stomach. The Crow King had gotten here first. Was Gwyn too late to save Kive?

'*Gwynter, look there. At the doors.*'

His gray eyes settled on the gaping portcullis. There, in the doorway, hunched a figure draped in tatters that rustled in the mild breeze. Tendrils of matted hair tumbled down the figure's shoulders like a mantle of black.

"Kive," Gwyn whispered. "He lives." He raised a hand and called out: "Kive! Ho there."

The figure canted his head but otherwise remained as still as the statuary stretching above his head.

"How piteous a sight he is," Celin murmured, tone thick with sorrow. "You should have seen him in the glory days of our kingdom. So beautiful, so gentle. Majesty beamed from his very soul. O son of Roth, fallen creature once fairer than the very moon, what cruel fate is thrust upon you? To what bitter end must you dance upon the Weave?"

The three companions reached the portcullis. Kive stooped into a clumsy bow. Rising again, his red eyes caught Gwyn's, but there was no hint of recognition within them. "Master is waiting. Come, rats. Come. Kive will show you the way." He turned and stepped beneath the portcullis and into the courtyard of Swan Castle. Gwyn urged Aluem forward, Celin on their heels.

The fountain remained standing in the courtyard, its bed heaped with decomposing leaves in putrid water. The trees stood naked. Weeds peeked through the crumbling cobblestones, shriveled.

Celin crossed the courtyard to the fountain and fell to his knees. "High King Aveon, fallen father of Roth. 'Twas in his reign that Ilid fell prey to dark magics, but he gave his life that his son could escape. Roth stole away in the night and returned many years later to reclaim his rightful throne, bringing Lady Shalesta here to rule for two hundred years in peace. This statue was erected to honor the memory of so great an Ilidreth. Now he stands alone, a last crumbling remnant of a once-great land. Oh, Gwynter. The grief I feel is deeper and sharper than a dagger to my heart. Can there be any hope left for such a ravaged world, so rife with wickedness?"

Aluem led Gwyn to the statue.

Gwyn lowered his hand to the kneeling Ilidreth. "Come, Celin. Let us find what hope remains, and we shall harness it to pursue a future of liberty and happiness. "

Celin took Gwyn's hand and rose. He nodded, saying nothing.

Gwyn released his hand and turned toward the towering

doorway of the castle. Kive hunched there, waiting, silent. Aluem cantered across the courtyard, Celin keeping pace, and they entered the ruinous castle. The shroud of cobwebs glowed against the trickle of sunlight snaking into the vestibule.

Kive led the company straight ahead, while Gwyn's eye strayed to the staircase he'd taken before, where above Lady Shalesta lay in eternal slumber.

At the end of a long gallery, Kive stopped before a set of white wood doors rising to the ceiling. He opened one door and slipped inside, then drew his head back out to stare at Gwyn and Celin.

"Come, hurry. Master grows impatient."

"Kive, wait," said Gwyn. "We don't need to see your master. Come with us now, and we'll go home. It's me, it's Shiny. Do you remember me?"

Kive shook his head. "This is no time for talking, little rat. Master is waiting. He has something for Rat. A gift." He slipped back into the room beyond, and Gwyn followed on Aluem's back, pushing the door aside to enter the throne room.

Carved wood shaped like white trees rose against either wall, great roots creating gradual steps that led to two winged thrones. Gwyn felt as though he had stepped back into the woods themselves, as though the chamber breathed. A gaping hole in the ceiling added to the effect, carrying the sweet breeze of autumn from beyond. Under a strand of sunlight stood the Crow King at the chamber's head. Behind him, bound and gagged, Nathaera sat upon one throne.

Gwyn cried out and Aluem increased his pace.

"Welcome," declared the Crow King, arms raised in perfect mimicry of the fountain statue outside. "I have long desired to meet you here, Gwynter ren Terare, even as I wished never to meet like this at all. Had you only followed me without defiance, had you sworn loyalty to your king and not broken faith — but alas, it is not in the nature of a Wintervale to bend the knee. You would rather die than serve another."

Aluem halted before the raised dais.

"That isn't true," Gwyn said. "Were you a sovereign worthy of fealty, I would bend the knee this very instant and serve you faithfully forever — whether or not you're Simaeri. But you're a tyrant and a warmonger. Indeed, you're mad." He unsheathed his sword and pointed it at the Crow King.

"Mad, am I?" The king softly laughed. "Ah, Gwynter. Do you know what madness is?" He turned his hand toward Kive. The fallen Ilidreth crawled up the dais steps. Kive groped the hem of the Crow King's robes and kissed his feet. "Madness is mindless subservience. Madness is cowering before one's terror. Madness is the complacency of softhearted fools. As such, *I* am not mad. Simaerin is mad! Kive is mad! But not I. I am powerful — therefore, I am sane."

Gwyn shook his head. "Spoken like a true madman." He patted Aluem's neck. The unicorn started up the steps while Gwyn kept his sword level with the Crow King's chest. "Release Nathaera. Release Kive. Let them go free."

"I shall," said the Crow King, smiling, "but only under two conditions. 'Tis fair. Two prisoners in exchange for two requests."

"What are your requests?"

"Firstly, you must serve me diligently all the days of your life, never wavering. Consequently, your rebellion must stand down. The days of Wintervale shall never come again to Simaerin. This must be sworn by magic and blood, for I well understand that your past oaths were not binding. Your royal blood saw to that."

"And secondly?"

"You must bind all magic across Simaerin, as you have unbound it. Only the mages under Corvus shall wield magic henceforth, and you shall oversee that so it remains."

Gwyn lifted an eyebrow. "But I didn't unbind magic."

"You did. A consequence of your heritage, likely unwitting. But there it is. You must bind magic anew, apart from those who serve me loyally. Though unbound in ignorance, you are adept enough now in magery that you could consciously contain it."

"Why can you not bind it? Didn't you once?"

Annoyance flitted across the Crow King's face, then vanished. He smiled. "I did, but I was not challenged by Wintervale then. You are the first in a very long time to cause me any trouble. I do not begrudge the change."

Gwyn shifted his grip on his sword. "You guarantee that your prisoners will be freed if I swear to your terms?"

The Crow King's smile faded. "My word is binding, as is any mage's."

"You once spoke of Kive as a threat to Simaerin," Gwyn said. "Yet you would let him go now?"

"On his own, he is no threat. If you are my man, and he fancies you as a substitute master, the threat is even less."

Gwyn frowned. "But he's your brother."

The Crow King fell still, so still he might be a statue. His gaze drifted toward his feet, where Kive groveled. "I have no brother. This *creature* is my slave. My pet. He is merely a nuisance I deem to tolerate for my amusement. My brother is dead. He fell long ago." The Crow King's voice rose as he spoke, losing the gentle tones as his eyes widened. "He fell beside his parents, long, long ago, as *Shaeswéath* burned at my feet. He is *nothing* to me now. Just a cur. *I have no brother!*"

Gwyn stared down at the Crow King, unflinching. "So adamant, Your Majesty. Why?" He brought his sword-point nearer. "Are you certain that your brother died so long ago? Or does a guilty conscience impede your memory?" He drew a breath. "Kovien."

The Crow King's eyes widened more. His breath caught. "Silence. Silence. Be silent, fool! Kovien is dead. Kive is dead. All fell before my wrath and glory! NONE YET LIVE!"

"Majesty."

The voice belonged to Celin.

Gwyn turned his head to find the Ilidreth on his knees before the dais, head bowed, eyes raised toward his ancient lord.

"Forgive me, sire," Celin said, "but you *are* Kovien. I remember well."

The Crow King let out a harrowing scream filled with rage and misery, longing and grief. He backed away from Gwyn, away from Celin, toward the throne. "They are all dead! I saw to that. I killed Kovien myself."

"Yet you are he," Celin insisted.

"NO!" The Crow King turned toward Nathaera and raised his hand to strike, black flames leaping from his fingers. Gwyn waved his sword. Torrential wind followed the path of his blade and flung the king aside. Gwyn and Aluem pranced forward and stepped between Nathaera and the fallen king.

"My answer," Gwyn said, "is no, Crow King. I shall not serve you, nor shall I keep the Weave bound. Nor shall I let you take Nathaera and torment Kive further."

The king squared his shoulders and lifted his hand. "Detestable Simaeri, stand down before your king."

"I see no king. You must stand down or we must fight." Gwyn dismounted and stood beside Aluem. The unicorn tossed his head.

A smile lighted on the Crow King's face. "Then we shall fight. *Avéas weth!*" Black flames leapt from his fingers and he lunged.

Gwyn raised his blade to block the attack. Wind rushed by his ears, responding to his defensive magic. The wind faltered as the king's flames formed a wreath and shot forward in a raging cyclone.

Gwyn leapt right and fell to one knee. Swung his sword, flinging wind at the king. The flames grew, fueled by the windstorm. Gwyn rolled and swept both hands inward, still gripping his sword.

Two strands of wind swooped in on the king, but the Ilidreth allowed his black flames to consume him as they swallowed the wind's ferocity.

As the flames died down, Gwyn found the king unharmed. Gwyn had heard of lesser mages consumed by their own magics, particularly the aspect of fire, but the Crow King was no novice.

"You still have much to learn, Simaeri mage," the king said. "Heed this lesson. When I have beaten you, bend the knee and swear fealty, else I will end the lady Nathaera's life and seek your beloved brother's next."

"You won't find Lawen so easy to kill," Gwyn said. He adjusted his sword grip.

The king chuckled. "Oh? Is that because he is a mage? This isn't news to me. General Cadogan already discovered Lawen's hidden talents, but as the man was dying anyway, we left him alone. And then you acted. Brave, reckless, young Gwynter dared to enter my woods, defile my mother's tomb, and take what did not belong to him."

"You admit to it," Gwyn said. "You call her mother, yet you say Kovien is dead."

"*He is dead!*" Fire burst from his hands, rising high over his head. "All the royal family fell. I am the Crow King!"

"You forsook your name to protect your magic. It was Kovien who dabbled with the unholy, and so you blame him — the name — for *your* actions. You refuse to be responsible. Is that not true?"

"Silence." The soft voice rang across the chamber, echoing with the voices of phantoms. "How little you understand."

"Tell me, then," said Gwyn. "Tell me all that happened and let me help you. Tell me that you were tricked or forced to destroy your father's kingdom, and I will endeavor to free you of the darkness. Are you like Kive, fallen against your will? Tormented by some vile force? Do you remember?"

A dark laugh filled the air. "Tricked? Forced? No. No, no, young Wintervale. I was not so naive as Kive is. Not so trusting. I well knew the prejudice and caprice of men's hearts. Simaerin stood to gain much in our demise. The Ilidreth were too peaceful, too soft, and they falsely believed that the oaths of old would hold evermore, even as rot and jealousy consumed valor and loyalty. Our people were being slaughtered. My father turned a blind eye. He blamed other lands, distant lands, for the deaths of the Ilidreth — but not Fraelin, not Simaerin. Not his allies!

"Yet I saw, when I rode out to protect the borders of Ilid. I saw all the horrors, the atrocities. I saw what none would dare to see. I became afraid — and fear led me to seek an answer. I found one. I found my answer, Gwynter. And I brought it home. Father rejected it. Mother — foolish Fraeli woman! — begged me to stay my hand. In that moment I knew: the Ilidreth were weak, fallen, and unworthy to be saved. I had transcended them all, and it was my duty to end them, before they fell of themselves. And so I did. I ended the Ilidreth, nearly all. The Vales fell, their keepers fell. It served them right for their *compassion* toward men. The fault lay with my mother. Such a weak, tenderhearted, frail thing."

"And your brother? What was his crime?" whispered Gwyn, staring at the mad king. How had his illness begun? How did a man reach such a place as this?

"Kive? Kive was weakest of them all. He chose to wed the princess of Wintervale — he intended to unite Simaerin and Ilid — to carry on the tradition started by our father. But I wouldn't have it. I threw the princess from her own castle and brought the pieces to my brother. His horror, his grief — they filled me with such ecstasy. I knew from then what I must do."

He laughed his gentle laugh. "Oh, Gwyn. To have such power — such strength. You cannot comprehend it. How could you? You are bound by the laws of mortality, but I? I grow stronger with each babe I slay, each dark deed I accomplish. Yet you think to stand against me? Oh, Gwynter, it is a fool's errand to try. There is nothing — not man, not magic — who can defeat me. Not even your Afallon — for I am a god."

Chapter Fifty-One

The wingbeat of a crow brought Lawen's head up from the trail. Adesta nocked an arrow and raised it to the sky, though the heavy foliage made it impossible to spot the bird among the burning shades of autumn.

The rustle of leaves ahead turned Lawen's eyes back to the trail. He met the gaze of Traycen ren Lotelon. The mage stood among the trees. A faint silver glow curled from his frame.

Lawen dismounted, steeling himself for an engagement he might not survive. His horse snorted, and Lawen patted the stallion's neck, keeping his eyes on Traycen. "Adesta, go on without me."

The Fraeli mage scoffed. "You cannot believe you would best him alone. No, my friend. I shall remain and aid you. I, too, am a mage, if you recall."

"Gwyn will need backup if I'm killed."

"Forgive me, Lord ren Terare," said Adesta, striding to Lawen's side, "but I feel very certain Gwynter would agree with me in this matter. He has the unicorn. You would be alone. Do not let noble sentiment stand in the way of good sense, *sui*? Besides, after all that your brother has done to spare you, should you not be less careless with your life?"

Lawen sighed and nodded. "Fraeli sentimentality is far superior to my own, so I shall yield."

As though he'd waited upon their decision, Traycen started forward only now. Orange flames licked his fingertips as he spread his hands at his sides.

"He wields the aspect of fire," Adesta murmured. "Such is very dangerous in these woods, even with the recent rain."

"It's all right," Lawen replied. "I can protect the trees, for my aspect is water."

"Ah, yes." Adesta nodded. "Conjuration. So you said. I use wind, just as Gwynter does. I am defense — though I am not so adept as your brother."

Traycen halted a few feet before the two young men, fingers engulfed in flames. "Which of you chooses to die first?"

"We fight together," Adesta replied. "If you seek an honorable duel one on one, you must first be an honorable man. That you are not, and so we shall battle you at once."

Traycen chuckled. "It matters very little. Crushing both of you will be like crushing two ants, rather than one. It's the same effort."

"Before we begin," Lawen said, "you should know that your master took Nathaera. For all we know, he'll feed her to Kive. She's your daughter. You can't turn a blind eye to that."

Traycen lifted a brow. "Why should I not? If the Crow King desires my daughter for any reason, he is welcome to her. The fool girl deserves to be punished."

Lawen stared, cold shuddering through him like a blizzard. "You're bluffing. Even you aren't so heartless."

"Even I?" asked Traycen, slanting his head. "You think my fealty to my king is so flimsy that I would defy his will? Do not lump me in with riffraff such as you. I'm no rebel. My loyalty to the Crow King shall never waver."

"The Crow King is a usurper," Lawen growled. "He stole the

throne from the line of Wintervale ages ago. He's not even Simaeri!"

"He's not human, that is true," Traycen said, smiling. "He is superior. Chosen of Afallon to lead Simaerin now and always, none shall stand against him for long." Flames raced up his arms, punctuating his words, adding heat to his tone. His eyes blazed, though the features of his face remained unruffled, even icy.

Lawen resisted stepping back. "Monster."

Traycen chuckled. The flames on his right arm shifted downward and dripped from his fingertips to form the shape of a sword. His hand closed around the burning hilt, and he raised his blade. "We are all eager to end this and hurry onward to protect what is precious to us. Shall we commence?"

"At once." Lawen summoned a blade of water from the palm of his hand, siphoning from the fluids of his body. It slid forward, hard like ice, but warm to touch. He grasped it and stepped forward to meet Traycen's charging blade. As the two conjured swords connected, no sound rang out. Instead, a pulse rustled the trees above, and the stillness of the woods deepened like a tuneless hum.

The rush of rising wind shattered the silence. Adesta lifted his hands. The gale obeyed, throwing Traycen into a nearby bramble. Lawen darted forward, sword lifted, ready to strike the man down — but a stream of fire exploded from the bramble, catching on the trees above. Lawen scrambled back to avoid being scorched.

Traycen emerged from the fiery wall of trees, eyes smoldering in the light. He raised his blade and leapt forward with a cry.

Lawen stumbled back as his sword met Traycen's fury. Adesta stepped in again, metal sword thrusting to strike Traycen's side, but the Corvus mage moved quicker. A wall of fire burst from the forest floor, and Adesta retreated. Wind would only feed the flames. Lawen hoped Adesta would realize his disadvantage and go on ahead to help Gwyn if he could.

But the Fraeli nobleman stayed. The breeze died down. The fires sputtered.

Adesta was no fool. Keep the wind level low, stifle the breeze, and the fires couldn't strengthen. The only missing element was water, and *that* Lawen could easily supply. They'd been following a little brook for several days.

Lawen stepped backward, freeing his blade. In the same moment, he stretched his senses toward the brook and tapped it. There wasn't a lot of water there, for the true autumn rains had yet to begin, and a drought had settled across the woods — but there was enough.

On command, the water climbed from its bed and into the air to form a fog bank. The air turned damp. Visibility shrank.

It wasn't much, but the fires would struggle against the dampness.

"Clever," said Traycen. "But fire is stronger."

The flames shot upward with renewed vigor and licked at the trees, reaching ever higher, like ravenous beasts not to be denied sustenance. A wave of nausea washed over Lawen as Traycen's will permeated the ground around him, nearly tangible.

"You're not bad for an inexperienced mage," Traycen said, "but Gwyn is by far your better. Even before he was trained, his will was stronger than yours, and thus his magic is greater."

Lawen grinned. "You needn't tell me. I know my brother's strength."

The fog curled around Lawen and Traycen, growing thicker, and the smoke of the fires rose higher. Adesta vanished in the haze. Sounds grew muffled. Lawen swung his sword. Traycen's met it with the same soundless shudder. Traycen's eyes narrowed and he leaned close.

"You're a fool to believe you can defy the Crow King. What could possess you to think you have a single thread of hope?" The question shone in his eyes, bright and disdainful. "Simaerin is stronger for his leadership. Greater by his will. Why destroy what he's built?"

"Because," Lawen replied, gritting his teeth against the other man's pressing blade, "no nation should be built upon the foundation of murder. Were the Crow King a just man, an honorable ruler,

I wouldn't care a whit what his origins are. But the Crow King kills the innocent. Oppresses the weak. Demands war. These things are wicked, Traycen. They're wrong. There's no justification for the murder of children. Not ever." He kicked out his foot and caught Traycen's knee. The man buckled with a gasp.

Adesta charged from the fog. Wind bolstered his step. He plunged a knife into Traycen's back. The mage grunted and collapsed.

Panting, Adesta looked surprised by his own good timing. He wrenched the knife free and straightened, pale hair stuck to his damp face.

Lawen knelt beside Traycen. The fire in the trees dimmed and lowered. Pressing a hand to the man's neck, Lawen sought a heartbeat. There, faint and growing fainter. Traycen coughed and struggled to move. He managed to shift his head until he could fix an eye on Lawen. He drew a ragged breath. Adesta must have pierced his lung.

"Save her, Lawen," whispered Traycen. A tear slid from his eye. "In life my loyalties could not...be swayed...but in death...he has no claim on my affections... Save Natty. Tell...her..."

The man fell still, his eyes dimmed, and the flames hissed and drifted away as smoke, leaving blackened trees in the fog.

"What a despicable creature," Adesta said. "He abandoned his daughter, and yet he pretends affection in the end. Did he truly think we would buy into so pathetic an act?"

Lawen rose to his feet. "I suspect some part of him was sincere. Who can say that he wasn't magically manipulated by the Crow King? Perhaps he had no choice but to serve, even at the cost of his family. Or perhaps he was a zealot who only saw truth in the last moment of his life. Would you judge a man's soul, Lord Gilhan? I dare not."

Adesta grimaced. "You're right, of course, but his treatment of Lady Nathaera was still egregious."

Lawen nodded, eyes resting on Traycen's body. "I don't like leaving him here, but we must press on."

"What good will that do? We're still days away from Swan Castle." Adesta sighed. "Already we are too late. Our part to play in this act is finished."

Lawen frowned. "Perhaps. But we must go on, nevertheless. If all we find when we reach Swan Castle is the remains of a battle, we must go to discover how it ended and help if we can." He glanced back. "Did the horses run?"

"No, I tethered them while you fought. I enjoy a good walk, but not for quite so long." Adesta moved through the fog and appeared moments later, guiding the horses forward. "They're a little spooked."

"Assist me with Lord ren Lotelon. I won't leave him here."

Adesta hesitated but nodded and helped drape the dead man across Nathaera's stallion. Lawen swung up into his saddle and clutched the reins of the other horse.

"Hurry. We've wasted a great deal of the day."

Adesta mounted his own horse. "Very well, Simaeri mage. But we will be slower with your baggage."

Chapter Fifty-Two

Flames filled Gwyn's vision.

He staggered sideways to avoid impact. The tongue of fire singed his sleeve and pant leg, tickling flesh. Gwyn stumbled and fell to his knees, sword clutched in his hand. He panted for breath, sweat dripping into his eyes.

Steps approached, sharp and resolute. Gwyn looked up through the smokey haze atop the dais and made out the shape of the Crow King coming near.

"I will give you one last chance to swear fealty, Gwynter, or I shall cut you down and slay your loved ones next. All of them. Even your little sisters."

"You can't." Gwyn lurched to his feet.

"Can I not?" The king chuckled. "Are you pretending to be wounded? Are you not down to the last ounce of magic you can muster?"

"You can't kill me," answered Gwyn, meeting the king's gaze through the smoke. "I am of Wintervale. By right of blood, you cannot cut me down, Kovien."

Fury flashed in the king's eyes. "An ancient oath whose potency is long deluded. It is time to test the last of its strength. I would wager that you shall die today, Gwynter, and at my hand."

"Try. I shall fight you to the last."

The king chuckled. "Little fool."

He lunged forward, quick as lightning. Gwyn barely raised his sword in time to block the slicing blow. He slid backward, limbs trembling, teeth gritted. The king stepped back and broke contact. Swung again. Gwyn caught the blade with his and forced it left. He tried his own strike, but the Crow King parried and thrust in the next moment. Gwyn couldn't block it. Wind encircled him — a last stand against the king's power, but the sword cut through it, heedless of Gwyn's magic.

The sword ran through him as easily as a sickle cuts through wheat. Gwyn heard Nathaera scream from far, far away.

He stood for a moment, stunned, and his eyes lifted to meet the Crow King's pale gaze. The king stared back, disbelieving. Warmth spread from the wound. Gwyn lowered his eyes to find his chest. A flower of red blossomed around the blade.

"I have killed you," the Crow King whispered, voice wavering with awe and horror. "I've vanquished the heir of Wintervale." He drew back and wrenched his sword free.

Gwyn held a hand over the wound.

Why do I feel no pain?

Wind swelled around him, and he realized he was falling. The ground caught him, strangely soft. The Crow King remained in his vision, silent and pale, regal and terrible.

A sweet, gentle voice whispered in his ear. "Hold on, Gwynter. You mustn't die." Golden hair tickled his face, and Gwyn turned his eyes from the king to find Nathaera's blue gaze. When had she gotten free? Did Celin loose her bonds during the fight?

Everything held quiet, so quiet, like a warm summer's night in Vinwen. Slow and lazy and wonderful.

He smiled at Nathaera, but his smile faded. Cold washed over him, stealing that summer evening.

"It's far too late to save him," said the Crow King at a distance.

Water fell onto Gwyn's face.

Nathaera is crying.

He tried to reach up, tried to wipe away her tears, but his arms wouldn't move. He couldn't move at all.

'*Stand aside, Lady Fair.*'

The voice sounded like the rushing winds of a storm.

Gwyn turned his eyes to find Aluem above him. His horn glowed faintly. His eyes shone bright. Beautiful, majestic.

'*Alone I do not have the power to save you, Gwynter, but there is no cause to fear. You are the heir of Wintervale, last of the line of Cygmund, dear brother of Lady Shalesta. By her grace shall you live, for the ancient oaths do not lose their potency through the ravages of time. What is immortal cannot be undone by what is mortal. Behold.*'

Aluem stepped aside. All Gwyn saw at first was the Crow King. But there, beside the mad king, swathed in white and silver that flowed like water and silk, stood the woman who had long slumbered in this castle. Long hair fell down her back, dark as ravens' wings, her eyes a piercing blue as clear as a summer lake reflecting an endless sky.

She glided forward. The Crow King cried out and cowered.

The woman knelt before Gwyn. Met his gaze. Held it steadily. "Blood of my brother," she said in tones like swansong, "lie still, and I shall see you mended." She lifted her head and reached a hand toward something beyond Gwyn's sight. "Kive, my son. Come."

"No, stop!" cried the Crow King. "You are dead. You cannot aid him." He turned toward the spot where his mother looked. "Kive, remain where you are. Master forbids you to go!"

Sobs, faint and miserable, touched Gwyn's ears.

He drew a breath, though the cold deepened. "Kive," he whispered. "Please."

Footsteps neared. The sobs grew louder.

"Come on, Kive," called Nathaera. "Help Shiny."

"Come to me, Kive," said the woman, smiling so sweetly the cold lessened within Gwyn, though his vision wavered.

The rustle of cloth suggested Kive knelt nearby. "Oh, Shiny Swan," he breathed, still weeping. "Warm, beautiful Shiny Swan!"

"Give me the stone, my dearest," said the woman.

Kive reached into his robes and withdrew a familiar blue gem, just the shade of the lady's clear eyes. He bowed his head and presented it to his mother, who took it with a smile.

"Thank you, Kive. You have done well to guard it." She turned back to Gwyn. "Few may wield this stone. Once already you have used it, and only thrice can it be invoked. This is the second event, wherein I shall use it to save your life." She pressed the stone against Gwyn's heart. "The oaths of old hold strong, and the line of Wintervale shall never fade by the will of others. But I give to you fair warning, Gwynter ren Wintervale. You are the last nonetheless."

His brow creased even as warmth spread through him. Before he could ask the question, the lady rested his hand against the stone, pulled back, and turned toward Kive.

"My precious child," she whispered, and placed her hand against Kive's cheek. "I am sorry for your pain. Your suffering has been beyond reckoning. But your strength and bravery have never failed. I am so very proud of you. Fight, dear Kive. Become well, and know that I love thee."

With that, she vanished as though she had never been. The ancient chamber fell still. Gwyn turned his eyes to find the Crow King, but he too had disappeared.

"Gwynter?"

He found Nathaera, who cradled him in her arms, tears shining in her eyes.

Gwyn smiled. "I'm all right for now," he whispered, clutching the stone tighter. "It seems I'm meant to live a while longer yet."

Chapter Fifty-Three

Lawen entered Swan Castle, his chest tingling, his throat aching as he thought of his brother. Cold nipped his fingers.

Adesta walked beside him. They'd left the horses tethered in the courtyard. Traycen's body had been buried in a shallow grave near the Crystal Way, perhaps to be fetched on the way back, should Nathaera still be alive and wish it.

The journey had been tiring, but apart from that, nothing had stirred to hinder or harm them. Lawen wondered if that was a good or ill omen, but he didn't dare voice the question. Adesta held his tongue as well.

Uncertain where to begin their search of the grand estate, Lawen made for the throne room along the wide gallery. His mind comprehended the ruinous grandeur that surrounded him, but his heart urged him on. He must discover what had happened to Gwynter. He mustn't stop for anything. Adesta seemed to understand, and he'd never complained that they slept for only an hour or two before pressing on. Now, hungry, weary, filthy, the Fraeli nobleman strode evenly beside him, eyes darting this way and that in search of answers.

Lawen suspected Adesta's motivation centered around Nathaera. He didn't blame the lad. Her fate might be worse than Gwyn's.

The doors to the throne room were more intact than others in this fallen realm. Lawen threw one aside. It hit the wall with an echoing boom. The chamber stood empty, but the scars of fire across the head of the room accompanied the faint, lingering scent of smoke. A battle had taken place here, but several days ago.

Lawen's heart sank into his stomach. He moved forward, Adesta on his heels, footfalls echoing off the walls. Blood stained the dais steps, dry now, and dark. Lawen crouched and touched the stain. His fingers trembled. Someone had lost a *lot* of blood.

"There you are!"

Nathaera's chipper voice brought Lawen whirling around as he straightened. She stood in the chamber's doorway, whole and hail, but for rich brown stains against the fabric of her borrowed dress.

Adesta rushed toward her, arms extended. "Thank Afallon you live!" He caught her and pulled her close, embracing her so tight Lawen thought she might turn blue.

He hurried to their side. "How are you? What happened? Where's Gwynter?"

She laughed. "I'm well. Perfectly well. As for what happened — well, that's a long story. I'll tell you as we go. Come along. Gwynter's what you really want to know about, anyway. He's doing fine now. A little weak from all his magic usery, but mending, just like she said."

"Who said?" Lawen shook his head. "Tell us everything from the beginning."

Nathaera guided them along a passage to the west of the throne room, and into a circular wing fitted with several rotting couches and dilapidated chairs. As she led them along, she recounted everything she'd seen since Kive brought her to Swan Castle.

She halted before a wooden door and finished her narrative before reaching for the knob. "I think the whole ordeal shook Gwynter deeply. How could it not? He nearly died." She smiled. "But he's whole again. Tired though, just as I said."

She pushed the door aside and stepped into the bedchamber beyond. "Kive hasn't left his side. I think he sees something of his mother in Gwynter." Nathaera chuckled. "Funny, I know. But there is a sort of similarity in their bearing. After all, they are distantly related."

Sunlight illuminated the chamber. Moth-eaten curtains at the windows had been tied aside and a faint breeze wafted into the room. Gwynter slept under the musty coverlets of a sagging four-post bed, a little gaunt, but breathing just as Nathaera had said. Kive lay curled up at the bed's foot, and Celin stood in the far corner, grim and still.

Lawen padded forward and sat on the bed's edge. He caught Gwynter's hand and held it tight.

His brother stirred. His eyes fluttered open and he stiffened. "Lawen?"

"Here and whole," Lawen whispered, smile broadening. "As are you, thank Afallon."

"It certainly took you two long enough to reach us," Nathaera said, not sounding as fierce as she probably wanted.

"We were delayed," Adesta said. "The Crow King sent someone to deal with us." His voice grew quieter as he spoke.

Lawen frowned and turned from the bed. "He sent Lord ren Lotelon, Nathaera. It was us or him."

She stared. "Oh." Tears filled her eyes. "Oh." She turned away. "Well, this is...difficult...I'm disowned, after all. Yet I'm crying..."

Gwynter tried to sit up. "Nathaera." He sank back against his pillows, quivering.

Adesta moved to Nathaera and wrapped an arm around her shoulders. "I am sorry, my lady. In the end, he said he loved you. He asked us to save you."

"You're just saying that," she murmured, her head bowed.

"No," said Lawen. "Adesta isn't lying. Whatever his feelings before, in the end, his last thoughts were of you. He called you Natty."

The girl let out a sob and threw herself into Adesta's arms.

Lawen and Gwynter looked away to give her some manner of privacy.

Chapter Fifty-Four

Three weeks later the bedraggled company stepped from the woods and into the lands of Vinwen. Gray clouds stained the midday sky with shadows. Celin remained at the border, and the company halted to bid him farewell.

"I shall speak with my people," Celin said, addressing Gwyn, "to see if they would follow the heir of Wintervale. I will tell them all that I have seen. Most of all, that the Fair Lady of *Shaeswéath* woke a final time to aid you. Perhaps we shall join with you upon the battlefield, but I cannot promise it."

Gwyn nodded. "Whatever the Ilidreth decide, you've stood with me once, and I count you as a friend. Thank you, Celin."

The Ilidreth inclined his head and slipped into the trees, stealing a single glance back. Gwyn thought he looked toward Kive, who stood beside Aluem, wordless and sad. Kive had said nothing since his mother vanished in Swan Castle, nor would he step away from Gwyn for any reason.

On impulse, Gwyn reached into his pocket and caught the blue stone. Its healing properties would work only once more. Gwyn must use it wisely if he must use it at all.

As he stared at the gem, it vanished from his hand. Gwyn curled his fingers around empty air. His chest panged.

Would the gem come to him again if ever he needed it?

"Shall we?" asked Lawen.

Gwyn looked up and nodded. The company moved toward Vinwen. He feared what he might find there. The Crow King had threatened his family, and in the weeks since their duel, he'd had plenty of time to tear the manor down, stone by stone, after slaughtering Gwyn's household. Would the Crow King spare the slaves or would he murder them too?

Eyes trained on the horizon, seeking any hint or wisp of smoke, Gwyn rode steadily toward home.

A single horseman appeared ahead, and galloped toward them. A white banner streamed above him as he raced the wind.

"Who is that?" asked Adesta.

"Towwen Stone," said Lawen after a moment. He laughed. "That bookish young man from Charquae. Remember him, Gwynter? He used to wrestle you when you were lads, and he always lost. Towwen moved to town to pursue the life of a scholar."

Gwyn smiled. His childhood friend, come out of the blue. "I recall him well. But what is he doing here?"

The rider soon reached them. Reining up, Towwen Stone bowed his head. "Greetings, Your Majesty. I've come to welcome you home, but first I bring news. Vinwen still stands and your army is gathering there. News of your birthright has spread across Simaerin and thousands have come to swear fealty to the rightful king. More come every day. Your lady mother and sisters are well, but they've left for safer lodgings."

Gwyn's hand found Aluem's neck and he rubbed it. "My army?" He glanced toward Lawen, then turned back to his boyhood friend. Towwen had been a lanky stick of a thing in their youth, but now he sat well upon his horse, a handsome red-headed gentleman, with clear, light eyes.

"Lead on," Gwyn said, adopting the tone of command he'd learned while serving at Keep Arch. With his friends at his side, and Towwen Stone leading the way, Gwyn wrestled with thoughts of his future. Like it or not, he was a king by blood. He didn't want that, but his people wanted it.

Simaerin needed a benevolent and righteous king. A young man, so flawed and inexperienced, could never lead them justly. But he could fight for them against the Crow King, and that would give him time to find a better answer.

Cresting a hill, Gwyn raised his eyes toward Vinwen Manor. In the fallow fields surrounding the estate spread a veritable army of tents and milling soldiers. Some — perhaps even most — were untrained peasants. But they wanted to fight. Wanted to defy a mad, tyrant king, and make Simaerin something better.

Gwyn wanted that as well.

Now he must pursue that dream, for there was no turning back. He must fight to obtain liberty or die in the attempt.

Gwyn nudged Aluem onward.

The boy king and his unicorn rode to meet their army as snow drifted from the wintry sky.

Continued in Book Two

THE WINTER KING

Dearest Reader

Thank you so much for picking up this book! I hope you've enjoyed Gwyn's story so far, along with that of Kive, Aluem, Nathaera, Lawen, Celin, and the rest of the *Wintervale* company.

May I ask a favor before you go? If you've enjoyed *The Crow King*, please take just a moment to leave an honest review online where you purchased this book. It's one of the best ways to support an author you enjoy, and it would mean the world to me.

I'd also love to see you on social media. My links can be found on the *About the Author* page of this book. Drop by and say hello!

All my love,

M. H. Woodscourt

Appendix

PEOPLE:

Adesta Gilhan [*uh-DES-tuh gill-hăn*] – A Fraeli Knight of Seabrelle in Fraelin.

Afallon [*ă-fall-on*] – The god of Simaerin and Fraelin. Also referred to as Sweet Afallon or Blessed Afallon. According to church doctrine, he sacrificed himself to redeem all men.

Aluem [*ă-loo-em*] – A unicorn who dwells in Ilid.

Aveon [*ah-vee-awn*] – High King of Ilid and the father of King Roth.

Bowrin [*bow-rin*] – An Ilidreth commander allied with the armed forces of the Crane King.

Brioc Ffyr [*bree-ock fire*] – A philosopher and printer in Charquae, and an associate of Towwen Brym.

Celin'Laen {*sel-LIN-lay-in*} – An Ilidreth. Also called Celin. {*sel-LIN*}

Crane King, The – Ruler of Fraelin.

Crow King, The – Ruler of Simaerin.

Cadogan ren Silverard {*căd-oh-gen ren sil-ver-ard*} – A General under the Crow King.

Gwynter ren Terare {*gwin-tur ren tur-RAIR*} – Second-born to the ren Terare estate in Simaerin. Mount Vinwen is his home. Also called Gwyn {*gwin*} or Gwynny {*gwin-ee*}.

Harrevin {*hawr-eh-vin*} – A Simaeri Captain at the Battle of Drakefield.

Hesegg {*hess-ehg*} – The family doctor of House ren Terare.

Kive {*kīv*} – An Ilidreth now fallen. He views people as rats and eats them. (Also see *Fallen* under *Terms & Phrases.*)

Kovien ave'al Edelin {*ko-vee-in ah-vay-all eh-dell-in*} – A prince of Ilid.

Kydess {*kī-dess*} – Simaeri General of Keep Arch.

Lawen ren Terare {*law-wen ren tur-RAIR*} – Lord of Mount Vinwen in Simaerin, elder half-brother to Gwynter.

Lishtil {*lish-till*} – Simaeri Captain, Battle of Drakefield.

Mair ren Terare {*mare ren tur-RAIR*} – Mother of Gwynter, second wife of Tynveer ren Terare.

Mavell (*maw-VELL*) – Head cook at Mount Vinwen in Simaerin.

Nathaera ren Lotelon [*nuh-thay-ruh ren lot-TAY-lawn*] – A young woman of Simaerin, betrothed to Windsur ren Cloven.

Neirin ren Terare [*nay-rin ren tur-RAIR*] – Gwyn's younger sister.

Pensivil ren Dorsen [*pen-siv-ill ren dor-SENN*] – General Cadogan's adjutant in the Crow King's army.

Rindermarr Lorric [*rin-der-marr lor-rik*] – A priest of Afallon in Simaerin.

Roth ave'al Edelin [*raw-th ah-vay-all eh-dell-in*] – High King of Ilid in former times. He is now deceased.

Rovare [*row-vair*] - Steward of Mount Vinwen.

Sila ren Terare [*sigh-luh ren tur-RAIR*] – Gwyn's youngest sister.

Shalesta [*shuh-LESS-tuh*] – A princess of Fraelin in former days, and queen of Ilid before its collapse. She was the wife of Roth.

Stefa [*stef-uh*] – A friend of Neirin ren Terare.

Tarven [*tar-venn*] - A knight in service to House ren Cloven.

Theolin [*thee-oh-lin*] – A resident of Vinwen Province.

Tia [*tee-uh*] – Gwyn's dappled mare.

Towwen Brym [*tau-wen brim*] – A printer in Charquae and associate of Brioc Ffyr.

Towwen Stone [*tau-wen stone*] – A childhood friend of Gwynter living in Vinwen Province.

Traycen ren Lotelon [*TRAY-sen ren lot-TAY-lawn*] – A member of the Order of Corvus under the Crow King.

Tynveer ren Terare (*tin-veer ren tur-RAIR*) – Deceased head of House ren Terare, father of Lawen, Gwynter, Neirin and Sila. His first wife died giving birth to Lawen, and he married Mair years later. Their union produced Gwyn, and later, the girls.

Windsur ren Cloven [*wind-sur ren kl-oh-vin*] – A knight of Simaerin and the man betrothed to Nathaera ren Lotelon.

Yiara ren Lotelon [*yee-AWR-uh ren lot-TAY-lawn*] – Mother of Nathaera ren Lotelon.

Places:

Bayton [*bay-tun*] – A port city in Simaerin.

Charquae [*char-kway*] – A trade city near Mount Vinwen in Simaerin.

Crane Castle – The castle of the Crane King in Fraelin.

Crow Castle – The castle of the Crow King in Simaerin.

Crowwell [*cro-well*] – The capital city of Simaerin situated on the southern coast of the kingdom.

Fraelin [*fray-lin*] – A kingdom to the northeast of Simaerin constantly at war with its southwestern neighbor. The Crane King reigns over these lands. Its people are called the Fraeli [*fray-lee*].

Ilid [*ill-id*] – The wooded northwestern kingdom of the fae-like Ilidreth [*ill-id-reth*], it has fallen into ruin and its fae are becoming wild and violent. (Also see *Shaeswéath* under *Terms and Phrases*.)

Keep Arch – A fortress near the northern Simaerin-Ilid border.

Keep Lirial [*leer-ee-all*] – A fortress near Siaan Wood, conquered by the Fraeli-Ilidreth forces.

Keep Lotelon [*lot-TAY-lawn*] – The estate where Nathaera ren Lotelon resides within the city of Crowwell in Simaerin.

Londolin [*lawn-doh-linn*] - The abandoned former capital of Simaerin during the age of the Wintervale Kings.

Mount Vinwen [*vin-wen*] – The agricultural estate and where House ren Terare resides, within Vinwen Province.

Seabrelle [*see-brell*] – A port city in Fraelin.

Simaerin [*sih-MAY-rin*] – The southern kingdom ruled by the Crow King. Its people are called the Simaeri [*sih-MAY-ree*].

Swan Castle – The human term for *Shaeswéath*, the legendary castle belonging to the Ilidreth.

Vaymeer Ocean [*vay-meer*] – The southern ocean in Simaerin. Crowwell sits upon its shores.

True Wood – The human term for the fae kingdom of Ilid.

Terms & Phrases:

Chesevwé [chess-ehv-way] – The Crystal Way; a path leading to Swan Castle.

Corvus, Order of [*kor-vuhs*] – An elite and mysterious order under the Crow King in Simaerin.

Fallen – A term used to describe the state of the Ilidreth when their souls darken due to the blight that has overcome their people and kingdom. A fallen Ilidreth loses his or her sense of reality and usually becomes violent until they fade into nothing.

Léathial [lay-AH-thee-all] – The Ilidreth name for the starstones in the *Chesevwé*. (Also see *Chesevwé.*)

Shaeswéath [shay-SWAY-auth] – Swan Castle and its enormous grounds within the fae kingdom of Ilid. (Also see Ilid under *Places.*)

Weave, The – The source of magic, both of fae and of human mages.

Ilidreth Tongue:

"Amondel ré tiéthwé Shaeswéath." – Awake yon (watery) path (to) Swan Castle!"

"Avéas weth!" – Come fire!

Fraeli Tongue:

Sui [swee] – Fraeli for "yes."

Acknowledgments

Though I've already dedicated this book to its inspiration, I can never say enough about my love and admiration for the Father of my beautiful United States of America. My passion for studying the Revolutionary War — in particular George Washington — inspired Gwyn's story.

While the scenes herein are fictional, I have borrowed from aspects of George Washington's life and historical events to lend strength and truth to its pages. And so I acknowledge its source with all my heart.

I must also, and gladly do, thank my family for raising me with an undying love of my country, and for supporting me in writing this tribute.

I also wish to express my great appreciation to all the voices who aided me in taking this labor of love and polishing its pages. In particular, to my beta readers: CJ Farley, Brett Starks, Heidi Wadsworth, Tawnee Wadsworth, Sheyanne Warren, and Jamie Wills. Your honesty, enthusiasm, and willingness to read this book (several times in some cases) means the world to me.

Also to my editor, Sara B., who hushed the demons of doubt in my head and encouraged me to share this labor of love with the world. Gwyn's story isn't for everyone, but it will resonate with those it's meant to reach.

To my Father in Heaven, my deepest gratitude for dropping this story into my head and not letting me abandon it.

Lastly, thank you, dear reader, for giving this book a chance.

—M. H. W.

About the Author

Writer of fantasy, magic weaver, dragon rider! Having spent the past two decades devotedly writing fantasy, it's safe to say M. H. Woodscourt is now more fae than human.

All of her fantasy worlds connect with each other in the Mithrinn Universe, forged with great love and no small measure of blood, sweat, and tears. When she's not writing, she's napping or reading a book with a mug of hot cocoa close at hand, while her quirky cat Wynter nibbles her nose.

Learn more at www.mhwoodscourt.com

facebook.com/mhwoodscourt
x.com/woodscourtbooks
instagram.com/woodscourtbooks

Also by M. H. Woodscourt

Mark of Valliath

High Fantasy/Young Adult

The Storyteller True

The Shattered Arch

The Marked Prince

The Blood Fountain

Record of the Sentinel Seer

Science-Fantasy/New Adult

Prince of the Fallen

Rule of the Night

Song of the Lost

Paths of the Broken

Heart of the Sentinel

Wintervale Duology

High Fantasy/Young Adult

The Crow King

The Winter King

Paradise Trilogy

Portal Fantasy/Humor/Young Adult

A Liar in Paradise

Key of Paradise

Beyond Paradise